The Winter Wolf

The Winter Wolf

★ ★ **WYATT EARP IN ALASKA** ★ ★

Richard Parry

A TOM DOHERTY ASSOCIATES BOOK
NEW YORK

THE WINTER WOLF

A Forge Book
Published by Tom Doherty Associates, Inc.
175 Fifth Avenue
New York, N.Y. 10010

Book design by Scott Levine

Forge® is a registered trademark of Tom Doherty Associates, Inc.

Library of Congress Cataloging-in-Publication Data

Parry, Richard
    The winter wolf: Wyatt Earp in Alaska / by Richard
Parry.—1st ed.
        p.   cm.
    "A Tom Doherty Associates book."
    ISBN 0-312-86017-X (alk. paper)
1. Earp, Wyatt, 1848–1929—Journeys—Alaska—Fiction. 2.
Frontier and pioneer life—Alaska—Fiction. 3. Gold mines
and mining—Alaska—Fiction. 4. Fathers and sons—
Alaska—Fiction. 5. Married people—Alaska—Fiction. I.
Title.
PS3566.A764W56 1996
813' .54—dc20   96-18269
                                                          CIP

Printed in the United States of America

0   9   8   7   6   5   4   3   2

This book is dedicated to the two women in my life:

Lillian K. Parry, my mother, who showed me the grandeur of literature, and

Katherine S. Parry, my wife, who showed me the value of faith.

★ ★ ACKNOWLEDGMENTS ★ ★

First, I would like to thank Tom Doherty, publisher of Tor Books, and Doug Grad, my editor, for their faith in this work long before it ever existed. Thanks also to Lisa Wiseman at Tor Books.

Second, my sincerest thanks to my agent, David Hale Smith of DHS Literary, for his tireless support and unflagging efforts on my behalf.

Third, I am indebted to Gretchen Lake, Virginia Bedford, Sarah Kavorkian, and Sharon Coulter for helping me with the historical research.

Finally, I owe a great debt of gratitude to Glenn Boyer, Bill O'Neal, and Bob Boze Bell for their works on Wyatt Earp; and Terrence Cole, Stan B. Cohen, and Murray Morgan for their books on the Great Alaskan Goldrush.

A special thanks is due the staff and instructors of Gunsite Training Center, Inc., for teaching me.

★ ★ AUTHOR'S NOTE ★ ★

This novel is an interwoven coil of historical fact and fiction. At times the distinction may blur, but the physical locations Wyatt Earp visited in Alaska and most of the characters he met there actually existed. Alexander McKenzie and Judge Noyes did run a corrupt machine that strangled Nome until their removal. That much is historically correct. Wyatt's part in overturning their "Spoilers" is open to speculation.

Newton Jim Riley was a real man who vanished after the gunfight known as Newton's General Massacre. Soapy Smith was indeed the scourge of Skagway and died as described in this book.

In 1898, Virgil Earp learned that he had a grown daughter from his first marriage in 1860. Mattie Blaylock, Wyatt Earp's common-law wife in his Tombstone days, died of addiction to alcohol and laudanum in 1888. Pinal, Arizona, the place of her death, is a ghost town now where most of the birth and death records have vanished.

And of Nathan Blaylock? Wyatt Earp never acknowledged having a grown son. I leave it to the reader to decide whether he lived or not. . . .

—RGP

The Winter Wolf

✶ ✶ ONE ✶ ✶

Glacial mist swirled off the Wrangell Mountains to tumble onto patches of morning fog that filled the basin of the Stikine River. Cloaked in this chilling vapor, the port activities of Wrangell continued unabated, identified by the clash and clank of men struggling to unload the latest steamer from Seattle.

Situated on the northwest tip of an island in Zamovia Strait, four nations had laid claim to this natural harbor. Tlingits, Russians, British, and now the Americans, all coveted Wrangell. But not for Wrangell itself. Whoever controlled its bay dominated the mouth of the Stikine River. The Stikine flowed swift and sure into the heart of the Yukon like a well-placed arrow. And this river's shaft aimed at a heart of gold.

Rough-hewn from a strip of land begrudgingly shared by the rock-strewn Wrangell Island and the gunmetal sea, this raw port of call had exploded in the wake of the latest gold rush. First of the painful stepping stones that led the bold and the foolhardy to their fate in the gold fields of the Klondike, Wrangell offered little comfort and no hint of the afflictions that lay ahead. Sitka spruce and cedar covered the land. Bracken and fern also thrived in the maritime climate. But this lush scene was a deceitful facade that masked another land of swamps, ice, and clouds of mosquitoes. The interior held only hardships. Those who extracted the Yukon's gold would pay a heavy price.

Still, the men flocked onward, driven by desperation as well as desire. A lingering depression in the states since the silver panic of 1893 further fueled the lust for easy riches in the land of Eldorado. Added to this stream were thousands of railroad construction workers set adrift with completion of the routes along the western shores and tidewaters. Soon, a flood of humanity poured northward.

A sharp sea breeze tore apart the haze to unveil the *City of Seattle* warped to the dock. Rusted, tired, and barely afloat, the steamship disgorged an unbroken stream of eager men. Workers, miners, drummers, and craftsmen jostled down the gangplank in a packed flow of bobbing heads. The crowd spread out to the tent saloons, stores, and crude bathhouses that packed the rutted street. A drink, a bath, and perhaps a woman to bolster their courage before the trek—that thought crossed many a mind.

Now the foredeck of the steamer was empty except for a woman and a man. Ramrod straight and thin as the ship's rail, the man nodded to his companion. A look of anxiety passed fleetingly across her face as she gazed into his eyes.

"Go on, Josie. I'll follow you down," he replied to her unspoken fears. "I'll be all right. This bum leg of mine will slow me down." His iron gray eyes softened momentarily.

Hesitantly, she kissed his cheek, smoothed a stray lock of silver hair, then started down, stopping midway to look back at him. He nodded encouragement.

At the foot of the plank waited another man. Half hidden beneath the brim of his hat, his pale eyes watched Josie with apparent disinterest. Although he pretended to study a list of names in his hand, she felt his eyes bore into her back. She hurried past. The hard manner, the gunbelt, and the badge—she knew the type all too well. A U.S. marshal.

Now the marshal stiffened as he watched her partner descend. His eyes narrowed. The dark figure with wide-brimmed black hat moved painfully down the gangplank, favoring his right hip. The lawman noted this man used the left handrail, keeping his right hand free and close to the pistol that rested in a worn holster. Cut down in front and worn with the barrel slightly forward, he observed. And he'll know how to shoot, the marshal mused. In response he shifted the list of wanted men to his left hand.

Halfway down the gunman halted. Light reflected from the sea lit a feral grin that flashed beneath the shadow of his hat. The peace officer's face split into a broad smile.

"By God! Is that you, Wyatt?"

" 'Buckskin' Frank Leslie," Earp said. The tension left his shoulders, and his right hand moved from his gun. "Who'd believe you'd be the first person I meet in Alaska?" Still, Wyatt glanced at the list of warrants in Leslie's hand and held his ground.

"Hell, there are a lot of our associates up here. Guess they figure gold is gold whether it's burning hot or frozen." Leslie followed his gaze to the papers. Shaking his head, he tucked the dog-eared sheaf into his coat pocket. "Come on down, Wyatt. I don't have a warrant for your arrest. Although I do recall that one for Frank Stilwell's death is still floating around in Arizona. But," he shrugged, "it didn't make it to Alaska. Besides, I'd never serve that one on you. I was there when you plugged the bastard."

Wyatt arched his eyebrows.

Leslie shook his head. "That's not unusual here. This Alaska is different. Why, I know things have changed since our Tombstone days. Sort of got all civilized and such, but not here. Alaska is as woolly as the Indian Territories ever was, and then some. This place is like some exotic, foreign country that the U.S. doesn't know what to do with." Leslie tapped his marshal's badge. "Look at me! Eight years in the territorial prison in Yuma for shooting a cuss, just pardoned for good behavior, and here stands 'Buckskin' Frank Leslie, U. S. territorial marshal. I tell you, Wyatt, it's a crazy place!"

"Sounds like a place to my liking," Wyatt said. He turned his head to locate the worried face hovering on the edge of the boardwalk. "Say, Frank, I'd like you to meet my wife, Josephine. She's over there about to explode with worry. When she saw you on the dock, she thought for sure I'd have to shoot my way onto Alaskan soil." With that he guided the marshal in her direction.

"When I first saw you, Wyatt, a few hairs raised on the back of my neck, I don't mind telling you. Leastways until I saw it was you." Leslie slowed his gait to match Earp's limp. "Horse throw you?" he asked, frowning.

"Would you believe I fell running for a damned cable car in San Francisco? Dislocated my hip."

"Well, I'll be damned!" Leslie knitted his eyebrows and massaged his chin like a physician perplexed by an unexpected diagnosis. "A trolley car?"

Earp cocked his head and sent a sharp glance at his friend. "Now, don't go spreading that around. It's real embarrassing."

"I won't, Wyatt," the marshal chortled. "Not until well after you leave town." Frank's mood sobered. "I killed Billy Claiborne, you know."

"No, I didn't. When was that?"

"Yeah, shortly after you left Tombstone. Eighty-two. He had it coming. I know he was in on bushwacking Morgan." Leslie shrugged. "Besides he drew down on me."

Earp stopped to look at Leslie's side. "Still carrying your Colt with that Bridgeport rig?"

"Yes, sir." The newly minted marshal patted his weapon. "Colt Frontier Model .44 that I special ordered from the factory. Twelve-inch barrel and carved ivory handle. Some people don't like the stiff pull of the trigger compared to the Peacemaker, but I've got used to the double action." He withdrew his coat to reveal the long, browned barrel hanging from the split metal swivel on his belt. Designed to pivot on its forked clasp, with a Bridgeport rig, the gun could be fired without drawing.

A split-second advantage, Wyatt thought. But only good if you used that time to aim. So Claiborne, too, was dead. Billy Claiborne. The name recalled an image of the O.K. Corral, and Billy running from the street. Both Claiborne and Ike Clanton ran that day, before the conflict.

Wyatt sighed. Nothing was the same since that fight at the O.K. Corral. In less than a minute, the entire world had changed, and no end was in sight. The killing had spread like a vicious stain, extending beyond the primary circle to mark more and more in an ever-growing snare. Less than the time needed to deal a hand of poker, yet years of retribution followed. Virgil with his crippled arm, shot from a darkened alley. And Morg . . .

For a fleeting instant his mind retrieved his brother, Morgan, spine shattered by a bullet, dying in his arms. He could picture the bloody billiard table, even the sweet smell of his brother's blood mingled with cigar smoke and gun powder. Had it really been fifteen years ago, or only an hour?

"Wyatt, aren't you going to introduce me to the marshal?" Josie's voice drew him back to the present. Earp looked down at her. Dark curls framed her sultry face, making her stand out like an island of serenity in the current of goldseekers that flowed around her. She had been the only good thing to come out of Tombstone, he thought.

"Josie, may I present Marshal Frank Leslie, a colleague from Tombstone, and late from, er . . . Yuma."

Leslie doffed his hat, ignoring Wyatt's sarcasm, and bowed deeply. "An honor, ma'am. You might not recall me, but I had the pleasure of seeing you on the stage in Tombstone. And may I say you are as beautiful now as you were then."

Josie turned smugly to her husband. "Now *there* is a gentleman," she gently chided him. "Thank you, kind sir." The light of recognition filled her eyes, and she pointed a gloved finger at Leslie. "I do recall you, marshal. You were called 'Buckboard,' isn't that so?"

"Ah, 'Buckskin,' ma'am, because I was partial to wearing a fringed shirt. I don't wear it much here in Wrangell because of the cold and damp. A mackinaw or a slicker is better suited for this place."

"Buckboard suits him better," Wyatt grumbled. "Best beware of him, Josie. Frank, here, is a nefarious lady's man." He shifted his weight, and a bolt of pain shot up from his hip. Standing in one spot was difficult with the leg stiffening.

"Untrue! Untrue," Frank protested. "But I do have an eye for beauty."

"Well, I am flattered, Marshal Leslie." Josephine took Wyatt's arm. She had noticed the flicker of pain in his eyes. "But all this excitement has made me giddy. Do you think we might take some refreshments?"

Leslie screwed up his face as he calculated which hotel was less offensive. Canvas tents and tin-sheeted clapboard eateries lined the main tract, but the difference from one to another was trivial. The Grand Wrangell might offer unbent forks while the Alaska House had a Chinaman who actually used soap to wash the dirty dishes. He sighed, the choice was difficult. Then, he remembered the little restaurant run by the Widow Bartlett and her spinster sister. Personally, he never went there because they served no liquor; but he'd never had to roust any drunks from there, and it was nearby. His face brightened. Widow Bartlett's place would be perfect.

"Just ahead, Mrs. Earp," he pointed to the modest wall with built-up board siding. "The Bartlett. They have tea and sandwiches." He scanned the swarming boardwalk, searching with the practiced eye of a lawman. The planks were packed with tired, dirty, and anxious faces, no staggering drunks nor tattered native beggars. The coast was clear. Besides, it was early in the day.

Deliberately the trio moved across the elevated plank trestle that rose on stilts to connect Front Street with the docks. Wooden slats nailed across spruce poles and supported at ten-foot intervals spanned the chasm. Their boots scuffling across the planks caused the green wood to groan and creak, adding that noise to the low rumbling of the men who negotiated the boardwalk of Front Street. The sheer magnitude of the whispers and mumblings of hundreds of travelers filled the street with a thunderous din. The oddly situated flat-fronted buildings reflected back the noise to throw it in the face of the people below.

The tide had pulled back to leave an eight-foot drop to the oily water. Within that moat bobbed half sunken skiffs, canoes, floating chunks of cedar logs, shattered crates, and boxes. A sharp, fetid smell, rank and musty, arose from the pit.

"Excuse the mess, Mrs. Earp," Leslie apologized. "Back in Arizona or Colorado, the dumps went out back of the town. Here you'd have to cut down a forest or dynamite the side of a hill to make room for one, so most dump their extras in the front of the town. You'll see a lot of things like that up here. Turned around, you know, putting the cart before the horse. That smell is rotting cedar and hemlock." The marshal pointed to the rough barked logs rolling with the wash. "They get ripe, people tell me, in the summer sun."

Wyatt squinted into the low clouds. The sun fought through to cast a handful of baleful rays upon the town and its slatted roads, but any warmth was soon choked off as the clouds regrouped and coalesced. He squared his shoulders and trudged on, driving his thoughts and ever-present pain deeper into the recesses of his mind. Alaska would take some adjusting, he thought.

Sitting in the tidy cafe, the three savored the strong coffee and waited for Mrs. Bartlett to section her fresh baked apple pie. Upon discovering that her guests included none other than the famous Wyatt Earp, the widow had insisted they sample her baking. Humming about the table, she basked in their limelight while appologizing incessantly for the lack of fresh apples.

At her insistence, Josie followed Mrs. Bartlett into the kitchen for an impromptu lesson in cuisine à la Alaska, namely cooking with nothing fresh except game meat and fish.

After his wife had disappeared into the back, Wyatt turned to Leslie. "Tell me about Billy Claiborne."

Frank nodded. "A bad egg, Wyatt. After you and Warren left town with Texas Jack and Bitter Creek, the Clanton boys drifted back. And Sheriff Behan, he just looked the other way."

"Behan," Wyatt snorted. "Worthless as a lawman."

"Well," Leslie glanced over Wyatt's shoulder at the women in the kitchen. His voice dropped to a whisper. "I think he was a mite flustered after you shot half his friends and took his woman."

Wyatt's eyes flashed a deadly warning.

"Easy, Wyatt," Frank held his hands out in supplication. "I'm your friend. But the truth's the truth. Hell, you don't have to tell me about those things. Didn't I kill Mike Killeen, my wife's first husband? Folks still say I did it so I could marry her a week later. As God is my witness, Wyatt, that wasn't my game. I love that girl, and her being married to Killeen *was* an obstacle, but I never planned on a .44 caliber divorce." The heavy hands smoothed the red checked tablecloth as if setting its wrinkles right would correct past wrongs. "After I shot him, I just couldn't see any reason for waiting."

Wyatt recalled Frank's wife, called the Silhouette Girl because Leslie practiced by outlining her profile with bullets. He doubted Josie would let him try that with her. On second thought, why would I want to, he reflected. It's stupid to take needless chances.

Earp nodded. "Sometimes things don't work out like we plan."

"Well, as I said, Claiborne came roaring back into town. He figured he could do as he pleased with you out of the way. I was in the Oriental Saloon having a drink when Billy comes in drunk and starts cursing me. I collared him and threw him out the door, hoping that would be the end of it. But a miner came in and said Claiborne was lurking outside. So, I slipped out the side door, real quiet like, and snuck up the side alley. By God, the little sneak was hiding behind a fruit stand. A fruit stand, would you believe it! And he's got his gun out."

Another alley, this one dark in the night, spitting flames. "A bushwack! Like Virgil and Morg," Wyatt hissed through clenched teeth.

"Right!" Frank's hand slammed onto the checkered table-top, disrupting the ordered world he had just created. Coffee slopped from the rattled cup to cast an ugly stain on the pattern.

Violence, striking suddenly and unexpectedly. Earp knew it well. His pale eyes observed the spreading stain. A split second to fire a slug, and a lifetime isn't enough to take it back.

The Widow Bartlett stopped polishing her flatware and cast a stern glance at the two men. Josie added a knowing glance at Wyatt. She knew this animated conversation held death and powder.

Leslie waved feebly to the ladies and lowered his voice, but his blood lust was up, reliving the moment and his triumph. His lip twitched, and he wiped a fleck of spittle from his mustache. "I eased my Frontier out and took careful aim. 'Billy,' I called out, 'Are you waiting for me?' He spun around, quick as a cat, and fired at me. He rushed it, Wyatt." Frank nodded sagely. "His shot went wild, clipped my hat, and hit a stove oilcan behind my head. But I had my bead on him, and I took my time. Drilled him through the left side below the heart. Came out his back and lodged in a crate of apples. I was making to plug him in the brain pan, but he dropped his pistol and said, 'Don't shoot again! I am killed.' And he was. I got him through the spine." Leslie studied his coffee, then he shrugged. "He died a couple of hours later."

Both men looked up as the women returned.

"Well, I hope you didn't miss me, Wyatt," Josephine smiled sweetly, but her words carried an added meaning. Her eyes reflected a trace of the worry she felt whenever her husband's violent past touched their lives. She had hoped to keep it where it belonged—in the past, yet his shadows reached back three thousand miles.

Marshal Leslie sprang to his feet. "Sorry, ma'am. I got a mite carried away. I was just telling Wyatt about how I—"

"About . . . hunting," Wyatt injected. He rose slowly and bowed to the ladies. "Mrs. Bartlett, your pie was delicious."

The proprietress blushed at the comment. "Why, thank you, Marshal Earp. I consider that a true compliment coming from a gentleman such as yourself. I'm afraid it's impossible to get fresh apples. I had to use the sauce from those horrid number-ten cans." She screwed up her face in distaste. "But, adding a little brown sugar and cinnamon helps."

"*Marshal* Earp." Frank's eyes gleamed at the idea.

Josie stiffened. Her gloved hands knotted into tight fists.

Leslie pushed his point. "Wyatt, I could sure use some help. Why, twenty thousand will pass through here this year, unless I miss my guess. I'm covering an area five times the size of the Arizona Territory. I'm authorized to pay thirty dollars a month, plus ten percent of the fines. And with your reputation, it'd be a sure thing."

"No thanks, Frank." The former gunman smiled reassuringly at his wife. "I'm retired from that line of work." He shifted to ease his sore hip. It constantly reminded him of his age. Was his draw slower? he wondered. He'd never been as fast as Bat Masterson or Doc Holliday. A steady aim and gentle squeeze of his trigger had always worked for him. That and his will. Not many would kill a man without hesitating. But he could. He could because once he'd set his mind to the task his resolution held him firm. Not like Doc, who killed because he just didn't care.

Precious good Doc's speed did for him. He couldn't outdraw the consumption that ate out his lungs. The picture of his virulent friend drew to mind, lying pale and small in the hotel in Glenwood Springs, Colorado, coughing bits of his lung into that handkerchief that he always carried. No one was more surprised than Doc about that. He never figured on dying in bed. That was less than ten years ago.

But, could Wyatt still kill without that deadly, life-losing pause? He wondered. Josie had changed him. Softened him, perhaps. She was too dear to him. That fact strengthened him . . . and weakened him as well. In a gunfight, the man with the most to lose stood at a distinct disadvantage, and Josie was something he didn't want to lose.

"My husband is retired from that line of work," Josie added emphatically. To emphasize her point, she hooked a protective arm around Wyatt.

"Retired," Earp nodded. "Gold mining, that's my game, and maybe, a little poker if Lady Luck denies us a strike." He'd carefully said *us.* Josie was weighing every word, and she knew mining was a joint venture while gunfighting was not.

Josephine's radiant smile was worth his choice of words. He felt her grip on his arm loosen.

"Marshal Leslie," she said, tactfully changing the subject, drawing him away from her fears. "I know Wyatt has explained it to me on at least a hundred occasions—at times I'm such a scatterbrain, I declare I'd be lost without his help." She struggled to keep her voice soft and level. "But could you tell me about the different routes to the gold fields? I recall something about a water route and a land route, but geography was not my best subject in finishing school."

Leslie shifted in his chair and propped his elbows on the table. Pretty women had always been his weakness, and Josephine Marcus Earp still retained all the beauty from her days in the theater. Furthermore, he reveled in the chance to play the expert. So what if he had been in this country less than two months. Wrangell had few authorities, barring the Chilkats, Tlingits, and a rare miner who had actually returned from the Klondike. The tight-lipped Indians and Eskimos guarded their precious trade routes into the Interior, and the miners matched them in vagueness. Vanity allowed him to think of himself as an expert. That same pretension made him easy game for Josephine's wiles. His descriptions, she knew, would lead the discussion far from any thought of deputizing her husband.

"Well, ma'am," Leslie began pompously, "there are several routes as you so rightly noted."

"Do go on, marshal." She fluttered her lashes to offer encouragement. The effect was instantaneous. Frank's chest expanded several inches, and he lost his train of thought, a fact Josie observed to her satisfaction. From the corner of her eye, she glimpsed Wyatt rolling his own eyes in disbelief. He knows me too well, Josie noted, making a mental note to be less transparent when dealing with her husband.

"Yes, do go on, Frank," Wyatt added levelly.

"First, there is the All-Water Route." Frank had regained his notions. "That sails from here across the Gulf of Alaska to slip between Fox Island and the Alaskan Peninsula at Unalaska. Then you cross the Bering Sea to St. Michaels on the mouth of the Yukon River. From there you'd have to travel by flat-bottomed scow up the Yukon to Dawson City.

"Then, there's the Part-Water Route. From here at Wrangell, you continue up the Inside Passage to Juneau, and then on the Skagway or Dyea. I'm told both those places are such shallow coves that the steamers stand off a mile or two and unload miners and gear onto barges for the trip ashore." Leslie paused to collect his facts. He had never been north of Wrangell, so he hoped his facts were straight. He emptied his coffee cup, wishing it were beer.

"And then you're there?" Josie offered encouragement.

"Hell . . . heck, no, Mrs. Earp. Not by a long sight. You've got two ways overland from there. Through Chilkoot Pass from Dyea or White Pass and Dead Horse Pass. Both are uphill, I'm told.

"A few come in overland from the Northwest Territories by the old Hudson Bay fur trade routes, but most who choose that way are Canadians. Oh, yes, I've heard a hardy soul or two are landing at a place called Valdez or Valdes and heading directly inland. But part of that is crossing a glacier and going up the Copper River."

"No railroads, marshal?"

Leslie chuckled, "No, ma'am. But, I've heard talk of them trying to build one through White Pass." He sat back exhausted.

"Which way would you go, Frank?" Wyatt asked. "If you had your choice."

"Choice doesn't enter into it, Wyatt. The All-Water Route hits some pretty rough seas. Not sheltered like what you just done. Most ships aren't strong enough to stand that kind of pounding. Why, your boat, the *City of Seattle*, would break apart for sure. So, the ocean-going ships are few and far between, and booked up." He wrinkled his brow. "And dangerously over-loaded, I'm told. To make matters worse, the rest of the way up the Yukon is only clear of ice from May to October. After that it freezes up." He looked at the two. "I don't think many consider skating to the gold fields."

Wyatt ran his hand over the knotted muscle in his right thigh. He knew what Buckskin was going to say next.

"That's why most take the Skagway or Dyea passage overland until they get to the rivers. But, I hear those passes are dreadful. Even before I got here the stampeders were packing supplies up the passes in snow and ice.

"You see, Whitehorse and Dyea are in U.S. territory, but those mountain passes belong to the Canadians. The Mounties guard the routes and check everyone."

"Those men in those red coats?" Josie questioned.

Leslie nodded. He jabbed a finger at Earp. "I've met a few of them, Wyatt. They may dress like sissies, but they're tough as nails. Not much on quick draw with those flap holsters and cavalry-type lanyards, but they're all business with their Winchesters."

"Bat and I met one or two when we crossed over from Montana after hunting buffalo for the railroad. The Blackfoot thought their red coats were big medicine."

"They're big medicine up here, that's for sure. What they say goes. They've got this idea that a starving man will kill or rob to stay alive."

"They're right on that score," Wyatt agreed.

"And they don't want that happening. So they have a list of what they think a man needs to survive for a year. You have to pack it up one of their bloody passes before they let you in. They check every matchstick and pound of flour. Most stampeders make thirty trips up the pass, carrying seventy pounds at a time on their backs. Slipping and sliding in the ice with all that gear. I couldn't do it."

Earp chewed his mustache in thought. Even now his hip was stiffening. The short-barreled Sheriff's Model .45 Peacemaker that he carried in his coat pocket weighed against his leg muscle like hot iron.

Frank Leslie leaned across the table to hammer home his point. "Two thousand pounds, by God, Wyatt," he hissed. "*A whole damn ton!*"

TWO

Josie awoke with a start. Something was very wrong. The sun was up, and she was still in bed. Had she overslept? The sporadic rattle of the night's rain on the corrugated roof of the Grand Wrangell had lulled her into her first decent rest since leaving San Francisco. But it was daylight! Had the *City of Seattle* left? She bolted upright.

"Easy there, Josie." Wyatt turned from the window to cast an amused look at his wife. "The hotel's not on fire—at least not yet." He let the lace curtain slide across the window pane, and backed away from the light. Viewed from this second-floor room, Front Street followed the curve of the harbor, its design dictated by geography rather than civic planning. Nothing in Wrangell involved civil engineering.

"This is some place, isn't it." Wyatt shook his head. "Seems like they took the worst of Dodge City, Globe, and Tombstone and stacked it along the water's edge. One good wind would sent the whole kit and caboodle floating away."

"But the boat? It'll be leaving." Josie ran her fingers through her hair, struggling to clear her head.

"No hurry on that account. We're stuck here for two weeks." He hid the irritation in his voice. Three weeks flat on his back in San Francisco with his hip, and now this. Every day's delay lessened his chances for a strike. At this rate all the decent claims would be filed on.

"Two weeks," his wife sputtered. "Did I make us miss the ship?" Her voice quivered.

"Nope. Remember that grinding noise we heard as we came through the Narrows? Seems the *Seattle* hit an uncharted rock. Stove in part of her keel. The captain doesn't want to take the chance of her breaking up in a storm. He says two weeks to haul her out and repair the damage. He's hopping mad and threatening to shoot the pilot. Frank tells me the pilot's hiding out in one of the saloons until the captain cools down."

"Frank?" Josie's antenna for trouble twitched. "You've talked to Frank Leslie this morning?"

"Honey, the sun comes up here by four in the morning. You were sleeping soundly, so I slipped out for a walk. That's when I heard about the ship, and ran into Frank.

"And you're wearing your gun belt," Josie noted coldly. "What does that mean, Wyatt?"

He came and sat on the bed by her side and placed his arm around her shoulder. In doing so, the edge of his coat opened to reveal the glint of a silver badge.

"Oh, Wyatt, no! No!" Her voice changed from fear to reprimand to anger. Beating her fists against his chest, she hammered away at the hated shield.

He allowed her to pound away until her anger broke, and she started to cry. Then he held her at arm's length to look at her. She looked lost and so very young. After all these years she still looked like she had the day they met in Tombstone.

"Honey, what was I going to do for two weeks? There's no poker to speak of here. The miners are guarding their money for a grubstake or heading out busted. Frank offered me a job as deputy marshal while we're here, so I took it. Besides, we could use the money."

"No we couldn't. We've got money," she protested.

"Your money, Josie," he reminded her of that sore point.

28

"I know you think it's foolish, but I do not want us to live on your wealth alone. A man has his pride."

"I don't give a damn for your silly pride if it gets you shot in the back!"

"Sadie," he said, switching to his pet name for her, "I won't get shot, I promise you. Whether I'm wearing a badge or not doesn't really change my odds. The men here are freighters and miners, not cowboys. They're more handy with a shovel and pickax than a six shooter."

"They're men, and they get drunk and mean." She jumped from the bed to turn her back to him. In doing so, she let her nightgown purposely slip off one shoulder, exposing her breast. She turned back to give him a good look, eyes flashing. "But you've made up your mind; so go ahead, get a pickax driven into your stubborn skull. I won't bring flowers to your grave!"

Wyatt turned to the door. No sense arguing the point when she was like this, he knew. "Well, that would make me sad, your not bringing me flowers."

Instantly she was on him, arms wrapped tightly around his neck, raining kisses on the back of his head. "I didn't mean it! I didn't! Wyatt, please forgive me. I just don't want anything to happen to you. I couldn't bear it."

He shifted her into his arms to look down at her. A grin crossed his face. "As long as I keep that eye in the back of my head open, you won't have to worry about flowers. I'll be back for lunch around noon. Now, don't go about exposing yourself, except to me. I doubt Wrangell's jail could hold all the men in this town, but I'd have to lock them up if they saw you naked like this."

While she did her best to seduce him, he kissed her and left. Josie listened to his boots going down the steps, then she stood for a long time looking at the door. *I'm not finished with this matter, Mr. Earp, not by a country mile. I have a few tricks left up my sleeve.*

Outside, Frank Leslie waited, trying his hardest not to seem intrusive. "Hello, Wyatt." The marshal feigned surprise at their "chance" meeting while in fact he had been pacing back and forth on Front Street since offering Wyatt the job of deputy marshal. Leslie squinted into the cloud filled sky. "Might turn into a fine day, yet."

"It's okay, Frank." Wyatt flashed his badge. "I'm still wearing it."

A broad grin split Leslie's face, separating his dark mustache like raven's wings. "But are you still wearing your scalp, too?"

Earp chuckled. "I think so. But I won't know for sure until lunchtime. Well, shall we take a stroll around town, like the old days, Frank?"

"Just like the good old days, Wyatt," Leslie said. "I sure am pleased to have your help. This place is way too much for one man to handle."

As the two walked along the planks of Front Street, the sun beat back the clouds to burn off the lingering fog except for meager wisps that clung to the clefts of the mountains. Emerald green hills sparkled in the light amid a backdrop of knife-edged mountains, sporting snow white crests. Sitka spruce and Douglas fir, straight as ramrods, aimed at the sky like a host of arrows. Verdurous carpets of shrubs and spring flowers flowed from the hills as far as the tidal edge where the brine supported its own flora. Warm times had come to southeastern Alaska Territory after long months, and now every living thing rushed to take advantage of the meager growing season.

Wyatt stopped to view the scenery. "First time I've seen it without the rain. Almost takes your breath away, it's so green. And look at those trees, bigger than any lodge pole pines I've ever seen."

The men's conversation ceased as a wedge of prospectors, laden with bags, burlap sacks, and boxes, drove between them. With the boiling stew of humanity came a melange of odors: sweat, French perfume, and stale tobacco mixed with coffee and lard from leaking tins to form a cloud that chased after the men. As this clot of men hurried past, the underlying odor of souring cedar returned. The narrow plank road groaned and creaked under the pounding feet, but held together and refused to pitch them into the waiting icy water.

"Like Tombstone during the silver rush," Leslie shouted over the din of the crowd. "Except all the stampeders are jammed between those mountains and the sea. I hear it's worse in the gold fields. Funny thing, this Alaska Territory—bigger than all get-out, but the land's built so ruggedly you're wedged along the water's edge—be it streambed or sea."

A prospector, undistinguished from the horde by his black slouch hat, baggy woolen trousers, and shapeless coat, slammed into Leslie. The man fumbled with the sack of flour on his back and started to swear. The words died in his throat, and his full-bearded birdlike face blanched when he saw the marshal's badge on Leslie's chest and the big pistol strapped to his side.

Wyatt watched the man laboring away under his burden. "That fellow looked like Soapy Smith," he said. "I hear he's up here."

Leslie watched the man's receding flour bag. "Yeah, he sort of favors our old friend Jefferson Randolph Smith. But you'd never find Soapy doing an honest day's labor."

"He's not gambling?"

"Not for a living, he isn't. He's a boss in Skagway. Got his own gang."

"Soapy?"

"Yup. He's set himself up in Skagway. Built a place that looks like a storefront bank, hoping some trusting souls would think it was a bank and deposit their money with him. When that didn't work, he named it Jeff Smith's Parlor and turned it into a saloon."

"That sounds like Soapy," Wyatt said as he backed against a pile of galvanized tubs to avoid a prospector struggling past with five shovels lashed across a bale. The tools poked ahead of the man like medieval lances, threatening to skewer the unwary. "Slippery as his name. Bat Masterson and I used to play poker in his gambling hall in Creede. Never gave me any trouble. Not that he was yellow, but a stand-up shoot-out wasn't to his liking."

"Con man is more his nature," Frank agreed. "The local politicians finally kicked him out of Colorado. Fortunately, he's not my problem. He doesn't come down to Wrangell, and the army is in charge of Skagway. But I hear he's got some sweet operation set up. His gang sells protection to the merchants as well as the prospectors, then robs them on the way to the gold fields. Would you believe it, Wyatt, he even has a Telegraph Office that charges five dollars to send a message anywhere you'd like."

"So?"

"Skagway hasn't got any telegraph lines."

Wyatt stopped beneath a sign that read Wrangell Studio. The flat-faced wood structure sported fresh paint and a corrugated sheet-metal roof, and abutted a hardware store covered with canvas. "Pretty fancy for a studio," he remarked. "They must sell a lot of pictures. How about having our pictures taken, Frank? To commemorate my coming to Alaska."

Frank held his hands up in protest. "Not in there. Not unless you really want Josie to scalp you! That's a whorehouse."

Wyatt smiled and continued along the plank boardwalk as it rose and dipped with the contours of the bay. The whole street seemed built on stilts with fingerlike crossings fanning out at random intervals to allow crossing to the docks. The tide was returning, and brackish water lapped at the base of the cedar poles that supported the street. Earp noted that the high water marks on the posts stained the wood a good six feet higher.

Leslie stopped beneath a prodigious marquee proclaiming the Sample Room and dwarfing the City Cigar and Tobacco Store and Mercantile Restaurant just beyond. Raucous laughter spilled from the open door of The Eureka Beer Hall.

"Sounds like the boys are whooping it up a mite early, Wyatt," Frank said. "Maybe we ought to pay them a visit to keep things peaceful."

Wyatt nodded. Instinctively, he checked his Peacemaker, tightened his belt, and patted the backup revolver in his coat pocket.

"Old habits?" Leslie commented.

"That's what keeps us alive, Frank."

Stepping inside, both men squinted through the cloud of tobacco smoke and beer fumes that filled the saloon. Mud-caked sawdust littered the floor, and faded pages of calendar girls patched the rough-hewn board walls. Packed shoulder to shoulder, stampeders jostled for glasses of beer and the local watered down whiskey.

"Looks peaceful enough," the marshal sighed. "Just starting out while the day is fresh."

No sooner had the words left Leslie's mouth than a squarish man with red hair poking from a felt hat set far back on his head spun away from the bar. Beer foam dripped from his matted beard onto his plaid vest, seeping under his grimy collar and soaking into his shirt. "Goddamn, you jogged my elbow," he snarled. "You made me wear my drink, mister!"

"Sorry," the man next to him responded in a thick Norwegian accent. His dress marked him more as a fisherman than a prospector.

"Sorry don't cut it, you Swedehead," the first man sputtered.

"Who you calling a Swede, you stupid man," the fisherman yelled. "I ain't no dumb Swede."

"You're a foreigner, ain't you? Come up here to steal all the gold from us Americans."

"Go to hell. I am fisherman."

"Hell, is it?" the redhead replied, drawing a Remington Frontier Model .44 from his belt. "I'll send you straight there yourself!"

The fisherman blanched as the muzzle centered on his chest, and his hands jumped for the tin ceiling. Backing away, he protested. "I got no gun."

"Well, find one fast," his adversary ordered. To underscore his point, he fired a shot between the other man's feet. Wood splinters from the floor stung the crowd, prompting them to bolt out the door or crush themselves into the corners farthest from the fight and away from the clean bullet hole in the barked cedar plank. The discharge added more smoke to the already hazy room.

"Don't be messing with me," the redhead shouted. "I'm a hellion from Fort Smith, and I've killed more men than I can remember." He spun around. "I—"

An arm shot through the smoke to jerk the pistol from his grip. Stunned by its quickness, he gazed dumbfounded as his revolver rose above his head, ready to crash across his skull. At the same time the powder smoke cleared, enabling him to see who held his weapon. The man's eyes bulged in his head, and his jaw dropped in bewilderment.

"Wyatt Earp!? Goddamn, is that you? Wait, don't buffalo me, Wyatt," he pleaded referring to the practice of applying the heavy-barreled pistol as a blackjack.

"Get yourself peaceful, and I won't," Wyatt ordered. As the man nodded, Earp lowered the revolver.

"I don't believe it," the subdued man stammered. "Here I go to the ends of the earth, and the first man I run into when

I let off a little steam is Wyatt Earp. If that don't beat all. You threw me in the pokey in Dodge City for the same thing twenty years ago!"

"You must be a slow learner," Wyatt answered.

"Aw," the man pleaded his case. "Once every twenty years ain't too bad, is it?" He lowered his voice as he glanced at the curious crowd. "And I never killed a soul, honest," he whispered. "I just wanted to impress these dirt wranglers. I bet half of them never saw a longhorn."

Earp smiled. "You can collect your pistol tomorrow from the marshal's office." He searched the watching faces for the fisherman, but he had vanished. "I don't think any charges are going to be filed."

The man face lit into a wide grin. "You know, Mr. Earp, I sure am thankful it was you who arrested me in Dodge City. Most other lawmen might have shot me at the time."

"I would have," Leslie said.

"You could have shot me just now, too, but you didn't," the redhead continued. "Or split my head open with that barrel. I appreciate your not doing that. Always thought you were a fair man. Can I buy you a drink? For old time's sake?"

"Would you buy me a drink, also?" Frank Leslie asked. "I didn't shoot you, either."

"Sure." The man sounded relieved.

"I'll let you buy me a cigar, instead of that drink," Wyatt said.

"My pleasure, marshal. Wait until I tell the boys back at the campsite that you're here. They won't believe it."

The men had their pick of tables before the crowd realized bullets and blood were not on today's fare and returned to jockeying for a drink at the overrun bar. They picked a corner one so both Wyatt and Frank could sit with a wall at their back. After a while the man wandered off.

Wyatt watched the man exit the door. "By the way, Frank, do we have a jail here?"

"I've been using a shack off Church Street. It's got iron grating on the windows. It's better than the one in Greaterville. I jokingly call it the Wrangell Territorial Prison, but it's not at all like Yuma."

"Greaterville? Greaterville, Arizona?" Wyatt burst into laughter. "As I recall that was simply a deep hole that Sheriff Bob Kerker used to lower his prisoners into with a rope."

Buckskin nodded. "Wouldn't work here with all the rain we get. The prisoners would either float to the top and escape, or drown."

"How was Yuma, Frank?"

Leslie shivered as he recalled the Arizona Territorial Prison. "Bad, Wyatt. You want to stay out of there. Hot as the devil with nary a hint of wind. I can still picture it in my mind, built on a finger of rock that poked into the Colorado River. Now, they made that one right, I'll tell you. Solid stone walls with inch-thick iron grating over each cell door, and another grate at the end of a long corridor so the guards could shoot through if they had to. But they never beat us, I'll say that for them. If you tried to escape you got a ball and chain to wear. Breaking the other rules landed you in the Dark Cell."

"The Dark Cell?"

"Yup. A steel cage dug into the side of the hill. Black as the ace of spades and as hot as Hades. Bread and water once a day. You just sat in there, fouled yourself, and cooked. In a day your own smell would make you sick. Drove more than a few mad.

"But I did wrong, Wyatt, and that landed me in Yuma. You might have guessed it was over a woman."

Wyatt took a long pull on his cigar and studied the ash. The tone of Frank's voice sounded like a small boy confessing his wrong doing. Earp studied his friend: A good man in a fight, steady and reliable, Leslie had ridden by his side after his brother Morgan was gunned down, but Frank could turn wild when whiskey and women mixed. So Frank had killed a woman, broken the law, and been convicted. But what was the law, Wyatt mused. Which side of the law a fellow fell on often depended on a judge. And if the judge was crooked? Well?

"I was ramrodding Frank Joyce's ranch outside Tombstone back in eighty-nine," Leslie said, talking almost to himself.

"Frank Joyce, the saloon owner, who Doc Holliday shot in the hand?" Wyatt asked.

"Yup. I was living with 'Blond' Mollie Williams. She worked at the Bird Cage. Well, I come back from Tombstone, drunk as a skunk in sour mash one night in July. We get into an awful fight, she comes after me with a knife, and I shoot her dead. There's a young ranch hand named Jim Neal, and I shoot him, too, but he gets away. His testimony got me sentenced to Yuma for twenty-five years."

"But they pardoned you?"

"Just this year. A cholera outbreak hit the prison and I helped the prison doctor. Worked like a trooper in the infirmary, day and night, until the epidemic was over. The governor added that to my service as an army scout and pardoned me. And now here I am, on the right side of the law again as a U. S. marshal." Leslie finished his complimentary beer and wiped his mustache. He stood up, picking at a speck of lint on his broadcloth coat.

Wyatt snubbed out the stub of his cigar on the battered table. It was time to go, time to continue their loop through town. Showing their badges and parading the law, that's what it was. Hoping their presence would be enough by itself. And all the while, watching their backs with that finely honed smell for danger that had kept them alive this long. That and luck, he half admitted. Why was he doing this? Josie was right, they didn't need the money. He wasn't exactly sure himself. Maybe I'm like an old plow horse who doesn't know anything else, he wondered. What a sad comment on my life.

The two men separated, taking opposite sides of the street.

Wyatt crossed over the canal to cover the dock side where he had a wider view of the alleys than Frank. Weaving through the crowd, the hairs on his neck prickled. Being closely packed like this favored the odds of a poor shot plugging him at point-blank range, or a knife sliding between his ribs from an unseen arm in the crowd. The hands, he reminded himself, concentrate on the hands. The threat always comes from the hands.

To his relief all the hands held supplies rather than weapons. But night would be different. Something about the dark prompted men to expose the darkness in their nature. Perhaps they expected that absent light made their sins less black.

Having lured the citizens of Wrangell out of their warrens, the sun now chose to forsake them, slipping behind a bank of clouds that rolled in from the bay. With the cloud, a fine mist spread over the town, followed by a biting wind. Wyatt shivered and turned the collar up on his coat. The chill stiffened his hip, and he slowed his walk to mask his incipient limp. It would be a long two weeks.

He had been right. Two weeks in Wrangell dragged by like two years, but now he stood on the dock in Juneau. The last stepping stone to Skagway, Juneau—just named territorial capitol—afforded more comforts than Wrangell. Surrounded by his steamer trunks, Wyatt folded his new tickets in his breast pocket and reflected on this leg of their journey.

Only once before in his life had he felt the uncertainty and thrill of so foreign a land. That was in the '70s while hunting buffalo with Bat Masterson. The thunder of thousands of shaggy beasts churning the prairie into dust beneath the painfully blue sky had stunned him. But even that had not prepared him for this. Alaska stretched past the limits of vision and beyond the mind's eye as well.

With each mile that the steamer's bow cut north through the emerald sea, the terrain grew more fantastic. The mountains gained an increasingly sharper edge along with an ivory hue that changed to rose whenever the sun set. Shrinking in comparison to their southern kin, the trees nevertheless now forested the coastline with greater determination. The water, too, grew heavy and threatening. Killer whales followed the ship, breaching the water in silent pods of black and white while black-and-white porpoises, looking like miniscule orcas, rode the bow wave.

Totem poles and cedar-planked longhouses of the Indian villages added to the alien sense. Once, as the steamer struggled through a narrow passage, dodging shoals and skirting overhanging trees, Tlingit or Haida canoes, sleek and carved with fantastic figureheads, sprang from undercover to flash past. Wyatt watched in awe as the seal-oiled hulls sped past in a blur of pointed paddles and berry red and soot black designs. These Indians were very different from those wandering about Wrangell selling trinkets. A fierceness and pride showed in their tattooed faces with the same easy grace their canoes mastered the water. *Like the Apache back in Arizona.*

Tomorrow we leave for Skagway, Earp thought as he tested his hip. That was the one good thing to come out of their delay—his leg was healed. Walking now felt good, and he paced the docks while he waited for Josie. She had insisted on going into town, an offer he declined in order to see their trunks safely transferred to the shallow draft paddle wheeler destined to take them to the shoals by Skagway. Tormented by massive tides, the boat would anchor off the coast while barges ferried passengers and goods ashore. Ashore meant deposited in the middle of miles of mud flats during low tide. Racing then against the incoming sea, teamsters demanded, and got, fifty dollars an hour to haul the supplies to safety.

Wyatt noted the difference between Juneau and Wrangell. Running from the water's edge up the side of Mount Juneau, this town grew with a gold strike in 1880—long before color was found in the Klondike. Now the town straddled Gold Creek, the original site of gold, and spread into every crevice capable of holding a shack. The gold mining activity presently centered about the Treadwell Mine across Gastineau Channel, but Juneau continued to thrive as territorial capitol and supply center for the Interior.

The place seemed to Wyatt as if an avalanche of houses had spilled down from Mount Juneau. Warehouses propped on stilts, shipyards, and elevated docks lined the water's edge while lesser fabrications like wall tents were forced to cling to the steep mountain side. The ever-present horde of dark-suited miners swept across the town like army ants.

The master of the packet steamer placed a megaphone to his mouth and announced the last boarding call. The ship was loaded. Wyatt stopped his pacing and ground his boot into the tar-coated planks. Where was Josie? Their steamer trunks moved slowly up the gangplank on the backs of two freighters. North across the channel the placid waters of the Lynn Canal beckoned, and beyond lay Skagway, door to the gold fields. Rays from the morning sun ignited the docks and waterfront into the color of burnished gold. All the tales of men returning with fortunes in gold sprang to his mind. This was their big chance.

"Hello, Wyatt. I'm sorry I'm late."

He turned to see her standing before him, small and smiling. The light illuminated her hair, casting a reddish hue to her chestnut brown curls, and her face glowed with an inner energy that matched the sun.

"Josie, we . . . we've got to board," he stammered, caught off guard by the sudden change in her appearance. "The boat is leaving. . . . " His words trailed off as his eyes locked onto hers.

"Wyatt, we're going to have a baby."

"Fine, but the boat is leaving." He wasn't listening, still mesmerized by her radiance.

"I'm pregnant, Wyatt."

"Pregnant?" The words hit him with the impact of a bullet.

"Yes." She nodded happily and slipped into his arms. She allowed him to hold her for a moment before she pulled away.

"You're sure?"

"Yes. I saw a doctor in town. Now we'd better board the ship."

Suddenly, his gold fever faded. A vision of her struggling over White Pass, bent beneath pounds of supplies, flashed to mind. Only once in their fifteen years of marriage had Josie got pregnant. Cruelly, their hopes had been dashed when she miscarried.

"All aboard who's coming aboard!" the captain shouted. He waved his megaphone at them. "Are you coming aboard or not? We're getting up steam." His mate underscored his point with two blasts of the steam whistle.

A family! Wyatt felt the pride swell in his chest. A son! Someone to carry his name. He had given up hope, but now his past dreams reappeared, driving out all thoughts of Eldorado. He would not risk Josie's health and his son for gold.

"Are you dumb and deaf?" the ship's master bellowed. "We're slipping our mooring! Your gear is loaded, and I'm not waiting any longer. Get on board!"

Wyatt grinned and shook his head. "Hand off our luggage. We're going back to San Francisco."

"No, Wyatt," Josie pleaded. "This meant so much to you. I'll be fine, you'll see."

"To hell with your luggage." The captain's face turned scarlet. "I'm not waiting while they find it. Pick it up in Skagway. And to hell with you!"

Wyatt's grin turned feral. He drew his Peacemaker and aimed at the captain. "Pass off our bags or the first bullet goes between your eyes while the other four sink your ship."

"You're crazy! You can't sink a stern-wheeler with a pistol!" The skipper shook his fist but looked worried.

"Are you dead sure I can't?"

"Better do it, captain," a deckhand warned. "That's Wyatt Earp."

The bags landed by Earp's feet.

The steamer backed away, leaving the two standing alone on the wharf, and when the captain felt safely out of pistol range he shook his fist. "You've missed your chance for a gold strike, fool. Now go to hell!" Not wanting to test his theory of ballistics, he ducked inside the pilothouse.

Wyatt watched the ship's smoke trail away. "The hell you say," he laughed. "I've got my own strike right here." His hand gently patted Josie's stomach. "Alaska will have to wait."

★ ★ THREE ★ ★

The fresh tracks in the dusting of snow led to a desolate hill overlooking the dying town of Pinal. Spring was late in coming to this high country, and a last storm had deposited winter's final attempt to hold the naked ground against the dormant plants that also fought to dress the country. A white spray covered the sage and catclaw bushes that grew among the junipers.

Linked to the trail's end and working his way to the mining town's boot hill moved a lad of sixteen. Shoulders hunched against the biting wind and cap pulled about his ears, the boy trudged upward. His shoes, hand-me-downs, bore cracks and scuffs from many miles of walking, and his ill-fitting woolen coat bore a series of patched repairs.

Under his arm he carried a threadbare carpetbag while his right hand clutched a packet of yellowed papers. He paused to read the faded inscriptions on the plots. Tilted and splintered, the headboards marked the graves of gamblers, gunmen, and whores, and reflected the neglect that covers the bones of the forgotten and unloved. Iron fences surrounded one or two resting places of the town's respectable, as if to shield them from Pinal's riffraff. But these gratings were rusting as well.

The mining camp of Pinal, sandwiched between the Superstition Mountains and the Pinal Mountains, was terminal, dying with the fall of silver prices. The Silver King Mine lay closed, its smokestacks silent. Goldman & Company Dry Goods long since shuttered. Pinal's newspaper, *The Drill,* extinct. Less than ten living souls inhabited a town that once held over two thousand. The honeycombs of mining tunnels lay empty, shops were vacant, and the remaining few prepared to flee. The siren song of gold discovered in the Yukon called, and the miners of Pinal flocked to its allure. It was only natural that these deceased dwellers of the town now forever locked to this land were quickly forgotten. Soon only the dead and the wind would inhabit Pinal.

The youth paused. White rocks encircled a small mound with a cleft plank for a headstone. He knelt to read the bleached epithet: CELIA BLAYLOCK, DIED OF HER OWN HAND, JULY 3, 1888. Setting his valise aside, he studied the papers in his hand. Back to the wind to shield the papers, he extracted a faded photograph. The wind tore it from his grasp to pin it against the headboard as if to say: This is who I once was.

Dropping to his knees, the youth recovered the picture. Intently, his pale, gray eyes studied the likeness. Leaning against a cloth-draped pillar, an unsmiling woman gazed directly from the print. Her tightly curled brown hair and plaid dress gave no indication of the demons that drove her to take her life.

The boy knitted his brow in concentration. The woman's features were alien to him. While her face was round, yet almost square, his was lean and angular. Her features were soft and pliant while his face showed a feral sharpness. Could this be his mother? he wondered. Surely, he should feel something as he studied the likeness, some deep stirring or glint of familiarity that would establish their linkage. But he felt nothing.

Next, he reread the letter, as he had a hundred times since his sixteenth birthday. One week and a different life ago, the orphanage at St. Catherine's in Denver defined his life. Seven days ago he was just another castaway, working in the kitchen with no skills, no family, no past, and no future.

The day he turned sixteen the mother superior gave him the parcel that fractured his world forever. Two photographs, a letter, and a bank draft. Now he had a past, and his future was up to him.

Dearest Nathan,

Happy birthday, my son, for this will be your sixteenth birthday. Your name is Nathan Blaylock, and I am your mother, Mattie Blaylock. When you read this I will be dead, but know that you have all my love, and I have struggled to provide for your future and well-being.

I wish with all my heart that I could have raised you as a mother should, but that was made impossible by the willful and selfish act of one man—your father.

That man alone is responsible for the torment both you and I have suffered. He abandoned both of us, and as a direct result my life has come to ruin.

But, my dear Nathan, I have better hopes for you. I have struggled to save every penny I could for you. In the Union Trust Bank in San Francisco is twenty thousand dollars. It is all for you, Nathan, in hopes you will live the full life we both have been denied.

To receive your just reward, you must apply in person to that bank with this letter. The mother superior has four hundred dollars for expenses.

One more thing, Nathan. You must avenge your mother and kill the man responsible for our sorry state. Nathan, I beg you bring retribution on the head of this vile man. Whether you do the deed yourself or hire another is unimportant, but to collect your reward, you must kill your father! I have enclosed his photograph and his name.

Do not be distressed. This man is a murderer. As proof
I have enclosed a warrant for his arrest for the murder of
Frank Stilwell. So your actions will be legal.

All my love.
Your mother, Mattie Blaylock

Nathan Blaylock stared at the accompanying picture. The
sharp features glared in profile. A stern, angular face, sporting
a thick, down-curving mustache, glared from the paper with
piercing, gray eyes. Eyes, Nathan noted, like his. Written beneath the face was the man's name: Wyatt Berry Earp.

As the sun settled behind the bluish outlines of the foothills,
Nathan trudged into Pinal. Coming down from the mountain,
he brought mixed emotions. No longer nameless, he now carried a greater onus than being a bastard.

Long hours listening to a biting wind that held no answers
left him tired and confused. Nothing in his orphanage experience could help him in this matter. He was trained as a cook's
helper, not a gunfighter. Even now the outside world was new
and rough to him. Killing someone had never occurred to him.
Pushing the mother superior down the long flight of steps had
crossed his mind after his numerous beatings, but he had come
to accept her violent nature.

Eventually, he reached a conclusion. He must kill this man,
Wyatt Earp. After all, Earp was a fugitive from justice. Nathan
would avenge his mother, wipe out the insult to himself, and
collect the fortune. Twenty thousand dollars would see him to
a new life. Without that money, only a dark and uncertain path
lay before him.

His fingers massaged the last piece of this puzzle, a pouch
with four hundred dollars in double eagles. The boy had never
held more than a few pennies at the orphanage, and the coins
warmed his hand with an unholy heat. Tonight he would sleep

in a real hotel bed instead of beneath the junipers as he did last evening. At the corner store he bought a new coat, a wide-brimmed hat, and a pair of black leather boots. Rattling the change from a twenty-dollar gold piece, Nathan followed his stomach to the Mother Lode Saloon. The smell of simmering stew drew him onward.

Crossing the wheel-rutted street, the boy stepped onto the sidewalk. The sun's warmth was long gone, and the bite of the night air prodded the boy toward the yellow glow of the oil lamps. Outside the doors he stopped.

The cold wind from the mountains stirred a bundle of rags huddled on the elevated planks. Patched, threadbare pants legs dangled from a sorry saddle blanket cut into a poncho. Its owner struggled to fold as much of his body beneath the blanket as possible. Shivers wracked the rag man, but his eyes watched the boy's every move from the shadows of a slouch hat.

Nathan handed his old coat to the beggar. "Here, I've got a new one. My luck's improved. I hope yours does, too."

The man's eyes glanced down at the woolen jacket at his feet, then back at Nathan. He said nothing.

Without thinking, Nathan slipped two dollars into the man's outstretched left hand, then stepped inside.

Another world greeted the boy, one far removed from his orphanage. Stale cigar smoke, sweat, and the pungent odor of sour beer assailed his nose. The painting of a naked woman over the bar caused him to blush, and a wave of uncertainty engulfed him, but he found himself at the bar.

"A beer," Nathan tried his best to keep his voice level and low.

The bartender scrutinized the boy from above a filthy rag he was carelessly wiping across glasses. He shrugged and passed a bottle of warm beer to the youth as soon as Nathan dropped a double eagle on the bar. Business was bad, the barkeep rationalized, and he was not the town's conscience.

Nathan nearly choked on the tepid brew. Half turning to hide the tears in his eyes, he took another drink, this time more cautiously. So this was the dreaded demon alcohol the sisters had warned about, he mused. Nothing to it. He emptied the bottle.

"Another." The warmth spread from his stomach into his limbs.

The bartender pursed his lips while he assessing his young customer. "Want something to eat?"

Nathan nodded. "Haven't eaten since yesterday." His lips felt thick and rubbery.

"Then a man like yourself knows that drink on an empty stomach can be a mite fearsome," the man replied. There, he had assuaged his moral sense. "Have a seat over at that table, and I'll bring some stew over with your next beer."

Nathan walked stiffly to the table, exercising great care to appear in control. But his stiff-legged stride carried him into its side. He plopped into the chair, blinking furiously.

A crocker bowl of stew appeared on the table along with another brew. Forced by habit he paused to say grace, but the puzzled stares of the half dozen men caused him to stop. Nathan unfolded his hands to spoon the lumpy mix into his mouth. The glop bit back, reflecting the cook's heavy use of chili pepper. Another mouthful of beer helped quench the fire. Spoon and drink, Nathan carried out the routine until he trapped the last greasy potato with a scrap of flour tortilla. Before him lay four empty beer bottles.

Tilting back in his chair, the boy expanded into his surroundings. This was the life, a world among men. No black-hooded harridans to whip him and warn him of hell. If this was a part of hell, he could do with more. His reddened face glowed to match the coal oil lamps, and his limbs stretched toward the potbellied stove in the far corner. Carelessly, he shifted the bag of coins from his coat pocket onto the tabletop and removed a handful to inspect. The gold glinted in the lamplight. The gold also glinted in the eyes of three other men. The three exchanged knowing looks as they closed the distance on the boy.

"Mind if we join you, mister?"

Nathan looked up into a bearded face. He had never been called *mister* before.

The beard split into a sly grin, exposing two missing teeth and several rotted snags. "Tuck Horner's the name." A calloused hand thrust into Nathan's face. "And this here's my brother, Grubb. This other fellow's Jack Dunn."

Nathan shook the hand as he focused his blurred sight on the face. It and its voice appeared fox-like, devious and indirect like Sister Mary Augustus when she crept into Sister Josephine's quarters at night. Grubb appeared open-eyed and dim-witted like a marmot.

Without waiting for a reply, the men dragged chairs across the sawdust-covered floor and surrounded the youth. "So, mister, what brings you into town?" Tuck asked. "Pinal's on its last legs with no silver being mined." He studiously avoided staring at the open pouch. But his brother sat mesmerized by the money.

"Just passing through," Nathan mumbled.

"Is that a fact?" Tuck continued evenly. "I thought as much. No one in his right mind would live here." He patted the youth's arm. "We was just passing through, just like yourself. That gives us something in common."

"Yeah," Grubb agreed. Subtlety came hard to him, but he was just grasping his brother's designs and doing his best to play along.

"Got any plans, mister? Mister . . . I didn't catch your name," Tuck probed as he signaled for another round of beers.

"My name is . . . Nathan, Nathan Blaylock." Nathan used his unfamiliar, new name.

"Blaylock?" Grubb's frowned in concentration. "I knew a

Mattie Blaylock once. She was a whore. Killed herself about ten years ago, with whiskey and laudanum."

"She was my ma." Nathan stiffened. His mother a whore? And his father a murderer? His head was spinning.

"Sorry to hear about that, Nat." Tuck shot a venomous look at his brother.

"Well, she was a good one, I'll say that for her," Grubb added feebly, trying hard to recover. He screwed his eyes in concentration and picked at his blackened fingernails. This cat-and-mouse business was too hard, he thought. It made his head split. Better we drag this whelp outside, slit his throat, and be off with his gold.

"Will you shut your gob," Tuck Horner snarled. "Can't you see the poor boy's grieving for his ma?" To punctuate his remark his fingers clamped on the front of his brother's shirt, twisting the linen into a tight knot. Grubb dropped back into his chair and closed his mouth.

Nathan looked at Tuck. "She killed herself because my pa left her."

"That's a dirty shame, Nat, leaving a woman and young'n in this country. Why, I bet she turned soiled dove jus' to put food in your mouth." The older Horner measured the effect of his words on the youth.

Nathan nodded as he accepted another beer Jack Dunn slipped into his hand. "I . . . I never knew. I was in an orphanage." He scanned their eyes for sympathy. Grubb looked ready to cry.

"Your poor ma, doing those things to feed you. You ought to be real proud of her. Hell, some men ain't nothing but rutting hogs with no thought to the misery they leave behind." Tuck craned his neck to look at the papers the boy clutched in his fist. He decided to gamble on his hunch. His eyes narrowed. "Someone did that to me and my ma, I'd kill the son of a bitch."

Nathan's head snapped upward to level his eyes with

Tuck's. "That's just what I intend to do!" he growled. He nodded to the bag of gold. "I've got the money to hire help, too!"

"Well, Mr. Blaylock," Tuck said, grinning as he thumped his chest. "This is your lucky day. You just happen to be talking to three of the best bounty hunters this side of the Hassayampa River. Have you heard of the Stiles-Alvord gang out of Fairbank in Cochise County?"

Nathan shook his head.

"We used to ride with them, Billy Stiles, Burt Alvord, and 'Three-Fingered' Jack Dunlap," Tuck lied, glossing over the fact that Billy Stiles had kicked them out and threatened to shoot the Horner brothers on sight.

"You've actually killed someone?" Nathan gasped in amazement.

"A lot, boy," Tuck nodded gravely.

"And we don't count Chinamen nor Mex's, neither," Dunn added. He was a slight, squirrely looking fellow with a plaid bandanna covering a rough scar on the left side of his neck and an opaque cast in his left eye.

"What about Cousin Jacks," Grubb questioned. "Do we count them?" The tally taxed his thoughts.

"Naw." Tuck shook his head. "Those Cornish miners can't shoot nothing. I don't count them, neither."

"So we're your men, if it's for killing," Grubb chuckled. His hands massaged his stubbled cheeks.

Young Blaylock's eyes narrowed. "How much do you want? I mean, you know, to do the job."

"That depends on who you want done in," Tuck bargained. "Some takes more killing than others."

"How about this murderer?" Nat spread the warrant on the table along with the picture of Wyatt Earp. He kept his attention fixed on the photograph's cold eyes. In doing so he missed the reaction of his friends.

Color drained from Jack Dunn's face like water from a

holed crock, and Grubb Horner's eyes bulged from his reddened face as if a noose had snapped shut around his beefy neck. "Wyatt Earp!" Grubb hissed the words.

Nathan looked up into the alarmed faces of the three. "What's the matter? Do you know him?" he questioned.

"Don't you, boy?" Dunn sounded incredulous. "This here's a picture of Wyatt Earp, himself. Ain't you never heard of Tombstone and the O.K. Corral?"

Nathan shook his head.

"I forget, you've been shut away in a convent." Tuck scratched his beard as he recovered his footing. "Earp's a tough nut, him and his brothers." For an instant he weighed the odds: three against three. With Morgan dead, there were Wyatt, Warren, and Virgil. But they had friends. Then, Tuck's mind returned to the reality of the situation. They had no intention of looking for Earp, only dry gulching this foolish whelp and pocketing his gold. The knot in his stomach dissolved. He forced his face into a painful look. Shaking his head, he replied. "Wyatt's a bad one, for sure. How much have you got in that poke?"

"Almost four hundred dollars."

"It'll take all of that."

"Okay." Nathan wrapped his fingers around the leather pouch. "But, I have to go along. To see it done."

Tuck nodded. He was tiring of this game. He pushed back from the table and stood looking down at the boy. "We better get cracking, then. Get your horse, Mr. Blaylock, and we'll ride for Apache Junction tonight. In the morning we'll head for Tombstone and pick up your daddy's trail."

"I don't have a horse."

"Never you mind." Tuck had figured as much from the boy's rig. He had walking, train, and wagon written all over him. "You can ride up behind Grubb, till we can find you a ride of your own." His glance silenced his brother's protest.

The three men and the boy, clutching his valise, moved as a group across the plank saloon floor and out the swinging doors into the chill of the evening. Moments later the sound of horses' hoofbeats trailed away.

In their haste to leave, neither the Horner brothers nor Jack Dunn noticed the pair of eyes that watched their every move. Cloaked in the shadows outside the cast of the oil lamps, the eyes burned unblinking beneath a weathered hat. Five minutes after the last sound of the horses disappeared down the empty street, the silent witness finished the last of his beer, rose slowly, and slipped unseen into the night.

⋆ ⋆ **FOUR** ⋆ ⋆

"Stop yer squirming, or I'll stomp you again, boy!" Grubb cursed down at Nathan Blaylock, struggling beneath his boot. Blood mixed with ocher dust matted the side of the youth's face where Tuck had pistol-whipped Nathan off his brother's horse. With Dunn's help Nathan was jerked to his feet and his hands roughly tied with a lariat before being shoved into a cleft in the rocks. There he fought to clear his head as his former friends ransacked his belongings and stripped him of his new boots and coat.

The attack came unexpectedly as the men stopped to water their horses at a shallow stream five miles out of town. The group had pushed their horses west for several miles before turning south into the foothills. All the while Tuck kept up a good-hearted banter with Nathan and the others. Once they entered the cleft of dark, rocky hills, the older Horner fell silent. Riding along the winding path, darkness swallowed the group as they entered the black shadows of the outcroppings and clumps of juniper and mesquite.

Uneasiness settled in Nathan's stomach as the route took this ominous turn. The creak of saddle leather, coupled with the horses' hooves on the rocky ground, did little to assuage his anxiety. Nor did the unexpected hoot of a screech owl help. Tuck was heading off the traveled roads and farther into the wilds. Frenzied thoughts of robbers and rustlers camped in the blind canyons and draws of these rocks flooded the boy's mind, but he pushed them back.

Finally, Tuck reined in his mount. The rising moon cast its beams over the buttes to light a trickling stream ahead. Flowing like molten silver, the creek meandered around strewn boulders and smooth worn pebbles. A cluster of cottonwoods flanked the clearing. Dunn walked his pony into the creek and let it drink.

As Nathan sat behind Grubb, watching the guzzling horse, the other Horner leaned from his saddle and struck the boy from behind with his pistol barrel. The eight-inch American Model Smith & Wesson caught Nathan behind his left ear, sending him sprawling to the ground. In a flash the heavier Grubb was astride him, kicking him senseless.

Nathan fought until instinct told him to stop and wait for a better chance. Now, trussed like a hog to be slaughtered, he glowered at the men.

"What you lookin' at, boy?" Grubb snarled as he aimed another kick at Blaylock. "Did we hurt yer feelings?" Raucous laughter erupted from the trio.

"Why? Why are you doing this?" Nathan croaked. The sudden and vicious attack shocked and confused him beyond any previous experience. Beatings in the orphanage by the sisters and the drunken cook had always followed tongue lashings, allowing him warning and time to prepare.

Grubb took another swill from the whiskey bottle the men now passed around and pushed his bloated face close to the youth's. "You didn't listen, did you? We told you, but you didn't hear too good. 'Cause we're *bad men,* boy." His words misted Nathan in a cloud of spittle and alcoholic vapors.

"Haw, haw," Dunn guffawed. "Bad men, rustlers, and bushwhackers."

Only Tuck appeared sober. He squatted by the small fire the men had started, alternating between feeding it twigs and counting the coins in Nathan's purse. His boot nudged a battered coffeepot deeper into the bed of coals.

"But we had a deal!"

"Boy," Tuck said squinting through the smoke, "you must be soaking wet behind your ears. Or plumb foolish. The only deal we got is to deal with you. Whether to slit your gullet or plug you in the brain pan, that's the *only* deal going here."

White hot rage erupted deep within Nathan, bubbling upward into a hatred he had never felt before. These men had tricked him. They would kill him, steal his gold, and leave him rot. He, Nathan Blaylock, would disappear forever, never to have a future or seek his fortune. Never to avenge his mother, never to be someone—never to be anything. And all because of his foolishness. That thought drove him wild. His fists bunched and the muscles in his arms corded. He would kill them all, with his teeth and nails if need be.

"You dog turds! You fucking scum!" His compendium of vile words, learned from the drunken cook, spilled out. It was a poor choice of words, for it raised ideas in Grubb's sotted mind.

Grubb blinked as he focused on the white flesh of Nathan's exposed back. He leaned closer, eyebrows raised in reflection, before sharing his thoughts with Dunn. "Hey, Jack, the boy do look all pink and tender, don't ya think so?"

"Jus' like that dolly in Chilito."

"Yeah. What do you say, Tuck? Can we take him for a walk in the park before we kill him?" Grubb wiped the back of his hand across his mouth, referring to the phrase for visiting a brothel.

Tuck Horner shrugged at his brother. "Don't make no never mind to me." He poured coffee into a tin cup, balancing the hot cup in both hands while he stepped in front of the fire. The moon was fully up now, a silver disk casting its light without warmth into the clearing. Black shadows draped across the boulders in fearsome shapes that slithered under the dancing flames of the campfire.

Dunn and Grubb jerked Nathan to his feet and stripped his trousers to his knees. Dunn produced a tarnished Bowie knife with a bone handle, turning it over slowly in his hand to inspect the notched blade. Dunn had taken it off a Mexican vaquero he had backshot along the border, and being lazy, never cleaned up its edge.

"My, ain't he pretty," Grubb drooled. His hand ran down Nathan's buttock. The boy stiffened.

Dunn pressed the tip of the knife against Nathan's back. His eyes glinted feverishly. "I might want to cut you a mite, boy. Make you squeal, you know?"

Nathan spat into Dunn's face. "Go to hell!"

"Haw, Jack," Grubb cackled, his fingers fumbling with his gunbelt and pants. "He don't like you. That means I'm first."

"That weren't very friendly, boy," Jack Dunn growled. To make his point he pressed the blade into Nathan's side and drew a crimson line in the skin. The lad never flinched, but flames blazed from his eyes.

"Bend him over, Jack," Grubb ordered.

"Mind if I watch?" the stranger's voice rolled across the clearing like a clap of thunder.

Dunn and both Horners spun to see a man standing just inside the rim of light cast by the campfire. Peering across the blaze only his shape and the dreadful nature of his worn boots were presented to the bandits.

"Go on, boys," the stranger continued evenly as he slowly crouched to pour himself a cup of their coffee. "Don't stop on my account. I'm *just passing through*. You-all playing some kind of game?" The man sipped the coffee, yet all the while his eyes bored unwaveringly into the group.

"Why, it's that saddle bum, Grubb," Dunn exclaimed. "The one what was freezing outside the saloon." Grubb Horner's face returned to its previous smirk, but his brother edged closer to the Winchester rifle in his saddle scabbard.

"I ain't freezing no more," the man replied, a trace of irritation creeping into his voice, "thanks to that boy you're fooling with." His eyes, cold and deadly, continued to appraise them over the rim of the tin cup.

Nathan gasped. The man was wearing his cast-off woolen coat from the orphanage. "Run, mister!" he cried. "These skunks are murderers!"

"*Bad men,* are they?"

"Yeah, you made a big mistake, you saddle sore piece of shit," Grubb challenged. "Sticking your nose where it don't belong. Now we're gonna kill you, too."

"But I don't think they're gunfighters," the stranger mused, talking out loud to himself. "This fat one's got his pants down and his gunbelt around his knees, way beyond reach, his brother's too far from his Winchester, and their friend is holding a knife."

Jack Dunn glanced at the Bowie in his hand. He'd never had much luck throwing the thing. The stranger was right. The heavy blade seemed to anchor his hand, holding it away from his revolver.

"Friend, I'd use that knife to cut the boy's hands free."

Dunn started to obey, then stopped. "What the hell for?"

"So's he can put his fingers in his ears," the stranger explained.

"The hell you say?" Tuck snapped. Hairs were rustling to attention on the back of his neck. This bum didn't sound right. Something was definitely wrong here. Facing three men, he ought to be peeing into his holey boots. "Why would you say that?" he stalled as he inched closer to his rifle.

"Because it's going to get real loud—"

"Look out, mister!" Nathan saw the move and drove his

shoulder into Tuck, knocking his hand away from the Winchester.

The tin coffee cup seemed to float in midair, abandoned by the stranger's fingers. Instead, the cold barrel of a Colt .45 materialized. A balloon of flame spurted from the muzzle. Once, twice, three times, before Nathan could catch his breath, the Colt barked. Sharp and sudden like a close-by clap of thunder, the sounds deafened him.

Each muzzle flash painted the campsite in stark images of black and yellow. Nathan's eyes captured each glimpse. The stranger, firing his revolver with both hands, held it almost at arm's length like a rifle. Tuck Horner, spinning back into a clump of prickly pears, the front of his checkered shirt turning red from a hole where his third shirt button had been. Jack Dunn, dropping like a sack of flour, face down in the dust. An ugly rent opened out from the center of his leather vest at the point the lead slug exited his back. And Grubb, leaping the fire in a cloud of sparks, his pistol blazing away before the stranger's bullet caught him square in the stomach. Smoke embroiled the campsite and the level of light was reduced to that of the feeble cook fire.

Nathan's ears rang as the silence threatened to burst his eardrums. He crouched, ready to flee if the thinning smoke revealed danger. But his fears were groundless.

"Goddamn," Grubb wheezed incredulously as he sank back on his heels. His fingers worked vainly to contain the dark stain that spread across his belly. "You gut shot me!"

"That's all you got to hit is gut," the standing gunman replied. "But, I shot where I reckoned your heart was." He aimed along his barrel and placed a round between Grubb's eyes. As the bullet cracked into the fat man's forehead, he flopped backward, whites rolling beneath his lids, to land in the fire. The back of his head started to smoke.

Nathan straightened slowly. The suddenness and extreme violence astounded him. Three to four seconds ago, Dunn and the Horners threatened his life. Now they lay dead. Warily he watched the raggedy gunman remove the Bowie from Dunn's stiff fingers and approach him.

"You got sand in your craw, son, jumping that fellow with the rifle, I'll say that for you. But, yer choice of traveling companions ain't too bright." The knife sawed through the ropes to free Nathan's hands. His rescuer frowned at the knife before sticking it in the ground. "Lazy sod," he remarked. "Kept a dull knife."

Nathan watched as the man pulled the smoking corpse of Grubb Horner from the fire and proceeded to rifle the man's pockets. Carefully, the man looted all those he had killed. Soon he sat beside the fire surrounded by a pile of booty.

"You aren't going to rob them, are you?" Nathan questioned.

The stranger shook his head. "They was a-robbing you, wasn't they?"

Nathan nodded.

"Well, I'm robbing 'em back."

"Well, it doesn't seem . . . right."

The man paused to watch a packet rat, eyes flashing like burnished copper beads, inching into the circle of the campfire. The gleam of gold from the half-spilled coins drew him like a magnet. Without warning a screech owl dropped from the night sky to fasten its talons into the back of the rat's neck. The rodent twitched once, and the light faded from its eyes. Beating the air with fletched feathers, the owl silently flew off with its catch. Only a riffle in the sand marked the passing event.

"Does that seem right to you?" The gunman pointed to the faint disturbance in the dust. "Why, I bet that there rat had a family, with young'ns and all. Maybe even went to rat church on Sundays, and never beat his wife nor nothing. And now he's gone. By sunup tomorrow he'll be owl shit."

"Don't you believe in good and evil?" Nathan's Catholic doctrine spilled to the surface. He marveled as he stood there shaking to the soles of his boots that theology could wedge its way into his jumbled thoughts.

The man smiled crookedly. "Seen my share of that, I have. Problem is sometimes good and bad gets all mixed up in the same person. That becomes a mite perplexing. Some days they's good 'n other days pure poison. Hard to separate 'em out when that happens."

"That's for God to do," Nathan said. "You do believe in God, don't you?"

The man's face clouded. "My ma taught me to believe in the good Lord," he added solemnly. "But, I don't think the Lord believes much in me."

With that the man walked to the horses and inspected the saddlebags. As he passed Nathan, he scooped up the spilled double eagles and dropped the bag at Nathan's feet. "Best not be flashing that to every Johnny Come Lately you meet, son," he said. "Now, like that owl, I'm hungry."

Conversation was over. Nathan hugged his knees and watched as the man stirred a chunk of sowbelly into a pan of beans until the bubbling sauce softened the salty slab. Unexpectedly, the youth felt hungry. In fact, he felt wonderfully alive. The inky night, replete with its sounds and smells, the cold wind, and the wood smoke all bombarded his heightened senses. A strange giddiness engulfed him. Was this how it felt to survive a gunfight, he wondered. Was it always this way? Would it be like this when he killed Wyatt Earp?

After dinner, while Nathan automatically scraped the plates and scoured them with sand, his erstwhile savior busied himself with his spoils. Screwing off his dilapidated boots exposed tattered socks more hole than not. Trial and error finally led to an acceptable fit of Jack Dunn's socks and Tuck Horner's boots. The same Horner's pants also fit nicely and covered a pitiful set of long johns.

Newly attired, the man donned Tuck's straight brimmed hat, but chose to wear Nathan's old coat. He frowned at the body of Grubb Horner. "Wasted a bullet on this hog," he grunted. "All's his stuff is burnt or way too big."

Nathan pointed to the buffalo coat lashed behind Dunn's saddle. "Why don't you wear that one? It's finer than my old jacket."

" 'Cause I'm partial to yours, young fella. I think it might change my luck. Weren't there some saint in the Bible that give his coat to a beggar? I recall my ma reading that to me."

"St. Martin, I think. But he divided his cloak."

"Close enough." He thrust his finger through a bullet hole beneath the right pocket. "No better protection than wearing a saint's coat in a shoot-out."

Nathan's eyes widened. "That must have been Grubb."

"Well," the shootist said as he inspected the damage, "I always say distance is yer friend in a gunfight, with six-shooters anyway. That is if you use yer front sight and don't be jerking the trigger. I figure I can outshoot most if they's blasting away at me from the hip. But that lardy jasper got a mite too close for my taste."

Nathan reached his decision. It was all so clear. This man was the solution to his problems. "Will you teach me to shoot? I want to hire you for a job. I have to shoot someone, and as you can see, I can pay well."

The man appeared not to hear. He disappeared into the darkness to return with a dappled pony that looked far better cared for than its master. Unsaddling the paint, he tethered it close by a patch of grass. Then he shook out Jack Dunn's bedroll and settled himself just outside the firelight.

"Goodnight, St. Martin."

Nathan couldn't believe what he saw. Wearing the clothing

of men he had just killed and surrounded by their stiffening bodies, the man was fast asleep.

"Mister?" Nathan whispered. "Mister? What do you say to my proposal? Will you teach me?"

He got no response. Now an unhappy thought crossed his mind. Had this stranger been shot? Perhaps he was wounded or dying and too proud to ask for help? Warily, Nathan crept to the still form. As gingerly as he could, he raised a corner of the blanket to make an inspection.

He looked directly into the muzzle of the man's Peacemaker. That same revolver less than an hour ago had snuffed out three men's lives. Looking above the barrel, Nathan caught those cold, unblinking eyes fixed on him. He froze in terror, the blanket corner slipping from his fingers to redrape the waiting death.

"Lesson Number One, Mr. Saint: Don't never let yerself git caught unawares. Not never."

FIVE

Nathan awoke from a restless night spotted with nightmares and dreams of gun battles seasoned with faces of his mother and father floating around. He sat upright and rubbed his eyes. The sun was outlining the distant hills into a golden ribbon set beneath an azure sky. Wisps of cloud rode high overhead while that same rising sun lit their underbellies into fiery veils. The air was crisp and fresh, and ice rimmed the edges of the stream.

He turned on his side and shuddered. The dead bodies were still there. His nightmares had really happened.

"Morning, Mr. Saint." His companion greeted him from an economical fire of crackling mescal and juniper. The dried wood made little smoke. The nutty aroma of coffee and chicory wafted his way.

"My name is Nathan, Nathan Blaylock, not St. Martin," the boy responded, rubbing his eyes. Masquerading as a saint struck him as obscene and slightly dangerous. "What's your name, mister?"

"Smith. Just Jim Smith."

"A week ago my name was Smith, too." Nathan stared directly at the man. "I was a nobody then, a nothing called Smith. Smith is an empty name. No one should be called Smith for want of their real name."

The man looked hard at the boy. In the morning light his iron gray hair and silvered mustache framed a face worn thin and lined by a hard life. White stubble sprouted between the seams that covered his face. He was far from young. As he sipped his coffee, he seemed to be weighing his next move. He carefully studied this naïve youth. In Nathan he saw himself when he was that age, chock full of hopes and promises. Just like he'd been once so long ago that it hurt to remember. That was really why he'd followed them to the creek, he had to admit. That was why he waded in against all his better judgment. The spring of his life had died in a similar gunfight, and he hoped to save this youth from a comparable fate. Perhaps he half believed he could save himself if he saved this boy.

"You're right, Nat. I ain't Jim Smith. My name is Jim Riley." He stirred the coals with the toe of his boot. "And I ain't told no one my real name for some time."

Nathan's eyes widened. "Newton's General Massacre. I read about you!" he exclaimed. "In a dime novel the cook had. He hid ones about Wild Bill Hickok, Buffalo Bill, and Calamity Jane behind the washboard. The mother superior said they were trash, but I'd sneak down after vespers and read them. Newton Jim Riley! There was a book just about you," Nat added quizzically. "You're supposed to be dead."

Riley frowned. "Well, I ain't laid down jus' yet, dead or not."

He handed Nat a tin cup of coffee, and the two sat in silence staring at the fire. Nathan tried not to look at the half-dressed bodies sharing their campsite. Already the warmth of the sun was coaxing the corpses to swell. The buttons on Grubb Horner's long johns strained to hold back the bloating flesh.

"I've given yer proposal some thought, Nat, but I just don't know."

"If it's more money, I've got more."

"You talk like you got yerself a smart education, son. Take my advice, use it to make something good of yerself, and don't get on no killing trail. Once you ride that way, there's no certain nor good end to it. I know. I've been running for twenty-seven years."

"But you're a legend like Wild Bill!"

"And look what it's got us. Hickok dead, and you saw me freezing near to death on those steps."

"Look, Mr. Riley. I've got to do this. If I don't I can't collect my inheritance. That's twenty thousand dollars. I could never hope to make that much money washing dishes. Without that, I've got no future. I don't want to be a cook's helper all my life. I'm willing to split the whole amount with you. Besides, my dead ma asked me to do it. I never met her, but I owe it to her. Didn't your mother ever hold you to a promise?"

Those last words caused Riley to grimace. His head sagged as he dropped his cup to wipe his hands on his newly acquired trousers. "Yeah, an' I ain't kept it, neither. That hurts me most of all."

Nathan sensed the man wanted to talk. He waited while Riley wiped his eyes on his sleeve and ran his fingers through his forest of rangy, steel-colored hair. "Want to talk about it?"

Riley started. Something about this boy with his open face and clear eyes made it easy, like he was talking to himself. "We was dirt poor, my family, scratching a living on a piece of stationary dust jus' north of the Sweetwater. Kiowas kilt my pa when I was twelve. That left jus' me and my ma and a half dozen range cattle. Rancho Riley, we called it. But weren't nothing to signify it but an adobe arch my pa built before he died."

He paused to draw his Colt and tap its front sight. "That's when I learnt to shoot, aiming with both hands the way I do and using my front site. All we had was my dad's six-shooter, so I educated myself with that. Couldn't afford more'n a few cartridges, so every shot had to count. Rabbits and sage hens kept us goin'. If I missed we went hungry. I couldn't hit nothin' one-handed, nor shooting from the hip, neither. Hell, I'd lie on my belly for an hour, waiting for two sage hens to git in line so's I could drill two in the head with one shot." He pointed his finger at Nathan to emphasize his point. "Blasting one of them scrawny birds in the body with a .45 don't leave nothin' for the cook pot, you understand?"

"Is it true what they say about you and Newton's General Massacre, Mr. Riley?"

"Don't know what they's saying, but I'll tell you what happened. The winter of seventy-one nearly did for my ma and me. We was down to stewing rawhide scraps for somethin' to keep our ribs from sticking together. This fellow big Mike McCluskie was heading north a-buildin' the railroad. He hired me to hunt game to feed the workers." Riley stopped. "I jus' shot food. I never kilt no runaway Chinamen, like some others done. Those poor Chinamen was as bad off as me.

"Well, McCluskie, he had his faults, gambling for one and a hair-trigger temper that matched his red hair for another, but he took pity on us an' paid ma my whole year's wages in advance. By August we was at the railhead in Newton, Kansas. Big Mike killed this Texas gambler over a card game. Don't remember the man's name. Trouble was, he had a slew of cowboy friends.

"It was August 20, 1871, a Saturday, jus' after midnight when it all boiled over. McCluskie was in Perry Tuttle's dance hall playing faro when this cowboy, Hugh Anderson, calls him a cowardly son of a bitch and shoots Big Mike in the neck. Mike got his gun out, but it misfired. Then Anderson plugged him in the leg and the back. All hell was breaking loose. The cowboys from Anderson's outfit started shooting at all the railroad fellows. Two of Mike's friends, Pat Lee and another named Hickey were shot down.

"I figured I owed Mike somethin' for helping ma and me. He saved our lives. It didn't seem right all those men pumping him full of lead like that."

Richard Parry

"Did you really lock the saloon door behind you like it said in the novel?" Nathan asked.

"Yup. Those fools even shot one of their own men, Jim Martin. He staggered past me to die in the street. I didn't want none of them getting by me, so I locked the door."

"What happened next?"

"I used my two-handed grip and my front site, jus' like shooting sage hens. Only these prairie chickens was shooting back at me. They was a-yellin' an' a-blazing their six-guns, fanning the hammers and firing from the hip. Bullets was tearing all over the place—mirrors, tables, and the door post. But, they weren't no better shots than them sage hens."

"They say you killed all five."

"Three, or five, I don't rightly recall which, now."

"Wow," Nathan gushed. "You were great."

"Not hardly. I put five men in the ground that day and put an end to any future I was hoping for."

"I don't understand."

"Once you pull that trigger a lifetime of wishing won't turn that bullet back. An' one killin' draws another like honey calls in flies. Ain't no stopping it then, no how. People you don't know from nothing fixing to make a name by killing you. Since that day, I've been running more or less as Jim Smith, working as a buffalo hunter, hiring as shotgun on gold shipments, riding protection in range wars. Putting folks under seems to follow me like a shadow." Jim paused to point his cup at the bodies. "See what I mean."

"But, you don't bend to anyone, do you?"

"No, I don't. But you make it sound richer than it is. I'm getting old in the tooth and casting a longer shadow than I ever expected. My bones are fretting over cold campsites something dreadful. The thought of a warm bed and a cabin occupies most of my thoughts, nowadays. I know the sun's setting on me."

"Ten thousand dollars would buy a lot of comfort."

"I'm sorely tempted, that I am. I've killed men for four dollars a day, an' this here's more money than I've ever seen, but I never killed nobody that wasn't trying to kill me as well. That much I think my ma would approve."

"But Earp is a murderer, surely that makes a difference? That would make it easier."

"Maybe he is and maybe he ain't. Remember what I said 'bout good and bad gittin' mixed up at times. There's lots would call me a cold-blooded killer, though I don't fancy myself one. I overheard yer conversation in the saloon. And yer pa, if that's who he is, ain't no simple killer."

"He's like the Horners and . . . and Dunn. You handled them all right."

Riley stared at the bodies. "Not hardly. These three, they's just rats. You can always tell rats 'cause rats travel in packs. I seen yer pa in Dodge City once, though he never knew me. I watched him work. Wyatt Earp ain't no rat. He's more like a wolf an' like me he's loping into the winter of his years. That makes him a wolf in winter, son." The gunman's voice took on an hard edge. *"There ain't nothin' so dangerous as a winter wolf."*

"Surely, there must be something I can do to convince you to help me," Nat entreated. His mind sorted what little information Riley had allowed him. "Think what the money could do for your family, your mother."

"When I rode back from Newton, Kansas, my ma was dead. Milk fever took her. She was the last of my family. I stood over her grave, asked her to forgive me for not keeping my promise to her. After Newton, being on the run, there was no way to ever make that happen. So I rode out under our adobe arch and never looked back."

"What was your promise? To your ma?" Nathan probed cautiously, sensing instinctively that this glimpse into Riley's soul was about to snap shut.

"Learn to read and write."

"Is that all?" Nathan blurted out in mixed relief and astonishment. The Sisters of Charity had schooled him well. Somehow they never saw the combination of a cook's helper reading and spouting Shakespeare while he peeled potatoes as incongruous.

"T'weren't something my ma took lightly," Riley warned. "She placed stock in being educated."

"I'm sorry. I meant no disrespect. And you never learned?"

"Not hardly. It's a mite burdensome to concentrate on yer lessons with bullets whizzing about. And none of my traveling companions went to college. Down in Horse Thief Basin we spent more time looking over our shoulders for posses than looking at books."

"But I can teach you!"

Riley studied the boy warily. "What would that cost me?"

"Nothing. I'd be happy to do it for nothing."

Jim Riley switched his gaze to the mountain tops. The sun was well up now, warming the jumbled red rocks and scattering the myriad crystals of dew that broke the light into sparkling little rainbows. The ice in the creek cracked and sailed downstream. He squinted into the blazing light, forcing the mist from his eyes. This day would be fine, bright and clear, with a warming wind from the southwest. And maybe, just maybe, he might patch a piece of his life that shattered twenty-seven years ago.

His calloused hand thrust out to clamp onto Nathan's boyish fingers. "You got yerself a deal, young Nathan Blaylock. I aim to be rich *and educated*. And if Wyatt's a hair faster then us . . . well, it won't make no difference to me then, will it?"

"Well, I think we put enough distance between us and yer former business partners," the gunman joked as he reined in his mount. Nathan and Riley, leading the two other horses, packed with his loot, had popped out of a gully and climbed a hill to disappear into a stand of cottonwood that encircled a minuscule waterhole. Time-worn in the sandstone, the basin held cool spring water. Surrounded by scrub pines and miles of chaparral, the mound also offered the best outlook for miles around.

The boy was happy to slide from his saddle. His experience on horses totalled less than a handful of short rides. Now chafed and saddle sore, he dreamed of walking, something he never imagined he would.

Hours and miles had passed since they left the bodies to rot in the heat. A shocked Nathan watched Riley scalp the three men before they rode off. "If these rats had friends, I'm hoping they'll think a band of Utes jumped 'em," was Riley's reply. "Less you plan on killing only orphans and social malcontents, you've got to watch for friends and family."

That was the last time he spoke, and that was hours ago. Always riding northeast and looking over his shoulder, they pressed on. This eerie silence, broken only by the creak of leather, the horses' muffled hooves, and a rare note from the rowels of Riley's spurs, infected Nathan so that soon he was swiveling his head and scanning for dust like his mentor.

After a hasty meal of coffee and cold biscuits, Riley gestured to the mound of gunbelts taken from Dunn and the Horners. He smiled and said, "The most important rule of a gunfight is: *Always bring a gun.* Pick yerself a rig, youngster, and let's see what you can do." He half suspected which set this reader of dime novels would choose, and he knew it would be wrong.

Nathan glanced at the older man, searching for a clue, and found none. He hefted the American Model Smith & Wesson Tuck had laid so unexpectedly across his head. Ornate scrollwork decorated the weapon, covering the barrel and frame. The holster, too, reflected the tastes of its dead owner with elaborate tooling and silver conches. The weapon, inscribed like a suit of medieval armor, suited Nathan's romantic nature. He was on a quest, and this was a noble armament. The boy looked back at Riley for his approval.

"Wrong," Riley shook his head, secretly pleased at reading the boy's sign.

"Why not? It's a beautiful pistol."

"Sure it is. And maybe best suited for a Sunday-go-to-meeting gun, but it's got its faults. You recall the jasper what owned it clubbed you with it instead of plugging you. An' when push come to shove, he went for his rifle."

Nathan looked longingly at the pistol. "I still like it."

Stubborn, Riley noted. That's good. He'll need all the grit he can muster. "It's front heavy with that thick barrel dragging down. You'll always be shooting low, and look at the way they've bent the pistol grip forward to help compensate for that. But that makes it hard to get a good shooting grip with yer fingers. When you draw, son, you don't want to be shifting yer fingers all around. Worse of all, the trigger's a real bear to pull. It's too damn stiff. Best you can say about the American is you can re-load it fast, being as how you can break the cylinder open."

"Well, that's good isn't it?" Nathan surely admired that Smith & Wesson.

"Most shoot-outs never git around to reloading, not 'less all parties concerned is dead drunk. You better hope yer first shots do the trick. No self-respecting pistolero is going to give you more time than that. And he won't be jus' picking his teeth while yer trying to plug him, neither." Riley paused for emphasis. "These Americans do have some supporters, though; but most is dead."

Nathan's face dropped as Riley retrieved a Colt Peacemaker. "Grubb Horner's gun?"

"This ain't Grubb Horner's gun, boy," Jim Riley sputtered in exasperation. "This here is his pistol! Grubb's gun is cooking back in that hollow, still inside his pants until the ants and scorpions git to it. Besides, it's yer *pistol* now," he added as he flung the rig to the youth. "Buckle it on! Time's a wasting."

Nathan strapped on the belt and holster. To his surprise the leather was well oiled as was the revolver. The cylinder spun easily, emitting a series of precise clicks.

Riley noted his consternation. "Funny, ain't it. I suspect Tuck did most of the thinking, but that porker, Grubb, was the deadlier of the two. His piece reflects that. He took good care of it, something you'd do well to continue. I've seen more than one pistol blow up in a man's hand for want of a good wiping down. And it don't never happen except when you really need it. Now"—he pointed to a saguaro cactus—"most pistol parties happen a lot closer than you'd expect. Less than fifteen feet, and more likely inside of seven. See what damage you can inflict on that cactus."

Nathan faced the plant and jerked the Colt from the holster. Fanning the hammer as he remembered from his novels, young Blaylock sent three bullets singing into the desert.

"I ain't impressed, and neither is that cactus. I don't see no holes in him. Below the Rio Grande they'd call that a *no bueno*. Try again, and use yer front sight."

Nathan got off another round before the hammer dropped on an empty chamber. Still, his jerking of the trigger whipped the barrel of the Colt aside as if the revolver had actually recoiled.

The older man shook his head in disgust. "Best you creep up on that old saguaro and screw the barrel into its side afore you jerk that trigger. Hopefully, the bullet will stay inside it, then."

"Let's see you do better at this . . . "

Before Nathan could finish, Riley's pistol flew once again into both of his hands where it barked from his rock-solid grip. When the smoke cleared, the cactus sported a hole at dead center. "One dead plant," the man added with finality.

"Okay," Nathan admitted defeat. "I'm doing it all wrong. But I've read about shooting from the hip."

"Pointing and shooting from the hip takes lots of practice, boy. Some's real good at it, I'm not denying that. But I can only teach you what works for me. You and I ain't got the time nor the money to make you good at hip shooting. Speed ain't nothing if you miss. Men like yer daddy keep alive by staying cool and making their shots count. That ain't no easy thing, not by a long shot. Jus' imagine if that saguaro was shooting back. Why, yer heart'd be pounding fit to jump outta yer chest, and you'd be pizzling down yer leg."

"So how do you stay cool?"

"Some do by flat not caring. Take the late Doc Holliday, for example. They used to say he was dead from the eyes down. He never got nervous 'cause it made him no never mind if he lived or died. Men like Wyatt have figured out all their moves ahead of time, so nervous or not they're following a plan. Sort of like a dance, I guess. They's especially dangerous."

Nathan slumped against a boulder, the pistol hanging limp from his hand. "I haven't got a chance, have I?"

"Sure you do, Nat." Riley's tone softened. This boy was like an Indian pony he once owned. Stubborn, but sensitive. Whipping did nothing but get its back up while its own expectations meant everything. This boy could wound himself more from within than anything life could toss his way. "I'm counting on you to provide me with a soft retirement. I'm betting on you, boy. Besides," he laid his finger aside his nose conspiratorially, "I've a secret that'll give you the edge."

"What is it?" Nathan spirit soared, refreshed by the mystery.

"Practice, son. Practice."

SIX

For the next four days, Nathan tasted life on the run and learned what practice meant: winding along creekbeds, using arroyos for screen, and bending their route to follow the contours of the foothills, and always looking back. Riding half turned in the saddle grew second nature, searching the horizon for a telltale cloud of dust that spelled angry men were pressing their ponies hard on their trail.

But no dust appeared, except for a string of freight wagons out of Copper Hill. Without silver prices for support, the mining towns of the Arizona Territory had collapsed. The land was emptying of humans.

Long days in the saddle toughened the boy's backside as much as it tempered his resolve. Something else happened, too. The clean scent of the pinnon pines and the sage fired an unaccustomed joy in Nathan for the majesty that surrounded him. The Sisters of Charity had been a world of darkness, of cloisters, of shuttering walls. Out here no limits met his imagination, and his spirits soared to match the mesas and buttes around him.

As they rode, he picked Riley's brain, and when they stopped he practiced. The gunman had a system which the boy absorbed like a sponge. Years in the orphanage memorizing his catechism had primed his mind for these deadly lessons, a thought that would have sent the mother superior into a fit, Nathan grimly noted.

Swaying in rhythm with the horse, the boy reviewed his moves. Step one, his right hand gripped his pistol while his left hand moved across his belt line ready to supply the two-handed hold that Riley so prized. Step two, draw and aim with the six-gun clamped in the two hands. Nathan had to admit this did reduce the barrel wavering. Step three, concentrate on the front sight and press the trigger gently. Front sight, press! Front sight, press! Riley drummed the words into his head. Even in his sleep Nathan dreamt of those words.

In those four days, a minor miracle occurred. Hours of dry firing formed blisters on Nathan's fingers until Riley worked the sharp edges smooth with a chip of sandstone. The gunfighter had run the Colt over his face afterwards, testing for rough edges. Now, Nathan could draw and fire in under a second. And when Riley begrudgingly parted with a few cartridges, the boy hit his targets. With each success Jim Riley concocted more challenging marks, turning, spinning, shooting from the off hand side. Quietly, yet inexorably, the teacher always pushed his student.

"Front sight, press," Nat mumbled as he gathered firewood.

"And don't you forget it," Riley barked from the fire. "Once you pick yer target, jus' keep fixing on that front sight while you squeeze that trigger as gentle as you can. No matter if a fancy marching band is playing to yer left, and Natches and the whole Apache Nation is screaming on yer right. Finish up yer target. Then, you can look to the others. More men got themselves killed by having their mind one step ahead of their trigger finger."

"What would you do, Mr. Riley? If the whole Apache Nation was on your right?" Nat entered the light from the fire. The older man was tracing the alphabet in the sand.

"Why, son, I'd run like hell. Even then I expect I'd be kilt."

Nat nodded. Being young he saw no end to his own life, so

he misconstrued Riley's acceptance of his mortality in that same light. He pointed to the figures that Riley arduously scribed in the dirt. "You've got the D backwards again, Mr. Riley."

Riley scrutinized his mistake. "Do I? Damn, I keep doing that. It comes of working for the Double D spread down near Nogales. One of their D's was always backwards, and I never knew which was the right one, so help me."

"Try your name," the boy prompted. It was ticklish work, he knew, the student teaching the teacher; especially when his teacher was a prickly gunfighter who could shoot the eye out of a gnat at twenty paces.

"J-I-M R-I-L-E-Y." The man carved the letters into the dust while his lips pursed in concentration. "But that ain't the same as writing yer name, is it?"

Nathan took another stick and connected the letters, underlining the name with a dramatic swirl. "See that's all it takes."

"God Almighty, will you look at that!" Riley's face split into a broad grin. "That's my name, in writing." He studied the script like a ten-ounce gold nugget before copying it carefully, even to the ending flourish.

After that Riley paused in his writing attempts only to wolf down some bread and the ever-present skillet of beans. Nat scoured the tin plates and rolled out their blankets. By the time the moon sat astride the mesa, the mesquite fire had died to glowing coals, and the small clearing was covered with Jim Riley's name. The man's stick snapped suddenly from sheer exhaustion, allowing Nat his chance to speak.

"How come we're working our way west?" he asked.

Riley's voice issued from beneath his Stetson. Prevented from writing, he had rolled himself in his blanket and moved his customary distance into the darkness. "Smart of you to notice, son. I ain't set us in this direction jus' cause I admire creosote bushes and cholla cactus. We're working west of the Mogollon Rim to Jerome. Over there a ride is the Verde River. We'll pick it up tomorrow and follow it into Jerome."

"Why Jerome?"

"Last I recall hearing of Wyatt Earp's whereabouts he was in Gunnison, Colorado. But that was some time ago. Wouldn't do to ride all the way over to Gunnison only to find Earp had moved on. It's a hell of a long ride. So, I figure to slip into Jerome and scratch about for more recent news. If anyone in the Arizona Territory knows where Wyatt is, the word'll be in Jerome."

"What if this Jerome is empty like Pinal was?"

"Jerome? Hell, kid, that place is founded on copper. And any fool knows copper prices is always heading up. I hear they're even trying to put copper on bullets. Did you ever hear of anything so foolish? Copper on bullets. Why, ain't no way a city like Jerome is ever going bust when they're doing things like that. Last year and the year before it burned to the ground, only to build back up better'n before. I've heard they now have over a dozen saloons and eleven restaurants."

A million questions flooded Nathan's mind, but Riley, worn out by his unaccustomed role as instructor, fell asleep. The boy lay on his back gazing at the canopy of stars. Offset by an inky black sky, the lights flashed colored signals at him until the moon stole their radiance. He was still imagining his life with money when sleep overtook him.

Morning found them weaving along the course of the Verde, climbing in and out of its river bed to cross the juniper dotted hills of the Colorado Plateau. Colder and more open, the land lacked the richer vegetation farther south. Deep-cut arroyos and tributaries of streams feeding the Verde sliced the flat-appearing plains into isolated segments. Wide enough to hide an army, the clefts heightened Riley's constant level of alertness. When a startled herd of antelope bolted from one, the gunman's horse shied, and he reacted. Half out of his saddle with rifle skinned from its scabbard, Riley tried to recover, casting a sheepish grin toward his companion.

"Jeez. This place makes me jumpy. Never know what might spring out of these damned gullies."

"Those were only antelope," the boy snorted.

"They could've been armed, though, boy," Riley grunted, trying to cover his embarrassment. "You can't tell me for sure they wasn't carrying weapons."

Nathan looked incredulously at his mentor. This man who cool as ice had faced three killers now spooked at the sight of a few pronghorn. But Riley burst into laughter before the boy could speak.

"That was a stupid thing for an educated man like me to say," he laughed. "If I can write my name with my hand, I ought to make better sense with my mouth." A worried look crossed his face. "I hope I'm not turning into one of those educated fools," he said.

Riley raised his hat to shade his eyes and squinted into the distance. "See that mountain over there? That's Mingus Mountain. Jerome's this side of it, hanging on the slope of Cleopatra Hill. Down there south of Jerome is Prescott. Being as that's the territorial seat and lousy with lawmen, we'll give it a wide berth."

"Why should we worry about lawmen? We haven't broken any laws."

"How do you know for sure? I swear, in some towns you break the law simply taking a piss. Speaking for myself, this educated fool's broke more'n a few. As for you, son, who's to say the Horner boys ain't got a judge in their family? Yer handsome face may be decorating half of Arizona by now on some wanted poster."

"Me, a killer? But I didn't do anything wrong. I was in the wrong place at the wrong time."

Riley winked at him. "Makes you think twice about that warrant for Wyatt Earp, don't it? Could be it's wrong, too."

"I don't think so. Killing him is a matter of justice."

"Justice?" Riley snorted and slapped the dust from his hat. "Justice, you say?"

"Yes, that and the law, too." Nathan didn't fancy having his motives impugned. He had enough of that in the orphanage.

"There's Justice and then there's the Law. Often the two ain't got nothin' to do with one another. I've seen more'n one man hung from a tree or riddled by a posse's bullets when Justice later said they was innocent. And I don't recall those dead men feeling any better for it. Believe me, boy, you best rely on yer Colt, 'cause Justice and the Law ain't got all their kinks worked out, yet."

"What's beyond that valley, the one between the mountains?" Nat asked, anxious to change the subject.

"Just past that valley is Iron Springs. And you know what happened there, don't you?"

"No, what?"

Riley tugged at his ear. "I keep forgetting you been living under a box. Iron Springs is where your father, Wyatt Earp, shot it out with 'Curly Bill' Brocius. As I recall he all but cut old Curly Bill in two with a double load of buckshot from a ten-gauge."

"A shotgun?" Nathan drew up his horse to look at Riley who was raking alkali dust from his mustache with his coat sleeve. Since the wool was also covered, the repeated passes did little to remove the powdery layer that coated his bristles. "Not a pistol? What a cowardly act."

"Boy," the older man blew a cloud off his upper lip as he snorted, "you've been reading too many of them dime novels. All eighteen holes was in the front of Curly Bill. That ain't dastardly. Right smart move on Wyatt's part, using that scatter gun. A rifle'd be just as good."

"But what about the six-gun?" Nathan asked, confused.

"Son, the best you can say about a pistol is you can always carry one, even in the outhouse. But a rifle or a shotgun beats a hog leg hands down in a shoot-out, every time. It ain't glamorous, but it gets the job done. There's a mean son of a bitch out of Texas named 'Killin' Jim' Miller, who's sent more than a dozen men south with a shotgun. But he's partial to bushwhacking, I'm told."

"No. I'm going to face Wyatt Earp with my pistol."

"Well, when that time comes, if he's holding that Wells Fargo special he used on Curly Bill, you'll pardon me if I don't stand too close to you," Riley replied sourly.

Following that acerbic exchange, nothing more was said for over an hour. In that time of riding, the town of Jerome grew until the structures crystallized into distinct buildings. The white-faced two story Little Daisy Hotel loomed above the main street, and storefronts and signs hovered in the afternoon haze.

Dozing in the day's warmth, Nathan rode his mount into the back end of Riley's horse. The gunfighter had reined in his pony and now stood in his stirrup gazing intently at a cloud of dust swirling about a clump of cottonwoods at a bend in the river.

"What is it? What do you see?" the boy asked.

"Trouble," came the sharp reply. "Looks like a lynching."

"What do we do?"

Riley loosened his rifle in its scabbard and tightened his pistol belt. He noted with satisfaction that Nat did the same. Boy's learning, he thought. "We best ride on in like we're returning from a church picnic 'cause they've already seen us. But keep yer wits sharp and be ready to use yer new skills if necessary."

Nathan squinted at the figures milling about the trees but could make out little except for a red and gold painted wagon. "Who are they hanging?" he asked.

"Can't see from here. Let's hope we don't know their guest,

and that he don't know us. Lynch mobs have a bad habit of adding to their roll call at the drop of a hat. Once the good citizens git their dander up, they tend to run amuck. Now ease yer pony in real slow." With that Riley coaxed his own pony into a leisurely walk.

Approaching the riverbank, Nathan saw a handful of angry men clustered about on horseback. The man in the saddle sported clumps of feathers stuck to patches of tar smeared across his shirt and face. His left hand was tied behind his back, and a noose encircled his neck from the stout branch of a black jack oak. Behind the man, the decorated wagon's side sported a gilded sign proclaiming: DOCTOR HENNISON'S WONDER ELIXIR. The painted sides of the wagon bore scattered bullet holes while a party of men cast bottles into a fire they were stoking beneath the cart. As each flask shattered in the flames, a miniature fireball erupted followed by the stench of burning creosote. To Nathan's shock, the man's right arm was missing at the shoulder, giving him the appearance of slumping to that side although he sat ramrod stiff in the saddle.

"Damn your hide, Hennison," a short man in frock coat and green bowler shouted as the riders drew within hearing. "You've poisoned half the town, and you're going to swing for it!" The short man shook his fist in the one-armed man's face, but his words changed to a strangled cry as he clutched his stomach, dropped to his knees in a paroxysm of vomiting. His green bowler fell from his head.

"Mayor, there is a terrible misunderstanding," responded the man about to be hanged. "I assure you these symptoms are not derived from my elixir. Someone must have tampered with my formula, or else your town's water is contaminated. There can be no other explanation, believe me."

But the mayor continued to retch uncontrollably. Bilious spittle stained his waistcoat while his rotund body, doubled so his head bobbed about in the grass, twitched in spasms. As if to further inflame the passions of the mob, the wagon burst into flames amid shouts from the arsonous townsfolk. Sensing he had lost his audience with the mayor, the doctor appealed to another standing over the official's body.

"Dr. Fry, surely as another professional yourself you can understand? Something went wrong. Perhaps this town is populated with those who are overly sensitive to my medication?"

"Something went wrong all right, Hennison," the pale Fry answered, shaking with rage. "You were so drunk when you brewed that last batch of your quack medicine you added too much kerosene. I've been up all night undoing your mischief. Most of the adults are stricken with the foulest flux I've seen since the cholera epidemic. And four dogs and two pigs are dead."

"I told them not to give it to pigs, as God is my witness," Hennison argued. "Pigs have far too sensitive a nature for my elixir."

"I'm against hanging," Dr. Fry added piously. "But this is beyond my control." He rubbed his hands and turned away.

"If you were half the physician I am, your patients wouldn't have begged me for my elixir," Hennison retorted. "It's you who are the quack. I see professional jealousy written all over your smug face. You'd love to have me out of the way."

Nathan noticed the condemned man kept his head high throughout, defending himself in resonant tones that emanated from his bruised lips. Despite the obvious beating he had taken and the patches of feathers glued to his hair, his face and trim goatee retained what little dignity circumstances allowed.

"Enough talk," voices shouted. "String the quack up!" The chorus rose and fell in magnitude as its members paused to drink some of the elixir they were burning or rushed into the bushes to throw up.

Jim Riley leaned toward Nathan and whispered, "Seems like the good folk of Jerome are embarking on another treatment plan, this one using Dr. John Barleycorn. I kin smell it from up here." He surveyed the group: burning wagon, a dozen half sick, half drunk merchants, and two buckboards. No saddled horses, except theirs and Hennison's tenuous link with life, he noted, and no shotguns.

No one had spoken to the two riders, but more angry eyes turned in their direction as Hennison nodded to them like long lost relatives, an action which caused Riley's concern to jump. Suspiciously, the crowd eyed the two saddled horses that Riley led. Imperceptibly, the gunman backed his horse into Nat's pony edging them away from the mob. Somehow, he sensed they wouldn't want to hear that his string of extra ponies belonged to men he had killed.

Several still standing in the crowd had marked the good doctor's greeting to them. The canvas sides of the wagon dissolved in flames and the wagon frame collapsed into the fire. The doctor took this as an ominous sign to vacate the premises.

Eyes sparkling and fixed directly on Riley, Hennison shouted loud and clear, his voice ringing like a clarion across the gathering, "Thank God, you've come to rescue me, brother Tom! I knew you wouldn't desert me. We've always been a team!"

"The hell, you say," Riley protested. But his words meant nothing to the inflamed mob.

The mayor's face snapped up from a patch of grass, his bloodshot eyes bulging with rage. "More of them, men! Get them! And get another rope!"

But the townspeople were inclined toward gunplay rather than ropework. Five or six drew their pistols and commenced firing at Nat and Riley. A bullet chipped the edge of the Jim's saddlehorn while more whizzed past Nathan like angry bees.

"Front sight, press, boy!" Riley bellowed as he drove his horse into the nearest man, knocking him sprawling into the fire. "Let's git the hell out of here!"

His words galvanized Nathan. Hours of practice directed his arms while his mind went blank. Without thinking he drew and fired at a man who leveled a rifle at him. His would-be killer staggered and dropped his Winchester, blood pouring from the hole in his chest. Nathan fired at the nearest threats as his horse bolted after Riley's lead. Two more men fell, and then Nat's horse jumped the flames, kicking a cloud of sparks that scattered the mob.

In midair something struck Nathan, but he hung on as his mount bounded away like a scalded jackrabbit. Looking back, the boy goggled at the sight of Doc Hennison close on his heels. The man had ducked his head out of the noose and escaped with them. More amazingly, Hennison appeared to be laughing.

The trio galloped away, Riley swearing a blue streak, Hennison laughing, and Nat following in bewildered silence. An hour of hard riding later, Riley led them into a streambed that was busily cutting a gully deep enough to screen them. Pushing his winded mount into a slow walk along the creek bottom for another twenty minutes, Riley finally reined in and let his horses drink while he rose in his stirrups to peer over the rim of the gulch.

"Damn, I was hoping you'd have fallen off by now," he growled at the grinning Hennison. "That way I wouldn't have to shoot you myself."

"Would never happen," the snake oil salesman boasted proudly. "My daddy taught me to ride as a babe in Tennessee. I can sit any horse, living or imagined."

Riley scowled at the man's left arm still tied behind his back. He had tried his hardest to spill this troublemaker without success. The man could ride, he had to admit. "Don't think much of yerself, do you? Who got yer other arm, more satisfied customers?"

"Yankees," Hennison said. He flashed a grin and bowed low

in his saddle. "It was so nice of you to see me today. Thank you kindly for rescuing me."

"You didn't give me no choice in the matter," Riley snapped as he checked their back trail again. The horizon appeared flat and calm without tell-tale dust clouds. "Well, they ain't coming," he said flatly.

Hennison shrugged. "Probably burying their dead."

"Did . . . did we actually kill anyone?" Nathan asked white-faced. He swayed in the saddle as even more color drained from his visage. He looked ready to pass out.

"Hell, yes," Hennison giggled enthusiastically. "But not enough to my liking. You missed that fat mayor and my professional associate, Dr. Fry."

Nathan looked searchingly at Riley.

"That's what it's all about, son. You did good. Drilled three of them dead center." He shifted in his saddle, knowing that his praise was somehow empty and inadequate consolation to the boy, no more so than the sound of his creaking saddle leather seemed comforting to him. " 'Course, I never cleared leather, so all three go to yer credit."

"Three?" Nat stammered. "I killed three men, Mr. Riley?"

"If they ain't dead, they're not fit for service."

"In my professional opinion, the wounds were fatal," the doctor added. "But I wish you'd killed those other two as well."

"Shut yer gob," Riley ordered. "This is the boy's first shooting. Go easy on him."

"The boy's a tyro? You could have fooled me. He shot like a real professional. But you say he's a virgin." Hennison nodded in appreciation. "Ah, there's nothing like the first time— for anything, love or murder."

"I murdered those three men," Nat whispered.

"Wasn't murder, Nat. It was self-defense, plain and simple. They was shooting at you, and they shot first. If you didn't shoot back, they'd be shoveling dirt in yer face right now."

Hennison rubbed his chin on his useless shoulder, easing the chafe from the hangman's noose. "I doubt the good folk of Jerome will accept your explanation. One was the minister, although he was a damned hypocrite," the doctor sniffed self-righteously.

"I shot a man of God," Nathan cried as he slipped from his saddle to crumple beside the creek.

"Weak disposition, eh? The boy needs some of my elixir. It works wonders."

"Normally, I got rules against hitting a one-armed man with his only flipper tied," the gunman growled. "But in yer case I'd make an exception." He dismounted to kneel over Nathan.

The boy lay face up on the gravel, pale and breathing shallowly, his feet submerged in the stream. Jim Riley grasped Nat and dragged him onto dry land. The older man's right hand withdrew with the glove soaked in blood. Quickly he rolled the youth onto his side and jerked up his stained shirt. An ugly hole marred the white skin of Nathan's left flank.

"He's been shot," Riley exulted. "He passed out from the bullet wound. I knew he weren't no sissy to faint jus' from plugging three men. Why, that makes me feel a whole lot better."

"I'm sure he'll bleed to death happily now, knowing how relieved you are about his manliness."

Riley frowned at the wound, then looked up at the unmoved Hennison. "Damn yer hide, you're a doctor. Ain't you gonna help him?"

"Please excuse my lack of feeling, but tending to the slaughter of thousands in the War Between The States burned all compassion out of me. One cannot saw off a forest of limbs without either going mad or becoming overly callous. I chose the later."

"He's only a boy, for Christ's sake, and you got him into this."

"When you've watched the entire youth of the South blown

to kingdom come, one more boy makes little distinction."

"Those thousands of others had a choice and made it same as the boys from the North. But Nat here didn't have no choice. That makes a difference."

"Sorry, I'm not moved by your less than eloquent speech. Why should you care, anyway?"

"You're messing with my meal ticket, that's why." Riley thought to appeal to the man's crass economic motives. "He's going to be worth a lot of money if he and I finish this job. Dead, he ain't worth nothing. I'm counting on this lad to provide me with a soft retirement."

Hennison shrugged his one shoulder. "Too bad. Remember what I said about my compassion. I am without feeling."

Riley approached the physician and drew his Peacemaker. In the silence that followed, only the metallic click of the hammer cocking was heard. "I'll bet you still got some feelings. Suppose I shot you in the belly and stood around while yer horse took off dragging you over the territory by yer one arm? Gutshot and bouncing all over the rocks could be mighty unpleasant. What would that do for yer compassion?"

"I see your point. Perhaps I might offer my medical services, after all. But Yankee roundshot took my right arm as well as my feelings, and that made me a one-armed surgeon, as useless a commodity as a cross-eyed whore."

"Maybe less so. A whore don't live by her eyes alone, and she can always shut them. I don't suppose you plan on growing another limb any time soon. But, you're the best we got, so get at it."

Riley cut the ropes and dragged Hennison from the saddle, but his right hand continued to hold his pistol. The doctor straightened his shirt, swiped his hand through his feathered hair, and knelt by the stricken youth. Examining the wound, he washed his hand, then sponged the blood away with the corner of his shirt.

"He'll live. The bullet went clean through the muscle over his kidney, but didn't hit it or his ribs. Mainly he's lost some blood, but he's young."

"That's gratifying to hear. Saves you digging two graves, one arm or not."

"Get a bottle of my elixir from that saddle bag," Hennison ordered. Tending to Nat produced an unexpected change in his manner. His haughty nature gave way to a no-nonsense practicality as he dressed the wound.

"You ain't giving him any of that poison to drink. He can't hardly handle beer."

"Where's he been all this time, in a nunnery?"

"Orphanage run by nuns. Just got released."

"That explains it." Hennison looked up at the gunman. "Because you don't look bright enough to have a son."

"Keep talking like that only makes my job easier if I have to plug you."

Hennison shook his head. "No. The elixir will cleanse his wound. It's got enough alcohol to kill any harmful humors. After that I intend to use it to remove these feathery decorations. It cuts tar like nothing else."

Riley fetched the bottle and tasted it. He spit his mouthful onto the ground. "What the hell is in this? Rattler piss?"

"Mainly grain alcohol with a little creosote, kerosene, turpentine, and shoe polish for coloring," the doctor replied matter-of-factly. "And a secret ingredient I'm not at liberty to divulge."

"Jesus!" Riley wiped his tongue on his sleeve. His tongue still burned, and he could feel his vision failing already, prompting him to scrub all the more furiously.

Hennison held the bottle up for inspection. He noted with satisfaction that it resembled the burnt sienna color of fine bourbon. Now that's the way it should look, he thought. "Not to worry. This batch is good. It was the stuff I mixed last night that has too much kerosene. I was pushed by demand, and I admit, I was rather drunk when I made it."

When the wonder elixir hit his wounds, Nat awoke with a groan. The world spun into focus, and he looked up at Riley's legs standing near his head. The fire in his side told him he hadn't passed out from fear, a fact he found somehow reassuring. "What happened?" he asked of Riley's boots.

"You was shot, Nat, by those crazy lynchers. But the doctor here says you'll be just fine, so don't worry," Riley's voice replied from above his boots.

"They shot me? They don't even know me."

"That's how it sometimes happens, and they started it," the gunman said. "But then you shot three of them and didn't know them either."

Hennison's dabbing elixir into his wound burned a blue flame of pain up to the back of his neck. Its torment brewed Nat's fear and confusion into anger. "They shot me without even saying hello, damn them. Get off me! I'm going back and shoot the rest of them!"

"Easy, Nat." Riley chuckled while his boot pressed gently on the youth's shoulder. "Leave it be. You're one up on them as it is. No sense being greedy. Leave some for another pistolero to plug."

Nathan realized his mistake when the ball of fire in his back exploded upon his moving. He slumped down and gritted his teeth as the physician dressed the wound. Using his teeth to hold the linen while his left hand wrapped, the man skillfully finished the bandage.

Hennison stood back to admire his work. "Not bad for one arm." Pleased with himself, he bowed to his patient. "Julian Crawley Hennison, physician and ex-surgeon, at your service. That will be five dollars, please."

"And it's five dollars for yer rescue," Riley cut in. "We're square on this account."

Hennison looked at the .45 in Riley's hand and sighed. "Okay, you need to keep him warm, and the more warm fluids you can pour into him the faster he'll heal. Wrap him in blankets and start a fire." With that he picked up his bottle of elixir took a swig, and started toward his horse.

"Not so fast. Where are you going?"

"Since you said we were even, and my work here is done . . . "

"Yer not crawfishing out of here like some swell at a Friday night social," Riley snarled. "I've seen plenty of gunshots, and most ain't all better in the morning. Some gets to festering. I figure yer five-dollar fee includes all the follow-up care Nat might need. So you fetch some firewood while I wrap the boy up. And don't get no green nor rotten wood. I don't want the good folk of Jerome spotting our smoke. We've wasted enough bullets today on account of you."

Throughout the night Nathan shivered by the fireside while both men tended him and fed the fire with dried juniper branches. A cloudless sky furnished their canopy, decked with brilliant diamonds for stars. With the clear night came a bone-chilling cold that settled on their camp. All their blankets went to keep Nathan warm, so Jim huddled inside his coat while the doctor wrapped himself in newspapers that he drew from his enormous saddlebags.

While he pretended to sleep, Riley watched Hennison nurse the youth. The gunman's practiced eye noted a carefully concealed vein of caring that the doctor took great pains to hide. Still, Riley kept one eye open and his Colt cocked beneath his coat. Most men have good and bad juices running through them, he reminded himself, and circumstances dictate which sap would flow. He was sure that the doctor could drift either way.

But morning came with the sun cutting a crimson ribbon through the layers of clouds to the east and Hennison snoring peacefully within his nest of newspapers. Riley lifted the floppy rim of his hat and surveyed the camp. A light rime of frost coated his saddle blankets and everything up to the smoldering campfire. He winced as he straightened his legs, working the cramps out of his lower back and legs. Pushing forty-five made sleeping on the ground a trial for him. Was he fortunate to have lived so long? The average age of death for his associates tallied up to about thirty by his reckoning. Living longer just made you slower and stiffer—not good attributes for staying alive. A few gunman he knew, long in the tooth and worn out waiting for that bullet in the dark, swallowed their own guns and shot themselves. Better that than wandering around like a snow-blind calf, waiting for the wolves to rip out your belly. Or was it? Riley wondered. Pinal had been the end of his rope, starving and half frozen. Two more days would have finished him.

Then Nat came along. One thing for sure, this boy was his last hope. Best not dwell on it too long, he reminded himself; things work out one way or another, regardless. A wry smile crossed his face, folding his leathery skin into silver-stubbled furrows. If I check out tomorrow, I've kept my promise to my ma, he thought. I can write my name, and now I can read a little.

Jim Riley sat up and inched toward the fire with his saddle blanket drawn tightly against the cold. Blowing on stiffened fingers, he coaxed life back into his body as he nursed the coals into flames. When the fire unlimbered his legs, he limped to the creek and filled the coffeepot with water from an opening in the ice that layered the banks with crystal shelves. Damn, this is one cold spring this year, he swore silently. But then again, he noted, the winters and springs just got colder as he aged.

Hennison's head surfaced from his library of papers. "Ah, breakfast in bed. Put a dollop of *creme de cacao* in my cup will you, my good man?"

"I ain't yer good man, nor nothing like that." Riley cleared his throat as he dumped a handful of grounds into the pot. "You're lucky I don't spit in yer cup for all the trouble you caused us."

"Still a bit grouchy, are we. Never mind, I'll get my own coffee. What's for breakfast?" Hennison crept to the fireside in his long johns, having removed his tarred shirt and trousers during the night. The faded red underwear stood in contrast to the man's impeccable goatee.

"Special soup for the lad," Riley said as he folded the scrawny carcass of a bird into a cast-iron pot. "Old Indian remedy. It'll make his bullet holes heal in no time."

"Chicken soup, nothing novel about that," replied Hennison as he squatted by the fire to watch the water boil. He juggled his hot coffee cup while ogling the cooking fowl. Yesterday's affair had left him with a hearty appetite. "But if I were you I'd get my money back. That bird looks as old as Methuselah."

Riley ignored his comments as he carried a bowl of the broth over to Nathan. He spooned the liquid into the boy. "Drink up, Nat. This'll fix you up."

With the gunman's back turned, the doc's hand darted into the pot to twist off a limb which he deftly stuffed into his mouth. "God's teeth!" He choked, spewing the stringy meat into the fire. "You call me a poisoner, do you? This is far worse. What did you do to ruin this chicken?"

"Ain't chicken," Riley grinned. Hennison had acted just as he expected. If I'd had a rat trap to put in that soup, yer fingers would be hurting as well, he reflected. "It's boiled owl."

The doctor flushed the taste from his mouth with generous gulps of coffee. He fixed his gaze on the gunman. "Only an uncouth oaf like yourself would try to make food of the symbol of Athena, Goddess of Wisdom."

Riley's face hardened. "Only Athena I ever met was a dance hall girl in Bisbee, and she never had no pet owl. And I ain't as ignorant as you'd think. I can write my name and read some now, thanks to that lad you almost got killed. So don't be calling me names. You was more trouble than you're worth yesterday, and you ain't improved none today. I didn't shoot you then, but that don't mean I can't correct that mistake now."

Nat sat upright although the action awakened the pain in his side. The air about the camp had grown dangerously charged. He realized Hennison had pushed Riley too far, but the doctor seemed ready to goad the gunman even further.

"Read, can you? I doubt that," Hennison sneered. "Go ahead. Show me."

Riley hesitated. *Read some* he had boasted, but he knew that was a generous assessment. Nathan's teaching enabled him to write his name and the alphabet, but even simple words came hard to him. Certainly his stumbling over simple sentences would give this troublemaker ample cause to mock him. "I think I'll just shoot you instead," he countered.

"I thought as much. You can't read. Besides, you wouldn't shoot an unarmed man."

Riley's hand dropped to his gun. "I could plug you for being a public nuisance. Bill Hickok did it all the time."

"Go ahead, Mr. Riley," Nathan said from his bed. The tension in the camp was explosive. "Read something to him. I'll help you with the hard words." The boy looked at this man of medicine who sowed disruption. "He can read, doctor," he insisted.

Nathan's words dampened their ire to a level below the flash point, causing the tension to diminish between the two men. His childlike faith in Riley gave the man courage to try, while that same faith reminded Hennison of something precious he had lost too long ago.

The doc looked bleakly at the newspapers piled about him, then at his horse hobbled near a patch of grass. This was the sum of his fortune: one horse and one saddle with bags containing six bottles of his elixir and handfuls of old newsprint.

Past brushes with irate townspeople had taught Hennison the need for an escape plan. For that reason he always kept this mount saddled with five hundred dollars, six bottles of elixir for starters, and wads of newspapers to filter the ingredients he would pick up at the next town. Let the fools spend their wrath burning an old wagon and a painted canvas sign worth only a few dollars. Hennison would be long gone, and back in business within a week somewhere else.

But this time he cut it too close. They caught him, and unwittingly the lynch mob recruited his getaway horse to hang him. Worse, one of the good folk also relieved him of his money, overlooking the bottles and papers.

"Here, read this," he mumbled, picking up a paper at random. Bereft of his money, the gloomy side of his nature rose to the surface with little desire to humble this bumpkin. "It's far from current. Might be over a year old, for all I know. I stopped reading the news long ago."

"What do you use all these papers for, Doc?" Riley asked. He too felt foolish. False pride was one thing his mother despised.

"Oh, I use them to filter my snake oil," Hennison shrugged. "People dislike drinking cloudy things. Somehow they equate clarity with purity, an understandable but imprudent blunder. A few pages of local tragedy do wonders for my elixir and its price."

Riley unfolded the paper. He frowned in concentration at the sea of words that covered the page. *"The Examiner,"* he read.

"That's the *San Francisco Examiner,"* Hennison piped in. "I like it better than the *Call* or the *Chronicle.* Less editorializing."

"I know that. It says 'Vol. LXIII, San Francisco, Tuesday Morning, December 3, 1896.' " The gunman paused to collect his thoughts. His eyes were snatching words from the page faster than his mind could sort them. He cast an accusing look at the doc. "This here paper is almost two years old."

"Like I said, I just use them when I need to. I don't sort through them for the more recent ones."

"Read the headline, Mr. Riley," Nathan prompted. Sitting up made his back throb, but he wanted this rift healed quickly. Yesterday's fight left him puzzled, and he needed time to sort out his feelings without more shooting. Nathan assumed killing three men, if indeed he had, would leave him with intense emotions. One way or the other he expected it to change his world. Surprisingly, he felt nothing—neither guilt nor fulfillment. Flat came closest to his sentiments, he noted. This lack of concern over the death of three men startled him most of all.

Riley screwed his eyes in concentration and licked his lips, well aware his childish reading made him appear all the more moronic. Picking the next largest type, he began. "Sharkey wins by a foul said referee Earp . . . "

"What?" Nathan sat bolt upright.

"Sharkey wins by a foul . . . " Riley repeated dutifully.

"No, the other part. You said Earp."

Riley's eyes widened. "Earp! Yeah, Earp. And there's his picture." He waved the front page at Nathan, his finger jabbing the lithograph of a dour face sporting a drooping mustache and wing collar and tie. Beneath the engraving read the caption: WYATT EARP, WHOSE DECISION MEANT $10,000.

"Yeah, the Tom Sharkey–Bob Fitzsimmons fight," Hennison said. "I lost fifty bucks on that. Fitz knocked Sharkey out, but Earp called it a foul blow and gave the match to Sharkey. I think it was fixed. So did most of the newspapers in San Francisco."

Nathan studied the print with narrowed eyes, Hennison's words unheeded. The youth turned slowly to Riley. "Wyatt Earp is in San Francisco. He's not in Gunnison," he hissed.

"I reckon so, but this paper is old. . . . "

"Last I heard he was still there racing trotters," Hennison

said. The grim exchange between the gunman and this deadly youth was not lost on him. His innate sense told him a deadly business was being discussed, and with all bloodthirsty business he perceived an opportunity for him to profit. "What business do you two have with Wyatt Earp?" he asked obliquely.

"Nothing to interest you," Riley snapped.

"You may be surprised what interests me, my friend. I have an intimate knowledge of San Francisco with many contacts there—many discreet contacts." He paused to let that sink in. "It's a big place, one that's easy to hide in," the doctor continued. "Of course, you could always go to the nearest police station to ask for directions." Having planted his seed, he carefully folded his newspapers, all but the one Nathan now studied like the road map to his soul. Then, he sat by the fire and drew pictures in the sand with a stick as he waited for his words to take effect.

"I ain't never been to San Francisco," Riley admitted to answer the questioning look from Nat. "Never been west of the Colorado River for that matter."

"What would you charge to find Wyatt Earp in San Francisco, Doc?" Nat asked.

Hennison stretched his hands toward the warmth of the fire and wiggled his fingers. "Well, seeing as how I am temporarily retired from my lucrative medicinal trade, and I do feel indebted to you all for saving my life . . . "

"Cut the crap." Riley interrupted Hennison's prepared speech. "How much?"

"How much do you have?"

"Four hundred dollars," Nat blurted out, before realizing his mistake. "Maybe, a little less." He ignored Riley's shaking of his head.

"Not enough, I'm afraid. I couldn't possibly do it for less than five hundred."

"We ain't got five hundred to our names, and we ain't never

gonna see that much, either. Not if we sold our horses, our rigs, and all our dirty underwear," Riley interjected. This was horse trading, something he knew about and the boy obviously didn't.

"I might consider four hundred."

"Seventy-five."

"Three hundred," Hennison countered, but he felt his position eroding with each round. He had not considered the older man would do the dealing. Well, he sighed inwardly, I've got nothing as it is. Anything would be an improvement. Still, he loved to haggle.

So did Jim Riley. Born without a penny to his name, and raised to scratch an existence from sandstone and sagebrush, he could squeeze a nickel along with the best. But, before he could offer one hundred twenty-five, Nathan surprised him.

"One hundred," the boy said. "And that's our final word. We'll need some left for expenses."

"And if I cannot accept?" Hennison turned to face his new threat, half amused by this amateur.

Nathan folded back his blanket. His right hand cradled his Colt Peacemaker. He grinned wolfishly at Hennison. "It would be your last word also, Doc. I have no doubt you'd sell your own mother for a profit, and knowing our intentions could bring you a profit. We can't allow you to slip that information into the wrong hands." Then to the astonishment of his mentor, he quoted Riley. "We don't ever allow ourselves to be caught unawares."

★ ★ SEVEN ★ ★

"Would you really have shot him, Nat?" Riley leaned from his saddle to ask young Blaylock. "I've been wondering about that for days."

The two sat astride their horses while the animals drank. Hennison sat on the cutbank beyond earshot, his horse nibbling the spring grass that flourished near the water. A hundred yards beyond lay the Colorado River, coursing to Mexico. Fingers of trapped and blind channels laced the grassy flats of the river's flood plain while across the river the sharp-edged low hills silently watched. A few years ago, Apaches would also have watched from these same rocks, but now the main threat came from the sun, rattlesnakes, and raiding bandits from Mexico.

Nathan shrugged. "Maybe, maybe not. I don't really know."

Riley nodded. It was enough of an answer to satisfy him. In the two weeks that followed the shooting at Jerome, the three rode south and west, away from that spot, keeping to back trails, and bypassing the major towns of Vulture and Ehrenberg where the telegraph and possibly the law waited. Once they encountered a prospector searching for his elusive El Dorado, but he knew nothing of the latest news. In those two weeks Nathan had changed along with the land, becoming rugged as the terrain grew dried and spiny like the prickly pear and saguaro that flourished. Bloodied by the fight at Jerome, the youth was becoming a man, a fact well recognized by Riley who saw the same changes in this lad that had happened to him so long ago.

Hennison had argued that a posse would expect them to ride either north to Oatman or to the rail crossing of the Colorado at Bullhead City or southeast along the plateau to Tombstone or Bisbee before hiding in Mexico. The natural barrier of the White Mountains and the Mogollon Rim dictated those choices. But no one would expect them to head for Fort Yuma right under the nose of the infamous Yuma Territorial Prison, he insisted. And that was the beauty of his plan. At Yuma Crossing they could catch the Southern Pacific to California.

Safely below Ehrenberg, the trio swung west to follow the Colorado toward Yuma. Weaving along its banks, Nathan enjoyed the cool breeze that blew off the water, and the scattered adobe and board shacks of abandoned miners. Camping at night in these offered a glimpse into a world previously denied to him. Bottles, boots, and skillets abounded, left in the scramble for elusive wealth, not to mention the pictures of naked women torn from magazines and tobacco tins and tacked to the clay walls.

Bedded down in an adobe hovel a day's ride from Yuma Crossing, Hennison caught Nat studying the reclining picture of a voluptuous beauty. In the flickering firelight the figure seemed to undulate alluringly.

"Ah, the raptures of Venus. Look at those enticing curves, my boy. Designed to snare the wariest of men."

Nathan blushed a deep crimson and pretended to arrange his bedroll. But Hennison persisted, warmed by healthy doses of elixir he had prescribed for himself to ward off the swamp fever he knew must frequent these lowlands. While they had been in the mountains, Hennison drank to guard against chills from the night air, so the net effect was that every evening found the doctor partially inebriated. But tonight Hennison had undertaken a particularly heavy treatment, and his tongue wagged more than usual.

"Come, boy, a handsome lad like yourself must have vast experience. How does she compare with your encounterings?"

Nat scratched his head in embarrassment. "Doc, I don't have any experience. . . . "

"What? Never? Not even behind the school yard?" Hennison wiped his benumbed lips and navigated his bottle to his mouth. Riley's fire, trapped within the adobe walls, was adding to the kick of his medicine. "Being a Methodist, I am unfamiliar with the vagaries of the Catholic Church. In the war I encountered Cajuns from the Tiger Battalion whom I believe were Catholic, but they were crazy as loons. Don't the nuns teach that stuff in school? How else do you get all those litters of papists."

"Sex outside of marriage? That would be a sin," Nathan stuttered.

Hennison tipped his head in mock salute. "Spoken like a true mother superior. I guess that rules out whores."

"Leave the boy be," Riley intervened. "Yer drunken tongue is an embarrassment. The lad's still pure, not fouled like you are. He's holding himself for the right girl."

"You'd do better just holding yourself," Hennison continued, poking Nat. "Let me tell you about right girls. Did you know I had one once, back when I had two arms?" The revelation sobered him so he tipped his bottle and drank until the pain of his memory lessened enough to continue.

"You did, Doc?" Nat asked wide-eyed. This was like the shining knights and their ladies.

"Annabelle Tarver," Hennison nodded. "From the finest family in Nashville—like me. We were betrothed, and she swore to be faithful and wait for me. I can still picture her waving her lace handkerchief while I rode off to war. It was a truly heroic scene, yours truly straight in the saddle, resplendent in my Confederate gray and gold braid, and Annabelle sparkling in her crinolines." He stopped and drew heavily from his bottle.

"What happened, Doc?" Nathan sensed a tragic tale of un-requited love.

"The bitch married a goddamned Yankee." The words choked in Hennison's throat, causing his eyes to bulge along with the veins in his neck. Riley watched curiously, wondering if the doctor would have a stroke. "When I limped back after the war, minus those parts I'd sacrificed for the Confederacy, she was bedding one of Sherman's thieves. Can you believe that? I'm shedding body parts to keep her safe, and all she shed were her underclothes with the first bluebelly that crawled into town!"

Riley chuckled. He knelt by the fire and unloaded his arm-ful of wood.

"Yes, laugh. It's amusing now. Take my word, Nathan, stick with soiled doves. You're better off renting."

Nathan looked to Jim Riley to agree, but the gunman shook his head. "A man who can't rope his own horse has got no choice but to ride another man's mare."

"We're not talking horses here, you buffalo chip–brained clod! We're talking women!" Hennison babbled.

"What did I tell you about calling names?" Riley warned.

"Get fucked, you ignorant peasant!" Hennison searched for another bottle.

Before he found it, the gunman wheeled on his heels and laid the barrel of his gun across the doctor's head. Hennison folded into his blankets unconscious. "Now that's a buffalo for you," Riley said.

Nathan bent over the physician. "You didn't hurt him, did you?"

"Naw. Jus' added to his headache. I doubt he'll even re-member what happened in the morning. Better get some sleep yourself. Tomorrow we hit Yuma Crossing and board the train to California."

With that Riley rolled up in his blankets, and fell asleep.

Nathan lay on his bedroll, hands folded behind his head and watched the dying shadows from the fire reflecting on the adobe walls and thought of what lay ahead. Would he be ready, he wondered. Daily practice had honed his draw and marksmanship to a lethal edge, and Jerome proved he could kill. But deep inside Nathan knew facing his father would be far more difficult. The shooting of the lynch mob erupted suddenly and unexpectedly, making his response unplanned, spontaneous, and unprovoked. The mob made it easy for him.

Silently, he unfolded the page of the *Examiner* and compared it with the photograph he carried. Disturbingly, the caricature with simian brow and bulbous head bore little resemblance to the sharp-eyed picture of his father. But what had Riley said about good and bad blending in some? Surely, his mother, the papers, and the warrant were right: Wyatt Earp was a cold-blooded killer and con man, many times more evil than good. Hadn't Earp abandoned him and his mother, causing her broken heart and death? What father would do that to his wife and son? Nathan ground his teeth. My father deserted me, he half whispered, dismissing me and all my feelings like trash in a dustbin, and forcing me to endure the life of an orphan. That alone was cause to kill him. But, I'm out now, and I'm coming to get you to pay you back for all that.

Killing Wyatt Earp would be an act of retribution for his evil deeds, and Nathan knew about retribution from his teachings in the convent. Wasn't the Bible full of stories of requital? Nathan slipped into a dreamless slumber secure in his new knowledge. Neither he nor his sleeping companions realized it was Easter Day, a day for hope and rebirth rather than vengeance.

✶ ✶ EIGHT ✶ ✶

The physician cracked the door ajar and peered into the sitting room. Behind him hovered two nurses, somber and stern in their black dresses with white starched aprons and caps. The severity of their dress matched their comportment. The older woman scowled and nodded her head in the direction of the man who sat in the parlor gazing at his folded hands.

"It's God's will, that's what it is. Punishment for all the men he's murdered," she whispered to the younger nurse.

"But he looks so sad," the younger and less hardened woman replied. "Surely, he can't be that bad."

"God's wrath," the other repeated, as a warning. "Mark my words, he's a cold-blooded killer. He could fly into a rage and murder us all."

Silently the doctor entertained a fleeting dream of Wyatt Earp shooting his one nurse, before wiping his hands on a blood-streaked cloth. He hated bearing misfortune, and this week had seen its full measure of tragedy. Still, that was part of his job. He squared his shoulders and opened the door.

The doctor walked slowly into the sitting room, uncertain what the reaction would be from the lone occupant who sat in the corner. After all, he was bringing bad news to Wyatt Earp, notorious gunfighter and killer. Didn't the Chinese kill the messenger with bad news? Would Earp react in anger against him, he wondered. As he approached, Wyatt stood up. The physician paused, twisted his neck awkwardly in his stiff collar, and extended his hand.

"I'm sorry to meet you under less than happy circumstances, marshal," the doctor said, using Wyatt's past title in hopes it might engender respect for the law.

Wyatt stood and gripped the physician's hand. His eyes searched the doctor's face for some hope but found none. "Josie?"

"She's had premature labor, I'm afraid. The baby was born too soon."

"Will she be all right, doctor?"

Dr. Evarts was impressed by the concern of this man who's steel gray eyes pierced his soul as his iron grip seized his hand. Not many men asked about their wives, but this killer of men did. It was confusing, and not in line with what he expected.

"Yes. She's young and strong. She's lost some blood and will need to rest." He paused, his voice faltering. "You . . . you can still have other children. . . . "

"Others?" Wyatt's grip tightened.

Evarts shook his head. "The baby is too premature, too small to survive. At most he'd have to be six, perhaps seven months along."

"He?" Wyatt asked.

Evarts winced and cursed himself for his unfortunate choice of words. Bringing the sex of the child into play only worsened the sense of loss.

"It's a boy?" Wyatt persisted.

"Yes, a male." Evarts tried to extract the emotion without success.

"May I see him, doctor?"

"Marshal Earp, It's highly irregular, and . . . and he's still alive. I strongly recommend against it. Best start over without painful memories."

"I'm no stranger to painful memories, doctor. I want to see him." It was a command.

"If you wish."

Dr. Evarts led Wyatt into the nursery off the bedroom where the nurses stood guard. Shocked to see the two men intrude into her domain, the older nurse positioned herself between Wyatt and the pillows that held his dying child. Arms folded, she prepared to make her speech, but one look from Wyatt, and she seemed to deflate. Silently she stepped aside.

Wyatt looked down at the pillows. A tiny pinkish figure lay in the center, diminutive arms and legs flailing weakly against the cold, alien air that scalded his sensitive skin. Every jerk reflected itself with twitching of the muscles of the father's jaw. Silently he was sharing the suffering of his son.

Without asking the younger nurse lifted the baby and pillow and placed him in Wyatt's arms.

"Thank you, I wanted to hold him," he said. Looking to the doctor, he asked. "He's cold. May I cover him with a blanket?"

"Better not to. He'll . . . he'll go faster if he's cold. It'll take more time otherwise." Disgusted with his clumsy handling of this moment, the doctor ran his finger through his hair and shrugged his shoulders helplessly. "Do whatever you want, marshal."

Wyatt lifted the softest cover within reach and folded it about the baby. "I'd like him to be comfortable. I've got all the time in the world."

With that he turned and carried the bundle and the rocking chair he and Josie had bought only three days before out of the darkened nursery. Dr. Evarts watched Wyatt sit beside the window in the sitting room, rocking his dying child.

"God's wrath on a cold-blooded killer, is it?" he asked the head nurse. "Are you so sure, Nurse Hobkins?"

The physician left, and the nurses turned their attentions to the convalescence of Josie while Wyatt continued to rock.

The sun shone through the glass while outside the town went about its business oblivious to the drama that played behind the second-story window.

Wyatt unfolded the blanket and studied the infant. The infant's hand caught his finger and held on tightly. The gunfighter rolled his index finger to inspect the tiny nails and fingers that clung to him.

"You've got a good grip, Nathan," he whispered, using the name he and Josie had picked. He remembered he had named the baby girl he so desperately wanted and lost two years ago in San Diego. "At least you won't have to hold a gun. I was hoping you'd make it, so we could build that ranch down near San Bernadino and raise horses. You know, I want to keep you out of gambling and gold mining—that and peacekeeping. That's been nothing but bad luck for our whole family. Your Uncle Virgil can back me up on that."

The hand weakened, lost its hold, then clutched again onto Wyatt's finger.

"Hold on, Nathan," Wyatt urged. "Hold on as long as you can. I'll stay with you as long as you need me."

The sun settled in the western sky while Wyatt rocked and spoke to his son. With the wearing down of the day the baby also lost ground. And shortly after sunset he died.

⋆ ⋆ **NINE** ⋆ ⋆

The cramped coach of the Southern Pacific rattled over the rugged railbed, and its conflict with the uneven rails and warped ties reflected itself in the agony of its passengers. Built in haste over unyielding terrain, the rail line held little in comfort for its occupants, yet this was the best way to travel when compared with the bone-jolting torture of stage lines or freight wagons. The stifling heat that lingered about Yuma followed the train as it fled westward and added to the misery. That and the fact that the car was packed far beyond its capacity produced an explosive mixture of heat, sweat, and ill temper among its occupants. Most on board sought the gold fields of the Klondike, but three men rode for a different reason.

Doc Hennison dodged the armpit of a miner and poked his nose into the stream of fresh air that flowed from a window among the sweaty bodies like a cool stream in the desert. The miner also noticed the breeze and shifted in its direction only to find the wily Doc already wedged into that space, thereby causing him to cast an angry glare at the doctor. Hennison shot the man a cold smile and realized the lack of one arm had some advantages after all. A bead of perspiration coursed into his left eye, stinging in its saltiness, before he wiped it away on his upturned arm. Packed as they were, Hennison's grasp on the overhead railing was his sole anchor in this confused sea of humanity.

"Boy, I knew this was a bad idea," Hennison shouted over the clack of the wheels. "We should have booked in the salon car as I urged, not this cattle car."

"Who you calling cattle, mister?" a short miner pressed into Hennison's back snarled. Although short in stature, he possessed a surly nature and five beefy associates.

The doc smiled sweetly at his accuser. "Not you, sir. Your wit and superb nature are definitely simian."

"Simian, eh? Oh, all right then," the man said as he sunk back into the human stew, not realizing he had been called a monkey.

"Doc, we didn't have enough money. You know that. We scarcely paid for this," Nat replied from Hennison's other side.

"Yes, but if you'd have staked me in that poker game back at Yuma, we'd be drinking champagne with the ladies in the salon car." Hennison jerked his head toward the front of the train where the first class rode, safe from the thick smoke and clouds of coruscating sparks that streamed back from the engine to envelop their car. The soot burned their throat and eyes while the cinders scorched their clothes and threatened to fire the tinder-dry railcar. The men traveled in torment from thirst while being forced to hold some of their precious water in reserve should a blaze break out.

"More than likely, we'd be broke back in Yuma if he did," Jim Riley added. "That poker deck was marked or I'm yer maiden aunt. Those sharpies was looking to fleece fools like you." Being packed like this ran counter to the gunman's nature and his life in the open spaces. He struggled to overcome a growing and unfamiliar feeling of claustrophobia. That fear rasped across his mind like a dull knife.

"We're broke as it is, saddler." Hennison used the term for a bum who lived in the saddle and survived from one handout to the next.

"No name calling, either of you," Nat said, mindful of the

explosive mix within this train car. "It's plain bad luck, that's all."

Not bad luck, Nat corrected himself, but bad timing. Any fool should have known the railroads would jack up their prices with the stampede to the Klondike. Gold fever was everywhere, burning into the unemployment that followed collapse of silver in Arizona and depressed hundreds of jobless rail workers and miners.

When the *S.S. Excelsior* landed in San Francisco on July 15, 1897, and dumped a ton of gold on the dock, fever struck and spread like wildfire. After that the race was on. Anyone able rushed to the coast to catch a ship for the Yukon. Only the first had the best chance of staking a lucrative claim, and the fastest way to the coast was by rail.

Three tickets to San Francisco took all they owned, and then they scarcely fit aboard. No sense complaining, Nat had noted. Their places would be taken in an instant by someone else. Men crowded every train stop, hoping for the chance to fit aboard. Still dressed in work clothes and Sunday suits, clutching carpetbags, feverish men jostled for a ride. Thousands of ordered lives had suddenly ceased as men rose from meal tables, dropped the reins of their plows, abandoned families, and rushed to the call of El Dorado.

Nathan looked at the slatted sides of the rocking railcar. Hennison was right, it was a converted stock car plain and simple. Freight boxes and crates of mining machinery served as seats for those fortunate enough to get one. The rest swayed standing in a congealed mass of gold maddened men. Measuring the fever gripping the men in his car, Nathan could hardly imagine the level of madness covering the actual gold fields. Silently Nat thanked whatever fates guided him. With gold fever everywhere, the death of Wyatt Earp in San Francisco would pass unnoticed. Best of all, with Nathan's revenge came a fortune, one obtained without the hardships of mucking for gold.

Hours passed and Nat and Riley dozed, lulled by the heat and close air. Hennison stayed awake and fretted about the first-class car and its cold champagne maddeningly beyond his reach. His mind also sorted his options. Financial prospects with the boy and the cowman had dimmed for him when all their wealth went to the purchase of their tickets. But Nathan confided to the doctor of the blood money for the killing of Earp. A considerable sum it seemed. Only the untimely arrival of Riley prevented Doc from extracting the exact amount from the boy, but he guessed it was in the thousands. The way Hennison figured, San Francisco offered greater opportunity than the emptying towns of Arizona, and who knew what else. The one-armed surgeon sighed again at the thought of iced champagne and closed his eyes.

Unexpectedly the train jerked to a halt. Bleary eyes opened as numbed bodies crashed together and fought for elusive handholds. Insult piled atop this affront when a cloud of smoke and sparks filled the car, igniting the jackets of six men and several burlap-covered bales. Cries of fire and swear words mixed with the smoke until canteens doused the blazes.

A man next to Nathan peered through a crack in the slats. "Water stop," he announced. "The tender is taking on water for the damned engine from a water tower."

Outside a fireman walked the rails to the pull rope for the water spout. As he passed he shouted, "Fifteen minute rest stop. Get out if you need to crap or get water. Next water stop in fifteen hours."

Riley tipped his empty canteen and watched the last drop clinging to the lip. "We need water, Nat."

"Should have let those muckers burn," Hennison answered smugly. "My bottle is still full."

"And we might have burned up with them, Doc. Did you think of that?" Nat countered. Through the separated board walls he saw the water tower, and its tantalizing cascade of water from the spout. He also noted the mob that clustered around the tower.

Riley followed his gaze. "Damnation! Looks like a party of miners here on the California side want to git on board. But there just ain't no room. They packed us tighter than a pack mule's cinch strap back in Yuma."

"You got that right, friend," an ex-shopkeeper chirped in. "Not hardly room to fart in here."

"Well, don't try it," the doc warned. "With all the sparks we might explode." A roar of laughter followed his remark from the men who welcomed any comic relief, and Hennison nodded in recognition.

"If we git off, we might not squeeze back in," Riley warned. "Especially if those miners try to git aboard."

"Well, we can't go without water, Mr. Riley," Nat said. "In this heat we wouldn't last until the next watering stop." He paused to think. "I'll fill our canteens. You and the doctor can hold my place until I get back, and you can keep an eye on the doc. I wouldn't put it past him to sell my place."

"Sir, I am deeply hurt by your accusation," Hennison said, but the thought had crossed his mind.

Nathan helped several others roll the door back and then jumped to the ground. Worming his way under the water tower, he dipped their canteens into a trough. The sides of the wooden stock tank glowed green with slime, and the water was tepid, but his first drink tasted finer than anything he could remember. Others pushed him aside, making his moment of enjoyment short-lived, although he managed to duck his head into the stream that gushed from the spout.

Outside the cattle car, Nat passed the canteens up to Riley. As he fitted a boot into the boarding rung, a scream caught his ear. It was a girl's cry for help.

"What was that?" he asked.

"Pay no mind, Nathan. Whatever it is doesn't concern us," Hennison said.

"Best git on board," Riley advised. "The doc's right. No need looking for trouble."

The entreaty sounded again, high pitched and strangely foreign, followed by raucous peals of laughter. Nathan stepped down and turned toward the sound. A crowd of the California miners clustered to the right of the water tower just below the door to the next railroad car. One burly miner hurled ornately inlaid chests into the dust of the railbed. One of the chests burst open, spilling gold and silver brocade dresses under the milling feet of the men. Dust mixed with water from the tower churned the clothes into muddy rags. Two miners grasped a struggling girl. Three others held a frail man in black silk pajamas while another beat him with ham-sized fists. With each blow, the crowd jeered, and the girl wailed.

"Oh, Lord," the former shopkeeper sighed. "The miners found a couple of Chinamen. This'll be bad for sure."

"Why?" Nat asked him.

"Why? Have you been living on the moon, boy?" the merchant snorted. "Don't you know nothing?"

"Convent," Hennison corrected the man. "He's only recently given up his vows. Just discovered he wasn't cut out for a nun's life. The boy's not stupid, just ignorant."

The man nodded understandingly and began his instruction in short jerky sentences. "Central Pacific Railroad and then Southern Pacific imported Chinamen to lay track. Cheapest labor there was. Promised to pay them when the job was done. After the railroad was completed, the companies hired men to shoot them so they wouldn't have to pay them off. After seventy-eight, the law stopped that. Now, the railroads just turn a blind eye to whatever happens to their Chinamen."

Nathan cast an accusing look at Riley.

"I never shot no Chinamen. Not in my whole life," the gunman replied. He winced as the girl screamed again. Riley was hurt that Nat might think him capable of such deeds.

"We've got to help them," Nat shouted. Out of the corner of his eye he saw the miners laboring to pull the girl's tight-fitting dress over her hips. Exquisitely fashioned and exotically dressed, the girl reminded Nathan of damsels rescued from danger by shining knights in the many books that sustained his hope during the dark days at the orphanage. Without waiting for a reply, Nathan pushed his way to the clot of miners.

"Lord, Lord," the merchant prayed.

"Keep praying," Riley commanded as he jumped out the door. "We're gonna need it."

"Let her go!" Nat ordered the men who now held the girl spread-eagled on the ground. Standing over her, an enormous miner loosened his pants and let them drop to his knees. Behind them the old man was rapidly disappearing into the watery muck, driven there by the raining blows of his assailant's feet. A third cluster rifled the traveling chests of the unfortunate man and girl, spilling precious teak and silk treasures into the dirt in their quest for gold or opium.

"Wait your turn," a weasel-faced man growled, grasping Nat's shoulder as he spoke and jerking the youth around. His right fist punched the air where Nathan's face had been moments before.

But Nat ducked and drove his knee into the weasel's crotch, connecting solidly. The man's eyes bulged, wind rushed from his open mouth, and he collapsed in front of the would-be rapist. There he lay groaning and blocking the others from rushing Nat. Diverted from their goals, the men released their grasp on the girl and turned toward this upstart. In that brief lull the girl slipped between the miner's legs and struggled to pull her beaten friend toward the railroad cars. The muddy ground aided her in sliding him away.

But Nat's action brought an unexpected result. The miners obviously worked together for they stopped their activities at once and faced this David who threatened their sport. A dozen hardened Goliaths surrounded the boy, brandishing ax handles, knives, shovels, and several pistols.

"Now hold on here!" Riley shouted, backing into Nathan to cover his blind side. "We don't want no trouble!" But he knew his words fell on deaf and angry ears. These men wanted the space the Chinese occupied on the train, and probably theirs as well. And they were willing to kill for it.

"You already got it, saddle bum," the giant miner answered Riley. Pulling up his pants with one hand, he jerked a short barreled .44 Schofield from one pocket and fired directly at Nat.

The charge exploded in Nathan's face, singeing his eyebrows and streaking his face with powder burns. Amazingly, the bullet missed the youth although he stood less than three feet away, passing over his shoulder to hit a miner to the left of Riley in the neck. Grievously wounded, this man clutched his throat, and fell thrashing into his friends while spewing blood from his mouth. His plight diverted the giant's attention for a split second.

Practice saved Nathan's life once again. In that fraction of time, Nat drew, centered his front sight on the miner's chest, and squeezed the trigger. The blast caught the giant square in the chest and ignited his vest. In that same time Riley capped off two rounds, dropping men who held pistols. Nathan fired again at the massive miner who staggered at him with vest ablaze and now sporting two blood-soaked bullet holes. His burning clothes appeared to perplex the miner more than the bullets in his chest. This lack of effect also puzzled Nathan.

"Head shot!" Riley screamed. "Shoot his damned head!"

That did the trick. Nat's third shot blew the miner's brains over his backup squad, and the man dropped into a smoldering pile without firing his revolver a second time. But that advice cost Jim Riley dearly, diverting his attention and allowing someone to bring a shovel to bear on the gunman. The flat part of the shovel caught Riley on the side of his head, knocking him senseless. A cheer went up, and the mob surged ahead. A windmill of hammering fists drove Nathan under. Momentary glimpses of the azure blue sky caught his eye briefly before fists and feet pummeled him into a black morass of agitating legs and arms. Instinctively he curled into a ball.

A clap of thunder rent the air. The noise of the mob subsided, the beating stopped, and the sky overhead reappeared as the miners fell back. Bloodied and confused, Nat rose to his feet. His pistol lay trampled in the mud, and he quickly retrieved it, although its lack of effect on the mob left him more deeply shaken than his beating. He looked about.

The miners were retreating, edging warily back from him and the body of Jim Riley. Nat shook his head to clear it, but the horizon still spun sickeningly around the train's tracks and the water tower. A peculiarly familiar voice issued orders from the direction of the rail cars. Nathan followed the sound, and nearly laughed in hysterical relief.

"Stand back, I'm placing these men under arrest," roared Doc Hennison from the doorway of their cattle car. While the tone of his voice commanded respect, the double-barreled shotgun in his left hand commanded more. But the major impact came from the silver star pinned to his coat lapel.

"Who the hell are you?" someone asked.

"Marshal Hennison from Culver City," Doc lied, hoping none of the miners came from there.

"Who are you arresting here, marshal? Us?" the weasel-faced man asked, still clutching his groin. A murmur ran through the crowd. He and the dead giant were the obvious leaders, a fact recognized by Hennison.

"Why, those two gunmen, man. I've been trailing them since Deadwood," the doctor replied, carefully avoiding any mention of Arizona. "They're wanted for bank robbery and murder, and I'm taking them back to stand trial."

"Why don't we just string 'em up from a telegraph pole?" someone offered. A roar of general agreement followed.

"Won't do, men." Hennison laughed easily. "Won't do at all. You'd lose the reward if I don't deliver them to Culver City."

"Reward?" A dozen men spoke at once.

"One thousand dollars apiece," Doc enunciated the words slowly for added measure. "You all captured them, so the money goes to you." He could see the men calculating their shares. Before the weasel could speak, Doc kicked a piece of rope from the car to the miners and continued. "Hand up their sidearms and tie them up. I'll telegraph at the next stop for your reward and a special train from Yuma to pick you all up."

"Telegraph from here, marshal," a tall miner suggested.

"Wish I could." Hennison nodded gravely as he strode back and forth. This role as champion of the law suited his perverse nature, and he was warming to the part. "But some fool shot out the wire. Probably that one, 'Gray Beard' Sullivan."

He pointed to the dazed Riley, then to the telegraph wire dangling from a shattered glass insulator. Hennison thought it best not to mention he had done it. His double-ought buckshot carried away half the pole as well.

"He and Kid Curry might have killed you all if it weren't for your brave resistance. This will make the papers for sure, boys. You'll be famous, that's for damn sure."

"Kid Curry!" A ripple of excitement went through the crowd.

"I've heard about him. Rode with the Hole in the Wall Gang and Butch Cassidy," another cried. "But don't recall no 'Gray Beard' Sullivan."

"He's past his prime," the pretend marshal added. "Over

the hill and just hanging on. Don't hear much about him."

The tall miner looked at the two men Riley had shot. "He don't shoot like he's past his prime."

"Well, he is. Now, get them on board, men. The sooner I make the next stop, the faster you'll get your money." Hennison continued his banter as Riley and Nat were quickly tied and pushed into the cattle car. Behind him their confused fellow travelers kept silent as Doc waved his ten-gauge in their direction.

"Hold on there," the weasel said. "How do we know you won't claim the reward for yourself, marshal? You might forget we caught them after the train gets around the bend."

"Forget? I won't forget." Hennison frowned. Slowly he pointed his shotgun at the man, causing his friends to edge away from him. "Are you calling me a liar?"

"Um, no, marshal, but we got no guarantees," the man replied defensively.

"Guarantees is it you need? You come along then to keep an eye on me," Hennison said matter-of-factly. "This car will hold one more. The rest will have to wait for that special train I'm calling for. It should be here by this evening. Then you can ride to the coast in comfort with a grubstake in each and everyone's pocket."

The spokesman clambered aboard and turned to grin at his friends. Obviously they trusted him for the group cheered and waved. At that moment the train started to roll, picking up speed with the grade. In the excitement the two Chinese were temporarily overlooked.

Hennison cradled the shotgun under his arm as his hand extracted a bottle of elixir from his right breast pocket. He tossed it in a soaring arc to the men below. "Have a drink on me while you're waiting," he crowed. "And may that wait last until hell freezes over," he mumbled under his breath.

The train struggled up the grade and passed through a cut

bank topped with scrub brush and cacti spared by the railroad builders. Curving to the right it accelerated on the flat for another two miles before swinging north in a wide arc that avoided a jumble of granite boulders to the south. The wind cooled the sweat from the occupants and kept the flies at bay. Leaving the scene of this recent violence farther and farther behind with each mile caused the riders in the car to relax and enjoy the cooling breeze.

The surviving leader of the rabble stood inside the open door and grinned down at the tied Nathan. He jabbed his boot into the boy's side. "Kid Curry," he jeered. "You ain't so tough now, are you?"

"Are you keeping an eye on them?" Hennison asked.

The weasel nodded.

"That's a big mistake." Doc grinned at the puzzled man. "I distinctly recommended you keep an eye on *me.*"

The steel butt plate of the shotgun caught the miner squarely between his eyes, knocking him backward into space. He gasped, hands and feet clawing the empty air as momentum carried him outside the car at the same speed as the train. Then he dropped onto the railbed to bounce along the cross ties for a hundred yards.

Hennison leaned out the door to look back at the inert body before it disappeared. "Told you I wouldn't forget," he said. Then he faced the packed car, scanning the faces for opposition. The men here wanted only to reach the Klondike, and showed that intent by shortening their memories and closing their eyes. This was not their problem.

" 'Gray Beard' Sullivan!" Riley snorted up at Hennison. "And over the hill! I ain't never heard such trash. Cut me loose, and we'll see who's just hanging on."

"What lack of gratitude," Doc chortled. "Here I save your worthless life, and what thanks do I get? Damn little."

"Cut me loose, damn you."

"Not until you thank me."

"Hell if I will. If you'd used that scatter gun earlier Nat and me might have missed our thumping."

"Maybe I'll just roll you out, too. Then I wouldn't have to listen to that ear-grating Texas accent of yours."

"Go ahead, but I ain't thanking you for something a partner oughta do for his trailmates."

Doc leaned over the fuming gunfighter. "Does that mean you like me, *partner?*" He accented the last word, imitating Riley's drawl.

"Go to hell. Kick me off if you're a mind to, but don't talk me to death. It's plain torture."

"I'll thank you, Doc, for Mr. Riley and me," Nat said. "You saved both our lives."

The boy's sincerity caught Hennison off guard, rendering him momentarily speechless. Candor and open honesty he found impossible to subvert. Lacking the words for a cynical retort, the doctor simply set his shotgun aside and cut the two men's bonds. Then he leaned against the slatted side of the cattle car and watched Riley and Nathan get to their feet. Dark blood, already caked in the dry air, stuck to the gunman's hair while the youth sported a swelling over the bridge of his nose and a darkening bruise at the angle of his jaw.

"Better let me look at that cut," Hennison suggested to Riley after he examined Nat and found no serious injury. "It might need stitches. Wouldn't want any of your limited brains to spill out."

Begrudgingly, the gunman sat on the rolling floor while the Doc probed the cut, cussing whenever the physician struck a sore spot. Both men looked up in amazement when the Chinese girl emerged from the packed passengers and placed her slim hand in Nathan's. Her dark eyes locked with his, holding him in her gaze like a snake holds a mouse. Taking his hand firmly, she led the youth back into the far corner of the car. The equally astonished travelers parted like the Red Sea for Moses to allow them passage.

"Where the devil did she come from?" Riley asked.

"Must have slipped aboard when you two were entertaining those miners at the water stop," the doc said.

"What she gonna do with Nat?"

Hennison watched the retreating backs of the boy and girl, then turned grinning to the confused gunman. "Riley, you've spent too much time with cows. I'd say she plans on doing an examination of her own."

Nathan followed the girl to the corner of the freight car where her older companion lay on the rough boards, breathing unevenly. Lying on his back with hands folded across his muddied robes, the figure struck Nat as incredibly small and incredibly old. The richness of his clothes showed through the splotches of dirt to accent the seamed and wrinkled face and hands, while elongated, lacquered nails sprouted from the bony fingers like animal's claws. The fingers moved imperceptibly, motioning the girl nearer. She knelt by the man and bowed her head as his lips moved. Her face appeared immutable, but a single tear coursed down her cheek to hide behind a strand of raven hair torn out of place by her recent calamity. Other than her soiled and torn dress and that solitary tear, she maintained her composure.

The lips whispered while one manicured hand withdrew a small jade figure from the folds of the robe. Nathan watched in fascination as the China doll received the figurine and bowed further until her forehead touched the hem of the dying man's robe. The ancient coughed once, his eyelids fluttered momentarily, and his breathing ceased.

An eternity passed as Nat stood over the girl swaying with the railcar, oblivious to the miners and teamsters who turned their backs to the drama unfolding in the corner, not for of lack of curiosity but due to fear of his pistol and his two equally deadly associates. The youth thought she was praying, but whether or not that was true, her uniqueness was sufficient to hold him in thrall.

At length she covered the dead man's face with his robe and rose to face Nathan. Her beauty startled him. Oval, and perfectly symmetrical except for the track made in her makeup by that errant tear, her face seemed constructed of porcelain with limpid brown pools for eyes. Those eyes surveyed him now from beneath slanted lids without fear or curiosity or trace of anxiety.

"I am Wei-Li," she said as she pressed the jade object into Nat's hand. "And this is for you to take to San Francisco."

Nathan started at her words. How did she know he was bound for that city? For a fleeting moment he feared her eyes had peered into his mind and read his thoughts. To cover his consternation he glanced at the cold stone in his hand. Milky green and translucent, it was an ornately carved dragon grasping its tail in its jaws. In the flickering light of the moving train, the figure seemed to glow with an internal pulsation. Suddenly another fact struck him: She spoke perfect English with an accent similar to one he had heard from a visiting bishop from England.

"You speak English," he blurted.

Her slitted eyes tilted slightly at the corners in amusement. "I learned English in Hong Kong. I also speak Mandarin and Cantonese. And some French."

Nat dropped his gaze again, unable to stand her scrutiny. She appeared roughly his age but infinitely more poised, more worldly than he could ever hope to be. The dragon flashed in his hand. "What has this to do with San Francisco?" he asked.

She turned toward the body. "It was his wish."

"I understand. My friends and I will see you safely to San Francisco. We're headed there, too." Nat looked at the corpse.

Dead, the man appeared even smaller. "I'm sorry I didn't save him. If only I'd been sooner . . . "

"If only . . . " she answered with the hint of a smile. "If only the tiger's tail would not twitch, perhaps he would not spring."

"What does that mean?"

She shrugged. "It is only a saying."

"Was he your grandfather?" he asked, fearful she was laughing at him behind those dark eyes.

"He was my master," she said simply. "I am . . . was his concubine."

"Concubine?" Nathan's face burned crimson.

"I believe the English word is mistress. He was a wealthy man. He bought me in Hong Kong. To warm his bed."

Nathan lost all powers of speech. The traces of jasmine perfume straying from her body with each gust of air through the boxcar perplexed him as much as her frank disclosure. Perhaps the girl expected this, because she took both of Nathan's arms and sat him down on the floor. Carefully her fingers explored his bruises and cuts. All the while the boy watched her, mesmerized by her beauty and her air of cool detachment, and all the while his face burned hotter with each feathery touch. At length she sat back on her heels.

"I regret I cannot treat your injuries with the proper ointments. All our trunks were stolen from the other car by those bandits who killed Won Lo."

"Won Lo, was that his name?" Nat gestured to the body, painfully aware of his croaking voice.

"Yes. He was a merchant dealing in silks and opium. We were returning to San Francisco from Denver. Bad joss brought us by this route instead of the Northern passage, but no other transport was available."

"Opium?" Hennison's voice came from behind Nat's shoulder. "That fellow ran opium dens?" Opium meant laudanum, and that meant he could be back in business making elixir.

Wei-Li turned her head to look at the doctor and then Riley. Her practiced eye categorized each. The one-armed man, while upper class, obviously drank too much, and the tattered gunman at his side bore the marks of a hard life outdoors with meager food. Clearly, this man was a hired assassin. One-arm would be easy to control should the need arise, but the other would not. He bore too many features of the man-eating tiger. "No. Won Lo arranged for shipments," she said.

"Do you have any opium left?" Hennison pressed. But his hope faded when she shook her head. "Damnit."

The girl bowed her head abjectly. "I am sorry. Everything was taken from us. Perhaps if you went back?"

Hennison snorted in derision. "And get hanged from the nearest pole? No thank you, lassie. That would be plum stupid." He spun on his heel, heading back to the cooling air at the open door while Riley backed slowly away to follow him.

Wei-Li watched them retreat, keeping her head low. The one-armed man reacted as she had hoped, and the gun-killer had the sense to leave them alone. She turned back to Nathan, purposely touching his swollen cheek in a way to cause him pain. Caught off guard, he winced in spite of himself. From a secret pocket in her dress she withdrew a small, lacquered vial.

"This medicine will ease your discomfort and help you sleep." She held the bottle to his lips, but he jerked back.

"What is it? If it's that laudanum stuff, I don't want any."

She shook her head, inwardly amused at the foolish pride that allowed this boy-man to prefer pain over any outwardly show of weakness. "This is medicine," she said firmly, directing the flask to his lips.

He obeyed, reverting to old habits from listening to the ordering nuns. The potion tasted bitter, but left a warm trail down his throat into his stomach. With another dose his head spun in time with the swaying boxcar, his lips tingled, and he allowed Wei-Li to place his head in her lap. While she stroked his brow, he fell asleep to dream of dragons and damsels in distress.

Time passed while Nathan slept, and the sun sank in the sky, casting longer shadows between the cracks of the car's siding. The interior cooled somewhat and took on hardened images of golden light and blackened shadows. Wei-Li watched the boy and wondered if he was the foreign devil the soothsayers had told her of when she first left Hong Kong. She thought back on the seventeen years of her life, reflecting on the bright lights and dark shadows that filled her past just as the light transformed this traveling car. Born into a starving peasant family, she was sold at the age of five to the House of Moonbeams to begin the rigorous training of a courtesan of the first class. Fine clothes and food erased the memories of crushing poverty and perpetual hunger, and her beauty and skill provided her with no small measure of control over her life. But her beauty sealed her fate as well when agents for Won Lo arrived from America and bought her.

Frightened and depressed at leaving all things familiar to her, she purchased poison and contemplated ending her life, but an ancient soothsayer read her fortune. True, she would suffer grievously in the cold land of barbarians, the old hag had said, but this would be a test of her worthiness. If she passed, a mysterious devil would bless her with a son who would rise to power. Pressed for more detail, the fortune teller saw nothing more. Wei-Li had taken heart at these hopes for her future, set aside thoughts of her own death, and sailed to San Francisco. Now, stroking this foreigner's brow she wondered, again. Was this the devil in her future?

Long after dark, Wei-Li slipped away from the sleeping youth and borrowed a blanket from a sympathetic miner to hang across the cattle car's corner. One meaningful look from her in the direction of the dangerous Riley and unpredictable Doc silenced any grumbling from men forced to relinquish another few inches of space for her privacy. Then she slipped back.

Nat opened his eyes. The swaying train and the constant clacking of the iron wheels over uneven rails told him the journey continued. Again he breathed her perfume and felt his head cradled in the warmth of her lap. Night light from the stars and a rising moon illuminated her face as she bent over him to study him.

"This Mr. Won Lo, was he good to you?" Nat found himself asking.

Wei-Li smiled at his curiosity. "Yes," she whispered, bending close to him so her hair touched his face. "He prized me, much like his gold and jade. He never beat me." She stopped for a moment. Was this young man asking something else? Perhaps, she had misjudged him. "He was old and easy to pleasure," she said, expecting to answer his unasked query. But the effect of her words was not what she expected. Nathan stiffened and sucked in his breath.

"You . . . you weren't married to him?"

She shook her head, then laughed. Her laugh at his ridiculous question tinkled near his ear like tiny silver bells, rung in the secrecy of their blanket walled fortress, and her hair caressed his face with each movement of her body.

Nathan found himself grinning. "Kind of a stupid question, wasn't it?" he chuckled. Then he turned serious while the laughing eyes watched him. "What will you do in San Francisco? Do you have someone to take care of you? Do you need money?" His whispered questions poured forth, coaxed by the laudanum, the touch of her jasmined body, and the release of these past weeks of anxiety.

Wei-Li pressed a finger to his lips to silence him. Did he not know Won Lo had given her to him with the jade dragon as his dying wish? Won Lo the Wise, had he made the right choice with his last breath? She ran her hand over his shirt and felt the muscles shiver from her touch. Won Lo was old and easy to please, she mused, and this one is young and also easy to please. The knot hidden in her own stomach relaxed with the knowledge that she was again in control.

"All I have was stolen," she whispered. "I have nothing but my clothes. You saved my life, and you saved my honor."

"It's okay."

"I have nothing." Her eyes narrowed in fixed purpose as her professional training came into play. "But I can still show you my gratitude."

A rustle of silk caught Nathan's ear as the train dipped into the inky darkness of a cutbank before emerging. When he looked up she sat naked at his head. Faint starlight fluttered over her naked body, causing her skin to gleam against the somber woolen backdrop.

"Sweet Jesus," he gasped.

This time she stoppered his words with her lips while her hands deftly undid his belt. Exploring farther she found him ready. In view of his injuries, and her judgment of his inexperience, and because he now possessed the jade figurine, she lowered herself on top of him in the position known as Ride the Dragon.

⋆ ⋆ TEN ⋆ ⋆

Wyatt stopped to light his cigar at the street corner. Over the flickering match he surveyed this bustling city. San Francisco, gateway to the gold fields, grew with each passing day as more and more stampeders arrived. With only Seattle to rival its docks and waterfront and with better links to other towns by railroad, the city by the bay enjoyed expanding prosperity as the predominate outfitter to most prospectors heading north.

But Frisco was like a gaudy wedding feast, Earp realized: all bright lights, dancing, and laughter that went on far too long and prevented the married couple from truly enjoying themselves. He was tiring of the city, tiring of the crowds, and tiring of the thin veneer of civilization where men killed one another with legal snares and secret deals instead of face to face with a smoking gun. Watching them stab each other in the back with an ink pen sickened him. His eye longed to search the horizon without bumping into a building that masked the sky, and he yearned to swing his arms without fear of knocking off the latest maribou feathered hat.

"San Francisco sure is something, isn't it, Wyatt? Goings-on every minute," commented his brother Virgil. "But it's too damn much for me. Allie and I are heading back to Prescott tomorrow. I aim to give the Grizzly another chance to make me rich."

"Your beloved Grizzly mine will only make you dead if you let her."

"Like the rooster in the henhouse said, I can't stop now," Virgil said as he grasped Wyatt's hand and directed the match to light his own cigar.

Wyatt puffed thoughtfully, enjoying the pungent smoke as he sized up his older brother. Life had dealt Virgil a harder hand to play than most, but the fire still burned in his eyes. His left arm dangled at his side, useless since that night in Tombstone scarcely eight weeks after the O.K. Corral when a shotgun blast in the night blew out three inches of the bone. Less than two years ago, Virg's precious Grizzly mine collapsed on him, leaving him half buried and unconscious for hours. Allie had nursed him back to health as she had done so often in the past, tending him while his dislocated hip and crushed feet healed. Yet here he stood, eager to try again with the scar on his face from the cave-in still an angry red. And Virg was still taking jobs as a lawman. Why did he continue, Wyatt wondered. What made him go on?

Stubbornness, he answered himself. All the Earps had it—to the point of recklessness. Bulldog blood ran in their veins, mixed with a love for taking chances. What else explained the penchant of the Earps for prospecting, gambling, and wearing a badge. God, Wyatt thought, what a formula for trouble. This bent would kill them all, including himself.

And with no one to carry on his bloodline, that black notion surfaced once more. Like a knife twisted deep in his heart, the ache returned with it. Wyatt's thoughts drifted back to his dead child, and the sad fact that neither he nor Virgil had children. Time was running out.

A ruddy man in tan bowler and checked suit, concentrating on the sports section of the *Call*, plowed directly into Wyatt's back. His paper crumpled into his face, knocking his bowler askew. "Watch where you're going, you idiot!" he snarled. His hat tumbled past his furtive grasp to settle atop a pile of fresh horse dung in the gutter.

Wyatt turned. "You ran into me, friend."

"Christ!" the angry fellow swore as he gawked at his soiled hat. Accustomed to bullying softer men and looking to vent his spleen, the man glared at this obvious dandy with cravat, stick pin, and stiff collar. "Look what you did now. I've half a mind to box your ears for that. Or take your hat instead." He grasped Wyatt's shirt front and raised his right fist. To his surprise his grip divulged a tightly muscled chest behind the fabric, not the flabby flesh he expected. Something else stopped his punch in midair.

Wyatt's left hand clamped on the man's fist in a viselike grip that sent slivers of pain up the arm, and his right hand gripped the butt of a short-barreled Colt tucked in his waistband. To one side Virgil already had drawn his revolver.

Outclassed and outgunned, the tough released Wyatt's shirt and stammered an apology. "Excuse me. I made a mistake," he said as he swallowed hard.

"We all do, at times, friend." Wyatt showed his teeth and released the man's crushed fist, but his right hand still rested on his pistol.

Virgil picked up the soiled bowler and placed it on the troublemaker's head. "Better keep down wind of people until you clean that hat." He nodded to the steaming manure decorating the bowler.

"Yes sir, I certainly will. Thank you," the man said as he hurried into the crowd.

Virgil released a hearty laugh that started in his ample belly and rolled to the surface. Wyatt joined him with a chuckle. The older Earp was gratified to see his brother smile. Wyatt, he knew, still blamed himself for Morgan's death and his own crippled arm. Why he did puzzled Virgil and the younger Warren because no one else did, and surely Wyatt had made those who were responsible pay. But Wyatt was always the serious one, even as a child, running deep like still waters, their mother would say. Perhaps this was the time to spring his newfound secret.

Virgil studied the ash on the burning end of his cigar. "You know, Wyatt, something amazing has happened, if it's true. I've been waiting for the right opportunity to tell you."

"Don't tell me you struck it rich, Virg?"

"Better than that, little brother. I may be a father."

"What? What do you mean 'may be?' "

"Well, I got this letter . . . "

"Allie wrote you a letter? Don't you two talk anymore?" Wyatt snorted, expecting one of Virgil's practical jokes.

"No, Wyatt. This is the gospel truth. I got a letter from a woman in Portland, Oregon, claiming to be my daughter."

"You've never been to Portland, Virgil."

"No, but you remember my first wife, Ellen?"

Wyatt nodded. Virgil had sown wild oats as a seventeen-year-old youth in Iowa and eloped to secretly marry Ellen Rysdam, a neighbor girl, in 1860. "Yeah, her father tried his damnedest to have your marriage annulled."

Virgil grinned. "But he couldn't because he never knew what names we used to get married nor what county we picked."

"But he sure kept you away from her after he found out."

"Yes. And you remember I enlisted in the Eighty-third Illinois in sixty-two, and some damned fools told Ellen and her family I was killed at Fredericktown where James was wounded."

"So?" Wyatt remembered his oldest brother, James, arriving home permanently disabled from his wounds.

"So Ellen was pregnant and had a baby girl, and I never knew it because her whole family moved away to Oregon. Would you believe it, Wyatt? I've got a full-grown daughter living in Portland. She read about us after Tombstone and wrote to me. I just got the letter."

"Well, I'll be damned, Virg. What does Allie say about this?"

"She's happy for me, seeing as how it happened before I ever met her. I'm going to write back and arrange a meeting. Her name is Jane, and she wrote that Ellen is there too."

Virgil studied his somber brother. Josie had told him of Wyatt's ordeal with his premature son. "You might have a child you didn't know anything about, too. Wouldn't it be wonderful if you had a son out there somewhere, Wyatt, looking for you!"

"Couldn't happen, Virg. Urilla died trying to have my baby, or have you forgotten how the Southerlands blamed me for her death?" Wyatt knew he had not. The years of 1870 and 1871 were two of the worst of his life. His first wife's death had driven him to lawlessness in the Indian Territory, drinking and stealing horses until he turned to buffalo hunting in 1872. That was the year he met Bat Masterson on the Salt Fork of the Arkansas River.

"No, Wyatt. And I didn't forget the fight Morg, James, and the two of us had with her brothers, either. I was thinking about you and Mattie."

Wyatt stubbed his cigar out on the metal lamp pole. This topic had turned its taste stale in his mouth. The image of Mattie, lurching about their rooms in Tombstone, her mind numbed on laudanum and whiskey, still seared his mind. He had loved her until the dope destroyed her and all that he found in her to love. Like a river roiled after a prairie thunderstorm, her addiction changed her overnight from a clear stream to one muddied, treacherous, and unreadable. Mattie blamed him for her problems, he knew that, yet he had done everything in his power to make her stop. But, was he truly responsible for Mattie? Had he driven her to use those drugs? Had he really killed Urilla? Would he bring bad luck to Josie, the only good thing to come out of Tombstone?

"I heard Mattie died in Pinal from opium and whiskey,"

Wyatt said simply. Showing his emotion came hard to him, no matter how strongly he felt, even to his family.

Virgil bobbed his head. "I heard that, too, from a cowboy passing through Prescott." His eyes lighted. "But, I also heard she had a baby boy in Globe or Pinal the year you two parted ways. But I'm not sure which town."

"Mattie would have written to me."

"I don't know. She was hanging around with Big Nose Kate, and you know how bitter Kate was that Doc Holliday dumped her. You'd be drawing to an inside straight to bet Kate didn't spill some of her anger into Mattie. It'd be just like those two to keep knowledge of your child from you. Sort of their best way to get even, I figure."

Wyatt pursed his lips and sighed. "She couldn't do much worse to me than keeping me separated from my rightful child. But Mattie wouldn't do such a terrible thing, I'm sure of it."

"You never know. Hate does strange things to people. . . . "

A deep sorrow shadowed Wyatt's face. "Virg, I know you're a born optimist; finding out you have a daughter has me tickled pink, but you're asking lightning to strike twice in the same spot. It just isn't possible."

"Maybe, maybe not. But if it did, and you had a son, he'd be almost grown. Wouldn't *that* be something?"

Wyatt turned away from his brother, wearied by this conversation. His keen eye picked two familiar faces out of the moving sea of men and women flowing over the cobblestones. Josie and Allie were strolling toward them, stopping at intervals to window shop and adjust the parcels in their arms. Inwardly he sighed in relief. Allie and Josie would monopolize the conversation and give all this speculation of undiscovered children a rest. Virgil meant well, but sometimes he could grate on sore nerves.

"Ladies," he tipped his hat and bowed gallantly. "What are two stylish ladies such as yourselves doing in this dangerous city without male escorts? May I place my poor services and that of my mostly useless older brother at your disposal."

Josie curtsied and flashed a gleaming smile at him while Allie commenced to spit nails.

"Wyatt Berry Stapp Earp!" Allie snapped, dropping her packages to ram her fists onto her hips. "What makes you think we need your help? Why, Josie and I can handle anything this overcrowded burg can throw at us, and wipe your runny noses as well. And don't you go calling Virgil old and useless."

Virgil grinned sheepishly as he gathered her parcels while Wyatt backstepped, cursing his foolishness in giving Allie an opportunity to spar with him. Looking at the two women, dressed so alike in silk bonnets and dark satin filled dresses, he wondered how it was possible their personalities could be so divergent. Miniscule Alvira was outspoken, opinionated, and as tough on the outside as a sun-dried yucca, while Josie was all soft and ladylike. Yet Allie's thorny exterior hid a tender core that had nursed Virgil back to health after Tombstone and repetitive disasters like the Grizzly cave-in.

It was Josie who was made of steel inside, so smooth and polished that it seemed soft, but she could be as strong as the finest tempered blade. Inwardly, Wyatt took comfort in that fact. Whatever hardships his life caused them, Josie would not break like his other wives had.

"Hope you two haven't been waiting long for us," Josie said, changing the subject. "But we saw some bonnets in a millinery shop and we just had to try them on."

Wyatt rolled his eyes. "No, not long, would you say Virg? About an hour?"

Virgil coughed, trying to straddle the fence between Wyatt's teasing and his wife's questioning look.

But Allie ignored that remark. "Wyatt, I suppose Virg has told you all about his long-lost daughter?"

"Yes," Earp nodded. From the corner of his eye he saw Josie

blanch. Damn Allie and her loose tongue, he thought. Josie was still grieving for their lost child, also.

"Allie's told me all about it, Virgil," Josie countered bravely. "I think it's marvelous."

Allie fidgeted with her lace gloves before emitting a long sigh. "I wish I were able to have children, but the good Lord shorted me on that end, so I'm pleased Virgil's first wife helped me out."

"He shorted you on both ends, Allie. No denying that," Wyatt quipped at the tiny woman, hoping his joke would lead them off this painful subject. "I suspect you got stunted from lack of enough to eat. Since my stomach has been growling all these three hours we were waiting for the two of you, I suggest we take some refreshments. Who knows? Perhaps Allie might grow another inch with the proper food."

"You just said one hour," Josie corrected him.

"Leave it to a man to be thinking about his stomach when he isn't thinking of making love." Allie giggled. "Let's walk back to Fulton and try that new restaurant. The Del Monaco, wasn't it?"

They strolled along the street, admiring the carriage trade that frequented this quieter part of town and knowing that closer to the wharves prospectors were stampeding about the docks in frantic last-minute maneuvers. The gold rush had transformed San Francisco into a two-faced entity like Janus the Roman god. In this posh section, San Francisco looked back on an era of gentility and refinement, yet all the while its other face looked ahead to new riches and new-sprung travails. Here polished brass hitching rings, etched glass door panes, and doormen closed a blind eye to the dockside madness.

Two blocks from the dining room, Josie clasped her hand to her stomach and clutched Wyatt's arm for support. Her eyes widened in pain.

"What is it, Josie?" he asked in concern.

135

She shook off his concerns, straightening herself with determined self-effort. "It's nothing," she said to the concerned faces. "Something I must have eaten. It's gone now."

"You don't look well," Allie said. "I've read about these type of recurrent labor pains."

"I'll be fine," Josie protested.

"Maybe we should take Josie home and put her to bed?" Virgil suggested. "She looks right peaked to me."

"I think so, Virg." Wyatt agreed.

"Oh, no. I don't want to spoil this lovely evening for the rest of you."

"Don't be foolish," Allie scolded her. "You have to take care of your health. We can dine out another evening."

"No, I won't ruin your night out."

"Look," Wyatt interrupted. His concern heightened with every minute his wife pressed against him for support. "Allie, you and Virg go on to the Del Monaco. I'll take Josie home."

Overriding the protests of his brother and sister-in-law, Wyatt sent them on their way before he flagged down a hansom cab. Helping his wife inside, he gave the driver directions to their residence at 720 McAllister where they stayed with Josie's sister. The carriage rattled down the cobblestones past Virgil and Allie. Wyatt leaned out the window to wave at them as they passed. Then he turned anxiously toward his wife.

Josie sat smiling smugly at him. One block in the cab had worked a miraculous cure. While the astonished Wyatt watched, she slid open the portal behind the driver and ordered him to change direction for the newly planted gardens near the Presidio. The worldly hack driver winked and gave a knowing nod as he accepted the twenty-dollar gold piece she slipped into his hand. Gentleman and their ladies often explored the gardens and each other in the privacy of a curtained hansom, and this lady looked ready, he reasoned.

Josie arched her eyebrows at his puzzled stare. "Don't look so confused, Wyatt. I was tired of listening to Allie, and I wanted you all to myself. Did you forget I was on the stage before we met?"

"Well, I'll be damned. You sure fooled me." Wyatt smoothed his mustache. "Darling, next time let me in on your next performance—in advance, if you don't mind. You scared the hell out of me."

Josie's Cheshire cat grin spread across her face. At thirty-seven she was still a ravishing beauty, aided by a mature sensuality that had supplanted her role as ingenue. Like a feline, she moved sinuously to his side of the cab.

"Besides, I have a surprise for you," she purred.

Wyatt focused his eyes in the dim light on two pasteboard cards Josie flashed before him. He raised his brows quizzically. "Tickets to the theater?"

"Guess again, buster. Think of someplace that rhymes with gold."

Wyatt's mouth dropped open. "Alaska! Are you sure about this, Sadie? Really sure?"

"I'm ready and strong enough for anything the Klondike can throw at us. And I'm getting tired of San Francisco. This place is too crowded to suit me." That last line was a lie, she knew, but she also realized her delivery had been flawless, making it credible. In truth, she hated watching her man shrivel inside while he watched others heading for the gold fields. Wyatt was a doer, not one to stand while the parade passed him by.

"Two first class tickets on the *S.S. Brixom* bound for St. Michael's on the mouth of the Yukon. None of this climbing over icy passes to get to the Klondike for you and me. We're traveling by the All-Water Route this time."

Holding the tickets just out of his reach, Josie slipped onto his lap. Her free hand directed his hand under her dress, and to his amazement he felt smooth skin. Josie was naked beneath her hoops and crinolines.

"But the tickets aren't free," she purred as her lips sought his. "You will have to earn them, Mr. Earp."

★ ★ ELEVEN ★ ★

Jim Riley leaned on the butt of his Winchester and watched the trolley crawl up Clay Hill as if by magic. Smartly dressed couples, arm in arm, paraded by this rustic bumpkin exchanging looks of mild amusement at his floppy hat and scarred leather chaps. The cable car clanged over the crest of the hill and disappeared just as the electric lights glowed to life.

"Lord Almighty," Riley exclaimed. "This place is magic! Did you see that trolley ain't got no horses pulling it? And who lit the street lamps? I didn't see no lamplighter here abouts."

"That's a cable car," Hennison replied. "An underground cable pulls it up, and the streetlights are electric. Throw a switch, and they all turn on at once. No need to have lamplighters since they don't use gas or coal oil."

"That sure puzzles me. I'd have thought with all these extra hands walking about they'd keep lamplighters just for something to do. Just what do all these folks do, anyway?"

Hennison shrugged, enjoying the gunfighter's discomfort. "Most are in business."

"Business?" Riley goggled. He waved his arm at the crowded streets. "You mean to tell me all these swells run whorehouses, saloons, and dry goods stores? Why, San Francisco must be the drinkingest, screwingest place on earth."

"It may be, my friend," Hennison chuckled. "It may be, but

most would never admit it. No, these decent folks run other businesses like . . . like selling life insurance."

"Life insurance? What's that?"

Hennison thought for a moment, searching for the most uncomplicated explanation. Pursing his lips he began. "With life insurance you pay money to a company. They hold it for you, and then pay it back when you die. The longer you live, the less they pay back. If you die earlier, you get more than you pay in."

Riley's face screwed up in disbelief. "If that ain't the stupidest thing I ever heard. You mean you give a stranger yer money so's he can enjoy it while you're living on the promise you can enjoy it after you're dead? And you get more if you croak early? Hell, what fool would bet on his own dying? How'd he collect? Do they stuff the money in yer coffin?"

"Well, the process is a bit more complicated than that."

Riley swatted his hat against his leg, raising a cloud of dust. "I'll bet it is. Unless all these folks are light in the head, these insurance agents must be moving that old pea around mighty fast in their shell game. And here I thought you was slick."

"It's big business."

Riley squinted into the dusk, measuring the passersby. "If they's so many fools that take this life insurance seriously, I ought to start my own business shooting 'em so they could die and make that profit."

Riley stood at the intersection with hands on hips, studying the city, and conveying all the natural nonchalance of a man who called his own shots. However, without saddle or tackle or horse, Jim Riley was lost. He had lived so long in the saddle he had come to the belief held by most cowboys that legs were made for standing while the only decent movement came from horse back. Back at Yuma Crossing he sold his horse and tack to raise his train fare, something he now regretted, for he was afoot in a strange land. But, minus a mount or money, there was no turning back.

With each day his destiny wrapped tighter around the fool's bargain he had made with a wet-eared boy. Well, maybe not wet-eared no more, Riley admitted. Not after that first night behind that blanket with that China girl. He'd heard the boy's heavy breathing and guessed that dolly was thanking him real proper. What puzzled Jim was that the thanking went on for the whole next week they spent in that filthy cattle car. Every night, until the bored miners started a pool as to how long the boy could last. He surprised them all.

After a quick transfer in Los Angeles, Nathan stepped off the train in San Francisco a man in love. The old gunfighter knew cowboys feared a bad horse or a good woman most of all in their simple lives, and it was plain to see the lad had run afoul of the latter. It made Riley sick to see Nat mooning over that foreigner, and worse of all he slacked off on his pistol practice. Being in love was bad enough, but shirking his quick draw could get them all killed, although Riley had reason to believe Doc Hennison planned to poison Wyatt Earp if the boy would let him.

Riley walked along, tagging after Hennison and overcome by the strange sights and smells. Thinking as he walked was much harder than thinking in the saddle, he discovered. His boots were built for holding a stirrup, and his feet kept hitting potholes that his surefooted pony would have avoided, and that distracted his thoughts. About the only thing he drew comfort from was the constant pressure of his Colt hanging from his waist and the Winchester slung over his shoulder. While his weapons drew a second look from the blue-hatted policemen he passed, no one stopped him.

Doc paused to study the scribbled notes he held in hand. Hennison looked to the left and pointed down the street. The descending cobblestones and brick walk led into another world. Jumbled shacks were stacked atop each other and wedged wherever space permitted. Even the air was filled. Banners sporting brightly colored lettering crisscrossed the street to dance in the breeze from the bay. Similar signs filled the glass windows of storefronts interspersed among the tents and shacks. Mainly red with black and gold intermixed, the Chinese lettering only added to the exotic and foreign atmosphere further enhanced by paper lanterns glowing like full moons. Odors of incense, garlic, and spiced cooking oil packed the spaces left by the banners.

"Chinatown," Hennison said simply. "I'll bet there's enough opium in one city block for a lifetime of my elixirs."

"Could be a short lifetime," Riley warned. "Look at all those Chinamen, and there ain't one of them smiling at us."

Lining the sidewalks, somber Chinese squatted outside their houses in groups of twos and threes. Uniformly dressed in black silk pants with tautly plaited queues and pillbox hats, they turned faces toward the round-eyes that were far from friendly. A dozen hulking men leaned against the buildings with thick arms folded across barrel chests.

"Not the warmest reception, I'll admit," Hennison quipped. "Well, faint heart never won fair lady. Onward and downward."

"I ain't in no mood for yer confusing sayings," Riley said as he tightened his gunbelt. "They's more of them than I got bullets, so think of something witty to say about that."

But Hennison wasn't listening. He bolted ahead, compelling Riley to follow until they were in the center of the Chinese enclave. In midblock he stopped, checked the sign overhead, and turned to a heavy wooden door in a dilapidated frame structure.

"This is the place. Won Chow's." Ignoring Riley's nervous scratching of his head, Doc hammered on the door.

"They's no doubt slit the boy's throat already, and are just waiting for us," Riley warned. His fingers continued to run through his graying hair while he wondered if these Chinese took scalps. With long hair like the Cheyenne, he reasoned they placed great stock in a fellow's topknot.

The door opened and two scowling giants stepped out of the darkened hall into the twilight. An evil scar pulled the lower lip of one into a perpetual scowl. Inside the sleeve of that man, Riley caught the glint of a knife. His companion wore similar pajamas but sported a brushed gray fedora on his head, making him look strangely threatening and comical at the same time. The gunman checked the knotted cords at both men's waists for scalp locks, but found little assurance when he saw none. Both men were muscled like oxen, and carried themselves like trained fighting men.

Scar Face pointed to the sign overhead and growled. "Tong! Tong!"

Hennison scowled. "Can't you read your own sign? It says Won Chow's. Won Chow's, you understand? We want see, chop, chop." He jabbed his finger into the paper for emphasis.

The guard became more agitated, his face contorting in rage and turning a deep purple. "Tong!" he shouted back. "Tong! Won Chow Tong! Won Chow Tong!"

"Excuse me," Wei-Li's voice came from behind the two guards. She spoke rapidly in Chinese, and the men stepped aside, but her words did little to mollify them.

"Ah, Wei-Li," Doc bowed to her.

"Please excuse these men," she said. "They are guards and this is a tong, usually off limits to white men."

"Tong?" Riley looked puzzled.

"It's like a private club," Wei-Li answered in her accented English. "But much more than that. Many business deals originate from tongs; some you might call illegal, even dangerous, so secrecy is paramount to the tongs."

"Sort of like the railroads," Riley nodded.

Wei-Li smiled enigmatically, not refuting his analogy of an organization known for heavy-handing the law, and led them deeper into the dank corridor of the building. She paused momentarily outside another door, this one lacquered a bright red, before ushering her companions inside.

The room floated in layers of smoke thick enough to make its far walls obscure, and the sickly-sweet smell of opium mingled with jasmine assailed the men with almost physical force. Flickering for lack of fresh air, several oil lamps sputtered in valiant attempts to illuminate the rank effluvium.

A rotund figure dressed in simple black robes sat in a chair facing the door. From his elevated position on the dais and the deference shown him by the others sitting below him, Hennison recognized him as the obvious leader. To his left sat Nathan, looking strangely out of sorts. Wei-Li bowed to the leader and led Hennison and Riley to cushions beside the lad. Then she knelt behind Nathan.

The fat man watched them with eyes containing all the animation of a day-old fish. Riley started at the object hanging from his neck: It was a dragon grasping his tail, identical to the one Nathan now held in his hand.

The man spoke, and Wei-Li translated in lowered tones. "We deeply regret the death of our brother Won Lo," she began. "That he was murdered by round-eyes makes his request all the more puzzling and difficult."

Riley cast a wary eye at Nat, who shook his head in confusion. Hennison merely focused on the girl's words.

The head of the tong paused to whisper to his advisors, obviously not wanting Wei-Li to translate that discussion. He turned back.

"So as not to anger Won Lo's spirit, we have agreed to some of his requests—but not all. To the youth Nat-tan who risked his life to save Won Lo, we allow him to keep the jade dragon, symbol of our secret tong, so that it may offer him the protection of our society should the need arise."

Wei-Li's voice faltered, dropping behind in the translation so that the fat man was forced to stop and look at her. She continued with shaky voice. "But the concubine Wei-Li cannot be given as a gift to Nat-tan. Won Lo's unfortunate death left his debts to the tong unpaid. The girl will be sold to offset those debts."

"What, no reward for helping that Chinaman's stinking hide?" Hennison blurted out, ignoring the angry muttering and incredulous stares his remark caused. "That's gratitude for you."

"But I want to marry her!" Nathan cried over the noise.

Riley shut his eyes at the boy's foolish remark while all the time feeling his pain. A good woman, the gunman thought: something to fear, yet something to desire.

"Impossible!" the fat man snapped in English, not waiting for the weeping Wei-Li to translate. "She is for sale, not for marriage."

"How much?" Nathan continued undaunted. "If she's only for sale, how much do you want?"

The tong's leader inclined his head to listen to the words of a thin scribe seated to his right. He wiped stubby fingers across his chin. "Four thousand dollar."

"Four thousand! Why I wouldn't pay that for a . . . " Hennison started to say.

"Sold," Nat shouted.

The fat man leaned forward to study the youth. "Agreed. Do you have the money?"

"Sir, I'll have it by the end of this week."

The head of the Won Chow Tong narrowed his eyes. "Why should we wait for you to secure the money, let alone trust you at all? Your people delight in burning our wash houses and killing our people. The police and firemen stand by and do nothing. We trusted the railroads, and we trusted the city officials, and that has brought us only sorrow. Have you heard them laugh at us and say we have not a Chinamen's chance?"

"I don't know anything about that, sir. But neither me nor my friends ever did any of those things. But we did risk our lives to save Mr. Lo and Wei-Li. And we did it because two people were in trouble, and it didn't matter that they were Chinese. Now you can say no, but I'm sort of a member of your Won Chow Tong because of this dragon, and I'm asking as a favor that you give me a week to get the money."

The leader allowed a slight smile to cross his face. His head bobbed as his gaze rested on the jade dragon gripped in the boy's hand. "The dragon speaks through you already. You have one week. Now, is there any other request we might honor for you?"

Nathan rose to his feet. "I need to know the whereabouts of a man called Wyatt Earp."

The smile vanished from Won Chow's face as fast as it had appeared. "What do you wish with him?"

"I aim to kill him."

Don't mention the money, Hennison screamed silently, or we'll all be dead men. But Nathan didn't.

"That may prove difficult," the tong leader said. "He is highly skilled with his gun. But we will find him for you. Our eyes see into every corner of San Francisco. His death would come as no great loss to this tong. We lost heavily on a boxing match because of him. If you kill Earp, my white dragon friend of the Won Chow Tong, you will surely also get the money to buy Wei-Li."

The Won Chow head stood, and the audience ended with the three men following Wei-Li down the maze of corridors into a smaller room with a door that opened into the back alley. The girl motioned for the men to sit before she left. Nathan watched her go with mounting anxiety. Being so fresh in love made moments of separation from her unbearable.

"Look at that. They didn't bother to lock the door. We can cut out of this opium den whenever we like," Hennison remarked as he opened the back door and peered into the gloom of the trash-strewn alley. The smell of rotting garbage assailed him, and he shut the door quickly.

"No need to," Wei-Li said. She stood inside the inner door with steaming platters of food. "The fingers of the tong touch every shadow of this city. There is no escape, even with open doors. You are to wait here while the tong searches for this Wyatt Earp. Meanwhile, I have brought you food."

Riley's stomach sounded a noisy wake-up call, breaking the air of uncertainty, and causing all to laugh.

"Guess my gut has more good sense than my head," the gunman grinned. "It's telling me to eat while I can." He remembered the Chinese cooking he'd had once at the end of the drive in Newton, Kansas, before his deadly fame forced him into the life of a fugitive. That was years ago, but his stomach never forgot the delicious taste. Many were the times as he shivered under wet blankets, hungry and cold, that the memory of that exotic meal would tease his thoughts.

The three men hunkered around the low table and fought with the unfamiliar chopsticks. Riley rapidly lost patience and resorted to shoveling the vegetables, rice, and chicken into his mouth with his fingers, but Hennison took this as a personal test of his one-armedness and soon mastered the wooden sticks.

Wei-Li knelt beside Nathan and fed him with selected morsels as was her training. While her outer face smiled serenely at him, inside her thoughts tumbled with troubled emotions. Nathan was unlike anything she had expected. Her years of indoctrination prepared her to pleasure and serve her master, yet he insisted on helping her. The few British she had met in Hong Kong were haughty and condescending, but

Nathan was none of those things. At one train stop to take on water and wood, he had jumped from the car to pick her a handful of blue cornflowers. None of the other men dared laugh because of his skill with the pistol he always carried. Only in bed did he remove his weapon.

Inwardly she smiled as her mind conjured up Nathan's muscled body intertwined with hers. He was an exciting and eager lover, not pale and flabby like Won Lo. Her new master's Jade Dragon awoke feelings in her Heavenly Gate previously unknown to her, and that frightened her. Was she losing control, something her teachers said must never happen? Was this round-eyed killer of men who brought flowers capturing her heart?

Wei-Li was too familiar with the tragic love poems of star-cursed lovers that ended badly for all. For herself she scarcely minded. If bad joss ruled her future she could do nothing to change that. But she shut her eyes whenever bad thoughts of Nathan arose in her mind. She could not bear to think of him shot down by this man-killer Wyatt Earp. Was that love? And what of the soothsayer's prophesy? Was Nathan the one?

Wei-Li looked up, and her thoughts vanished. Sam Lee, the tong gatekeeper with the gray fedora, stood at the inner door. He beckoned to her. The girl rose with utmost care to disguise her shaking legs and glided to Lee's side. He whispered to her then vanished.

"Well, I could do with a nap," Hennison yawned. "I don't suppose they'd have fed us so well if they planned on cutting our throats while we slept." He stretched his one arm over his head, looking curiously lopsided in the process.

But Nathan caught Wei-Li's pale face and tight-set lips. "Wei-Li, what is it?" he asked.

"Sam Lee has returned with news. They have located the devil that you wish to kill."

"Earp?" Riley stopped with his mouth half full of noodles.

The girl's trembling voice sounded warning alarms in his head. "Is he here?"

"No," Wei-Li shook her head. "But . . . "

"But what Wei-Li?" Nathan held her trembling body at arm's length.

"He is leaving tonight on a boat to Alaska Territory. . . . "

★ ★ TWELVE ★ ★

Wyatt leaned against the stern rail of the *S.S. Brixom* and watched the last of the cargo slings load the horses on board. Neighing in fright and kicking their legs through the nets, the animals disappeared into the aft cargo hold where their plaintive cries became sealed under the battened hatch.

God help those poor creatures, Wyatt thought. Half had ribs poking from their sides and sores covering their bony haunches. Alaska was hard on horses, he'd heard, yet these wrecks were being shipped there. San Francisco and Seattle had nothing left but broken-down nags to send, so send these they did. Most would die, he knew, overloaded and starving, crossing the icy passes to the gold fields. When gold fever struck, men's values washed away faster than the dirt in the sluice boxes. The Mounties were right to order a year's grubstake for each prospector, Wyatt agreed. Any man who would flog his horse to death would kill his partner if the need arose. Alaska was grinding up men and horses at lightning speed.

Wyatt thought of his favorite horse, Dick Nailer, named as a ribald jest. When he first laid eyes on Old Dick the horse was trying to propagate his line with a pretty filly. Someone had said, Look at that dick trying to nail her, and the name stuck.

A sure-footed racer, old Dick carried him faithfully across Arizona in his ride for vengeance after Tombstone. Oddly, Dick was one of the causes of that fight, too. Billy Clanton stole

Dick once; and when Wyatt caught Billy with Nailer in the corral in Charleston, the kid almost cleared leather on him. The idea of Dick in that stifling hold made Wyatt wince.

While Wyatt watched, a cold wind carried more swirling fog in from the bay, obscuring wide sections of the dock in bone-chilling mists. Lighted segments of the pier illuminated the vapors in lines of yellowish orbs, adding to the surrealistic nature of this night scene. He shivered and turned his collar up against the salty air.

Earp checked his watch as the stern lines were warped: 9:30 P.M. right on time. At least the captain was punctual. That was about all he could say for this ship. Absentmindedly, Wyatt's fingernail flaked off another piece of paint that covered a badly rusted railing. He hoped the hull was not as bad.

Josie had moved mountains to book their passage, but the *Brixom* was no luxury liner. Barely decommissioned as a troop ship for the Spanish American War, the *Brixom* sorely needed a major overhaul. Instead she was heading to Alaska by the All-Water Route through the Gulf of Alaska to the mouth of the Yukon River.

As if reading his thoughts, Josie appeared like magic and pressed against his side. She smiled and stood on tiptoe to kiss his cheek, then turned her face to follow the lines snaking on board as the ship slid away from the wharf. Inches at a time the ponderous vessel sidled from the dock until a twelve-foot gap of dark water separated them from land.

"Too late to change your mind, Josie girl." Wyatt watched the black rift widen. "It's too far to jump now."

"I'm excited and so are you, Wyatt. I know you are."

He smiled at her. But a commotion on the pier caught his attention. Josie followed his gaze.

"Look at that, Wyatt. What is it?"

Two-thirds of the way from the end of the pier, a party was battling their way through the crowd of well-wishers and disappointed hopefuls that packed the platform. Pushing and shoving, this group plowed against waves of reluctant people. Shouts and curses from the dock led to encouraging cries from the stampeders that packed the stern of the *Brixom*. The departing passengers waved these stragglers on knowing full well their efforts were futile, but a mood of elation filled those lucky enough to be on board. Compounding this drama, the *Brixom*'s screws now inched the vessel forward in an agonizingly slow crawl alongside the wharf. The boat itself seemed to be tantalizing and teasing the people struggling to overtake it.

"Looks like someone literally missed the boat," Wyatt quipped.

"What a curious bunch," Josie said, staring at the four who fought their way alongside the ship. "Look at them. They don't look like miners, do they? Is that girl with them Chinese?"

Wyatt stared at the four, and hairs prickled on the back of his neck. Leading their charge were a tall youth and a mangy cowpoke carrying a rifle, followed closely by a Chinese girl and a one-armed man. Both men in the lead sliced through the throng with the grace of professional killers. Clearly they spotted him for the man with one arm was pointing directly at him.

"Do you know them, Wyatt?"

"Get behind me, Josie," Wyatt commanded. His right hand swept back his coat to clear his pistol in a move more reflex than planned. His Colt was little good at that distance, but the tattered gunman could still reach them with his rifle.

Wyatt watched as the rifleman raised his Winchester, drawing a bead on his chest. Packed against the railing on the crowded upper deck, Wyatt was wedged in this exposed position, unable to seek cover. All he could do was shield Josie and hope the man was a poor shot. From the look of the man, Wyatt knew he wasn't.

Unexpectedly, the younger man shouted something, and the rifleman turned to look at the youth, then lowered his rifle.

At that moment the *Brixom* wallowed in the trough of a wave, side-slipping closer to the end of the pier and cutting the gap in half.

"Oh, God!" Josie cried.

The youth sprinted from the end of the battered dock to leap at the ship. He fell short of the lower railings to tumble down the side of the vessel. His fingers caught the rudder chains, clawing for a handhold on the swaying links. There he hung suspended above the churning propellers and their seething wash. His iron gray eyes locked with Wyatt's before the roll of the ship tore his grip loose, and he dropped into the boiling sea.

A collective groan arose from the deck of the *Brixom* and the dock, and both sides cast life rings into the darkening bay, but no head broke the greasy waters. The ship continued on, leaving the wharf to shrink into the fog.

Shaken, Wyatt watched the Chinese girl slide to her knees, face pressed into her hands to hide her tears while the rifleman searched the waters helplessly. But the boy's eyes still blistered his mind.

"Did you see his face, Wyatt?" Josie cried, fighting to understand this sudden, violent confrontation. "Did you see his face? And those pale eyes? *He looked just like you!*"

✶ ✶ THIRTEEN ✶ ✶

An anemic sun abandoned all attempts to burn away the early mist and slipped behind a cloud bank, relegating the bay to the dimly illuminated gloom of another summer day. This early in the morning the dockside crowds were gone, the actions of that foolish youth forgotten, and a rain shower had driven the few stragglers for cover. Human voices were gone leaving only the timeless lapping of the waves against the rotting pilings.

Slipping silently toward the dock and taking advantage of the cover of the fog drifted a skiff loaded with wet, wriggling canvas sacks. Hunched over the oars sat a young man shivering in his spray dampened slicker. After studying the docks, he headed toward the inner pier where flotsam rolled in the oil-slicked water. The youth had good cause to seek the quietest dock: He was plying his trade as an oyster pirate.

Sliding into the shadows beneath the tarred planks, he tied his skiff to a piling and inspected his haul. All night he braved the currents and wakes of cargo freighters to pilfer the oyster catches of others. Working alone and under cover of darkness, his theft was hardly noticed when compared to the swift ships of larger pirate groups, but the man preferred it this way. This way he was responsible to no one, and it allowed him more time to indulge his dream—to become a writer.

But now he would rest before hawking his oysters at the back doors of San Francisco's restaurants where the chefs appreciated his low price and asked no questions. Then he would return to the driftwood shack he inhabited near the docks to practice with pen and pencil. That was John Griffith's life: stealing oysters, writing, and struggling to educate himself at the public library.

Something stirred beside a piling, causing John to draw his knife. Others were not above slitting his throat for his meager catch, and a stint on the blood-bathed sealing ships that worked the Pacific coast for fur seals had schooled Griffith well in using his knife and defending what was his. In John Griffith's world savagery was the rule, not the exception, and only the strong survived.

Griffith looked at the white object that clung to the wood amid the sea lettuce and barnacles. It was a hand. Quickly he poled his boat closer, and peeked cautiously around the wooden structure.

A white face, eyes half-opened, stared at him from a swirl of kelp. The eyes followed him, and the lips moved weakly.

"Help me," Nathan whispered.

Griffith leaned closer, impressed that this half-drowned fellow's words sounded more like a command than a plea.

"You're one tough gent," John chuckled. "Waterlogged like a dead rat and still giving orders. I like that."

"Then get me in your boat. . . . "

"What if I just slit your throat and empty your pockets?"

Nathan released his right hand from its slippery grasp and drew his revolver from the kelp. "Go ahead and try, friend."

The oyster pirate looked at his knife and then the pistol, wondering if the weapon would still fire. It was a Colt Peacemaker with metallic cartridges, not the older Navy Colts that used cap and ball. The thought intrigued him.

"Different weapons," he said. "Sort of like the gladiators of ancient Rome."

Nathan dipped his gun barrel momentarily. "Hail Caesar. We, who are about to die, salute thee."

Griffith's mouth dropped. "By God, you got an education! This is glorious."

" 'The paths of glory lead but to the grave.' That's Thomas Gray, if you must know; but if you want a fight, get on with it, I'm freezing. The sooner I shoot you, the faster I can get in your boat and out of this damned cold water."

" 'Elegy in a Country Churchyard!' I know it well."

John Griffith threw his head back and roared. His dark hair fell from beneath his wool watch cap, and his broadly spaced eyes twinkled. He sheathed his knife and extended a hand to Nathan.

"I can't let the crabs feast on so educated a mind as yours. Come aboard."

Griffith dragged his newly found literary friend into his skiff and wrapped him in a burlap sack. The frozen Nathan watched his rescuer while he struggled to wipe the water from his pistol with shivering hands.

John cocked his head at the waterlogged weapon. "You'll have to rinse the salt water off and coat it with lard, or it'll rust by tomorrow. I learned that the hard way on a sealer. My knife rusted solid in its metal scabord. Never could get it loose until I cut the sheath open with a hacksaw."

"Lard?"

"Yup. Lard or axle grease. Lard's easy and cheap. Only thing is it attracts all the shipboard rats, so you have to keep an eye on your things. Old salts claim they saw rats carry off a cannon that way, but I never believed them. But I have seen starving rats eat a sick man's ears once—that's for sure the gospel's truth."

"I have to get ashore. Now," Nathan stuttered through chattering teeth. The hours spent in cold water seemed to have penetrated to his bones, causing his limbs to quiver uncontrollably.

"Hold on, my educated friend. First, you have to get thawed out. If you don't, you're a dead man. I've seen it too many times. You need hot coffee and hot blankets, but no spirits. Spirits will lead you to seizures. I don't know the reason for that, but it has something to do with the cold from the water driving deeper to your heart even though you've been taken out of the water."

"You sure talk a lot, don't you?" Nathan said, but the words stuck in his mouth like treacle while his lips failed to form the sounds properly. He started to object even as his vision faded, and he slipped into a warm dream with Wei-Li laughing at his side. He smiled at her until the man on the stern of the freighter pushed her aside and began to choke him. Wei-Li faded into the background as Wyatt Earp continued to apply a suffocating grip.

Nathan awoke sputtering and spewing hot coffee into Griffith's face. He focused on the young man, wiping the dark brew off, and on a driftwood shack filled with crab pots, partially repaired fishnets, and stacks of books and newspapers. The heavy smell of fish was everywhere. His Colt lay on the gouged wooden table, gleaming under its new coat of lard.

"Damn," John cursed. "You're the one that needs this coffee, not me." He sat back and allowed Nat to feed himself.

Nathan squinted at the oil lamp on the table, then swivelled his head toward the cracked pane of glass that valiantly defended its position in the window frame against the lashing rain. Outside, the night was black as pitch.

"Did I sleep all day?" he asked.

"Three days is more like it. I thought you were a goner, but you fooled me." John looked wistfully at the revolver. "No chance now of inheriting your Colt, I guess. Say, what is your name? You never told me."

"Nathan Blaylock. What's yours?"

"John Griffith, but I'm going to take my stepfather's last name instead of my mother's, and I'm calling myself Jack instead of John. It sounds snappier. I think a slick name is important for a writer's success. What do you think? Doesn't Jack London sound better?"

"You're a bastard?" Nathan asked.

Jack's eyes narrowed. "I've thrashed anyone who dwells on that point, Mr. Blaylock."

Nathan shrugged. "I'm one also, so there's no point in taking offense."

"Well, I'll be damned, Nat. We do have a lot in common. Here, drink the rest of this java instead of puking it in my face and tell me about yourself. I'm collecting stories for my writing, and I'll wager you've got an interesting one to relate."

The wick on the oil lamp guttered, sending trails of smoke up to the tar paper roof as John Griffith listened to Nathan's tale. At length he tipped back in his chair and scratched his mop of unruly black hair.

"Damn!" John said. "I thought I was living on the razor's edge, but you've packed just as much action into your life as I have. Whatever possessed you to make that crazy jump for the *Brixom?*"

Nathan buried his face in his hands. "When Doc pointed out Earp standing on the back of the boat. There he was, slipping out of my grasp. Getting him meant everything—having enough money to be someone, fulfilling my mother's last wish, and getting the money to buy Wei-Li. But, he was getting away. I just couldn't let Riley shoot him from the dock without Earp knowing the reason—that wouldn't be right. So I jumped for the boat. I almost made it, too."

Griffith rubbed his hands together. "What a colossal story! Two great forces clashing for supremacy like wild beasts in the forest with only the strongest surviving. I'm very partial to that theme; it plays out in the animal world, and I figure mankind is still part of that world in spite of electric lights and railroads. Hell, look at the railroad moguls crushing all the men they used like ants to build their fortunes."

"But I didn't make it." Nathan sighed. "He got away, and now I've lost everything. I'm lost as well."

"Steady, old chap," John said. "Without great travails there can be no great gain. You're down, but not out of the fight. We just need to regroup and make another plan."

"But Earp is on his way to Alaska."

Griffith studied his newfound friend's utter despondency with mild disbelief. The boy folded too easily, but then he was still young. Nat was made of good steel, he reasoned; nevertheless, he still needed some tempering.

"Alaska's not the other side of the moon, Nat. I've been there myself."

"You have?" Nathan's hopes soared. "But how come you're not rich?"

John's eyes danced in merriment. They mirrored his mercurial moods, changing to dark pools of depression one instant only to be replaced by flashing lights of joy in another split second.

"Didn't pan out, as they say. So I'm back here. Most don't strike it rich, Nat, only a few, I'd say, but that doesn't stop thousands from trying. It wasn't a total loss, though. I've got a headful of great stories to write about." Griffith swept his arm around the hovel in a grandiose gesture. "That's what I'm doing now. Writing. This is my studio."

"I thought you were stealing oysters."

"Leave it to you to see only the pessimistic side, Nat. No, I'm a full-time writer, but pirating an oyster or two meets my overhead."

Griffith placed his hand on Nat's shoulder. "I know how you feel, Nat, but you can't give up now. The lowest I ever felt was when I was arrested for vagrancy. I spent thirty days in jail for being a hobo."

"You were a hobo?"

"Yup. I grew up on the Oakland docks, fighting in gangs and stealing oysters. Ran away to sea when I was seventeen. I worked on a fur sealing ship. God, those vessels are a bloody hell on earth. But that time in jail turned me around. I realized I was the only one who could change my life. No one else could. So I worked my way through high school and read every blessed page in the Oakland Public Library to educate myself. Now, I aim to be the highest paid writer that ever was. It's the same with you, Nat. No one is going to just hand it to you. You have to fight for what you want."

"Will you help me find my friends?" Nathan asked as he rose to his feet. He had to find Riley and Hennison and Wei-Li. John was right. Together they would find a way to get the money before the week was out, or if need be, fight for her. But only four days remained.

Griffith pointed at the door. "The best place I know to start is in the bars along Fisherman's Wharf. Get your greased revolver and we'll be off."

Doggedly, Nathan followed John Griffith into a dozen seedy saloons and watering holes along the waterfront until his head throbbed from the rotgut fumes and his clothing reeked of stale beer and cigar smoke. But no clues to the whereabouts of his friends were found. With deepening fears, Nathan slogged on.

In the last tavern the barkeep listened intently before gesturing to a table blackened by the shadow of the bar. Face down on the chipped table sprawled a man whose rain soaked clothing still dripped water onto the sawdust floor and whose wet hair spilled across the table like wild brambles. Babbling half-mad phrases to no one but his carafe, this wreck was like a hundred others they'd encountered that night—except for his one and only arm gripping the drink.

"Doc!" Nathan rushed to the table to shake the wet form while John lifted the bottle. "Doc, it's me Nathan! Where are Riley and Wei-Li?"

The drunken Hennison raised his head to stare with red-rimmed, watery eyes and slack-jawed lips that dribbled saliva over three day's growth of beard. Seeing the boy, he started as if in a convulsion and pawed at the air between them.

"Oh, God! Nathan boy, you've come back to haunt me," he cried. "I can't blame you. Forgive me, I beg of you."

"Doc, what happened?" Nathan asked but Hennison wrenched free of his grasp and fell to his knees sobbing pitifully.

"Forgive me, Nat," he pleaded. "I didn't know the game was rigged."

"His eye teeth are afloat in booze," John said. "You'll get no sense out of him until we douse his innards with black coffee." So saying, he hoisted the quivering Hennison back into his chair and signaled the barman for a pot of the tarlike brew that simmered behind the bar.

One and a half pots of coffee later, Hennison vomited up the last traces of whiskey in his stomach. He continued retching until only greenish water coated the sawdust; then wiping his eyes, he squinted at Nathan.

"You're not dead?" he asked incredulously. "But I saw you drowned."

Nathan shook his head.

"Not a ghost, then?"

"No. Now tell me what happened. Where are the others?"

Hennison gathered what pieces of his composure he could find. He looked at John standing with his fists balled, then back to Nathan. "I . . . I'd rather not."

"Tell him," the writer ordered. "Or I'll keep pouring more of this joe down your gullet until its squirting out of both your ends.

Hennison waved his hands in front of his face. "No more of that tainted brew. It's more vile than anything I could ever conceive. It makes my elixir seem like milk and honey by comparison."

With sobriety came added impact of what he had done, and Hennison's face reflected the pangs of guilt for his actions. The Civil War had scarred him so deeply that blame had been burned from the meager list of emotions he allowed himself. What he did since then was for survival until fate had linked him with Nathan Blaylock. During these last weeks he'd felt traces of companionship stirring beneath his hardened core like spring grass twisting free of the grip of winter-hardened soil. Head bowed, Hennison related his story.

"We thought you had drowned, Nat. We saw the propellers suck you under, and you didn't come up. I never saw Riley so agitated. He paced that dock for hours and would have killed anyone who tried to stop him. I looked with him, It's the God's truth. We finally knew you were dead."

"What about Wei-Li?"

"She just knelt there the whole time, crying her little heart out while we searched. When we gave up, she just got to her feet and stood there like nothing else in the world mattered. She wouldn't even speak, just stood there in some sort of trance.

"Riley growled something about having a real score to settle with Wyatt Earp now as he had caused your death. I saw his eyes, Nat. They were angry as hellfire. He just took his rifle and stomped off without another word. I haven't seen him since. I think he's going after Wyatt himself, money or no money."

"But what happened to Wei-Li? Did the tong take her back?" Without thinking, Nathan's fingers felt the cold jade dragon in his pocket.

Hennison shook his head. "Worse than that. I did her in, but I never meant to. It seemed like the best idea at the time. . . . " Doc's words trailed off, lacking persuasion.

Nathan's heart turned as cold as the jade piece in his pocket. "Did her in? Is she dead?"

"She might as well be. I was leading her along the waterfront when we passed a saloon, the Land's End."

John nodded his head. "A cutthroat dive."

"Well, I needed a drink, and I thought the girl might benefit from one, too. I hoped she would snap out of her trance. So I took her inside."

Griffith pushed his cap onto the back of his head and began kneading his wide brow with his fingers. His eyes darkened into a scowl that spread across his face. "Lord! I bet I can tell this tale from past experience. They got you liquored up and into a poker game, didn't they?"

Hennison hung his head in shame. "They didn't seem that good. At first I was winning big. Two thousand dollars, and I started with the fifty I kept hidden in my boot for emergencies." He stopped and turned to look pathetically at Nathan. "I figured I could raise enough money to set Wei-Li free and . . . and maybe buy passage for Riley and me to Alaska." Doc paused to wipe his nose on his sleeve.

"You're probably wondering why a moral wreck like me would want to do something worthwhile. I've asked myself that same question, and I don't have the answer. Maybe those card sharps put the notion in my mind. But seeing her there like a bird with a broken wing touched my heart. I knew you'd want her free too, Nat."

John beat Nathan to the punch. "You lost the girl in the poker match. You used her for stakes, and you lost. Right?"

"Yes . . ."

The saloon and the hazy movement of its inhabitants squeezed close around Nathan, and its undercurrent of talk and laughter faded to mere whispers behind the pulse thundering in his ears as his mind recoiled in disbelief. Unexpectedly, he felt no anger, only a steely resolution: He would get

Wei-Li back, whatever it took, whatever it cost. It would be so simple to put a bullet in this broken and emptied husk, but that would prove nothing. Hennison may have meant well. Nathan would sort that out later. Now he had to get the girl back.

"When did this happen, Doc? Do you know where she is now?"

Hennison cast a grim look at his friend. "Three days ago. I realized what I'd done the next morning, but she was gone. Sold to someone named Soapy Smith to use in his whorehouse in Skagway. They're holding her on a ship called the *Dazzler* on the south dock. It's heavily armed."

Nathan touched the handle of his greased Colt. "I'll get her out," he said grimly.

"Hold on, Nat," John gripped the youth's shoulder. "The *Dazzler* sailed yesterday. . . . "

★ ★ FOURTEEN ★ ★

Slipping between the dockside shadows with an easy grace that comes from familiarity, John Griffith paused to study the fog-slicked wharf. Nothing exceptional moved in the damp morning mist. Other than the doleful tolling of the channel marker's bell, no other sounds merged with the creaking of the ship riding against the salt-soaked timbers. Moored some distance from the other ships, this vessel's masts rose from her darkened hull like charred timbers.

"There she is, the *Constance*, but she's far from rosy and not constant at all," Jack whispered to his friend. "She's a sealer, plying her trade up the Alaskan Coast and the Aleutians, and killing fur seals and what sea otters are left. I've shipped on her kind, and they're hellholes the likes of nothing left afloat. I suppose slave ships would compare favorably with fur sealers if they still sailed. But the slavers were all burnt, and so should these dreadful wrecks.

"See how the deck is painted black? That's to cover the blood that's soaked into every crack and seam. The sun bakes the blood into dark stains that mar the topsides with marks no holy stone can touch, so they hide it with pitch and black paint. But that doesn't fool the flies and the gulls. They smell the blood and follow. You pray for a storm to drown the bugs, but the birds always come back to mark you as a blood ship."

Nathan shivered at Griffith's description, but he told himself it was the damp night air. As he blended into the shadows he reflected back on the long night. The tenacious strings of fate were pulling him north to track down his father, Wyatt Earp, north to claim his fortune, and north to rescue Wei-Li.

Nathan also pondered the change in Hennison, who continued to be repentant and contrite even when sober during these last, dark hours. Something in him was different. The knife edge of his cynicism, while far from blunted, had nevertheless dulled. Nathan attributed this subtle change to Doc's rediscovering his long-lost morality. At least the youth hoped that was the case. He could not believe this man to be all bad, despite Hennison's insistance to the contrary. He shrugged at the thought; only time would prove his theory right or wrong. For now, it was enough for Doc Hennison to follow him north.

It was Griffith who hatched this plan. With Wyatt and Wei-Li both sailing north, Nathan had no choice but to follow by sea—immediately if he wished to save his love from a dreadful fate. However, without money or influence, such passage was impossible. Stowing away was the only way. Not a novel idea, many others had also thought of slipping aboard if they couldn't book passage. Gold fever drove men to reckless acts. So the steamers and freighters posted guards, checked and rechecked passenger lists, and locked their cargo holds. Their vigilance made unpaid passage unattainable.

But no one in his right mind stowed away on a blood-washed fur sealer. Most of these sailed shorthanded; and once underway, extra able-bodied hands would be pressed into service. With luck and favorable winds, the *Constance* would follow the Alaskan coast. Once close to Skagway, John suggested the two take French leave and jump ship.

Griffith started as the ship's bell broke the silence. He extracted his pocket watch, but the face was obscured by the darkness. "Eight bells! The four o'clock watch is changed. Now's the time to slip aboard. I'll help you find the cargo hold and then be off. My face is too well known on these wharves. No use raising the crew's suspicions by my hanging around.

Stealthily, John led them over the bow rails, past the raised cabin and forward hatch, to the canvas battened cargo hold. He drew the tarp back and slipped into the inky space. Doc tumbled after him. Nathan paused at the rim as a rush of foul air from the hold assailed his nose. Fighting back a wave of nausea, he slid inside. Nathan dropped to the lower deck, barely missing the sprawling Hennison.

"God's breath, what a stench!" Doc gasped, pinching his nose while he scuttled after John. He paused to assess the three bottles of elixir crammed in his pockets. The solid clink of the intact bottles and the absence of wetness reassured him they still survived. Nathan had his gun-handling skills, the one-armed surgeon noted, so it was natural for him to carry his weapon, namely his all-powerful elixir.

The two landlubbers felt their way over unfamiliar coils of cordage, sail canvas, and barrels in the darkness as John led them on. Finally, he directed them behind a stack of stout rope.

"This is the spare anchor rope. They won't even look at it unless they lose the anchor chain, so you should go undetected until the ship is too far to turn back. After that . . . " Griffith flashed a white grin through the gloom. "Well, it should be interesting."

"I don't like the way that sounded," Hennison grumbled. "Are you sure they won't throw us over the side?"

Griffith patted Doc's shoulder. "You two will be all right. You're proving my theory of survival of the fittest."

"The last great social experiment I partook of cost me my career, my sweetheart, and my arm," Hennison said. "You can understand my loathing to cooperate with any others. I'm running out of essential body parts."

John snickered. "As long as your tongue still works, Doc,

Richard Parry

you'll do fine. Now, I'm over the side. Good luck to both of you."

Nathan clasped John's hand. "I don't know how to thank you. When I get the money, if you need any—"

"No need, old fellow," John said, cutting him off. "Just keep an eye out for my pen name, Jack London. I aim to be famous."

His coat brushed against Nat's cheek as he slipped past, and then he was gone.

The two stowaways waited in the foul darkness of the hold and counted the passing of time with each ring of the ship's bell. Starting at two bells, the sounds of movement reached their ears to increase with each additional strike. The ship was coming awake. Muffled voices and feet scraping topside swarmed about the vessel until Nat felt lines cast off and the *Constance* shift and wallow as she headed out to sea.

Encased in the forward hold, time passed without distinction as the ship sailed north, each moment and each hour being identical except for a mounting thirst and hunger that tortured the stowaways. Still, the ship's bells tolled on hour after hour, marking the passage of time and distance. After uncounted hours, the orderly waves changed to deep swells of the open water that the ship rode, rising on the crests and dropping into the troughs with teeth-jarring crashes. The timbers groaned and protested as rogue waves battered the sides; through the battened canvas sealing the hold, Nat and Doc heard the keening of the wind lashing the decks and the sails aloft.

"Lord," Doc groaned, flashing the whites of his eyes in the darkness. "I hope we didn't work this hard just to get ourselves drowned. If that's in the cards for us, I'd have been happy to stay in San Francisco. There I could roll off the pier while drunk and drown in comfort."

"I hope not," Nathan said. From the sound of it, Doc was

168

actively sampling his elixir. "Maybe we should come out of hiding, Doc. What do you think?"

Before Hennison could answer, the *Constance* lurched suddenly, snapping the line that held an enormous barrel to the base of the fore mast. The cask tipped over with a crash and rolled directly at the two men's hiding place.

"Look out!" Nat yelled. He leapt from his nest of coiled rope and jerked Hennison with him. A second later the butt vaulted over the Manila hemp, demolishing its orderly coils before wobbling into the portside ribs of the hull. With a sickening thud, the loose cargo struck the planks, opening a seam in the caulking through which green sea water poured.

The commotion below decks did not pass unnoticed. Harsh shouts and curses cut through the howling wind, and instantly the canvas cover was thrown back to reveal anxious faces.

"Damnation! Who lashed that water barrel?" a voice growled. "I'll give 'em a taste of the cat for this! Frenchy, get below and secure it before we're stove in!"

In response a wiry man in rain-drenched oilskins dropped into the hold. Landing on all fours like a cat, he spun to face the barrel which charged back across the deck with the ship's next roll. In his hands he carried a length of line, but that caused his undoing for it tangled his sea boots and sent him sprawling directly before the massive barrel.

"Look out, you stupid frog," the voice shouted. "She'll mash you for certain."

But Frenchy could only look up as his impending death advanced on him. The seaman's mouth opened to form a wordless scream. Yet in that instant, a hand gripped the collar of his oilskin and jerked him from undoubted destruction.

Nathan flung the startled sailor aside as he dodged the deadly cask. It rammed the starboard timbers, opening more seams before heading back. With light spilling into the hold along with rain, Nathan spotted a pile of repair beams stacked to one side of the hold. Seizing a timber from the pile, he thrust it beneath the barrel as it passed. The runaway stock stopped, but started to spin off this impediment. Frenchy, having regained his feet, thwarted this attempt to escape with another beam. Together Nat and the seaman continued to wedge the barrel until the sailor could lash it to the foremast with his lines. All this was watched with keen interest by the loud-voiced captain and three other faces who appeared at the mouth of the hold.

The little sailor wiped his hand through oily ringlets of black hair before flashing a smile of tobacco-stained teeth at Nathan. "You save me," he said in heavily accented English. "Old Frenchy think he was a goner for sure. I don't forget this."

"Rats in the hold, eh?" the captain yelled down at the three upturned faces. "Bring 'em topside, Frenchy, so's we can wring their necks."

Hauled on deck by the crew, Hennison and young Blaylock stood witness to a scene far more horrifying to landlubbers than a runaway cask in a pitching hold. Low lying storm clouds skimmed above the waves to cast slanting veils of rain onto an angry sea while the wind shrieked through the tangled lines of the running rigging. Shreds of canvas beat on the yardarms, struggling to tear free of their lashings and popping in the wind with smart, pistol-like cracks. Those that broke loose were rewarded for their pains by being ripped into tattered strips that vanished astern.

A mountain of green water rose and fell in deliberate march, encompassing the vessel in ever-changing ridges and canyons that towered above the beleaguered square-rigger. From the tops of these waves, windblown spindrift filled the air with foam. Their world had turned to water. Water choked the sky and blurred all reference for the senses until it seemed that the juncture between air and sea dissolved before this tempest.

"God Almighty!" Doc exclaimed when he saw the surrounding tempest. "We're lost for sure."

"You think so, do you?" laughed the captain. "You two must certainly be landlubbers to be frightened by this little blow."

The ship raced forward then shuddered as she climbed out of a trough only to have her bow dig into the back of a mountain of verdant water. Hennison lost his footing and slid across the deck with his one arm flailing for a hand hold. Nathan snatched the tail of his friend's coat in time to prevent Doc from going over the side.

The captain looked aloft. "Take down the fore topmast staysail," he shouted. "We're carrying too much sail. Another round like that, and we'll pitchpole for sure or else be sailed under. We'll run under the fore staysail along with a reef in the mizzen, too."

Nat watched in amazement as the men scurried about, pulling on various lines until the rectangular sail at the stern folded to one third its original size and the dagger-shaped wedge of canvas flying from the bowspirit was hauled down, all the while protesting and whipping in the wind.

The ship slowed its wild sledding and settled into the rolling pattern of the sea. Satisfied that his ship was now safe, the captain turned his attention back to his two stowaways. His sharp eye caught the holstered revolver beneath Nat's opened coat as well as the hapless Hennison clutching to the security of the foremast.

"Land rats for sure," he muttered, squinting his eyes and drumming his fingers as if calculating their worth pound by pound. "Search 'em, boys, and mind the lad. That one's an armed rat."

Nat braced himself as the seamen relieved him of his Colt and rifled his pockets for valuables. Hennison struggled until struck with a belaying pin across his back.

"Nothin' much, Captain," Frenchy reported. "Only this pistol, some papers, and these bottles."

He handed the gun and elixir to the captain. The captain's face lighted as he pulled the cork and took a long swallow. A moment later his face turned crimson, his eyes filled with tears, and he doubled over with a fit of coughing.

"Mother of God! What manner of poison is this?" he rasped between coughs and sneezes.

"It's death to pigs, I'm told," Hennison sniffed, still out of sorts from his search. "So I reckon it should be lethal to you, Captain."

The captain cast a suspicious glance at Doc before taking another swig. The results were less spectacular than his first drink. "Ah," the captain burped appreciatively. "I've got its measure now." He managed another protracted swallow, coughed again, and said simply, "I've had worse."

An awkward silence settled between the captain and the stowaways as he studied them with beady black eyes. Nathan felt his gaze pass over him like a butcher judging where to make the first cut in a hanging carcass, and he wondered if the captain would order them thrown overboard. Hennison seemed unmoved by their dilemma, glowering as the captain finished off the bottle of elixir. Doc exhibited a peculiar tunnel vision at times like these, being able to focus entirely on a trivial matter which annoyed him to the exclusion of any and all life threatening exigencies. Pressing needs meant nothing if his ire was raised.

The captain wiped his lips on his stained oilskin and belched heartily. He tossed the bottle into the foam. "So did you enjoy the hospitality of my forward hold?"

"It reminded me of an exceptionally dismal Yankee prison where I once resided," Hennison said. "It was named Fort Douglas, as I recall. Since you asked, I'd rate Douglas a leg up over your smelly pit."

"A crippled, old Reb, are you?" the captain said. "I was a midshipman with Farragut when he ran the blockade at New Orleans. Nothing more glorious than the sight of Reb ships burned to the waterline."

"I doubt you served any honorable service," Hennison replied. "You have the stench of a pirate and a smuggler."

"Do I?" the captain said with forced nonchalance, but his cheek twitched, revealing Hennison's barb had struck dangerously close to the mark. He squared his shoulders and thrust Nathan's revolver into his coat pocket. "This gun by itself won't pay for your passages," he added ominously.

"We're willing to work," Nathan interjected. It was obvious Hennison and the master of this vessel were close to violence. "This ship hunts fur seals, I was told. I can help you there. I'm a good shot, and Doc here is a physician. I assume this boat has no doctor on board."

To Nat's astonishment the captain threw back his head and roared with laughter. Frenchy and the crew laughed, too.

"By the devil's teeth, boy!" the skipper chortled. "We ain't about shooting the buggers. Not hardly. The *Constance* don't hold enough bullets for all the beasts we plan to kill. Bless me, no. No shooting for us. We clubs the dumb buggers."

"Bashes their heads in," Frenchy agreed. "No holes in the furs that way."

"A pity the seals can't shoot back," Hennison quipped. "But then who would pay a penny for your mangy hides?"

"Please, Doc," Nathan warned. "You're not helping things."

Hennison shrugged. "The truth is the truth. What more can I say?"

"You don't have to shout it out loud, do you?"

"Son." Hennison fixed Nathan with an earnest look. "I've done so many things I regret that I've decided to indulge myself by exposing fellow hypocrites when the fancy moves me. You see, it takes one to spot one, and my credentials are of the first rank, thereby qualifying me as an authority on the subject."

The captain smiled crookedly as he fixed Hennison with his outstretched index finger. "Mind your name calling, *doctor*. I'll wager you're the biggest butcher on board the *Constance*. Cutting, sawing, and probing—deny that a trail of corpses mark your passage."

"You bastard!" Hennison lurched at the skipper with his fist balled. "A doctor can only do so much! Faced with the efficiency of gunpowder and grapeshot, a physician will always lose."

The captain neatly sidestepped the blow and drove his elbow into Hennison's side, knocking him to the deck. To the physician's humiliation, the captain pinned the man beneath his heavy sea boot. Doc twisted in agony more from this act of degradation than from any physical pain. All the while the skipper studied his prey with the detached objectivity of a fisherman watching a wriggling fish.

"Please, let him up," Nathan urged. "He meant you no harm. He's disrespectful to everyone. The war cost him his profession as well as took his arm."

The captain stared piercingly at Nathan. "You're his shipmate, then?"

Nathan nodded. "He saved my life once." Watching this exchange, Hennison glowered as his inner weaknesses were dissected.

"Well, lad, he goes over the side. I don't allow intractable rats on my ship. You can sign on with me, or stick with your shipmate and follow him over the rail; it makes me no nevermind."

"I stand with my friend," Nathan replied firmly. "But you'll not find us an easy toss."

The captain stared at the double-barreled derringer that appeared without warning in the youth's hand. It pointed directly at his belly. "Blast your liver, Frenchy!" he cursed. "I told you to search them. A school girl couldn't miss that pocket cannon."

"I did, Captain," the first mate blurted. "God's truth, I frisked 'em good. I don't know where he hid it."

Hennison looked just as amazed. "Where did you get that?" he asked.

Nathan smiled. "A present from Wei-Li."

"Bless her warm, little yellow heart," Doc said. "Remind me to thank her."

The captain studied the two, paying particular attention to the derringer in Nat's hand. His keen eye noted no tremor. The barrels pointed steadily and unerringly at the second button of his brocade waistcoat. His men might overpower these troublemakers, but he would take a bullet in the gut for certain. The *Constance* was two days from land at least, and the captain had seen enough men die from belly wounds. Days dying in a rolling sea bunk with peritonitis was something he didn't relish. He had not survived and risen to master of his own ship by taking unnecessary risks. From the first day he stepped aboard as a cabin boy, he had clawed his way to the top by scheming and exercising a cold, calculating will.

"Well, lads," he smiled. His boot slid off Hennison's back. "What we have here is a Mexican standoff for certain. I don't relish you putting no seacock in my guts, and you two don't strike me as long distance swimmers. Perhaps I was a bit hasty. You look like honest fellows to me, ones that need a passage, and I could use two more hands. Would you consider stowing that deck gun of yours and signing aboard for this passage?"

"What does it pay?" asked Doc from his location on the deck.

"My, but you've got balls, even short-handed and all." The captain chuckled. "I'd have liked to have seen you with two flippers."

"Then, I needed a wheelbarrow for my balls," Hennison said.

"It's settled then." The skipper extended his hand slowly for Nathan's weapon.

"I'll keep the derringer," Nathan countered. "Since I don't have a knife, and you already have my Colt."

"But a seaman's knife is tipped to take off the stabbing point," the captain protested.

"Not all of them," Nathan nodded at the pointed blade the seaman beside Frenchy held. "Besides, this derringer is blunt-tipped, too. You won't have to worry about my stabbing anyone with it."

The captain shrugged. Another standoff to be tacked around until the winds were in his favor. He turned his back on Nathan and stomped aft to where a reed-thin sailor with faded red hair drenched and lying limp atop his head struggled to keep the *Constance* nose into the waves. The sailor's legs were spread wide apart as he used every ounce of his body's weight to fight the rudder. The skipper measured the sails before shouting to another seaman. At his command the tension vanished, Nature being more of a threat now than the two stowaways, and the other man sheathed his knife before rushing to throw his body against the wheel.

Frenchy winked at Nathan and wiped the salt spray from his dripping nose. "Good, good," he said. "It's good you're crew now. Ever sail before?"

"No." Nathan watched Hennison struggle to his feet. His heart went out to his friend, but he knew he dare not offer him assistance. That would only deepen the wound in the physician's pride. Nathan was beginning to wonder if Doc Hennison's deliberate flouting of authority was a ruse to hide a desperate need for order. Certainly, the War Between The States had deprived him of his normal existence. But Frenchy interrupted his thoughts.

"Come help me with this sheet," he directed the youth.

"She needs to be cleated off Bristol fashion. Old Red plays good music, but he's slack when it comes to his lines." He pointed to the helmsman who shot back a crooked grin and made an obscene gesture.

For the next two hours Nathan followed the wiry Frenchy as he sprang from deck to deck checking lines, adjusting blocks, and sorting the coils of rope scattered by the sudden storm. The little man seemed without fear or fatigue as he swung out from the wooden railing to snatch flogging rigging, giving no thought to the racing sea that boiled and hissed past the black hull. Nathan found himself digging his fingers into lifelines and rails whenever his shadowing of Frenchy brought him closer to the water than was comfortable for him. Surely one misstep would be fatal for a man overboard would be lost far astern as the storm drove the ship along without recourse to turning back.

Frenchy laughed good-naturedly at him while his hands coiled lines as if with a mind of their own. "You get your sea legs mighty quick if you watch old Frenchy. I teach you to be finest sailor. My papa an' his papa before him all good sailors. That's because we're Portuguese. All men in Portugal the best sailors. It's small country, very poor—poor land, poor crops, poor everything. Only the sea is left to feed us, so we sail all over. To the Portuguese the sea is our land, our home. We learn not to be scared by the big water. You can't be afraid of your home, can you?"

"But they call you Frenchy?"

"Ah, these stupid sailors. They don't know nothing about my country, can't even spell it right; so they log me as French. French, they can spell." He dug a calloused finger into his ear to force out the saltwater, then arched his eyebrows resignedly. "So Frenchy I am now. But I'm Portuguese."

Nathan kept a firm grip on the rigging. "Henry, the Navigator, he was from Portugal," he said. "I read about him in a book in the orphanage library. He realized the importance of maps for sailors."

Frenchy's face illuminated in delight, glowing through the drops of water and salt rime lacing the furrows of his swarthy skin. "You know about King Henry, eh? That's wonderful. You sure you not Portuguese?"

"No."

"Maybe your papa, then? Or your mama?"

Nathan's past rushed into the present to drive its talons into his stomach. Even in a place as alien and removed from the desert as these wild coastal waters he could not escape it. The neglected gravesite at Pinal, the photo of the woman in the checkered gingham dress for whom he felt nothing, and the steely gray eyes of the man on the stern of the departing steamer, shielding his woman companion, hand resting on the butt of his pistol, and calmly waiting for Riley's rifle shot—all flared up before his mind's eye.

"No," Nathan lied. "I'm an orphan. Don't know who my father was, or my mother."

Frenchy studied the lad. His dark eyes had sagely noted the fleeting look of pain Nathan quickly hid. "I bet you'd be surprised if you ever met them. You got good metal in you, I know. You save my life and stand up to Captain Coffin for your shipmate." He paused to spit into the sea after mentioning the skipper. "That takes guts—the kind you only get from a strong papa or mama. One or both give that to you, that's for sure."

Nathan had no ready answer for that. If Frenchy was right, did his mulishness come from the man he planned to kill? Not from his mother, he surmised. Before he could give the idea more thought, Captain Coffin loomed menacingly behind him like one of the waves outboard of the railing. Frenchy skipped away, chasing a flogging line and leaving the boy alone as if their conversation never took place.

Coffin seized Nat's arm, judging the thickness developed from being assigned the heavy work at St. Catherine's. "Got good muscle in your flukes, I see. You ought to swing a club all day without batting an eye. I'll put you on the shore crew while your one-armed friend can clean the slops and skin. Being a surgeon he ought to do real well at that, and he won't need to worry about losing a single patient 'cause they'll all be dead as a parson's itch for a whore." Enormously pleased with his gallows humor, Coffin wended his way forward, shaking with laughter.

Nathan half slid, half rolled to where Hennison, still brooding over his humiliation, had wedged himself between the foremast and the stained aft section of the forecastle. Timing his next move with the roll of the ship, Nathan slid down beside the physician. There the two of them sat, waiting out the weather. While the rain pelted and lashed the two, they huddled together for warmth, each man ruminating on vastly disparate thoughts. Mixed feelings churned in Nathan's mind, those of lost love for Wei-Li and a growing hatred of the man at the stern of the vessel. Weeks of grooming his enmity for Wyatt Earp naturally made it easy to blame him for Wei-Li's loss rather than ascribing anything to his foolhardy leap at the departing vessel or Hennison's drunkenness.

Unlike Nathan, Doc's thoughts were acutely focused on revenge. Only once before at Fort Douglas, the federal prison camp on the windblown sand dunes of Lake Michigan, had another human laid a foot across his neck. Then he was weak from his wounds, dispirited, and shaking with fever; he never forgot the humiliation, and he had vowed as he lay on the fouled straw pallet that night to never allow such indignation again. The world might steal his fortune, ruin his body, and make him an outcast, but his pride was his alone to command. Locked safely inside from external forces, he'd resolved that night to preserve at all costs this shrine to his very being.

179

Now Coffin's boot had revived this promise. As they struggled to keep warm, Hennison plotted his retribution.

Eventually the storm passed like all things in a restless world, and so did the days at sea. The *Constance* continued unerringly north, seeking colder waters where only the hardy sailed and seal fur grew thicker for protection. In that time the two stowaways learned the boring routine of shipboard life, and the youth took heart that each league sailed north brought him close on the heels of the vessel that carried his love. Doc helped the Chinese cook, relegated to washing dishes and scouring pots, while Nat learned as much as Frenchy could teach him as seaman apprentice. Delighted to have an eager pupil, the little Portuguese filled the boy's head with stories and knowledge gleaned from a lifetime at sea.

Even the narrow wooden cribs—as narrow as coffins—that served as bunks grew familiar. Falling out from watches, both men learned to sleep on the wooden pallets. On finding his blanket alive with bedbugs, Nat followed the advice of Frenchy and collected a handful of cockroaches from the abundant supply in the galley. The roaches ate the bedbugs, but proliferated themselves, darting about his bunk—something Nat learned to accept. But food was a problem, and he lost weight while he forced himself to eat what Frenchy called grub and Doc labeled swill. Breakfast was interminably hardtack crawling with weevils, chicory, and scouse, a paste of boiled potatoes and salted beef with the consistency of glue. Dinner was more of the same.

Nathan learned to read the dark moods of the captain as he did the changes of the sea while Hennison also craftily awaited his opportunity for revenge. In turn, Coffin watched them, and while he approved of Nat's learning seamanship, he misjudged Hennison's surly compliance as submission to his will.

The Winter Wolf

Without visible signs of warmth, Captain Coffin was a man without a single living friend, yet his office and skill commanded due respect. Nathan could find no one aboard who spoke to the skipper unless directly addressed and no one who spoke of him in private. Coffin's eyes and ears pervaded the very planks and caulking of the *Constance.* A misdeed by a seaman named Hicks led immediately to Coffin redressing him with the knotted end of a rope. Somewhere in his murky past, Coffin had read of the British Navy's use of the knout and adopted it himself.

Besides Frenchy, Nat grew to know the helmsman, Paddy Coniff, the redheaded Irishman who carried an endless supply of clay pipes which he bit in half whenever the steering turned hard and who played a tin whistle and the Irish bagpipes when off his watch. The mournful sounds of the bellows-powered pipes matched the heaviness that oppressed the *Constance* with each day that passed. To Nathan it seemed as if all of the crew but Hennison carried some black secret that grew to weigh on them like the iron links of the anchor chain in the forepeak lockers as they neared their destination.

What this secret was he could not discover until one night when he and Hennison sat listening to Paddy's mournful rendition of "Lilibulero" on his pipes. Fingering the keys while his knee worked the bellows, tears suddenly erupted from the Irishman's blue eyes and coursed down his windburned cheeks until they mingled with his curly red muttonchops. Nat noticed the others chose to ignore Paddy's state of despondency, but his tune seemed to mark the dark mood that pervaded the ship. At last Paddy finished playing and paused to wipe his runny nose on his sleeve. When he looked up, his eyes met Nat's questioning gaze.

"Ah, lad," Coniff sighed, "tomorrow it might begin."

"Begin what?" Nathan asked.

"Why the killing, of course. Killing those poor, wee bairns

in front of their own mothers—and killing their mothers as well. 'Tis a hard thing, a cruel thing, and it breaks me heart."

Hicks, Frenchy, and even the Chinese cook nodded solemnly in agreement.

"Why do you do it, then?"

"Because we have no other choice, me boy," Paddy blew his nose. "Because we're marked men, all of us. You see, we have the mark of Cain on us, and sailing on this blood-cursed ship is all that's left open for us. We're like physicians who bleed a patient, hating every drop we spill, yet having no choice."

With that mention of doctors, Hennison raised his head from the lower bunk where he had lain in the dark, ruminating. "Marked? What the devil do you mean?" he asked.

Paddy glanced at the others before replying. "All of us, in one way or another. You see, we have no papers. Me, I'm wanted by the law for striking a landowner back in Ireland. I stowed away on the first ship I could to avoid hanging. Worse luck, it took me to Canada instead of America. The authorities got wind of me there, and I smuggled myself to San Francisco on a cattle barge. But I've no official papers, being illegal, so no other ship will sign me on. And Frenchy here lost his first mate's papers when he drew his knife on his last captain."

"He was a pig," Frenchy interjected. "I should have stabbed him good. They treated me like I did."

"Anyway, Nat," Paddy continued, "Only sealing ships like Captain Coffin's will take us. It's the *Constance* or nothing. On the beach there's no money, and Frenchy and I have to feed our families in the old country."

"Sounds like the *Constance* is true to her name," Hennison remarked. "Her grip on you is constant for sure."

Coniff shrugged. "She's fast and black, and Captain Coffin slips in quiet like, and we're gone before anyone takes notice. He avoids the authorities, too, whenever he see 'em since they ain't too partial to the slaughter we do."

Nathan's eyes gleamed. "We could take over the ship and sail her to Alaska to find gold! You could do it, Paddy. You and Frenchy could sail this ship all by yourselves, I know it."

"Bless me," Paddy laughed, but the sound was forced and carried a note of warning which Frenchy's face reflected. "Don't do no more talking like that, lad, even in jest. Mutiny is a sure hanging offense. Besides, I can man the helm sure enough, but I ain't never learned celestial navigation. The skipper's sextant is as foreign a thing to me as the House of Lords. Without proper bearings, we'd sail in circles until the water ran out. No, we're signed on for good, no taking command, and no taking French leave. These islands are barren."

"French leave?" Hennison said. "What's that?"

"Jumping ship," Paddy explained. "Put it out of your mind, Doc. Queen Charlotte's are harsh as a kitchenmaid's knees. Wild forest and natives that'd slit your gullet in revenge for all the mischief done them by whites. You'd be dead in the water and dead on the land as well. Why d'you suppose Captain Coffin sails this route? No one dares jump ship."

Frenchy grasped Nathan's arm. "Better get some sleep. Tomorrow we should sight the Queen Charlotte Islands. You better hope we find a big herd of seal there, or else we'll be sailing north to Alaska."

"Alaska!" Nathan's hopes soared. "Will we make port near Skagway, Frenchy?"

The little man shook his head. "No. If we have to we sail straight to the Aleutians, a God-cursed land of fog, fearsome wind, and icy rains. No land, no nothing between—a good two thousand miles from Skagway."

Frenchy's words fell on Nathan like hammer blows. Two thousand miles from Wei-Li! The distance sounded like the other side of the world from her. An aching hopelessness churned in his belly, threatening to overwhelm him. Would he ever see her again?

As if on signal the gathering broke up with Frenchy going topsides, Paddy replacing his bagpipes in their box, and Hicks turning his face to the wall. Nathan pulled his moth-eaten blanket about his neck and settled into a despair as dark as the shadows that filled the corners of the forecastle. For hours he lay awake, staring at the shadows cast by the solitary, swinging coal oil lamp near the companionway. Battered and dented by years of faithful service, the brass lamp's warm glow offered the only source of hope for him. Somehow he would rescue Wei-Li, but exactly how escaped him. So he consoled himself with thoughts of her. In the forecastle's darkness he visualized the raven's wing hair of his lover; and with the rhythmic thump of the waves against the wooden hull, he remembered her heart as it beat against his chest.

While Nat dreamed of Wei-Li, Doc sifted through his own jumbled thoughts. Before ending his watch, he had stood on the quarterdeck and watched the horizon swallow the copper sun. The wind had lowered and the sea glowed fire from the reflected scarlet sky for half an hour before night quenched the flames. The beauty of the sunset held Hennison in thrall while he hated every minute of it. Since a surgeon had sawed off his arm, sunsets and sunrises brought nothing but pain to him. The fresh birth of a new day only served to remind him of his failures and the sorrowful fact that his life would never be as he so dearly wished. Sunsets drove home sharply his impending demise, having failed to fulfill even the smallest of his dreams. So Doc hated the birth and death of each day as he despised what he was and what he would always be.

Tonight, his malice focused on Captain Coffin and his ship. Something Paddy said had hatched a new and deadly plan in his mind. Now Hennison nurtured this kernel into a budding machination. With luck and proper timing, he would make it work.

Before weariness overtook him and doused his schemes, he

remembered Paddy mumbling something in his sleep about the killing beginning in the morning. . . .

Nathan awoke to a change in the roll of the *Constance.* The hissing water under her keel died away, and the hull commenced to wallow in the following seas as her nose dropped into the swell. Muffled voices topside and the thudding of feet on the decking prompted him to leave his warm blankets and scramble up the ladder.

Sliding back the hatch he emerged into a surreal world of dense fog. Bundled in wool sweaters and oilskins, the crew hurried about like black-hooded wraiths, disappearing and emerging from the grayish-yellow mist that shrouded the ship so that even the bowsprit could not be seen from the forecastle companionway. The masts and cross spars rose upward like stripped and fire-blackened trees to disappear into the haze.

Perplexingly, the fog amplified all sound from the creak of the rigging to the thunder of surf breaking on rocks close by while masking its true direction. Nathan spotted Frenchy leaning over the starboard rail, listening intently to the splashing surf.

"What is it, Frenchy? What's happening?"

"Shhh, a Canadian revenue cutter. She spot us at first light." He paused to wink at Nat. "We not pay for Canadian license, so they want to seize old *Constance.* But Captain Coffin, he one smart fox. This schooner plenty fast. We make dash for fog off Anthony Island rocks. Now those Canucks sniffing around, but they don't see us, and their skipper too yellow-livered to come in after us. He know if he put his vessel on rocks it's a life on land for him, and one stinking sealer ain't worth ruining his career.

"Listen, you hear her motors." Frenchy pointed into the fog, his eyes glistening and his face bright with excitement like a fox outsmarting the hounds.

Nat turned his head from side to side until he caught the low growl of the cutter's engines pacing back and forth. All the while the *Constance* slid through the fog with Coffin directing Paddy by hand signal. The youth shuddered as he caught sight of jagged rocks looming out of the mist like dragon's teeth off their starboard quarter, but Coffin guided them safely past.

In time the revenue cutter drew impatient and soon its rumbling screws faded into the distance.

Luckily, soon after their pursuer had left, the fog thinned, allowing the rock-strewn shores to emerge. Nathan started as he caught sight of giant and grotesque wooden carvings spaced along the beach and thrusting from the spruce forests. Painted in garish ochre, black, and white, the poles consisted of stacked creatures, glaring back at him with wide eyes, protruding tongues, and bared fangs.

"Totem poles," Frenchy explained. "This old Haida village." He nodded to the crumbling long houses beyond the totems. Cut from colossal cedar logs and planks, many of the houses dwarfed their seventy-two-foot schooner, but their state of disrepair was obvious with many having caved-in roofs and shattered lintels. The size of the village stood in mute contrast to the lack of human activity.

"Where are all the people?" Nat asked.

"Dead or run away," Frenchy answered. "They get sick and die like flies. Those that survive think this place cursed and flee."

"Cursed by us," Hennison replied. Unnoticed before, he now stood behind his young companion and gazed forlornly at the dead village. "Smallpox wiped them out, a gift from us. Another tribute to progress, like the rifled musket and high explosives."

Coffin walked forward from the helm. "Don't waste your pity on these heathens, doctor. They were damned warlike. If you'd been shipwrecked fifty years ago on this beach, these

Haida would have bashed your brains out with a war club or strangled you to catch trade shells."

"Trade shells?" Nathan asked. "What do you mean, Captain?"

Coffin grinned tensely. In spite of himself he liked teaching this boy. "Trade shells, lad. Dentalium shells, long and curved like claws. The inland tribes placed great stock in them, would trade their sainted mothers for 'em. They grow well on corpses that still have blood inside, so the Haida would strangle their slaves between logs and hang 'em in the sea to catch Dentalia. With their great war canoes the Haida roamed far on raids for slaves. An old sailor told me they could catch unwary merchantmen."

"And that justifies salting them with the pox, I suppose," Hennison retorted.

"It don't justify nothing, quack," Coffin snapped. "What happened is over and done. What happens next is our concern. You'd do well to remember that. I'm surprised that hunk of honest New England steel that nipped your fluke didn't learn you that lesson."

"It only taught me that fighting for your ideals is a sure way to lose. Your honest New England merchants sold molasses for slaves and then jumped at the chance to play pious savior of the slaves they helped create."

"Ah, that's it, quack. You miss your slaves, do you? Can't wipe your bottom by yourself?"

"I never owned slaves. I fought for Tennessee, but as I said I've learned my lesson. Now I only fight for myself."

Coffin nodded approval. "That the first sensible thing come out of your mouth, quack."

"I'm learning."

Frenchy's head snapped suddenly to one side. He tilted his nose into the wind, and shouted. "Smell 'em, skipper! Seals! There's seal ahead!"

Coffin sampled the wind and bobbed his head in agreement. He doffed his rumpled fisherman's cap and ran a hand through his thinning hair. "Aye, you greasy frog, your big nose is true as a compass. Nothing stinks like that but seals."

Nathan sniffed until the pungent odor of rotting fish and offal hit him. It hung heavily on the air like a banner, betraying the doomed animals and leading straight back to their hiding place. The smell galvanized the schooner's crew. The sails were furled, anchor chains slipped to splash into the green water, and the longboat swung over the side on its davits. The ship's crew mustered on the quarterdeck clothed in oilskins and heavy sea boots while Coffin passed out stout ax handles and poles from the stores. Frenchy motioned Nathan to join the line. Only Doc and the Chinese cook stood aside.

"Here we go, kid," Frenchy said. "Get on oilskins and get a good club."

Paddy nodded gloomily. "Better hope there's a big herd, so's we can skip the Aleutians." He directed Nathan to the middle of the pitching longboat which now rode impatiently alongside the schooner.

Nathan took his seat and handled an oar as the longboat slipped its davits and rode the waves toward the roiling surf, skipping over the surge as all men put their backs to the oars. Silently, like a hunter stalking his prey, the skiff cut towards the looming gray-green island that lurched through rents in the mists. In minutes the longboat's keel crunched on a coarse gravel beach sheltered between to massive rock outcropings. Coffin grounded the boat, and all hands splashed ashore in the hip-high surf.

Nathan followed Frenchy as the party clambered across the rock to fan out along the shoreline. The ax handle felt waxy in his grip, and he stumbled over the loose scree in his oversized sea boots. No one spoke as they clambered along, slipping and cursing beneath their breath, so the only sound he heard was the eerie grunting of the unsuspecting seals growing louder, mixed with the crunch of sea boots on shell and gravel.

Topping a rise, the men spied the herd of fur seals scattered over a rounded tongue of gravel. Thick-throated bulls guarded clusters of females in clumps of harems while smaller white-coated pups lolled close by their mothers. Quickly, the men rushed over the crest and splashed through the surf to cut off the seals' ocean escape. Disturbed barks and squeals erupted from the male beachmasters as they watched the men advance. Uncomprehendingly, the males mistook the threat to come from rival males and so they added to the turmoil by lurching and slashing at their nearest rivals. This action drove the females and young inland en masse, resulting in the crushing death of the smaller pups.

Heads turned back toward their pursuers and soft, rounded eyes wide in alarm, the seals flopped inland, away from their only means of escape and survival—the sea. Nathan followed this route with a leaden heaviness swelling in his heart.

Then the slaughter began. Coffin struck first, his club slicing down in an arc that smashed the head of a fawn-colored female. She dropped onto the sand, blood frothing from her nostrils and flippers twitching convulsively while her calf bleated plaintively nearby. Another swing of Coffin's club silenced the pup, smashing him senseless in the shadow of his dead mother.

Coffin's signal loosed the others in a dance of mayhem. Whirling clubs rose and fell as the men waded into the panicked seals. Each blow left an animal dead and twitching until the corpses themselves acted as a barrier to the survival animals' escape. While the low, scudding clouds cast a darkening pall on this carnage, the beach turned red from the blood seeping into the stones, and this blood ran into the tideline to stain the waters.

Nathan moved among the seals with the rest. His first blow killed an old, battle-scarred beachmaster who lunged at him with bared fangs, but it was no contest. His second strike missed the head of a female, stunning her without an instant kill. She flopped to one side, vainly trying to protect her infant. Sick to his stomach, Nathan finished her off. But killing the pup was beyond him. He stared at the bleating cub as it sought the warmth of its twitching mother, but nothing could make him raise his arm to smite the child.

Standing, looking down at the pup, tears filled his eyes to match those brimming in the brown eyes of the baby. For what seem like an eternity, youth and seal stared at each other, sensing yet not comprehending the evanescence of life. Then Paddy killed the pup.

"Better this way, lad," he explained. "He won't survive without his ma. He'll only starve or be eaten alive by the foxes and gulls. I know it's hard, but a swift death is a kindness." The helmsman turned away, shifting his grip on his bloody club, but Nathan saw him pause to wipe the tears from his own eyes on his blood-soaked oilskin.

An hour later the butchering was done. The beach that a short time before held several generations of fur seals now lay covered with corpses—none escaped to the sea. But the indignity continued. The crew moved among the still forms, slitting the round bellies and severing the wrist bones of the flippers so the valuable fur could be stripped from the bodies.

Nathan stood by having discarded his weapon, numb from the slaughter, and watched the bodies turn into pink shapes that bore no semblance to the soft, warm creatures they once were. Scattered in random family units, they littered the cove and imparted a dark obscenity to the entire island.

Under Coffin's terse command the men filled the longboat with piles of the raw furs until there was room for only two men to man the oars, then the skiff headed back to the *Constance* to unload before hastily returning. Four trips reduced the pile of skins to one last load.

But by now the surf had risen as if in protest to their deadly work to lash the small beach and the encircling rocks. Handling the light skiff turned perilous as wave after wave turned her broadside in the surge, threatening to capsize her and drive her onto the rocks. To Frenchy fell the difficult task of manning the skiff's tiller while the final pile of furs was loaded. Time and again the small boat broached in the waves, causing the sweat to drip from his brow although the air was cold and laden with salty mist. Gritting his teeth and with veins popping in his neck, he threw all his weight against the rudder as a rogue wave struck the longboat—but to no avail this time. The skiff slewed broadside to surf across the beach toward a rock-strewn outcropping.

Nathan, arms filled with dripping hides, saw the boat driving toward them and dove to one side. His foot tripped on the kelp and sea grass, and he went under, still clutching the pelts. Rolled helplessly underwater by the surge, he caught sight of the murky shadow of the longboat as it passed directly over his head. Lungs bursting for air, he shot to the surface behind the skiff just as it crashed into the rocks. The gunnels splintered with a sickening crash that echoed around the cove, but fortunately the stove-in side held together.

But Paddy Coniff was not so lucky. Caught unawares, the boat carried him before it to crush him against the rocks. Nathan watched in horror as the boat hammered him against the anvil of jagged stone and razor sharp barnacles.

Without a sound from his open mouth, Coniff slipped under until only the top of his red hair glowed faintly beneath the green sea. Frenchy gave a cry of anguish as he leapt after his shipmate. Nathan also waded to the Irishman. His hand locked with Paddy's fingers in a desperate grasp, and together they dragged him ashore.

Laid on the still warm furs with his feet slewing in the water, Paddy looked wide-eyed at Nathan while his mouth worked desperately to form his dying words. But nothing came from his crushed lungs save bloody froth. He coughed once, and then died.

"Paddy, Paddy, I'm sorry! The skiff got away from me! Forgive me!" Frenchy sobbed, all the while his hands moving about the dead Irishman's face, smoothing his disheveled hair, and wiping the pink-tinged stain from his mouth.

Nat looked down at the death grip Coniff had on his sleeve. Gently he pried the fingers loose. Death had struck once again, unexpectedly. Since he left the orphanage, the violent outside world had repeatedly shown its true nature to him like an unwanted but accustomed visitor, but each time left him with a different feeling. And this time a sense of deep loss twisted in the pit of his stomach.

Here, in a field of slaughter where these men had discovered over a hundred seals by chance and clubbed all to death, chance and bad luck had added a human life to the tally. Somehow Paddy Coniff's body, lying alone on the sand and surrounded by the skinned animals, made his death on this forlorn and bleak island all the more poignant and wasteful to Nathan.

Captain Coffin's shadow loomed over them. He bent down to examine his crew member. "Damned lousy luck. He was a good helmsman," he said.

When only the sorrowful stares of Frenchy and the youth met his retort, he shrugged. "Well, he's finished. Leave him be. We got work to do. That stove-in longboat won't hold together much longer if we let her ground herself again. Then we'll all be stuck on this godforsaken heap to rot along with Coniff."

No one moved. An angry hiss escaped from between someone's clenched teeth. Coffin frowned at the tightly balled fists surrounding him. "Get going!" he ordered.

Frenchy shook his head. "No, Captain. We don't leave Paddy to the gulls. He comes on board for a Christian burial."

The tone in the little Portuguese's voice made Coffin stop.

He looked at Nathan and saw the same firm resolve. His face darkened like the squall line that broke to the south of the island, and he knitted his brows in anger, but he nodded his head. "All right, toss him in the lighter, but let's get moving. That Canuck cutter might just swing back, and I can't outrun her with both my feet planted on this stinking beach."

For all of two hours the *Constance* buried her nose in the waves, tossing spindrift over her forepeak, as she headed north. Despite the killing less than half the forward hold lay filled with pelts. Cursing them all, Coffin ordered the ship to the Aleutians. As if on signal the sun burst forth from the low clouds to cast its cheerful rays paradoxically on the gloomy vessel. Paddy's death and the seal slaughter left the crew somber and silent.

Below decks Doc Hennison helped the Chinese cook sew Coniff's battered corpse into sail canvas with an arm's length of anchor chain wrapped around his feet. When they had completed their task, Frenchy steered the ship directly into the wind, putting her in irons for the funeral. There the *Constance* lay, wallowing in the swells while Coffin read rapidly from his ship's bible. It was obvious to Nathan and the others that the skipper considered the service a wasteful exercise. He finished in record time, the plank was tipped, and Paddy Coniff, late of Ireland, slid forever beneath the waves.

For the next week the *Constance* slogged northward, but fortune no longer cast so much as a wry grin on her after the Irishman's death. The winds died unexpectedly on the seventh day, leaving her to roll in the oily sea while hordes of flies and seagulls descended on the craft.

The flies settled on everything, moving or not, buzzing in protest whenever Hennison smashed them with his bare hand and humming in excitement whenever the now rancid hold was opened. While the gulls soared incessantly alongside, they added to the sense of attack by swooping in when least expected to steal food from the sailor's hands or scraps as the men fleshed the seal hides. Their constant presence left Nathan with the impression the ship carried three types of crew: birds, flies, and humans.

"Must be why this tub is called the *Constance,*" Hennison remarked one evening as he pursued his personal vendetta on the insects. "These bastards are *constantly* with us."

"Why not ignore them, Doc," Nathan suggested as he leaned against the leeward rail and watched Hennison cutting his way through the black cloud that dodged him with equal exuberance. "They're all over the ship. You just end up chasing them from the bow to the stern and then back again."

"Because I hate them!" Hennison answered with exceptional vehemence. "During the war they were everywhere after the battles, in the hospital tents, on the dying, on the wounded, crawling in the wounds I was treating—every damn where. And when it came my turn, they were there for me, too. I remember lying on the grass outside the hospital tent watching the flies landing on my amputated right arm. It was on top of a pile of legs and arms outside the tent. I recognized it as mine because the little finger still wore a filigreed gold ring given to me by my mother. The orderlies were either too busy or too tired to steal it. Later that night someone took the ring—perhaps it was the flies themselves. But I remember lying there as the laudanum wore off and wondering if those flies were Yankees or Johnny Rebs. I decided they were neither, that they worked for themselves without handicap from useless dogma. And they were definitely the only ones having any success."

"Doc," Nathan frowned.

"Really, Nat, my boy, it's the gospel. I vowed right then and there to be just like those insects, to profit from the avarice and stupidity of the human race, and to put all grandiose but unproductive motives right out of my head. It's worked well for both of us, the flies and me. So you'll understand why I endeavor to kill as many flies as possible. I'm only trying to eliminate my competition."

Nathan turned Paddy Coniff's tin whistle over in his hand. After the funeral the men had divided up the dead man's possessions, and all decided Nat ought to have the penny whistle. The instrument, battered and shorn of its nickel plating in spots, lay cold and inanimate in his grip. Nathan recalled how Coniff could make the forecastle ring with music. Now only the hiss of waves remained.

Despite his cavalier attitude, Nathan knew Hennison grieved for the helmsman. His crazy bellows-operated bagpipe and rambling good humor somehow complemented Doc's laconic nature, and as a sign of rare magnanimity, Hennison had treated the Irishman's boils. Nathan also realized Doc would rather die than show his soft side, yet the physician's relationship with Coniff brought to mind his begrudging acceptance of Jim Riley.

"Where do you suppose Riley is, Doc?" he asked.

"Hopefully, burning in hell," Doc muttered. He punctuated his remark by smashing a dozen flies that had followed him from the hold.

"You don't mean that, I know."

Hennison inspected his palm, counting the number of squashed insects. Satisfied with his tally, he wiped the fly specks on his pant leg. His youthful companion was probing for tender chinks in his armor, so Doc chose to ignore the issue. He squinted at the sun splashing its colors of mauve and crimson over the glasslike water. Another beautiful evening to rub salt into his crosscut memories.

"Well," he drawled. "If he's as good as his word, he should be hot on our friend Earp's trail." He paused to glance about. Only Frenchy was on deck with them, and he manned the wheel well out of earshot. "And so are we my boy," he added slyly.

Nathan's ears pricked up. "How so?"

Hennison's eyes grew furtive, and a guileful look came over his face. His voice dropped to a whisper. "I've been checking the captain's charts each time I remove his dinner dishes. He marks the ship's course on the map each day. Right now we're one day south of Skagway. It's over there off the right side of this stinking bucket of blood. Why, I suspect these damned flies could make it to Skagway from here."

His revelation had the opposite effect from what he expected. Nathan's face dropped, his hands gripped the rail, and his lips pressed into a drawn line. "It might as well be a thousand miles away," he sighed. "You heard Frenchy. Coffin's sailing straight for the Aleutian Islands. No stops in between, and there's nothing we can do about it."

Hennison's remarks had brought Wei-Li to the forefront of Nathan's thoughts, although she was never far from there. While Hennison hated the evening, especially those that demonstrated any beauty, Nathan also suffered at these times. It hurt all the more knowing his love was just beyond the horizon, and he was powerless to do anything about it.

Hennison smiled grimly. "Where's your faith, Nat, my boy? Trust old Doc, and he'll solve the problem. Besides, I owe Captain Coffin for his ill treatment of both of us, so what I've planned will be a pleasure."

"We can't try to take over the ship. He's got all the weapons locked in his cabin, even my derringer."

"Your derringer? I thought he let you keep it?"

"He did. But this morning when I awoke it was gone. I'm sure he took it."

Hennison thought for a moment before waving his hand like an earl dismissing an inconsequential servant. "No matter," he said. "We won't need it, anyway."

"What are you thinking about, Doc?"

Doc's face looked positively foxlike. "I can't tell you just yet. You'll know what it is when the opportunity arises. So be ready to act. . . . "

FIFTEEN

Three hundred nautical miles and many days north of the fur sealer, the *S.S. Brixom* puffed steadily onward. Unknown to Nathan and his companion, those on board had no intention of sailing to Skagway. The *Brixom* was taking the All-Water Route to the mouth of the Yukon River. From there its gold seekers would travel back along the winding Yukon to Dawson, bypassing the saw-toothed mountains of ice that discouraged the less hardy. It would penetrate to the heart of the Klondike by mastering the giant river that pumped from the heart itself.

Over ten days the ship's daily routine soured from dull to remarkably tiring, except that those days at sea exposed the vessel's glaring flaws. Portholes leaked, one engine died, and the *Brixom* was forced to cut her speed in half. Before long, sullen knots of passengers clustered around lifeboats, cursing the skipper and complaining of the vile food.

Josie looked up from the book she was reading as her husband opened their cabin door. She smiled warmly at him as he hung his coat on the brass hook inside the entryway.

Wyatt surveyed the cramped cabin. A drab blue curtain halfheartedly covered the only porthole above the tiny bunk that barely could hold them both. Besides the chair in which Josie sat, the only other furniture was a battered writing table bolted to the bulkhead below a sputtering electric light.

"Damn, my dear," he said as he flaked a chip of peeling

white paint from the bulkhead and inspected the rusted metal beneath. "I sure am glad we're traveling first class. I've seen the second-class staterooms, and I doubt your big feet would fit in the bed."

Josie pretended not to hear and returned to her reading. "If you're going to be nasty, I'm going to ignore you, Mr. Earp."

Wyatt sat heavily on the bed and studied his wife. The striking beauty that first had attracted him in Tombstone was still there, in her face and in her body, but she had changed with the loss of their last child. Now a quiet elegance overlaid her features, making her all the more desirable and all the more precious to him.

In Doc Holliday he had found someone willing to take a bullet for him. Other than his brothers, Holliday had been his only friend. John was gone now, but Josie had taken his place. Her quiet courage filled that void. As long as she lived, he knew he would never stand alone. He shook his head in amazement as he studied her. A lover and a friend, he mused. What a combination.

"Are you going to be sweet?" she asked, studying him over her book.

"I'll let you in on a secret, if you like," he teased.

Her eyes widened. "You know I love secrets. What is it?"

He leaned close enough to her to smell the lilac in her hair. "This ship is not all it is cracked up to be," he whispered.

"What do you mean? Are we sinking?" she asked in alarm.

"No, Josie, but I've been poking around, and I discovered something very interesting about the *Brixom.*" Wyatt paused to scratch behind his ear.

"What?"

"You know the flyer that described this ship as brand new, with the latest, up-to-date conveniences?"

Josie pointed her toe at the miniscule water closet. "I don't call that up to date. The toilets in Tombstone were better than that—that pillbox. And I can stand in here and touch both walls with my arms outstretched." She picked delicately at the frilled collar at her neck.

"Absolutely correct, my dear. The *Brixom* isn't new at all. Just look at all this rusted plate. It's an old freighter used to haul our troops down to Cuba for the Spanish-American War last year. One of the black gang came on deck for a breath of fresh air, and he told me. This ship steamed directly to San Francisco from the Caribbean to carry passengers to the Klondike. It wasn't even cleaned out first."

Wyatt stopped to dig furiously at his shirt front. His fingers dove between the buttons to seek out a series of itches. Josie was wriggling about also, trying to scratch in a manner as lady-like as possible. Wyatt frowned. Then he jumped up from the bunk.

"What the hell! Why are we scratching like a dog with . . . "

"Fleas!" Josie completed his sentence, leaping to her feet. She snatched one of the folded blankets and held the brown wool cloth beneath the lamp. The words U.S. ARMY were stenciled clearly in one corner. "The steward brought the extra blankets that I asked for."

Wyatt scrutinized the blanket. Tiny specks somersaulted across its textured surface, launching themselves into the air in all directions. The blankets were loaded with hungry fleas. He tore the blankets from Josie's grasp and flung them out the door. Rapidly, the two stripped to their underwear, kicked their clothing into a far corner, and doused each other with the bottle of rubbing alcohol Josie kept at the bedside.

When she was satisfied her fleas were dead, Josie looked up from inspecting her chemise to find Wyatt buckling on his Colt Peacemaker over his long johns. "Why, Wyatt, you look positively fearsome dressed like you are. Are you planning to call someone out?"

"I think I'll start with the captain. After I shoot him, I'll work my way down through all the crew and then those obnoxious Phillips brothers who sit at our dining table." He growled. "Where's my damned hat?"

Josie snatched it from the hook and held it behind her back so he had to reach around her to get it. "You're right, darling," she purred. "You can't go without your Stetson. You'd be positively undressed."

Earp looked down at his gunbelt slung low on his right hip, then past it to his long johns bagging at the knees and his gray woolen socks. "Damn, I even got a hole in my sock." He looked up at her and started to laugh. "We do look a sight, don't we, Josie. I'll bet you a twenty-dollar gold piece all those I was aiming to plug would die laughing first if they saw me dressed like this."

She stood on tiptoe to kiss him. "I'm not laughing," she said. "I think you look quite handsome." She barely got the words out before she began to giggle.

Wyatt eased his revolver from the alcohol-soaked holster and wiped it on his leg. "I suppose now I ought to oil my Colt. I don't want it to get rusty."

Josie's movement on the bed caught his eye, and he paused to watch her empty the rest of the rubbing alcohol onto the sheets. Deftly, she slipped out of her chemise to lie naked on the wet bed. She held out her arms to him.

"Come here, Mr. Earp, and oil me," she whispered, her voice turning husky. "You wouldn't want me to get rusty, either."

Later, they lay together in the drying bunk, her head resting on his chest, and listened to the labored drone of the single engine. More delays, Wyatt thought. With one engine down the captain was hugging the coast, adding extra miles and extra time to their voyage. Two days ago they had left Kodiak and sailed along the Alaska Peninsula. That jagged scythe of windblown mountains stabbing into the throat of the Pacific almost to Japan resembled collections of broken glass more than land. Silently it watched them, waiting off their starboard rail for the right gale to blow them onto its rocks. One day ahead lay Unalaska, a wild settlement still more Russian than American that straddled the gap in the rugged Alaska Peninsula and the chain of Aleutian Islands. From there the *Brixom* would turn sharply north, leaving the security of the land behind to head across the Bering Sea with its penchant for fog and sudden storms to St. Michaels. And even then, we're only halfway there, Wyatt calculated. Each day's delay cut into the perilously short Arctic summer.

The boy's face flooded into his thoughts. As suddenly as his attack had come, his image jumped into Wyatt's mind as it had time and again since that night in San Francisco. The straight brown hair, iron eyes, and lean face haunted his thoughts. Wyatt frowned. Another added to the list of those who would rather see him dead was no novelty, but what was hard to understand was the youth's grim determination . . . and his face. Wyatt had seen that face a thousand times before. *It was his own countenance over thirty years ago.*

Josie tilted her face to look up at him. "You're thinking about that boy again, aren't you, Wyatt? The one at San Francisco? It wasn't your fault he drowned. He . . . he must have been drunk or so crazed with gold fever that he gambled on a wild jump to get aboard," she lied, knowing the truth was something far different.

"Josie," he said, smiling grimly, "Your pretty nose will grow if you don't stop fibbing. You know as well as I do that youth was with the other three on the wharf. That fellow with the rifle was no stampeder. He was a gunman, and that boy was trying to get to me. It was written all over his face."

"Well, you shouldn't blame yourself."

"I don't. What puzzles me is who was behind it all. And why."

Josie sat up. "You ought not to lie to me, either. You can say it. What really puzzles you, and me, is how much that youth looked like you. He could have been your son."

Earp nodded. His fingers tapped the knuckles of his other hand as he thought.

"Maybe Mattie—" He cut her off.

"I don't believe that rumor, Josie, not for one minute. If Mattie had had a baby she would have written me."

Josie snorted contemptuously. "You've still got a lot to learn about women, my darling husband. Thank God you still hold us on a pedestal, but we don't deserve your adoration. We can be as mean-spirited as weasels. Don't you know that Mattie hated us, and that Kate Elder fueled that hatred? I have no doubts in my mind the two of them would do anything to hurt you."

"Perhaps. But keeping my child from me—if there even was one—seems very hard." Wyatt stirred uneasily. This talk about offspring breached his self-imposed barrier about children. Since the death of their infant son last Easter, he'd taken great pains to avoid any talk of children with Josie. Yet she persisted.

"Well, that young man is past history, anyway," she said flatly. "We all saw him drowned."

Wyatt squinted past her to look out the porthole. The sunlight was playing across the crests of the waves. Rolling endlessly, the swell doggedly followed the ship, and Wyatt wondered if his past was following him as tenaciously as the water chased the vessel. A nagging sensation, more perception than firm idea, troubled him. Deep in his gut he sensed that disturbing youth still lived. And, like the waves, would be following him.

SIXTEEN

"Spoiled!" Captain Coffin's voice cracked with rage and a violent red color suffused his face as he spit the water from his mouth. He dipped the copper ladle again into the water cask and gave it a vigorous swirl before withdrawing another sample. This time he cautiously sniffed its contents before letting a drop fall on his tongue. The result was the same. He almost gagged until he wiped his mouth on his coat sleeve. He flung the dipper along the deck where it clattered over the planks before perversely slipping between the railings to drop over the side.

"Christ Almighty!" He punctuated that comment by kicking the entire water barrel over. Its emptied contents cast a nauseating flood across the deck. All the crew blanched at the smell, except the flies who went berserk in a mad effort to sop up the rank spillage.

"All the water barrels are the same. All the water has turned bad," Hennison responded, working hard to keep his manner deferential. "I checked them this morning."

The Chinese cook bobbed his head in agreement, his queue wagging like a dog's tail. In his hand he held the ship's teapot, the sole remaining supply of drinkable water for the entire ship. He held it like his life depended on it—which it did.

Coffin eyed him suspiciously while his fists clenched and unclenched in fury. He ducked his head into the overturned cask, fighting back the stench emanating from the bottom, to search for the causative agent. He suspected Hennison of poisoning the water with spoiled meat or tar. If this obnoxious bastard had, he'd hang him from yardarm, Coffin vowed.

But he found nothing. He wiped his hand along the bottom of the staves and withdrew it. His fingers bore a brownish stain that seeped from the wood and definitely smelled bad. Gingerly, the Captain touched one finger to the tip of his tongue. The stuff burned like acid.

"What is this?" he demanded of Hennison, presenting his fouled hand to the doctor. "Have you seen this before?"

Hennison winced as the fingers waved beneath his nose. He shook his head. "I have no idea, Captain. Something they used to seal the barrels, perhaps?"

"Damn their eyes! You're saying those bastards in Frisco sold me green kegs caulked with this crap to keep them from leaking before the wood swelled?"

"Quite possible," Hennison fought to strain the amusement from his voice. "I'm not an expert on water barrels," he added, keeping his tone as emotionless as possible. "But it appears to have just seeped out into the water. Yesterday, the water was fine."

Coffin tried to calm himself. He had survived many a disaster by holding on to his wits while others lost theirs. "What water do we have that's fit to drink?" he asked the cook.

Cook offered the teapot. His face remained expressionless but he measured the distance to the galley steps where safety and his meat cleaver resided. Coffin snatched the dented two-gallon pot, cradling it in his arms like the precious treasure it had now become.

Hennison leaned his back against the cookhouse hatch. " 'Water, water, everywhere, nor any drop to drink,' " he quoted.

"Shut up!" Coffin snapped.

"Merely quoting Samuel Coleridge's 'Rime of the Ancient Mariner,' sir," Doc said.

"I know what you were doing, and this is not a poetry class. You're trying to incite a mutiny, aren't you? Or scare me into turning back to Frisco? Well, it won't work." Coffin opened his sea coat and withdrew Nat's Colt Peacemaker, which he leveled at Hennison's grease-smudged apron.

"Not at all, Captain," the physician replied while he slipped behind the frightened cook, using as much of his squat body for cover as possible.

But for the tension in the air, Nathan would have laughed at the comical yet expert way Doc Hennison contorted his lanky frame to match the shape of the trembling Chinese chef. A laugh might cause the panicked Coffin to pull the trigger though, so he kept still. Carefully glancing over his shoulder, he saw the fear in the other crew member's faces. Even Frenchy's swarthy complexion appeared blanched. Nat recalled the talk in the forecastle by the sailors. Dying of thirst at sea ranked highest on their list of fears, up there with the ship catching fire and shark attacks. But to them death from thirst was the worst because it took an agonizingly long time, driving men to acts of madness.

"Everybody drop your knives on the deck now!" Coffin barked, waving the pistol in wide circles. "Then sit on top of the forecastle where I can watch you while I figure this out."

Grumbling their loyalty and innocence, the remaining five men clustered atop the sliding hatch and roof of the raised fore cabin that led to their quarters. Coffin retreated to the quarterdeck to lash the wheel, as the wind was freshening. Even from there the flickering of his beady eyes was noticeable to the men. Several minutes passed while Coffin ran below to return with his sextant and shoot the sun. After conferring with a tattered nautical almanac, his face lighted like the sun that illuminated the sky overhead. Stowing his instruments, he marched back to confront his crew.

"No reason to panic, men." He waved his chart authoritatively, poking his finger at a spot marked on the worn paper. "I've checked our position. We're one—two at the most—days out of Skagway. If these winds hold we'll be there by tomorrow night. We've enough water to see us there—if Frenchy doesn't take a bath."

A laugh erupted from the men. The tension dissolved like fog before the warming sun, and wide smiles lit the men's faces. Everyone knew Frenchy hated bathing.

"Now pick up your knives and get back to work. I'm not paying you to sit on your asses while there's work to be done," he commanded. Jamming the Colt back into his waistband, Coffin patted the shoulders and goodnaturedly cuffed the ears of his crew as they returned to their duties. But Nathan noticed his eyes watched them icily.

"Look at the pig," Hennison snorted. "Acts like he's running for mayor. No matter. He's doing just what I expected."

"You planned this, Doc?" the youth whispered. Coffin was not that far beyond earshot, and he was casting furtive glances at them.

"Yes, I did," Hennison replied proudly. "One of my more subtle applications of science, I must say. Shall I tell the captain how I did it?" he crowed. "He might appreciate it."

With that Hennison took a few steps in the captain's direction, but Nathan grabbed his sleeve.

"For God's sake, no! He's itching for a chance to hang you or shoot you, Doc."

"Posh, I'm not afraid of him." Hennison shrugged off Nat's restraining grip and took another stride toward the quarterdeck.

"Look." Nat realized a different tack was required to stop

Doc's headstrong self-destructive bent. "I know Coffin doesn't frighten you, but he'd only shoot you with my gun—*and that would make me feel bad.* You don't want that on your conscience, do you?"

Hennison looked crestfallen. "Well, I just have to tell someone. It's really clever, actually. Shall I tell you?"

"Okay, but keep your voice down. What did you do?"

"Gall bladders," Hennison announced proudly.

"Gall bladders? I don't understand."

"It's poetic justice, really. Perhaps call it the seal's revenge. Divested of their fur, I noted the similarity of the seal to the human body. So I dissected their internal organs to satisfy my curiosity." He paused to look up and cast an angelic smile in Coffin's direction. "I harvested a handful of those wretched animals' gall bladders while the others were busy skinning them. Remarkably similar, you know."

"You put the seal's gallbladders in the ship's water supply?"

"Yup. They don't float, so I dropped a few in each barrel yesterday. They promptly sank out of sight and did their dirty work. Their bile appears to have an affinity to the oak and attaches to the wood before dissolving into the water. I retrieved them before dawn and threw them over the side. How many damned bells that is, I can't keep straight. I think it was about four o'clock."

"Eight bells," Nat said. But his mind was racing through the possibilities. Skagway meant finding Wei-Li, and Earp would be there, too. When they got to Skagway, he and Doc would jump ship, quietly if possible. Otherwise, he'd fight his way off.

Doc continued, unaware that Captain Coffin was moving toward them. "I knew Coffin would have to put in at Skagway. It was the closest port to our position. Once there we jump . . ." He stopped as Nat directed a warning look over his shoulder.

"Did I hear the word *jump*, lads?" Coffin chortled as he strolled down the deck with the teapot in hand. "You boys wouldn't be thinking of taking French leave from the *Constance* once she hits Skagway, would you?"

"Certainly not, your honor," Hennison lied. He felt compelled to answer first as he felt no compunction about lying while he knew Nathan did. Why, the fool boy might feel honor bound to *ask for permission to leave.* "We're quite fond of this boat, aren't we, Nat?"

"She's a ship, not a boat," Coffin snapped. "Will you landlubbers never get that straight!" Then he caught himself and smiled with all the warmth he could muster. But the effect was that of a rattlesnake grinning at a pair of doomed mice. "Ever been to Skagway?" he inquired sweetly. "Either of you?"

Both Nat and Doc shook their heads.

Coffin patted the youth on his shoulder while still guarding his precious water. "It's an interesting place to visit. You'll see."

Warnings sounded in the back of Nathan's mind. "Why is that, Captain?" he asked.

"Well, lad, Skagway's at the mouth of a long, shallow inlet. With the great tides in Alaska, most of the inlet dries out at low tide. Did you happen to notice the moon lately?" He was enjoying this immensely and worked to prolong his surprise.

"The moon?" Hennison grunted. "No, I suppose its still up there, isn't it?"

"It's almost full," Nathan said.

"Ah, good lad. Very observant. We'll make a first-class seaman of you yet. Yes, it's a full moon. That means extreme tides."

A knot tightened in the depths of Nat's stomach. He began to grasp the reason for Coffin's glee.

Coffin read his mind. "Right, lad. The harbor will have low, low tides when we arrive. That means the *Constance* will be anchoring out from the town—*far out*—to keep out of shoal waters."

"How far?" Hennison asked. He'd finally realized Coffin's trap.

"One, maybe two miles offshore," the captain chuckled. "You might get a good look at Skagway through my telescope, but most you'll see is two miles of mud and muck across the mud flats. So the only visiting we'll be doing is taking on water from the flat-bottomed barges that'll bring us fresh water. They're the only things that have a shallow enough draft to make way." He tucked the teapot under his arm and backed away, still smiling.

"Damn!" Hennison swore.

Coffin's smile broadened until it threatened to crack the skin of his cheeks, being as that skin was unfamiliar with this facial maneuver. "Oh, and don't be thinking about taking a stroll over the flats. That's been the end of many a fool's life. The silt and muck will suck you down worse than quicksand. If it doesn't swallow you up entirely, it'll hold you until the tide rolls back in, and you drown in the icy water. But don't take my word about it. You'll see for yourself tomorrow night. You'll see I'm right."

The captain watched the shock register on Nathan's face with interest. He congratulated himself on second-guessing the boy, but his greatest satisfaction came with the show of rage that colored the physician's countenance. The man was close to being apoplectic, he noted happily. Unduly pleased with himself, Coffin sauntered back to the quarterdeck to supervise the change of course to Skagway.

But Coffin was wrong, at least about reaching Skagway by the next evening. The winds died, leaving the *Constance* to wallow in an oily sea that scarcely reflected a ripple of wind. Without wind the morning fog remained, turning into a golden haze as the sun rose. The sails hung limply from the spars, wafting weakly with the ship's roll like seedy laundry. The lines drooped and swayed, and the men's thirst grew.

Two days passed, then three, and the weight of the two-gallon teapot lightened with each half gill of water Coffin rationed out to the drying and cracking mouths of his crew. As their tongues swelled, the sailors' moods darkened. Hostile stares and odd mumblings followed the captain as he stalked about the deck, keeping an increasingly tight grip on the water pot. In response Coffin took to his cabin where he propped himself facing the door with Nat's loaded Colt in hand. There he sat, dozing in fitful starts and jumping at the slightest unfamiliar sound.

But Nature tired of a calm sea and the winds returned on the fourth night. Blowing briskly from the port quarter, they drove the ship toward land. All evening the winds held, and by sunrise the *Constance* came in sight of land.

Nathan had the deck watch when the sky in the east turned from mauve to a creamy orange. Watching Nature display its own fireworks while thinking about Wei-Li, his heart jumped when jagged mountain peaks abruptly rose out of the morning mists along with the sun. He blinked, but the peaks persisted, rising in layer upon layer, each shimmering in the distance with hidden promise.

"Land, land ho!" he hailed, and instantly Frenchy was at his side.

"Land she is, Nat. Alaska Territory, a land of sudden riches and sudden death," he rasped. Already his tongue jumped at the thought of drinking water and passed the news to his parched throat, causing him to swallow. "That's Cape Spencer, I'll wager. With these winds we'll take the North Passage through Icy Strait and then turn north off Rocky Island to head up the Lynn to Taiya Inlet."

The little Portuguese was correct in his assessment of Coffin's route. All that day Nathan watched the dark forested sides of Chichagof Island pass to starboard while the *Constance* wended her way between serrated islands that sprung from the sea like dragon's teeth. Rounding Rocky Island, the wind shifted due south to blow the sealer north along the Lynn Canal. By evening the ship entered the mouth of a narrow fjord leading to Skagway and Dyea, its northern neighbor. That was when Hennison astonished Nat with his next revelation.

"Ahead should be Skagway, Nat," the snake oil specialist announced like some tour director as he slipped alongside the youth. "Just beyond it is Taiya. It used to be mainly an Indian trading site with a narrow pass into the interior, but the gold rush has changed it into one more boom camp. Even the name is changed—to Dyea to make it easier to spell." He paused in his geography lesson to look astern. "Thank God we're way past Juneau. I was afraid Coffin might try to reprovision there. Luckily the wind's stayed southerly. He'd have had a hard beat to weather to turn down to Juneau."

"Juneau's the territorial capitol, isn't it?" Nat asked.

"Yes, it is. And it's got more law there than Skagway, so I figured Coffin would prefer to give it a wide berth if possible. This place only has an army garrison."

Nat frowned. "Seeing where we're heading, I don't understand why Coffin chose to go to Skagway, although I'm grateful whatever his reason. We're heading way into a narrow channel. Surely there must have been other places to take on water."

"Correct!" Hennison beamed. "But our noble skipper has a more compelling reason for visiting Skagway than water alone."

Nat searched his friend's glowing face for the answer to his extraordinary remark. "Are you so friendly with Captain Coffin that he now takes you into his confidence?"

Hennison feigned a hurt look. "Perish the thought. No, I simply read his ship's logs and diaries. For a closed-mouth lout, he's surprisingly detailed in his secret papers. I suspect he worries about missing a chance to turn a profit and annotates all his business to that aim."

Nat laughed at Hennison's childish glee. "You read Coffin's secret papers?"

"They were locked in his sea chest, as expected, but . . . " Doc paused to roll his eyes skyward. In doing so he sighted more of his faithful squadron of flies, prompting him to smash another dozen against the rigging. "I have a passion for opening locks. It's one thing a man can still do one-armed. Our friend is carrying a shipment of opium which he planned on dropping off to one Mr. Jefferson Smith in Skagway. Only he figured on completing the transaction on the way back from his sealing activities. Well, I changed those plans. I guessed he'd try to kill two birds, so to speak, by sailing here instead of Juneau or Douglas when I buggered his precious water."

"Jefferson Smith?" Nathan's brow knitted into a tight frown. "That's Soapy Smith, the man who bought Wei-Li."

Hennison winced at the reminder of his latest folly.

"I've been watching the shoreline, Doc." Nathan pointed to the bands of green sea lettuce and brown rows of mussels lying half exposed at the interface of each inlet with the now emerald green water. "Contrary to Coffin's predictions, I don't think we'll be reaching Skagway at extreme low tide. The slack winds foiled the skipper's plans by three days. There may be enough water to reach shore after all."

"Coffin will be guarding the skiff closer than his own purse. How do we get it away from him?"

"We don't. At the right time and with a little luck, Coffin might give us a ride ashore. That's if my plan works out."

"Great! A plan," Hennison chortled, rubbing his one palm against his pant leg in anticipation. "I love plans. What is it?"

"I'll tell you later."

"But . . . " Hennison protested. Disappointment filled his

213

voice, and he sulked like a three year old just denied a ginger cookie. "I want to know now. Don't you trust me?"

"No. I saw the way you baited Coffin over the water barrels. Another minute and I swear you'd have told him everything just to see him rage. We can't take that chance. This is too important."

★ ★ SEVENTEEN ★ ★

Twilight mixed with alpen glow, the arctic summer's rendition of night, flooded the tidal flats that split the low notch in the snow laced mountains surrounding Skagway. Two years before only Captain Billy Moore's trading post had marked this site. Now all that had changed. Every square inch of the lowlands between the tidal mud flats and the steep foothills held a building or a human being or both. Most were canvas-covered wall tents pitched shoulder to shoulder with wood framed flat-faced stores and sheet metal roofed saloons. Stores of goods, sacks of flour, tins of canned peas and soap stacked as high as the first stories filled whatever spaces remained. Poor Moore's house now sat squarely in the center of Fifth and State streets, causing a perpetual traffic problem.

Skagway's confusion extended to the water's edge and beyond. A mile offshore, freighters, square riggers, and vessels of all descriptions swung at anchor while a continuous string of barges, lighters, and flat-bottomed boats ferried goods and gold seekers around the clock. Trailing from the water's edge, continuous lines of men and mules trekked goods to the higher ground of the town. Like the mindless march of army ants, the strings worked day and night.

"Damn those teamsters!" Coffin stood in his grounded long-boat and swore at the men packing supplies across the shifting mud flats. Their feet churned the ooze into furrows that reeked of salt mixed with the pungent stench of rotting sea grass, yet they worked against the clock and the incoming tide.

"I don't give a rat's ass if it is a flood tide, I'm not paying five dollars an hour to these damned teamsters. It's robbery."

"But they have to pack twice as fast to beat the incoming tide, Captain," Frenchy said.

Coffin spit. "And they don't have as far to pack at high tide, either. No, it's robbery, that's what it is, and I won't pay one cent more than the two dollars they get for low-tide work. Kick those barrels out of the skiff. You and I will roll them ashore ourselves. While they're filled I'll complete my business with Soapy. His men will help us load the water—and for a decent price, I'm sure."

Frenchy's fears that Coffin would order him to roll the barrels across the tidal flats had come true. He had hoped to slip away to a saloon for a drink or maybe a quick roll with a whore while the casks were filling, but now he saw that dream fade. His heart sank. The next leg to the Aleutians would be long and dismal. Reluctantly, he wrestled the first oak barrel onto the seat of the longboat while Coffin checked the five-pound chest of opium in his arms. With a heave the seaman kicked the cask over the boat's gunnel where it spun crashing into the muck.

"Jesus Christ, be careful!" the barrel complained.

"What the devil?" Coffin snorted. "Who's in there?" He kicked the cask around to face the sealed bunghole. "Who's there?"

"No one but us sensitive hogsheads," the barrel answered. "Do treat us gently, I beg you, or we'll leak."

"The hell you say!" Coffin pried open the top with a crowbar and stood back with the bar raised to strike.

Doc Hennison popped up from the interior of the vat, smiling devilishly. "Perhaps I should say I'd piss myself if you gave me another such tumble rather than leak."

"Trying for French leave, eh?" Coffin cried. "But you've given me opportunity to stave in your head."

"Me first!" Hennison said. He struck first, delivering a lightning blow with the bungspreader he held in his left hand. The maul nailed Coffin squarely between his eyebrows, knocking him senseless. Coffin's eyes crossed and, emitting a hissing sound like air escaping from a balloon, he flopped backwards into the mud.

Still ensconced in his keg Hennison leaned forward to inspect his handiwork. "That's for your foul treatment of my friend, Nathan, and this is for mine. . . . " He raised the bungspreader over his head.

"Drop the striker!" Frenchy commanded. In his hand he held the Colt Peacemaker that had fallen from Coffin's waistband with Doc's first blow. "Drop it or I'll blow a hole in your guts."

Hennison's arm stalled in midair as he turned toward the First Mate. "You can't be serious, Frenchy," he said. "You'd shoot me to save this scum. I don't believe it."

"Believe it. He's still my captain."

Hennison's eyes narrowed as he inspected the inert Coffin. "This may be a moot discussion. I may have done for the tyrant already."

"Then I shoot you now," Frenchy said flatly. "Nothing personal, but I don't want hang for mutiny—not unless I start it myself. And I didn't start this."

Before he could pull the trigger, the second water barrel opened, and Nathan emerged. From Frenchy's position beside the skiff, his pistol barrel now covered Nathan. The youth's body stood between him and Doc.

"Move aside, Nat. I don't want shoot you," the little man commanded, waving the gun in tight circles. The whole process unnerved him, and Nathan's presence simply made matters worse. As a young sailor himself, he had witnessed the hanging of three mutineers. That left a lasting impression with him, but he had no stomach to shoot his young friend.

"I can't let you shoot Doc, Frenchy. Can't you just let us go? We don't belong on the *Constance*, you know that. Just let us slip away," Nat pleaded.

"How do I say I got a dead skipper, tell me that?"

As if on cue Coffin groaned.

"Damn," Doc swore. "I hit him hard enough to break my arm, and it didn't split his skull."

"See! He's not dead," Nathan exclaimed. "Now you can let us go. Tell him you found him unconscious, that he must have slipped getting out of the skiff. He won't remember what happened."

"Hopefully, he won't even remember how to piss," Doc added. "But I suppose that would be too much to ask for."

Frenchy struggled with the dilemma, torn between years of forced loyalty to his hateful captain and his desire to help this lad who saved his life. The indecision flowed across his face like roiling clouds until he heaved a great sigh and nodded his head. The pistol shifted down to point at the shallow waves lapping at their feet and threatening to cover Coffin's mouth.

"Go," the mate ordered. "Run fast and hide. You save my life, and I told you I don't forget it. Now, we're squared. Maybe the captain think you two not worth the trouble to look for. I think there plenty men here who need passage out of Skagway, and Doc's a lousy sailor."

Nathan grinned and extended his hand, but Hennison shuffled closer also, eyeing the revolver, and that scared Frenchy. While he knew Nathan wouldn't shoot him, he lacked the same trust in Hennison.

"Go, quick," he directed, stepping back while waving the gun barrel in the direction of the high ground where harried teamsters and natives were racing against the tide with their loads. A few cast curious looks back at the doings around the longboat, but no one stopped or offered to intervene. Skagway was a wide open town, and these men knew a blind eye kept one healthy.

Nathan grabbed Doc's sleeve and backed away from Frenchy. When they had moved beyond a reasonable shot, the two spun around and dashed across the tidal flats. Hennison loped along, grateful to have solid ground beneath his feet, while Nathan skipped beside him in unrestrained joy, spattering his trousers with clods of mud. He was on land, in the same town as his beloved Wei-Li, and near to a showdown with the one man whose death would settle past wrongs and make him rich. How he would rescue his love, he had not the faintest notion, but he knew he would.

In his youthful exuberance, skipping over the musky flats, Nathan Blaylock failed to note he had set foot on the mysterious soil of Alaska. Little did he realize this was the beginning of strange and frightening adventures in this frozen land. The footprints he left in the mud would soon vanish with the incoming tide, but Alaska would leave marks on him that would never fade.

EIGHTEEN

"Now let me do the talking, Nat," Doc cautioned his friend. "This Soapy apparently owns this town. That sounds like he's a first-class con man. Someone of my own stature. We talk the same language."

The two stood outside a square-faced, white-frame building with a shiny tin roof. A door to the right of two curtained windows still sported red, white, and blue bunting from the Fourth of July celebration four days ago. Across the facing hung a huge sign proclaiming JEFF SMITH'S PARLOR.

"It looks like a bank to me," Nathan said. "Are you sure this is the right Jeff Smith?"

"No doubt about it. He built this place to look like a bank, but no one was stupid enough to deposit their money with him. It seems his past brushes with the law in Creede, Colorado, caught up with him. So he turned this into an oyster parlor with gambling, liquor, and ladies added to the menu. The bartender boasted this Soapy has his fingers in every confidence game and protection racket in Skagway. And he's apparently not adverse to murder if it suits his purpose."

"Do you think Wei-Li's in there?" Nathan asked, his voice sounding unnaturally high. "Being so close to her gives me a lump in my throat," he explained.

Hennison shot him a disgusted look. "I'll bet it gives you a lump in your pants as well, but for God's sake don't let on you know her. If you do, we're sunk. Soapy's probably got a nose like a ferret for profit, and if he finds out you're love-struck over this bitch, he'll ransom her for the queen's jewels."

Nathan gave his friend a sharp look. "She's not a bitch, Doc. I love her, and I plan to marry her."

"God help us!" Hennison swore. "Can you hear yourself, lad? Marry her? What would your father, Wyatt Earp, say about that? I doubt he'd give you his blessing. But, then I forgot, we won't need it since we plan to kill him."

"Damn you!" Choking with rage, Nat clutched the muddied front of Hennison's shirt, his right hand cocked in a fist.

Hennison saw the hurt his words had caused and instantly regretted his acid tongue. "I'm sorry, Nat. I . . . I've got too sharp a tongue for my own good. I didn't mean that. If you want to marry Wei-Li, more power to you. I'd be happy to stand as your best man."

Nathan released his grip as the door to Jeff Smith's opened. Two burly men wearing bowler hats and ill-fitting suits stepped onto the boardwalk followed by a short man with a wide-brimmed white hat. The hat sat on the back of the man's head at a jaunty angle, exposing a forelock of dark brown hair that matched the thick beard covering his face. The man's equally dark suit and loose tie combined with his lanky frame gave the illusion that he was much taller. The rest wore bowlers or soft slouch hats.

"You boys look the worse for wear," he said, appraising them with small, darting, weasel eyes. His henchmen grunted in chorus.

Hennison brushed the dried segments of mud from his coat. "Looks can be deceiving, Mr. Smith. We're actually eccentric millionaires in search of adventure."

Soapy's startled look dissolved in laughter. "So you know who I am," he said. "I suppose you'd like to invest some of your millions in my bank."

"Actually, no. We'd rather make a deposit with your whores." Hennison stood stock still as Smith stepped into the rutted street to walk slowly around the two. His gang of bodyguards parted their coats to expose revolvers stuck in their belts. From the doorway another appeared with a Winchester clutched in his hands.

"You boys wouldn't be sent here by the Committee of 101, would you?" Smith asked. A hard edge crept into his voice, although he acted unconcerned. His hands remained in his pockets, but the sound of the Winchester chambering a round reached them. "That wouldn't be your game, would it? To make trouble for old Soapy?"

"Never heard of this committee. No, we've just arrived in town, and I heard you were the man to see. Personally, I'm not partial to committees. They tend to be overly puffed up with themselves and prone to piles."

"You're a doctor?"

Hennison bowed. "The best one-armed surgeon in Alaska. At your service."

"Probably the only one-armed surgeon in Alaska," Soapy retorted. "But you've got sand, I'll give you that. Who's your silent friend?"

"Nat Blaylock." Hennison dropped his voice. "As deadly a killer with a six-gun as I am with a scalpel. Don't let his baby face fool you. We're offering you our services."

"I've got all the help I need."

Hennison played his trump card, sensing Smith feared this committee he had mentioned. "I wouldn't place my life in the hands of these rabbit turds, not with the Committee of 101 riled up."

Soapy stepped back. "Hear that, boys? This fool here thinks you-all are rabbit shit." Smith's Georgia accent drawled the last word. "What do you think about that?"

One of the henchmen, a square-jawed fellow with ham

hands stepped forward and thrust his face close to Nathan's. "I'm Skagway Jim," he growled, exposing a mouthful of rotted teeth. "I was killing men while you was sucking on yer mama's teat."

Nat watched the man. He studied the Schofield stuck in the man's pants. The hammer was cocked, but the revolver had slipped down so that only half the trigger guard and the grip were visible. Skagway Jim would be hard pressed for a quick draw with it buried the way it was. Still, as tired and hungry as he was, Nathan had no wish to fight. He decided to apologize for Doc's troublesome tongue. But before he could, Hennison slipped behind him and leered at Skagway Jim over Nathan's shoulder.

"I heard he was sucking on *your* mama's teat," Hennison snickered.

Skagway Jim's face turned purple, and he reached for the revolver in the front of his waistband. Jim Riley's training and hours of practice saved Nathan. Instantly his own hand shot out, holding the revolver immobile while his fingers clamped down on Skagway's hand. The pistol exploded in a muffled roar. The front of Skagway Jim's pants erupted in smoke and flames, and the man dropped to his knees clutching the dark stain widening in the front of his smoking trousers. His lips formed a perfect circle moments before high-pitched screams spilled from its opening, and then Jim flopped face down in the dirt to lurch about in agony.

Smith's gaze snapped up from his wounded henchman to see that Nat held the gun now, and it was aimed at his chest. His eyes widened. "Goddamn! He was my best man," he stammered. Soapy stepped over his wounded guard to extend his right hand. "Damn, that was slick. But now I'm shorthanded, and it couldn't come at a worse time. Do you want a job?"

Nat kept the pistol on Soapy while he cocked his head toward the man with the rifle. "Tell him to drop the Winchester, and the same goes for the guy behind the lace curtain."

"Do as he says, boys," Soapy shouted. The guns clattered onto the wooden walk. A glint of admiration filled his dark eyes as he straightened slowly, being careful to keep his hands away from his sides. "I'm not packing a gun. What was your name again? In all the excitement I missed it."

"Nat Blaylock," Hennison repeated. "We're a team."

Smith paused to chuckle. "Up until now I thought I didn't need another man with all the help I'm paying for." His mood changed abruptly like a clap of thunder, and he stopped to plant a vicious kick into the back of the moaning Skagway Jim. "But I was wrong! Almost dead wrong!" He waved his right hand cautiously at his other men while keeping his eye on Nat. "Boys, drag this worthless piece of shit out of my sight. I hope he dies. He almost got me killed."

Hennison squatted over the groaning Skagway. He pulled up Jim's shirt and opened the front of his pants to examine the wound. "He may if infection sets in. Looks like the bullet went through his thigh just below the hip. But it missed his family jewels. He'll be laid up for some time, I'm afraid."

Smith just shrugged. "Skagway Jim's past history now. I have to deal with the present, and the present is giving me a pain in the behind. I offered you a job, do you want it or not?"

"Like Doc said, we're a team," Nathan said.

"Fifty dollars a week for the pair of you and I'm being generous. I don't need a doctor on my payrolls right now. I'm concerned with *undoing* the health of those damned committee members more than anything else."

"Okay, you got yourself two new men," Nat said. He twirled the revolver in a road agent's spin for effect and handed it butt first to Soapy.

"Good. Let's have a drink inside. I don't like to be standing out in the middle of the street while you two make my men look bad. It's bad for my image. You never know who's watching."

Nathan followed Hennison and Smith into his parlor. The interior was long and narrow, with a polished wooden bar running half the length. Swirling wallpaper contrasted with a gaudy circle and square patterned linoleum covering the floor. In the front corner a potbellied stove glowed smugly while the smoke disappeared out a stovepipe that ran up the far wall then snaked along half the ceiling before exiting through the roof.

Soapy leaned against the bar while a white-coated bartender hurried from the other end with a bottle of whiskey in hand. "My own private stock," Smith boasted. He looked hard at his reflection in the mirror behind the bar. Nat followed his gaze as it covered the crossed American and Cuban flags on the walls and the framed pictures of bare-chested prize fighters and alluring women in seductive poses.

The gang leader emptied his shot glass with one swallow as did Doc. Nathan only sipped his. The last time he drank in a bar his world had been a very different place: Both it and he were guileless then. That almost cost him his life. He was learning that caution was a valuable item to have in saloons.

Soapy encircled the room with his wave. "Just four days ago, I was cock of all of Skagway. I rode my white horse at the head of the Fourth of July parade. Even got a letter from the president of the United States. McKinley himself wrote thanking me for my offer to raise a company of volunteers to fight the Spanish. Of course he turned me down, but he wrote me, and that's the important thing. Me! Jefferson Randolph Smith, king of Skagway!"

He paused to down another shot. Doc, wishing to demonstrate his good manners, matched him. Smith stared glumly at the curtained back of the saloon. "Even got a brand new China whore. A real looker! Just off the boat. But, I haven't had time to even piss since that son of a bitch Stewart's been whining all over town. He's stirring up a damned hornet's nest of trouble for me. Now the honest citizens want my hide. They took my money readily enough for their stupid charities, but now they're banding together to run me out."

Nat's back stiffened, and his fingers tightened imperceptibly on his glass while his eyes searched the back for signs of Wei-Li. Doc noted his change, and so did Soapy, but the man misread Nathan's actions.

"Oh, you like yellow girls, boy? They come with lots of tricks. Maybe I'll let you have first crack at her. Sort of a signing bonus. You'd like that, would you?"

Nathan forced himself to grin.

Smith nodded to the barkeep, a wide-shouldered man with equally wideset blue eyes and a black hedge for a mustache. "Boners here wouldn't," Smith snickered. "He's taken with her, himself. Offered to pay two hundred dollars in gold to be first. Didn't you, Jack? Maybe I should let the two of you fight for her."

The bartender glowered at Nat. He deliberately raised a shot glass in his beefy hand, held it before Nat's face. His fist tightened, his neck muscles stood out like cords above his shirt collar, and the glass broke to pieces with a sharp crack. Boners opened his hand and let the blood-flecked shards of glass rattle to the bar in front of his rival. Hennison studied the fragments intently while Nat simply grinned. Doc patted his friend on the shoulder.

"Very impressive Mr. Boners, but Nat here can break a shot glass with his dick," Doc said.

The bartender swore and turned away. Soapy Smith laughed, and Nat turned a bright red; but it broke the tension.

"Maybe later," Smith said. "Right now I need every hand."

"What started all this?" Nathan asked, glad the conversation had moved away from Wei-Li.

"Hell, nothing unusual. We fleeced this miner, J. D. Stewart, of his poke. Not much either. Twenty-seven hundred dollars."

"That's what you get for being nice, Soapy," the henchmen named Tripp growled. "We should have cut his throat and dumped him into the sea."

"You're right, Jim. I act kind and look what it gets me," Smith agreed. "That wimp Stewart is whining to anyone who'll listen about how he got robbed instead of taking his loss like a man and keeping his mouth shut. I bet he's told every living soul in Skagway."

"Get rid of this Stewart, and things should quiet down, I'd think," Hennison opined.

"It ain't so easy now. The Committee of 101 have got hold of him. That damned vigilante crowd is down at the wharf now drinking up their courage to come up here and kick my ass. Did you see any suspicious activity when you came through?"

Nathan shook his head, realizing full well that he and Hennison were running flat out from Captain Coffin when they passed the wharf. "No, we didn't see anything."

"Well, Frank Reid is the only one I worry about. The rest are storekeepers who'd shit in their pants at the first gunfight. But Reid's different. He helped survey the town and thinks he owns the damned place. He's tough, used to fight Indians, but I think I can bluff him." Smith paused to rub his beard in contemplation. "Reid packs a pistol, though. How would you handle him, Nat?"

"Talk to him alone. Get him away from the others, so they can't hear what you say. He won't have to act brave for them that way. Buy him off if you can. And bring a rifle, just in case. . . . " He ignored the incredulous stares from Doc.

"Good idea, kid. That ought to trick him. But maybe I should bring the boys—for backup."

"I'd keep them out of sight, if I were you," Nathan continued. "Reid won't come out alone if he sees the whole gang.

He'll bring the rest of the committee, and they'll probably follow him. If what you say is correct, this Reid is their leader. Without him the others will fade away."

"Damn, kid." Soapy beamed. "I like the way you think. I was figuring the same thing: Buy off Reid or bluff him into leaving town. And carry a bigger gun, that's a great idea."

The saloon's door burst open and one of Soapy's men, Jackson, dashed inside. "Soapy," he gasped while trying to catch his breath. "You better do something quick! Half of the committee are talking about running you out of town tonight!"

"Are they still meeting down by the wharf?" Smith asked.

Jackson's head bobbed. "Yeah, and Frank Reid is guarding the walkway. He's got his pistol on, Soapy, bold as brass."

"By himself? Is he alone?"

"He was when I ran here."

"Great!" Soapy rubbed his hands together in anticipation. "Now I've got him. Boners, give me that Winchester you keep behind the bar. I'm going to pay Reid a little visit. Nat here thinks I can bluff him, and I agree. It's time to put an end to this committee crap, boys."

Boners handed the rifle to his boss. "I don't know, Soapy. What if this kid is wrong? I hear Reid's a fair shot."

Soapy smiled. "I'm not stupid, Boners. How do you think I built my gang—by not taking risks? You know that. Hell, I'm no gambler. All my games are rigged, and I plan on rigging this game, too. You and the rest of the gang slip down Broadway. Hide out somewhere near the Burkhard House or Getz and Donovon's and sneak around behind our friend Reid. Get the drop on him, but don't let him see you. If I can't buffalo him into playing along or leaving town, you plug him."

Boners smiled crookedly. "Great idea, boss. But what about these two? I still don't trust them."

Soapy scratched his beard. "Bring them along with you. Give them ax handles instead of guns. That way you can keep an eye on them, and they can still be useful if a fight with the others breaks out."

Smith opened the door, shifted the repeater in his hands, and winked back at his men. "Okay, men. You all know the plan. If Reid even looks at his pistol, help me out."

Boners and another man, Slim Jim, watched Soapy saunter down the planked walk that led to the wharves. The half dozen others grabbed weapons and filled their pockets with cartridges. Someone handed Nat and Doc wooden ax handles.

Boners cast a withering stare at the two while he fingered his shotgun. "Don't shoot yerselves with those clubs, boys," he joked maliciously. "They might be loaded. And we'll put you gunfighters in the front row so's you can get a good look. You never know, you might have to dodge lead from both sides. Then we'll see how good you are."

"You'd like that wouldn't you, Boners?" Hennison retorted.

"Yup. It'd suit me just fine."

Without another word the gang herded their two new recruits toward the back door. Ducking under a curtain, Nathan caught a glimpse of a narrow hallway off to his right leading to a row of doors.

Hennison saw them, too, and whispered to his friend. "Those must be the cribs for the dollies, Nat. My bet is she's in there."

Boners stopped at the head of the group. "Give you guys a look of what you ain't never gonna have," he gloated. "Bring out that China girl," he shouted down the corridor.

The third door opened and a bucktoothed girl with a face pockmarked from smallpox emerged. Dressed in a frilly nightgown still sporting remnants of marabou feathers near the neckline, she smiled knowingly, then dragged Wei-Li into the hall. The Chinese girl's eyes widened as she saw Nathan.

"Nathan!" she cried as she broke free of the woman's grasp and dashed to his side.

"Goddamn! It's a trick!" Boners cursed and swiveled in the confined hallway. The double barrels of his twelve-gauge swung up to blast Nathan.

But Hennison drove his knee into the bartender's groin while he guided the butt of his ax handle into the center of Boners's face. The seasoned oak slammed the gang member's head against the wall, splintering his nose, half blinding him with splattering blood, and causing him to jerk the triggers. Both barrels of double-ought buckshot exploded with an ear-splitting roar to shatter the first door and fill the narrow passage with acrid smoke.

Pandemonium erupted. Men, dazed by the blasts and frightened by the bellows of the wounded Boners, slipped and tumbled over themselves as they struggled to use their weapons in the packed hall. Adding to the chaos was Hennison, wielding his staff like a true musketeer. With Nat dragging Wei-Li behind him, Hennison hacked an escape route through the very center of the gang, lopping half-drawn pistols out of hands and repeating his successful thrusts to any available face.

Nathan shattered a window frame with his shoulder and plunged through the side window with Wei-Li wrapped in his arms. He hit the dirt rolling. Instantly he was on his feet and running down the alley with Hennison close on his heels. Behind them, Soapy's gang came pouring out the back door like angry hornets. A rifle cracked and a bullet snapped past Nathan's ear, leaving the smell of rotten eggs in its wake.

"Over there!" Doc shouted, pointing to a cleft in the frame buildings to their left. "Make for that opening!"

Nathan darted for the bolt hole like a scalded rabbit; but his boot skidded on the loose scree, and he slid sideways into the space.

Suddenly a figure loomed over him, filling the opening. Wei-Li screamed and twisted out of Nathan's grasp. The blued barrel of a rifle flashed in the man's hands while the shadows hid the rest of him. Nathan swung at this new threat, but he was off balance, and the figure easily parried his blow. The other man's fist caught Nathan on the side of his jaw, stunning him. Nathan dropped his stick and sprawled onto his back, head spinning. The sun still backlit the figure, hiding his face in shadow.

The man raised his rifle, turned, and sent a volley of shots crashing into Soapy's gang. Several crumpled, and the rest retreated back into Jeff's Parlor.

"Ain't you remembered nothin' I taught you, boy," the figure drawled. "First rule of a gunfight: Always bring a gun!"

Nathan looked up into the weathered face of Jim Riley.

"Jim!" Nathan blurted. "Am I glad to see you! I thought I'd never see you again!"

"Yeah." Riley glanced down at the youth, halfheartedly hiding his delight at finding his friend alive. "And I thought you was dead. Here I'm walking down a sidestreet, looking for Soapy Smith, and you nearly knock me down."

He paused to fire at a gang member foolhardy enough to open the back door. The bullet splintered the door frame, and the door slammed shut. Riley cast a disapproving look at Hennison who was trying his best to fit his body into a three-inch space between the buildings. Soapy's men had regained their wits and were returning sporadic fire. Each bullet that struck close by prompted the doctor to redouble his efforts to achieve the impossible.

"And as usual, yer up to yer ass in wolverines. I suspect it has a lot to do with the company you keep." Riley snorted. "Associating with this snake oil salesman will only git you hung."

"I'm glad to see you, too, Mr. Riley," Doc replied sourly. "Next to hemorrhoids and being shot at, you're at the top of my list of disagreeable things."

"Well, I'm glad we're all together, again," Nat said. He leapt to his feet and hugged the grizzled gunfighter warmly. "And I know you and Doc are too, even if you'd rather die than admit it."

Both Riley and Hennison made nondescript grumbling noises. Nathan knew his assessment was correct. But a hail of bullets from Smith's saloon forced an end to the reunion. The three men edged deeper into the side-alley and formed a protective shield around Wei-Li.

"Why were you looking for Soapy Smith, Jim?" Nathan asked.

Riley squinted down his rifle barrel and fired into the saloon's back window. "I heard he was a gambling buddy of Wyatt's, and I thought he might know his whereabouts."

"Wyatt Earp's not here?" Nat stuttered.

"Nary a hide nor hair of him," Riley replied. "And I've combed this burg for the last three days. He ain't been seen by nobody."

Hennison slid down the wooden-slatted side of a wall tent to sit disgustedly in the dirt. "What happened to our cakewalk into Frisco to blast Earp and collect our easy money? Since then we've fought off angry miners, a sea captain who's Ahab's mad brother, and Soapy Smith's gang, and all we have to show for it is the tattered shirts on our backs. I'm thinking of resigning my exalted commission in this claptrap army."

"Before you do," Riley said, poking a suspicious bulge in Doc's shirt with his rifle, "why don't you open yer poor, tattered shirt and show us what the lump yer carrying is?"

"What? Oh, this?" Hennison withdrew a packet wrapped in oilskin. "Bless me! In all the excitement of rescuing the little lady and seeing your kind face again, Riley, I . . . I plum forgot about this. I was meaning to share it with you-all, honestly."

The pouch clinked as Hennison set it in his lap and unfolded the corners. Wei-Li gasped as the greasy edges opened to expose a mass of golden double eagles. Hennison smiled up at them apologetically.

"Forgot, did you?" Riley growled.

Doc looked to Nat for help. His grin turned sheepish. "Ah, Captain Coffin had this locked up with his papers. It's small restitution for the way he misused us, Nat. Don't you agree?"

"Well, who am I to judge. I'm basing my future on killing my own father for a reward," Nathan answered. "But if Earp isn't here, where is he?"

"He ain't in Skagway," Riley said. "He could have slipped past and landed in Dyea to go inland by Chilkoot Pass, but that don't seem likely. My guess is he's taking the All-Water Route."

"Christ!" Nat swore. "We can't chase him that way."

Hennison refolded his stolen gold pouch and slipped it back into his shirt. He saw a chance to redeem himself. "Look, gold is the key. Earp is heading for the gold fields in the Klondike, by whatever route. If we get to there, we'll find him. He'll come to us."

Riley scratched the back of his head. "I guess yer right. I didn't think of that. How did you two get here, anyways? Last I saw of Nat, you was playing fish, and Doc, you was drowning yerself in whiskey."

"It's a long story." Hennison bristled at the reminder of his folly. Somehow, letting Nathan down by selling Wei-Li hurt more than anything he could remember in a long time. Of course, that didn't prevent him from cheating his friend out of Coffin's gold. Hennison found this dichotomy puzzling and strangely unnerving. "And how did *you* get here, I might ask."

"First class all the way," Riley said, beaming. "I went looking for passage down at the Frisco docks, and they was looking for bodyguards for this German duke and his lady going to Skagway on a lark. His agent gave me a hard time till I shot the cigar out of his mouth. His Dukeness hired me on the spot. Champagne and cigars and pretty girls for the whole week." He looked appreciatively at the silk sheath dress that clung to Wei-Li as tightly as she clung to Nathan. "I tell you, Nat. I'm feeling younger and friskier than I thought possible. Old age is a heap easier to take if'n you got money."

"Where's your duke now? Maybe I might interest him in some poker," Hennison asked. Money always attracted him.

"No chance. He landed at Skagway, took one look around, and slipped in the mud and fell flat on his royal arse. Right then and there that spoiled Alaska for him. He seemed to think everyone here would hear about that, as if we gave a fart about what he done. So he paid me a month's wages in advance and sailed back to civilization. Don't that beat all?"

Sporadic rifle fire continued to chip and splinter the doorway where the four of them huddled. A close shot sent a wooden sliver knifing across Nathan's cheek. Wei-Li dabbed at the red line dripping down his face, but he waved her hand away.

"Those boys are getting our range," Riley commented. "Must be all the practice they're putting in taking potshots at us. We better think of something fast. Got any ideas?"

"Let me try this," Nat said. He selected an egg-sized stone from the alley which he lobbed across the alley. The stone arched high into the air before striking the side of a hardware store on the far side of Soapy's place. After two more attempts, Nathan succeeded in getting the rocks to ricochet off the store into the opposite side of the saloon. Riley used the opportunity to fire back from their side of the alley as well. With all the shooting from both sides filling the air with smoke and sound, the stones gave the illusion of Jeff Smith's Parlor being caught in a crossfire. Some of the gang began firing at the windows and doorway of the hardware store.

"Hot damn, that's got them confused, Nat, boy," Hennison crowed between the noise. "Where did you learn to throw rocks like that?"

"The orphanage," Nat replied. "Where did you learn to use

a stick like you did back there? You looked like the greatest swordsman in all of France."

"Reverend Baker's Preparatory School for Young Men back in Tennessee," Hennison answered proudly. "We learned fencing, equestrian skills, manners, and moral principles. I regret to say I have forgotten the latter two."

"Hold your fire!" a voice inside Soapy's shouted while a white bar towel waved through the doorway. "Hold your fire! We got some wounded men in here."

Hennison jumped to his feet and boldly exposed himself, waving his ax handle like a commander's sword. "We've got you surrounded. Come out with your hands up, or we'll set the place on fire and burn you out!"

"Who the hell are you, anyways?" a voice yelled.

"Special detachment of the Committee of 101, and we got over fifty men surrounding you."

"Shit!" the voice retorted. "Don't seem like fifty is shooting at us. Ain't more than twenty of you, and that's a fact."

"We're not all shooting because we don't want to hit each other by accident. Only our sharpshooters are firing at this time," Hennison lied. "Surrender or we'll burn you rascals out." He enjoyed center stage and couldn't resist hamming it up.

"Damn! Sharpshooters!" another voice responded.

"You ain't gonna burn us out. You'd set half the damned town on fire if you did," the first crook replied.

"We're prepared to rebuild," Hennison shouted. "You have five minutes to answer."

Riley reached out and dragged Hennison offstage. "Damn, Doc, if they all surrender, what are we gonna do with 'em? Could be a dozen men in there for all I know. They'll see there's only the four of us."

Hennison raised his eyebrows. "Good point. I hadn't thought of that. Got any ideas?"

"How about a truce?" Nathan suggested.

In an instant Doc was back in the alley, addressing the gang and hammering out his terms for a ceasefire. The gang was to stay put until "his committee" sent medical help while the four "Special Agents of the Committee of 101" were to be allowed safe passage back to the wharf. Any violation, such as a gang member sticking his head out of the saloon, would be met with an instant fire attack on the parlor, Hennison warned sternly.

Those inside quickly agreed, and "Colonel" Hennison just as rapidly escorted his special agents down the alley toward the wharf. Any minute Nat expected to feel the impact of a bullet striking his back as he shielded Wei-Li, but that never came. They darted out of the alley at the first opportunity and hurried down Broadway turning onto Fifth Street. Ahead lay the timbered posts and planked sidewalk leading to the wharf. Hennison suddenly thrust out his arm and stopped them just inside the shadows of the shops.

"What is it?" Nathan asked. Being just behind his girl, he was third in line while Riley covered their rear. He slipped past Wei-Li to look where Doc was pointing.

"Soapy Smith," Doc whispered.

Immediately ahead Soapy Smith stood facing a squarish man with a dark mustache drooping past the corners of his broad chin. A short tie hung from his neck to end a good hand's breadth above his ample belly. Smith held his Winchester in both hands pointed low at his opponent, while the other held a pistol in his right hand. The scene gave the appearance of a coyote confronting a bear.

Riley squeezed past the girl to look over Nathan's shoulder. "That's Frank Reid," he said. "I met him once in Arizona. He used to fight Indians. He's a tough nut."

"I'm not getting out of town!" Soapy yelled. "No matter what!" He swung the rifle menacingly at Reid. "Get him, boys! Shoot him down!"

"What the hell! An ambush!" Reid raised his pistol directly at Soapy's chest, and his finger pulled the trigger. The hammer dropped, but nothing happened. "Misfire!" Reid snarled.

"Wait! Don't shoot!" Soapy cried.

But Reid thundered his hammer again, and this time the pistol fired. The bullet hit Smith square in the left breast. His finger jerked reflexively, and his Winchester exploded.

"Soapy got it in the heart," Riley judged impassively as he watched the two men fall to the sidewalk.

"He was planning to have his gang bushwack Reid," Nathan said. "We threw a monkey wrench in his scheme when we pinned them down in his saloon."

Smith lay flat on his back, arms outstretched, staring up at the empty sky with unseeing eyes. A dark stain spread slowly across the left side of his starched, white linen shirt. Only his right foot twitched for a second. Reid knelt on the boards, bent forward until his head touched the walk while both hands tried vainly to staunch a bright, red flow pouring from his groin.

"Gut shot, poor bastard." Riley finished his analysis.

Hennison nodded solemnly. "I agree. He'll probably last a week or two in great pain. I think Soapy won that hand, or at most I'd call it a draw."

These latest and closest shots brought the rest of the committee boiling out of the nearest warehouse. The distant gunfire between Riley and Soapy's gang alerted them that something was up, and Frank Reid had gone to check on the disturbance while his committee of shopkeepers, tradesmen, and disgruntled miners waited.

Soapy, too, had wondered what was happening, but he made the fatal assumption his gang was outflanking a probing party of the vigilantes. Confident that his trap was set, Jefferson Randolph Smith walked boldly into his destiny—a bullet from Frank Reid and a secure place in the turbulent annals of the Alaskan gold rush.

Now the vigilantes rushed onto the walkway, armed to the teeth to find their leader grievously wounded and Soapy dead. Long pent-up feelings of fear and anxiety exploded into rage. Shouts for tar and feathers as well as ropes filled the air as Reid was helped to the nearest doctor. Soapy was dragged ingloriously like a dog to the undertaker where he was photographed and autopsied with his astonished eyes still open.

Clusters of citizens spread out to hunt down the demoralized gang. Soon the road by the wharf was filled with righteous citizens herding suspicious characters back to the warehouse. A group of eight heavily armed men marched toward the alley where Nathan and his friends watched.

"Uh-oh," Doc whispered. "This doesn't look good. We better make a run for it. Those gentlemen have fire in their eyes, and they won't remember us being at the last church social. Besides, that short fellow has a rope in his hands, and you know I'm allergic to hangings. I can't breathe well suspended from my neck without my feet touching the ground."

"We've done nothing wrong, Doc," Nat argued. "We'll just tell them who we are. I'm sure they'll listen to reason."

"I hate to agree with this whiskey drummer, but they ain't got no look of human kindness in their faces, boy," Riley hissed. "We'd best make tracks. They got lynching in their minds, and you recall what good talking did for those citizens at Jerome. You still got that hole in yer hide from that conversation. Besides, look at us—three scraggly hombres and a China doll. Who'd believe we was spotless?"

"I sure as hell wouldn't," Hennison added. "And I've got more of an open mind than most."

Nathan turned to Wei-Li, and she gave him a knowing look that dashed any objections he had. Wrapping his arm around her shoulders, Nat led her back into the alley, across the foot bridge over the Skagway River to Market Street. Dodging a noisy party of committee members coming down Ninth Street, they quickly crossed Main Street and headed up State Street to mingle with the long, drab lines of gold seekers trudging along the mud-churned road.

Ahead, State Street merged into Broadway, and Doc looked longingly back at the clapped-together saloons, whorehouses, and bathhouses along that road. Trudging northward with this line of drones, he felt his heart tugging him back to that street brimming with the prostitutes, confidence men, and gamblers where he fit in so nicely. A dance hall girl waved enticingly at him, but all Doc could do was sigh.

Broadway ran into the tract being cleared for the narrow gauge railroad to White Pass, the first formidable test of a stampeder's will. Nat removed his coat and draped it over the shoulders of Wei-Li as the chilling wind from the mountain pass blew down on them. Picking their way over the wagon road, he paused to view what lay ahead.

Hastily hacked out of the wilderness by a company headed by former Minneapolis mayor George Bracket, the route existed more in name than anything else. Gnarled tree stumps, sawed off four feet above the ground and left for later removal, peppered Brackett's Wagon Road as a last sign of the forest that once grew there. Cursing teamsters guided their wagons around the obstacles only to have the wheels fall off the irregular tracts of corduroy logs into sinkholes of knee-deep mud while those on foot sloshed out of harm's way.

A year before Brackett had tried to charge a toll for his road, but the miners rebelled and refused to pay. One of the four companies of army infantry now guarded the road.

"Look at all them Bluebellies," Hennison groaned under his breath as he passed a black soldier leaning against a stump. "Makes me homesick for Tennessee. I haven't seen so many since we lost the war. These Yankees look a fair bit younger. They must be robbing the cradle nowadays."

"They ain't robbing no cradles, Doc," Riley said. "Not no

more than usual. These troopers ain't no younger. We're jus' a damned sight older, that's all. And my knees are reminding me with every step. Mother Riley'd turn over in her grave if she saw me off my horse. She didn't raise no walking Johnny."

Nathan stopped. To do so he had to step out of the moving line and stand aside. Hennison, the girl, and Riley joined him and instantly their places in line disappeared as the gold seekers closed ranks. The youth looked back toward the town. Skagway appeared even more surreal from that distance. Half-finished wooden walls and tin roofs arose at odd intervals from this tent city, giving the appearance of a toy town scattered about the ground by a petulant child. And from this jumble an unbroken line of gold seekers trudged to the very spot where Nat stood, and then beyond to wind into the firs.

No sign of the vigilantes, he noted happily. When his gaze returned to the line of men, he noticed something different about them. He and his friends were unburdened, carrying neither sacks nor provisions, while everyone else was.

"What are we going to do for supplies?" he asked. "We're the only ones without packs."

Without replying Hennison darted behind a Douglas fir stump wider than his arms could encircle and reaching above his head. The sound of water spraying the ground followed by his sigh of relief issued from the other side of the stump. He emerged, buttoning his fly.

"Whew, thought I was going to explode. I shouldn't have snuck that beer at Soapy's." He sighed.

Nathan repeated his question. "We don't have any provisions, Doc. We don't even have a canteen between the four of us."

Riley loosened his gunbelt and leaned on his rifle. "The boy's got a point. I didn't plan on hiking over White Pass, jus' wanted to talk to Soapy Smith. But I heard fellows complaining in Skagway about the Mounties not letting nobody into the Klondike without a year's grub stake."

"Have no fear," Hennison chuckled. His hand clinked the coins he carried. "We can buy what we need."

Riley nudged his head in the direction of the mountains. The plank and timber-covered road wound through strands of spruce and fir to climb steeply up into the hills. Whenever gaps in the forest appeared, a dark river of men, dogs, and horses filled the void. Seemingly endless waves of them rolled across the swamps and streams to flow up the side of the mountain range.

"Are you going to pack it up there? I ain't got the faintest notion how far it is," Riley added. "But it ain't no Sunday walk in the damned park, that's for sure."

A Chilkat packer, weathered face and hands burnished to a ruddy bronze, stopped before Riley and pointed back in the direction of the pass. He smiled, exposing perfect white teeth and adding a half dozen more wrinkles to the corrugated pattern of his face. Sooty tattoo lines traced alongside his furrows. His hand made sweeping motions like those made waving goodbye, and he spoke four of the few English words he knew. "Forty mile to lake," he said.

"Jesus! Forty miles!" Hennison choked.

The Chilkat shook his head. "No Jesus there. Forty mile."

Nat looked at the man. Decked in a battered, green felt hat and torn houndstooth trousers, his attire amounted to discarded rags, yet he seemed content and fit. Half the size of Nat and barely taller than Wei-Li, his bowed legs and muscled arms spoke of great strength. But he looked half starved.

The native turned to continue his trek back to town when Nathan touched his arm. He stopped and looked expectantly at Nathan. His eyes fixed on the jade dragon hanging from Nat's neck. In their escape from Soapy's henchmen, the pendant had slipped outside his shirt. The Chilkat fingered the polished stone while his eyes sparkled and his grin widened. He tapped Nathan's chest then his own, repeatedly poking as he spoke rapidly in his own tongue.

Wei-Li peered around Nat. "He must think you and he are related through the dragon," she said in her accented English.

"Damn," Riley shivered. "That China girl talking like some English earl gives me the creeps. It don't seem right."

"You'd prefer she talked like some ignorant Texas sod-buster, I suppose?" Hennison snorted in derision. "I find it rather charming. Her voice is like a tinkling bell—far more pleasant than yours, Riley, which grates on me like a rusty hack-saw."

"Well, her tinkling bell didn't pull your chestnuts outta that last fire. It were my Winchester, by God, and yers truly, Rusty Hacksaw Riley," Riley replied.

Nathan waved them both into silence. "Wei-Li has a point. He's acting like we both belong to the same tribe or clan. Look at the way he's looking at the dragon. Jim, you know sign language. See if you can talk to him."

For half an hour Riley and the native waved their hands at each other with varying degrees of frustration and success. But slowly, they began to communicate. Before long both men had the outlines of the other's thoughts.

Riley stepped back and shook his head. "He must think I'm some kind of half-wit from the way I sign, but his kind ain't like nothing used by the plains Indians. It's more a cross between something I ran into once in the Powder River country with a crazy Cree who spoke mostly French and something else. Best I can figure his name is Two Bears. He packs supplies over the pass with his family for eats since all this gold rushing has scared the game and muddied the waters so's the salmon's left. Business ain't been too good in spite of the rush 'cause most of these stampeders are foreigners—Swedes and Germans—who think he'll scalp 'em or steal their goods.

"He thinks your China dragon is a killer whale. That's his clan, so you must be brothers. He and his family are hungry, and he wants to pack for us. We must be important, he says, because we're not carrying anything."

"Or stupid," Hennison interjected.

"Anyways," Riley said, ignoring the physician. "He thinks we ought to help him. That's what family is for, he says."

"Doc, give him one of your gold pieces," Nathan ordered. "Jim, tell him to buy some food and meet us at that trading post ahead." Nat pointed to a two-story structure with a curious peaked roof jutting from the center of the store front and straddling the wagon road. A black-lettered sign read BRACKETT'S TRADING POST.

"What! Give *my* money!" Hennison protested. "Twenty dollars will keep this savage in whiskey and sugar for a month! We'll never see his face again."

Nat looked at the tattered native then back at his friends, who were wearing a weird mix of torn, mud-spattered sailor's oilskins and riding gear. Hennison still carried his wooden rapier. He ran his fingers over the dried blood on his cheek from the splinter cut. "Doc, he looks a lot less savage than we do. Give it to him."

Begrudgingly, Doc parted with a coin as if he were giving up his life, and Two Bears disappeared down the trail.

"Damned foolish waste of our money," Hennison grumbled.

The four made their way to Brackett's and went inside. Stepping through the doors they entered another world. No finer emporium in Seattle or San Francisco held a greater variety of goods than did Brackett's, despite it being situated thousands of miles from civilization and alongside a treetrunk paved road hacked from the wilds. Spoons, saws, candles, tubs, and all manner of canned goods filled the aisles and every inch of floor space while gunracks and clothing hung from the walls. Exotic smells of tea and tobacco mingled with the aroma of cedar coming from the potbellied stove near the door.

Nat's heart melted as he watched Wei-Li, drawn to the selection of perfumes and scented bath oils. Like a child she smelled each, smoothing samples on her chapped hands. Hennison shed his bloodied oilskins and slipped into a wool jacket with a fox-fur collar. Even Riley, who prided himself on being spartan, gravitated to the gun collection.

"Your lady has good taste in perfume," a voice behind Nathan stated.

Nathan turned to study the speaker who was also studying the four of them. The man wore a high starched collar surrounding a tightly knotted black tie. A brown brocade waistcoat with gold chain and watch fob and striped trousers completed his attire. Everything about him screamed of exactness from the even part down the exact center of his anointed hair to the shine on his leather boots.

"I'm George Brackett, the owner," he said, extending his hand to Nathan. "Like I said, your lady knows her perfumes. She went straight to the finest samples I could find this side of Paris."

"I'm Nathan Blaylock and these are my friends, Mr. Riley and Dr. Hennison, and the lady is Wei-Li."

"I'm pleased to make your acquaintance, Mr. Blaylock. You'll excuse me if I say you four don't look like the usual stampeders."

"Well, sir." Hennison stepped in to help Nathan. "Normally you would be correct. But we've decided to try our hand at finding the mother lode."

Brackett laughed. "Spoken like a true gambler, which I think you are. I'd mark that lanky fellow peering into my gun

244

case to be a dead shot of animals—the two-legged kind. But I'm at a loss to place this young man and his beautiful lady. Although rumors have it that someone of his description broke into Soapy Smith's place and rescued a Chinese girl of similar beauty."

Hennison started to protest, but the owner cut him off. "No need to concern yourselves. Those same rumors say Soapy's dead, killed by Frank Reid, with his gang being rounded up by the committee, and I say good riddance. Soapy was bad for business, and that's what I'm all for . . . business. Money he stole from the miners was coin that didn't get spent in my store. So if you contributed to Jefferson Smith's fall, I'm indebted to you."

Nathan relaxed. "Your store is incredible, Mr. Brackett. I never expected to see all this merchandise in Alaska."

"Thank you, son. I've worked hard to make this a first-class trading post. More people are coming, by the thousands, and soon a narrow gauge railroad will carry gold seekers directly to the gold fields. I just sold my toll road to a consortium set on building just that railroad."

"Soon, I hope," Hennison commented. He was trying on beaver hats in front of a full-length mirror.

"Not soon enough for you, I'm afraid. My wagon road only goes part way up White Pass. It may take another year to cross Tunnel Mountain and bridge Dead Horse Canyon."

"Dead Horse Canyon?" Riley grunted. "That don't sound good."

"It's a dreadful place. You'll see soon enough," Brackett sighed.

★ ★ NINETEEN ★ ★

Captain Ericsson pounded on the stateroom door with his right hand while his left hand mopped his sweating brow. Ericsson's face would turn florid when faced with a crisis, and this one beat all others hands down. One deck lower his crew was mutinying.

To Ericsson a mutiny was something that happened in navies or rumrunners off the Tortugas, not on a rusted freighter, but his men were currently arming themselves with the four pistols and two rifles broken out of his stateroom cabinet. They had stripped all the fire axes from the bulkheads too, as well as what carpenter's tools might pass for weapons. All the captain had was his pocket .36 Navy Colt, a rusted, ill-used thing that still required black powder. To make matters worse, the rebellious men had broken open the medicinal brandy stores and now were drunken sots.

The door opened and Ericsson found himself facing a beautiful dark-haired woman, something he had not expected and was even less prepared for.

"Yes?" she asked. "May I help you, Captain?"

Ericsson swabbed his dripping forehead and gathered his wits. "Ah, sorry to disturb you, Mrs. Earp, but we seem to have a . . . a sort of problem. And, well is your hus—"

The door swung completely open and Ericsson found himself staring up into the gray eyes of Wyatt Earp, standing beside his wife. For this late in the evening he already had his frock coat and waistcoat on and buttoned, and a thick, worn gunbelt buckled around his waist.

"A sort of a problem, Captain Ericsson?" Wyatt's voice was flat as slate. "I'd rate a mutiny as more than a sort of a problem, more on a par with a lynch mob, wouldn't you think?"

"Yes, I'm afraid you're right." Ericsson sprang inside to safety with the noted marshal and sat on their bed without being asked. Josie looked slightly amused at his behavior, but he was past caring. His voice trembled and sweat dripped onto his navy blazer, rolling between the two rows of brass buttons. "But it's not my fault, marshal. Really it isn't. I had no control over what food was purchased."

"It spoiled regardless," Wyatt countered.

"For God's sake, marshal, do you think I would buy rotten meat and flour with weevils for *my own ship!* I have to eat the same food as everyone else."

"I'm not a marshal anymore," Wyatt corrected the distraught man, "so I don't see what I can do to help with your problem."

"Please, talk to them, Mr. Earp. You have a reputation as a . . . "

"A gunfighter?"

"No, no, I didn't mean that. But the men might listen to you. You have a reputation for upholding the law. They've got into the firearms and now the brandy, and who knows what harm they might do."

"Well, you can spread the word, my wife and I are about to sit down to our evening meal of coffee and moldy crackers—thanks to your parsimonious purser—and we have no wish to be disturbed. So the first man who comes through this door uninvited will get a bullet between his eyes."

Ericsson rose slowly to his feet like a condemned man. "I'm

ruined." He sighed. "When the crew turns this ship around and heads back to San Francisco, the owners will hang whatever's left of me."

Josie stiffened. *"Back to San Francisco?"*

"Yes, ma'am. That's what they're plotting."

"Oh, no!" She stomped her foot. "We're not going back. Not this time. Wyatt and I have been denied our chance at a gold strike before, and this time we're going to make it."

The captain spread his hands hopelessly. "That's what they plan."

Josie grabbed Wyatt's arm. "You talk to them, Wyatt. If we have to turn back, I'm not trying again."

Ten minutes later Wyatt stood on the top of the ladder facing an angry cluster of sailors armed with clubs, mallets, and the stolen firearms. Behind him cowered the captain.

The mob's self-appointed leader, a lumpish man named Carney, strode up the stairs with rifle in hand. "Stand aside," he commanded. "We're headed for the wheelhouse."

Wyatt studied Carney. With a beefy face pitted from small-pox and a full beard to hide those scars, he could have been forty or he could have been twenty. Coal dust coated his cov-eralls as well as every exposed pore on his body, and the hand that held his revolver matched the gunmetal in hue. In addi-tion to smelling of sweat and coal, Carney reeked of brandy.

"Stand aside or we'll use these." Carney repeated his order, backed now by waving his pistol to the four points of the com-pass. From the way he handled his weapon, Wyatt surmised that Carney's finesse was with a coal shovel rather than a revolver.

"What's your grievance?" Wyatt blocked his path and asked, coming straight to the point. His hands rested on the brass rail-ing, away from his holster.

Carney faltered, taken aback by this challenge. Everyone on board knew about Earp, and he had been pointed out to Car-ney on two occasions. Seeing him allied with the captain was disturbing to this engine room man. Still, his men pushed him on.

"Stand aside, Mr. Earp. We've no desire to harm you or any of the passengers. Our grievance is with this penny-pinching skipper. This is no concern of yours."

"I'm surprised to hear you say that, Mr. Carney. After all, we are on the same vessel, and we are eating the same rotted food."

Carney blinked in astonishment. Wyatt Earp knew his name. He was done for.

Wyatt continued slowly, lowering his voice imperceptibly, thereby forcing the men to strain to pick up his words. As he had hoped, everyone now was listening to him instead of shouting curses and making threats. Forcing them to pay attention had the added effect of making them stop waving their weapons about. The last thing he wanted now was an accidental discharge. That might ignite a frenzy of shooting. "We may even have shared the same bedbugs."

Carney blinked again. Behind him, scattered guffaws and laughter erupted. He turned to glare at his fellow mutineers, and they quieted—but only somewhat. The fireman was not the only one reeking of brandy. When he turned back to face Earp, a few drunken titters resumed.

Carney looked at the Peacemaker just peeking from the edge of Wyatt's coat and decided to try logic. "It's a bad thing we have here, Mr. Earp, a shameful thing, and there's no denying it. We, the others and me, signed on fair and proper for the whole All-Water Route. We done our work as best we can on this run-down freighter they passed off to all of us as a first-rate ship. You've got eyes, Mr. Earp. You can see this is not no White Star Line vessel."

Wyatt nodded. "Get to the point, Mr. Carney."

"Well, any fool knows this passage might take a whole month, and they should have provisioned the ship properly."

"Which it ain't, if you'll pardon my saying so," North, the steward, added.

Carney shot North a venomous look. "Pipe down! You elected me spokesman, and I'm doing the talking for all of us." North slipped back into the cover of the others.

"But he's dead on," the fireman continued. "The food is rotten and the water brackish. We don't ask for much, but we expect a square meal. That's fair, isn't it?"

"Yes, it is," Wyatt agreed.

"Good," the relief was almost palpable in Carney's voice. "So we're turning the ship around and heading back to the first port of call. Then we're jumping this rustbucket because Captain Ericsson says he doesn't have the funds to buy food or pay us off."

Ericsson poked his head from behind Wyatt. "It's true, marshal. The owners shorted my cash box. I couldn't buy fresh provisions from Neptune himself if he were to surface off our bow and open his treasure house to us this instant."

"So, like I said, we're turning her about." Carney grunted. His point made, he placed one foot on the first rung of the ladder.

"I'll shoot the first man who enters the wheelhouse without Captain Ericsson's permission," Wyatt snapped. "This ship is going ahead!"

Carney flinched at the sharpness of the words, and his eyes moved quickly from his pistol to Wyatt's hands. Disturbingly, Earp's hands still rested easily on the brass railing, a good two feet from his revolver.

"You can't shoot us all," he said, but his voice sounded hollow, and he noticed his fellow seamen were already edging back, widening the distance between him and them. "And you haven't drawn your pistol, Mr. Earp. We could rush you. . . ."

"That's true, Mr. Carney." Wyatt agreed while slowly pushing his coat back with his left hand to reveal another Peacemaker in a holster under his left armpit. This one was a shorter barreled Colt .45 known as the Police Model, and it rested butt forward. "You could rush me. But I took my coffin money out of both my revolvers, so I've got six rounds in each now, and I'll kill twelve of you at least." Wyatt referred to the practice of carrying a rolled up twenty-dollar bill in the chamber beneath the hammer. It served the dual purpose of preventing shooting oneself if the hammer were accidentally struck as well as providing money for a decent funeral, if need be.

"What do you mean at least twelve?"

Wyatt's lips curled into a fearsome grin, showing his white teeth like a graying wolf turning on his attackers with plenty of fight left inside and years of savvy on how to conduct that fight. It gave all—Carney—most of all there the feeling that Wyatt *knew he would win.*

"Some of you are directly behind the others," Wyatt answered. "At this range, a .45 can pass through more than one man. I aim to make use of that opportunity if it comes to a showdown."

In a flash the men sorted themselves out of columns, but the narrow corridor prevented their spreading as wide as they would have liked.

"But I have another suggestion if you'd care to listen to it. If not," Wyatt shrugged, "well, then just place your foot on the next rung of the ladder, and we'll open the right ball here and now."

Carney was visibly sweating now. The pistol in his hand weighed ten tons. "Another suggestion?" he stammered, painfully aware of the higher pitch his voice had taken.

"I'll pay for fresh provisions for the whole ship if we head on to Unalaska."

"You'd do that, Mr. Earp?"

"Sure. I'm tired of eating this swill as much as you are, and Captain Ericsson will reimburse me when we arrive at St.

Michaels. You boys can get paid your wages there. That won't be a problem, would it, Captain Ericsson?"

Ericsson found his voice. "No, no, marshal. The money's there in St. Michael. You have my word on it."

"Suppose we don't trust the skipper's word?" The fireman searched for flaws in the idea.

"Well, then," Wyatt studied the shaking captain. "You and the crew can hire me to collect from Captain Ericsson and his backers. I guarantee you I will get our money. . . . "

★ ★ TWENTY ★ ★

Jim Riley gritted his teeth and gave the horse another whack on its rump, but the animal refused to move. It just stood there blocking the trail and shivering.

"She ain't gonna move, Nat." He sighed as he slipped out of his packing frame and flopped onto a rock outcropping. "The poor beast is plumb tuckered out."

Riley mopped his sweating brow with the brim of his hat and surveyed the twisting trail that squeezed through jumbled boulders the size of a house. Scarcely the width of their starving horses, the path wound along the side of a steep hill covered with similar boulders with short-limbed spruce stabbing at them at every turn. All along the trees defended the hill, ensconced behind rocky ramparts and using their stubby branches to stab and tear at the travelers.

"No wonder they call this place Porcupine Hill," Riley mused. He checked his torn coat sleeves and congratulated himself for having the good sense to buy a pair of leather chaps from Brackett's. "It's a damned prickly place. It's poking me more than I care to admit. Reminds me of the story of the raccoon that seduced the porcupine. . . . "

Nathan emptied a handful of water from his canteen and washed Wei-Li's wearied face. She gave him a grateful look and smiled. Exhausted to the point of collapse, she never complained. "What happened then, Jim?" Nathan asked.

"He had to quit when he endured as much as he could enjoy." Riley emitted a round of halfhearted guffaws. It was a lame joke he knew, but anything said on this mountain would be lame.

"Spare us your homespun humor, Riley, and just shoot the damned horse," Doc grumbled.

"If I do that, Doc, she'll be wedged in the trail like a cork in a bottle.

Hennison eased himself past the jutting ribs and crates of his own pack horse. His spine scraped along the granite rock, but he made it. Moving toward Riley, his boot caught in a spruce root and he tumbled into the mud-churned track. His new beaver hat sailed into the muck just as Riley's horse lurched back. The horse's hind hoof ground the hat further into the dirt.

"Jesus Christ, my new hat!" Doc swore as he retrieved it. He rubbed it on his equally muddied sleeve before replacing it on his head. The battered and soiled hat no longer resembled its original shape, however it did match perfectly with Hennison's ruined coat and torn pants. He stepped back and his boots made a sucking noise in the churned muskeg. "Jesus Christ," he said softly.

"No Jesus, forty mile," Two Bears added solemnly, pointing upwards to the mountain pass. The native and his two sons brought up the rear of the party, loaded with packs almost equal in size to those borne by the horses. Moosehide straps ran from their foreheads to support the weight. To Hennison's chagrin Two Bears and his sons had been waiting outside Brackett's in the morning. The savvy Chilkat even brought four square-chested malamute dogs with pack frames. Now the three Indians and their dogs waited patiently for the trek to resume.

"Thank you for that fascinating geography lesson, Mr. Bears," Doc replied.

"Hey! Keep moving up there," a voice from the column behind them shouted. Their followers were bunching up while those ahead disappeared around another bend.

"Hold your damned horses," Hennison snarled back.

"I *am* holding my damned horses, mister," the voice responded. "That's the problem. If they stop moving, I'm afraid they'll lie down. Then I'll never get them back on their feet again."

Riley grasped a twisted cedar that jutted out from the trail's ledge and swung around the outside boulder. Then he climbed over other rocks until he got in front of his horse. His heart nearly broke as he faced the mare, standing there shivering, covered with sweat and flies that busily bored holes in her hide.

"What's the matter, old girl." He spoke to her soothingly. "Something got you spooked? I ain't smelled no bears, so it must be these rocks. Is that it?"

The horse whinnied pitifully at the sound of a kind voice and hung her head so the froth dripped from her nostrils. Her brown eyes rolled at Riley in fright.

Riley patted her neck. "They say we're almost there, girl," he said, drawing a sugar cube from his pocket and slipping it into her mouth. He wiped the flies away from her eyes. "Why don't you follow me, eh? I'll scare these stone bears away; and when we get to the Mounties, I swear I'll set you free. Would you like that? You won't never have to climb this God-cursed trail no more. That's a promise."

Riley took the reins and walked forward. The horse took a step, then another, and slowly the column moved on.

Picking his way between the boulders, Riley and his horse led the others first up one side then down the other side of Porcupine Mountain, edging between rocks stained dark brown with the blood of previous hopefuls and thatched with tufts of horse hair. On either side lay only lichen and reindeer moss as all edible forage had been cropped and eaten by the starving pack animals. Coming down off the mountain's side, they entered a muskeg bog where the way was clearly marked by deep ruts carved into the taiga.

Jim and his trusting horse slogged on. But soon Riley found that with each step he sank to his thigh. His horse struggled with equal difficulty. Behind him Nathan and the others fought the sucking bog that tripped them at all turns. Compounding their effort were the tussocks that rose like tufted turtle shells at irregular spacing. Clambering atop one of these, one risked slipping off the worn moss into the next suck hole. Yet jumping from one high tussock to another was impossible because of their random alliance. The horses fared even worse because of the unsure footing. They were forever lurching or slipping or falling on their haunches until their legs were cut and bleeding from the sharp stones concealed in the muck. And their blood just attracted more flies.

In the center of the swamp a cloud of mosquitoes rose from the brush and attacked the party in a whining, undulating black cloud. The horses shied in terror as the insects savaged their eyes and ears. Riley swatted at them with his hat, but to no avail. His own neck and face soon was covered with welts and blood from those he squashed.

Hennison flailed the air with his battered beaver hat. "Go away," he commanded. "Bother the people behind us. They're much more juicy and tender than me." But the mosquitoes didn't listen.

Nathan stripped off his jacket and covered Wei-Li's head while using his shirt to shield himself. He pulled blankets from the horse packs and wrapped the stricken animals' heads. That caused the horses to stop bucking and follow him out of this battlefield. Only Two Bears and his pack dogs escaped unscathed. He and his dogs instinctively trotted through the tussock maze, wending their way around hillocks and suck holes. Being smaller and more agile, the dogs skirted the worst areas to thread themselves along the outskirts of the ruined trail.

When they saw the mosquitoes rise in attack, they dodged up-wind of the cloud.

Just past this last marsh, they entered a forest of stunted spruce. Slow growing in the harsh Arctic, many of these were dwarfed ancients, several hundred years old. But men with gold fever burning their minds cared nothing for these trees' struggles, and hundreds were trampled and cut for the poorest excuse for a corduroy road. Those trees that survived did so because they lay outside the trail and were too spindly to use.

As Riley emerged from the forest, he stopped dead in his tracks and stood open-mouthed at the scene before him. Never in his life had he witnessed a spectacle of such magnitude and such horror.

"Lord God Almighty," he swore. "Protect us. . . . " Instinctively, he looked heavenward to silently ask forgiveness. His mother never tolerated swearing, but ordinary words were inadequate here.

Below him, the land descended into a deep canyon, lined on both sides with shale and loose scree and scattered boulders. Other than rock, nothing living filled the bowl nor grew on its hostile sides, and nothing moved except for the icy water of a shallow stream that cut across the floor. The trail led straight into the depths of this pit and then snaked up the far side.

Nothing moved in the canyon, and yet it was not empty. Lining the sides of the stream and filling the canyon were the bodies of thousands of dead and dying horses. Carcasses in all stages of decomposure lay scattered about in the random poses of death. Newly dead lay beside the bleached ribs and backbones of those of the past winter. Clusters of ribs rose in such concentration that they resembled whitened fields of unmoving grass.

Sooty clouds overhead hid the sky from this shame, blanketing all signs of the cheery blue sky except for scattered pinholes in the clouds. Even scavengers like the fox and the raven no longer came to this awful place, perhaps due to the constant human passage or perhaps because the animals were tired of horse flesh. Whatever the reason, their absence only added to the morose aura of this place of death.

Hennison moved up behind the dumbstruck Riley. Even his jaded and calloused soul was touched by this terrible site. It brought to mind the carnage of the Bloody Angle or Frasier's Farm from the war—something he hoped never to witness again except in his nightmares. All the dead horses were there; only the men and the artillery caisson were missing. Yet even those meat-grinding battles paled before the magnitude of animal loss seen here.

"Dead Horse Canyon." Doc sighed.

Two Bears stepped to his side. "No Jesus here," he said sadly. "Too much dead."

Hennison nodded solemnly. "I have to agree with you, Two Bears. There's no Jesus here, not in a million years."

Hennison patted the suffering Riley on his shoulder in a rare moment of empathy and turned back to tend his animal. Jim had chosen the weakest animal of the four, and now he might pay the piper for this gesture.

Regaining his senses, Riley led his pack animal down the trail with great foreboding. Descending into this valley of death, he fought a nagging truth that festered in the back of his mind. All these corpses had died in this valley, littering its slopes and bottom with their bones. The horses they had purchased at Brackett's were the best he had to offer; nevertheless, like all those that went before, they were ill, half starved from their sea voyage, and probably chosen from the dregs back in Seattle or San Francisco. It stood to reason than no man would sell his best mount. This valley then, Dead Horse Canyon, was the final hurdle for many an animal. Riley wondered if his horse would founder here like so many of the others.

One hundred yards up the far slope he got his answer.

Stumbling over a cluster of rocks, his mount gave a piteous groan, somewhat akin to the sound of air escaping from a collapsing bellows, and dropped to all fours. Then she rolled onto her side and stretched her neck out on the loose scree.

Riley knelt by his horse's head and moistened her lips with water from his canteen. But the old gunfighter knew the end was near. He had seen too many horses founder in the barrens of Arizona and the Indian Territories to miss the unmistakable signs. But he tried to get her to her feet nevertheless.

"Come on, girl," he begged. "We've almost there. You don't want to stop here, not like all the others."

But the stricken animal could only roll her eyes and flair her nostrils with each wheezing breath. Nathan helped Two Bears transfer the horse's load to his dogs, but still she refused to stand.

"Anything I can do to help?" Nathan asked.

Riley shook his head. "She's down for good, Nat. This damned canyon broke her heart and her spirit. She won't get to her feet no matter what. You best go on with the others. I'll catch up."

Nathan backed off as Riley sat beside his animal and smoothed the hair on her forelock. As he turned, he saw the gunman draw his revolver and check the loads while he sat petting the animal.

"Well, old girl," Riley whispered in the horse's ear. "I ain't gonna let you lie here for the wolves and foxes to rip open your belly while you're still alive—not like some of these other callous bastards done. You done yer best, an' that's all I can ask. It's jus' a shame it weren't good enough, but maybe my life ain't gonna be good enough either. Right now I don't seem to be doing a lot better than you myself, 'cept I'm still on my feet. I jus' hope when my time comes there'll be someone there to finish me off quick."

Riley paused as he laid the barrel behind the horse's ear.

He looked around at the hateful canyon. "This is a hell of a place to bring a horse," he said. "Sad thing is you never got no say in coming here, and I did. Well, old girl, I promised you you'd never have to climb this trail no more, and I aim to keep that promise. . . . "

Halfway up the hillside, Nat heard the report of Riley's revolver. Its sharp crack shattered the air and reverberated around the sides of the canyon. A few minutes later Riley came trudging up the slopes, head bowed so he appeared to be watching his feet. As he passed Nathan he simply shook his head.

Later that evening when they finished the beans and rice Wei-Li had prepared over a cheerless fire of spruce and alder branches, Riley slipped away from the circle of light cast by the campfire. When he didn't return first Nathan then Doc went searching for him. They found him back down the trail sitting on a boulder overlooking Dead Horse Canyon.

The moon shone into the canyon, turning everything into sharp contrasting black shadows and bleached white highlights that could have been the bones of all those horses. The two others slipped onto the rock to sit beside him. No one spoke for the longest while until finally Riley broke the silence.

"Killing a dumb beast like a horse that don't know no better always strikes me harder than killing a man who should," he said simply.

Hennison noticed the tears in the old man's eyes as he spoke. "Again I have to agree with you, my friend. No four-legged creature I ever met seemed to warrant shooting as much as the two-legged variety, excepting mules, of course." But Doc's cynical stab at humor fell on unsympathetic ears.

"This is a god-awful place to bring a horse," Riley reiterated.

"Well, if you won't take my cheery words, at least try a swallow of my cheering prescription." Hennison uncorked his last bottle of elixir and passed it around. To him it was the supreme gesture of generosity, and to his surprise both Riley and the boy took a long drink. "It looks like a god-awful place to bring anyone."

"Then why are we here?" Riley asked.

"We're here to see justice done," Nathan replied. "And in the process gain a fortune for the three of us—a fortune none of us would stand much chance of seeing otherwise."

"The boy's got a point," Hennison said. "What chance have you or I got, Riley, of seeing that much money? Why, you know the truth of it, man. You're a cowboy, and the only cowpunchers with a nickel to their names are those that took to robbing banks."

Riley rubbed his hands together, and in the darkness his chapped skin made the sound of dry twigs being rolled together. "Justice? How do we know that? You two seen the justice we run across. Doc would be hanging from the end of a rope, and so might you, boy, for all the justice we seen. Maybe what we're talking about here is revenge."

Nathan bowed his head. "Yeah, Jim, I've been thinking about that myself. Maybe we'll strike it rich before we ever meet up with Wyatt Earp in Dawson. Then we won't have to make that call."

Hennison seized on Nathan's point. "Wouldn't that be grand? After all, the Mounties are making us pack all this gear. Wouldn't it be a shame to let it go to waste?"

Riley nodded halfheartedly.

Doc continued. "They say there are nuggets the size of my fist just waiting to be picked up."

Their conference broke up with each man dragging his bone-weary body back to their tents. Two Bears and his sons sat by their small fire, feet facing in toward the semicircle of warmth. Riley ducked into his canvas tent, but Hennison insisted on stoking his "white man's fire" with more logs until it illuminated the night and sent great columns of sparks funneling into the darkness. By the light from Doc's beacon one could see the tent city pitched about the summit of White Pass at the place called Log Cabin. Here the Mounties guarded the pass and checked each gold seeker's supplies.

Nathan paused at the door flap of his tent and looked past Doc's fire to the hundreds of pinpoint lights winking from Log Cabin. Somewhere up ahead, was Wyatt Earp waiting for him? Would he be faster? The young man wondered. Since being separated from Riley, his practice had gone to pot. Nat made a mental note to practice dry firing every day. Cartridges were too costly to waste on daily practice and he wished to avoid the Mounties' suspicions.

Was Earp ever the cold-blooded killer his mother described? He *was* wanted for Frank Stilwell's murder, and there were those string of killings following his brother Morgan's murder. But maybe I'm wanted for murder now, too, Nathan thought. Funny how those fights happened, sort of out of the blue, yet those men are dead just the same, never to take another step or another breath, ever again.

Back in Pinal the idea of collecting his reward for shooting his father was cut and dried. Now it no longer was. Wei-Li made it different.

As if she had read his mind, Wei-Li appeared at the tent opening. A single candle burned behind her in the tent, silhouetting her slender figure with its warm light and outlining her raven black hair with a golden line that traced its straight fall to the high collar of her dress. Her perfume, with its faint smell of jasmine, wafted past all the unpleasant odors of their toil. She slipped into his arms, and her fingers gently traced the furrows on Nathan's brow.

"Worrying about what lies ahead, my love?" she whispered as he gathered her in his arms and buried his face in her hair, driving back the stench of those thousands of dead horses and the reek of rotting muskeg.

"Yes," he admitted. Funny, he thought, two months ago

he'd never have admitted that. His boyish bravado was wearing thin. "I'm also worried about Jim. I've never seen him so low. All those horses piled in Dead Horse Canyon effected him terribly. Do you know, he told me that when he was a boy back in Texas, he and his mother would have given anything for a horse. With one they could plow a few more acres of their dust bowl or do odd jobs to raise money. But they couldn't afford one after his father left. He said he used to watch the cowboys ride by and dream of owning a horse. After Newton Station he rode his horse back to Texas, but his mom had already passed away."

Nat paused to search the brown pools of her eyes, so dark he felt he could never see their bottom, and he offered a prayer of thanks she was by his side. "Before I came along, I think his horses were all the friend and family he'd ever known."

She smiled up at him. "But now he has you and the bitter peddler of obnoxious medicines. You are his family, and they are yours."

"No . . . well, yes, I suppose they are. But you are the most important thing to me." He held her tighter.

Unexpectedly, she pushed back from him and searched his face for any signs of insincerity. Everything in her training warned her against this. Men were fickle creatures who followed their Jade Dragons like a compass needle, without regard for where it led them—even if it drew them onto the rocks. "Do I please you, Nathan?" she asked.

"Please me? Wei-Li, I love you!"

She chose to ignore his last statement. Love was only for the foolish, her teachers had stressed. Something to occupy the dreams of foolish maidens and pimply boys. Love had no place in her profession. Love led only to disaster, she repeated to herself.

Nathan's face burned at this rejection. He expected her to return his affections, and her failure to do so sorely stung his pride. He was about to force the argument when a cluster of would-be miners trod into their camp.

"How much for the China whore?" a cow-faced man leading the group asked. "I've still got some energy left after packing my goods up to the Cabin. She ain't got the pox or nothin', does she?" He smiled at Nathan and shot a grubby paw out to grasp Wei-Li's arm.

"She's no whore," Nathan snarled, his anger finding a focus. "She's . . . she's going to be my wife."

The man tightened his grip on her arm and burst into laughter. "Don't nobody marry them, you fool boy!" He stopped, and his eyes narrowed. Then his face turned nasty. "Wait, just a minute. You don't think we're good enough for yer dolly, *Mr. Pimp?* Is that it? Our money ain't good enough?"

"I'm not a pimp. I *am* going to marry her, mister," Nathan hissed through gritted teeth. He tore the man's grip loose from Wei-Li and pushed her behind him. "Now go away before you get hurt."

"You?" the man chortled. "There're five of us, boy. And any one can whup yer scrawny ass on their worst—"

He never completed his sentence. Nathan whipped out his Colt and laid it across the man's head with a crack that reverberated among the rocky slopes. The man dropped to his knees like lightning had struck him. His eyes rolled backward in his head, momentarily reflecting Hennison's giant fire in their whites before he toppled over backward. There he lay, staring up at the stars with his wool cap sporting a deep cleft that struggled to soak up the blood gushing from his opened forehead.

His friends whipped out knives, cudgels, and pistols. But their rush was checked by Jim Riley stepping from the shadows with a ten-gauge shotgun clamped in his hands.

"Evening, boys," Riley drawled. "You boys lost, or just looking for something?"

The second in command swung his pistol at Riley, but thought better of it when he saw the man's grim face and his shotgun. Instead he lowered it and backed into the security of his friends. "We got no quarrel with you, just with this kid here," he said. "Stand aside."

Riley ignored the order, but he also lowered his shotgun. He studied the men's faces in the firelight. "Ain't I seen you fellows back in the canyon?"

The man shuffled about unsure how to answer that question. Two of the others helped the buffaloed man to his feet where he leaned heavily against them. "Maybe. What's it to you?"

"I thought I recognized you," Riley continued. "You was having trouble with yer horses same as me. I was climbing out of the stream bed when I looked back and saw you unhitching yer pack animals."

The men relaxed. The number two spokesman found his tongue. "Dead Horse Canyon, you mean? Yeah, our nags gave up there like most. 'Course they was half starved when we bought them back in Skagway, and we didn't buy no grain nor feed for them. So I figured they was only good for a one-way passage."

"And you boys just left them there to starve," Riley commented evenly. Only Nathan was close enough to see the muscles knotting in the gunman's jaw.

"Hell, yes. They wasn't worth wasting a bullet on. I figured the wolves and foxes would get 'em."

"You figured wrong. I went back this evening and put the poor beasts down myself."

"Well, you just wasted yer own time and money, mister. Don't expect us to thank you."

"Funny, I thought you'd say that. No, I didn't expect no thanks from you. But yer horses told me to give you somethin'."

"What . . . !?"

"Just this—" Riley snapped his scattergun up and fired the right barrel from the hip. The balloon flash blinded the group momentarily; and when the acrid smoke cleared, all five men were doubled over clutching their bellies and dancing about in agony.

"You killed us!" one shouted as he vainly sought to hold his intestines in place. But his hands found no slippery coils, only scattered droplets of blood and sharp white crystals.

"Yew ain't gutshot with no more than rock salt," Riley said. "It'll burn like hell for a few days, 'less you prefer to spend the night digging it out of yer mangy hides. But it might remind you what starving to death would feel like."

The men wriggled backward in pain. The two closest received the lion's share of the blast, yet those on the wings also caught the spread of salt.

"Now, this other barrel, well, she's loaded with a double charge of buckshot. If I ever see you mistreating a poor, dumb animal again, I'll kill every one of you," Riley swore. "Now git the hell out of our camp."

The lesser wounded clutched their friends by the arms and dragged them doubled in two, their knees scraping across the rocks. Riley watched the men disappear outside the cast of the fire, and then spent another ten minutes listening to their moans recede into the darkness. When it seemed certain they weren't mounting a revenge attack, the old man turned to face Nathan and Wei-Li.

"You did good, boy, and I'm proud of you. You could have killed all five of them dirt busters, but you didn't."

Nat wiped the hair and blood off his gun barrel and inspected the weapon for damage. Finding the barrel still straight, he holstered the gun, but his face appeared puzzled. "I don't understand," he asked.

"A real gunfighter only uses his piece when nothing else will do. But he don't never let on that's his game. Half yer advantage is not letting the others know that. If they think you'd rather plug them full of lead than spit, you got 'em right where you want them. You got yer point across this time without pulling the trigger. That shows you was using yer noggin. Sort of like that King Henry the V I read about."

"Henry the Vee? Henry the Fifth? Shakespeare?"

"Yeah, the king. That German swell on the ship to Skagway had a load of books by that Shakespeare. I read some of 'em on the way up."

Riley peered into the dark where the groans could still be faintly heard. He settled his wide-brimmed hat on the back of his head, and a wry grin spread across his face. "Damn," he said. "Giving those dudes their comeuppance makes me feel a whole lot better."

The next morning the group stood in a bleak drizzle while a sergeant in the Mounted Police checked and rechecked their piles of provisions down to the last pound of sugar. Dozens of similar piles surrounded the meager shed called the Log Cabin where the Mounties endured as grim an existence as those that packed their loads to this border checkpoint. Wedged in the cleft at the pinnacle of White Pass, the outpost suffered from winds that lashed the pass and frequent snowstorms that struck even in the brief summer. Even now the clefts and crevices of the rocky site held snow from the last storm.

The Mountie gave Hennison and Wei-Li careful scrutiny, but as their names were not on his list of undesirables, he waved them through. Within minutes Doc had disappeared.

Riley leaned on his rifle and surveyed the chaos as Wei-Li boiled water for hot tea. "Gold ain't got no second in driving a man crazy," he said. "I seen it in Arizona, and it's the same here. You know, you could open a skillet store with all the dern frying pans we seen along the trail. Why, I counted over three hundred before I got tired and lost count. Some was big enough to feed a whole cattle outfit."

"I suspect they got pretty heavy the farther their owners climbed," Nathan agreed. "I know even my gunbelt got to weighing me down."

"And rubber boots and shovels," Riley continued. "You could collect them and sell them to the next gold-struck stampeder."

Nat sipped on the tea, blowing on the metal rimmed cup to keep from burning his lip. "I heard the men ahead of us talking about the Chilkoot Pass. They said the checkpoint there is above a place called the Scales where the Chilkat packers weigh the goods they're hired to pack. All the supplies got stashed around this Scales place, and the men have to wait their turn there. They said an avalanche buried sixty-three men there last April, and only just now are some of the bodies poking out of the melting snow." He stopped as he heard a voice shouting their names. Weaving through the clusters of people came Doc Hennison, breathless and waving jubilantly.

Hennison drew up beside them and struggled to catch his wind. Huffing and puffing, his words amounted to fragments and wheezes which they could not understand. Watching Doc deprived of his speech struck the others as amusing, and led them to laughing. Hennison immediately took umbrage.

"See if I tell you what I found just around the bend," he pouted.

Nathan apologized while Riley turned away, unable to keep a straight face. Wei-Li returned to her cooking fire.

"It's marvelous, Nat, my boy. Just around that lake over there, I think they call it Summit Lake, is a railroad. Would you believe it! A railroad up here in this frozen hellhole."

"Where does it go, Doc?" Nathan asked. "We passed the

construction crews for the Skagway and White Pass line back at Tunnel Mountain. They were blowing a hole through the mountain and carting the rubble down the trial by wheelbarrow. They said it would take another year to get to the summit."

"Absolutely correct," Hennison said. His head bobbed in excitement, and his legs shuffled around like some bizarre jig, causing his torn trousers to flap about in the wind. "But the Canadians, God bless them, were building from their side. And they've reached Summit Lake. Their track goes all the way down to Lake Bennett. We can load our cursed supplies and ride like gentlemen down to the lake. No more of this masquerading as a pack mule." He clapped his hands together in glee.

"You ain't carried yer fair share, Doc," Riley complained. "So don't go pretending to be no pack animal, 'cause you weren't even trying."

"I did my share," Hennison sniffed. "My forte is in allocating the work."

Riley spit a slug of tobacco into a snow-filled crevice and watched it disappear beneath the surface, leaving only a faint brown-tinged hole. A man could disappear just as fast in this snow, he realized. "If the fancy word means fixing it so's yer pack is lighter than the rest, you got that right. Why, Two Bears and his boys done most of the hauling."

As if on cue, the sinewy Chilkat clambered over a pile of goods and shook everyone's hand. He nodded and pointed past Summit Lake. "Sunday," he said. "No work. Good-bye."

"Would you believe it. He's a damned Presbyterian and won't work on the Sabbath," Doc muttered. "Anyway, we don't need him anymore."

Two Bears agreed. "Work finish," he said.

Nat shook his hand and gave him an extra five pounds of coffee to take home.

"You good man." Two Bears smiled, but his grin vanished as he gestured to beyond the mountains. "Plenty bad water there," he said. "Bad place, then you find Jesus man."

Nathan pondered the native's puzzling words as he watched Two Bears and his entourage of sons and dogs stride back down the trail.

★ ★ TWENTY-ONE ★ ★

ST. MICHAEL, ALASKA.

Wyatt Earp watched the *Brixom* vanish into a low fog bank that further smeared the vague line between horizon and leaden sky, leaving its smoke trailing behind in a wispy thread. The thread followed the ship into the fog, emerging above to mark its position like the inverted tail of a kite before it broke apart into disjointed segments. Eventually only the sky, the color of a beaten pewter bowl, remained.

Well, Sadie, he thought, we're into it now, but exactly what we're into I'm damned if I know. This is the strangest country I ever did see. But he kept his doubts to himself and simply smiled at his wife. She in turn recognized his terse grin and patted his arm.

The massive emerald forests and knife-edged fjords lining the coasts of Wrangell and Juneau had vanished as if some wrathful shaman had spirited them away from these gold-seeking intruders. The mountains and their covering growth were now gone. In their place stood nothing, nothing at all—no mountains, no cliffs, not even a tree.

St. Michael sat on a low gray spit that extended like a curved scimitar into the sea, its buildings appearing to rise directly from the restless water. Boxy wooden frame buildings, none over three stories high, littered the spit at random. At one end, the compound of the Alaska Commercial Company clustered together like a walled fortress. Extending out from the company a low boardwalk ran to the other edge of land and connected with its rival, the North American Trading and Transportation Company. Balancing each end of the spit like giants on a teeter-totter, these trading companies reigned over the site, guarding the plank road between them. Along this link the rest of the town camped. Sternwheelers, flat-bottomed scows, and any conceivable thing that might float littered the water and scattered themselves over the limited beach.

Unlike other towns along his route, Wyatt noted the monotony of St. Michael. Without a sizable tree within a hundred miles, all the structures were framed with board facings and tin roofs. Rare canvas tents huddled beside the wood houses, perhaps realizing their lives were short-lived. Soon the fall would bring gales to shred and rend their fabric. Then only the billowing fields of sea grass carpeting the low rises would be left.

Before he let his uncertainty well up out of control, he thrust his hands into his pockets and walked down to the beach where the small boats were being built. These flimsy crafts would carry them up the Yukon, fighting its current all the way to their destination. Without them, he and Josie were stuck on this pile of sand, no closer to their dream than in San Francisco. Their future and maybe their lives depended on the boat.

Following the sound of hammering, Wyatt and his wife walked along the curve of the spit to stop at the site of frenetic building. Twelve boats, flat-bottomed for the shallow draft of the Yukon and fitted with steam-driven stern paddle wheels, were in various stages of construction amid piles of lumber and harried builders. Some of the nearly completed boats rested atop wooden skids or lay tied up in the silty water, while others existed in name only. The bare ribs of a keel defined a vessel in more than half, but nothing more. Clearly, the constant stream of steamers disgorging gold seekers in St. Michael exceeded the supply of riverboats needed to carry them over the second leg of the journey.

"Marshal Earp! Marshal Earp!" A rail-thin man in his midtwenties with silt-dusted bowler and equally silted black suit scampered toward them.

"Oh, no," Josie sighed. "Here comes that dreadful, little Mr. Pingree from the *Brixom*. Why do you encourage him so, Wyatt? It's so obvious how he revels in your acquaintance. Besides, I find him so dull."

Wyatt squeezed her arm. "Oh, he not so bad, darling. He's just trying hard to get out of the shadow of his brother, the governor of Michigan."

"Well, I wish you wouldn't encourage him."

"Josie, after all, his brother is a governor. You never know. I might need a pardon in Michigan sometime," Wyatt quipped.

The man dabbed at his sparse beard with the back of his coat sleeve, trying to keep the silt blown from the beach out of his mouth. All the fresh lines in his face pointed down, and he looked to be nearly in tears.

"It's criminal, Marshal Earp!" he sputtered. "Absolutely criminal! That's all it is!"

"Good morning, Mr. Pingree." Wyatt tipped his hat. "May I remind you it's just *Mister* Earp, not marshal." The repeated litany was tiresome, but he was done with law-keeping.

"Well, you'd do better staying a marshal. There's no law or order here. None at all," Pingree huffed.

"What is the trouble, Mr. Pingree?" Josie asked sweetly.

"Oh, excuse me, Mrs. Earp," Pingree tipped his bowler. "I'm forgetting my manners. You see, this place is turning me into a barbarian like all the others. How are you today?"

"I am fine, sir," she replied. "And how are you?"

"Terrible, Mrs. Earp. Do you know those thieving schemers in San Francisco sold us tickets to a riverboat that doesn't exist.

Would you believe it! Doesn't exist!" The man started hopping about on one foot in his agitation, stirring up the powdered glacial silt that covered the beach. His dance further dusted his coat. Wyatt tactfully moved Josie and himself upwind of the cloud.

"Are you sure of that?" Wyatt asked.

"There! Look there!" Pingree rasped. His voice had raised an octave in the last minute. His finger jabbed repeatedly at a pile of lumber stacked beside the water's edge. "There, sir! There is our boat. *It hasn't even been built!*"

Wyatt scanned the wood, and the muscles in his jaw twitched. He carefully removed Josie's hand from his arm, leaving her standing there while he circled the woodpile. The timbers looked sound—without rot, he noted. Now all he needed was a good ship's carpenter. As Pingree continued his dust dance and fumed to Mrs. Earp, Wyatt studied the name on his bill.

"Where is this Mr. Bruger?" he asked. "Have you talked with him, Mr. Pingree?" But Wyatt already knew the answer.

"He's vanished," the governor's brother replied. "Nowhere to be seen in St. Michael. The bartender at that saloon over there thought he saw him heading up the Yukon himself in one of the completed boats." Pingree shrugged hopelessly. "Apparently, gold fever got the best of him."

The wind shifted and a sharp breeze engulfed the party. Wyatt stiffened. There it was again, the smell of autumn. He had sensed it this morning outside their rooms. Clear, cold, and sharp from the north, carring with it the smell of unseen leaves storing energy for the winter. It was just August, but winter came early in the Arctic, he reminded himself. Time was running out.

"Did you find out who was supposed to build the boat? Bruger was only the contractor."

Pingree shook himself out of his depression enough to

point to two men working nearby. One was caulking a finished hull beside the other, who was driving nails into the upper deck. Both men looked like sturdy burgermeisters thoroughly burned a bright red by the sun and constant wind. Both also looked as though they could break an ax handle in two with no trouble.

"Those two over there. Hall and Larsen. Bruger even paid them in advance. But it won't do you any good to talk to them, Wyatt. I already did. They just laughed at me. Ship's carpenters are worth their weight in gold here. Why, people are bribing them with whiskey and money and . . . even women!" Pingree blushed. "Oh! Excuse me, Mrs. Earp. I do apologize for that crude remark. This whole thing has got me unnerved. It's . . . it's not like back in Michigan, I can tell you. And it's not what I expected."

"I understand completely, Mr. Pingree," Josie smiled. "But I was on the stage, so I'm not completely blind to the ways of frontier towns."

"Well, in that case . . . " Wyatt winked at Josie. "Maybe you should go talk to Messrs. Hall and Larsen for us. I'm sure our boat would be built overnight."

To Pingree's horror Josie jabbed her husband in the ribs—hard enough to make him wince. "I might just do that, Mr. Earp." She purred like a cat extending its claws. "If no one else is man enough to rectify the situation."

Wyatt watched Pingree blanch. "She's only joking, sir," he reassured the dumbstruck man. "But, I assure you she would get immediate results." He smiled broadly as Josie blushed a deep crimson.

"We're doomed." Pingree returned to the problem. "Nothing I said or did could convince them to build our boat. We're not even on their list anymore. It's plain highway robbery, that's all it is!"

Wyatt removed his coat, carefully folded it, and handed it

to his wife. He was wearing his gunbelt with the worn Mexican loop rig. While Pingree's mouth dropped, Wyatt cinched his belt and checked the cartridges in his pistol. The midwesterner goggled.

"Are you going to shoot those two?" Pingree asked.

Wyatt adjusted his tie, squared his shoulders, and walked away. Josie and their companion watched him walk down the beach to where the boat builders were working away. Both men appeared happily at work, stopping from time to time to swig whiskey from their generous cache and swap humorous asides. Earp strode up to the men and tipped his hat. Josie strained her ears, but they were too far to catch the conversation. She saw the men's heads bob as they laughed at her husband. Wyatt pointed to pile of lumber that was to be their boat, and the man with the hammer waggled it about like a metronome, aiming it at all the surrounding and unfinished boats.

Then she saw Wyatt remove something slowly from his belt and carefully hand each of the builders an item. The men stared fixedly at the object in the palm of their hands, and their faces lost all traces of mirth. For a long time they stood looking at the gift as if weighing its consequence, then they gazed at each other, then back at their hands. Without another word both men set their tools aside and walked over to the Earp's pile of wood and began to lay out the lumber in the shape of a flat-bottomed keel.

Wyatt strolled back and retrieved his jacket from his astonished wife. He slipped the coat on and adjusted his lapels. "Two weeks and our boat will be ready," he said.

"That's amazing, Mr. Earp," Pingree sputtered. "What did you say to them? What could you have possibly offered to them that no one else had? What would make them change their minds?"

"Hold out your hand, Mr. Pingree," Wyatt commanded. He dropped something cold and heavy into the man's upturned palm. "I simply gave them this and told them a more direct one would be forthcoming if our boat wasn't completed in the shortest possible time. They decided to come around." With that Wyatt offered his arm to Josie and strolled away.

Pingree stared down at his opened hand. Nestled in the palm of his hand was a Colt .45 bullet.

Two weeks to the day the *Governor Pingree,* named after young Pingree's brother, chugged ponderously out of St. Michael and across the wide mouth of the Yukon River. Rumors had it that the *Pingree*'s two ship's carpenters had worked around the clock the last three days to make the deadline, and the spit was a-buzz with admiration for those men's dedication to work.

As the stern paddle wheel churned the waters, driving the boat deeper into the silt-laden waters flowing from the Yukon, Wyatt stood on the foredeck with his arm around Josie. All around them watercrafts of various descriptions wallowed and lurched across the windy gulf. Some consisted of nothing more than barrels lashed together to make crude rafts while others appeared to be whaleboats modified with sails and oars to row upstream. Half were hardly seaworthy.

Wyatt studied the western sky where dark storm clouds gathered, and he felt the wind shift on his cheek. Far on the horizon his eyes spotted the wind whipping the sea into a boiling froth. Like an approaching dust storm on the desert or the telltale smoke from a prairie fire, its presence spelled danger.

Josie watched her husband. In all their years together she had never seen him off guard, and she had learned that it was as if she lived with a coiled spring. She supposed it came from years of living in the Indian Territories and working as a lawman, or perhaps it was always in his nature. Whatever the cause, alertness was cast into his very fiber, but at times it made her edgy.

"Oh, do stop chewing your mustache, Wyatt," she scolded.

"At the rate you're going, you'll have it and your eyebrows gone by the time we reach Dawson City."

Wyatt smiled benignly at his wife. For all her compact stature she carried a feisty temper. "Yes, ma'am," he said. "I'll try my best to be more stupid, if that suits you."

Josie chose to ignore his remark and tightened her shawl about her shoulders. "Well, I do wish you'd blow your own horn at times. You're too modest. Look at Bill Cody and Mr. Hickok. They knew the value of self-promotion."

"I'm no showman, Josie," Wyatt stated. They'd had this discussion before, but something was obviously in his wife's craw. "And Bill Hickok never saw a dime from those dime novels. All they brought him was a bullet from some glory hound."

"You could have let them name this boat after you like they wanted to!" she huffed. "You, and you alone, caused it to be built. Without your intervention we'd still be back at that dreadful St. Michael."

So that was it.

Wyatt's face crinkled into an enormous smile, his eyes almost disappearing beneath his brows and his mustache curling up with the corners of his mouth. "Well, darling," he laughed. "If this scow sinks, wouldn't you rather it wasn't bearing my name?"

She started to laugh in spite of herself. "I guess you're right, Wyatt. I'd much prefer the governor sink than you. We could do with one less politician."

Wyatt pointed to the west. "I don't like the looks of that storm. It'll hit us before we make the shelter of the river."

Josie turned in time to receive the full force of the rising wind. The chilling blast cut through her, and she shivered as she watched whitecaps spring forth across the milky water. "Oh, Wyatt, to sink in these frigid waters must be a terrible way to die," she said. "I dipped my hand in and it nearly froze, the water was so cold."

"Don't worry." He joked to lighten the tension. "If it comes to that, I'll shoot us both."

She sighed. "Thank you. I feel so relieved knowing that, but I'd prefer to make it safely to Dawson City."

The wind mounted and soon the *Governor Pingree* was rolling and rising with each wave. The stern paddles growled in protest as they shot free of the water and groaned when they bit back into the sea. The whitecaps grew to dancing horses and foam-spewed mist streaked the air to mix with sheets of icy rain. A gale had struck.

Around the *Pingree* those boats cobbled together in haste suffered dearly. Barrels broke loose from their lashings, cargo shifted, and boats capsized, flinging hapless stampeders into the frigid waters. The lashing rain and a rising fog masked the bay so that only swatches of the disaster were revealed and the howling wind snuffed out cries for help. Here and there Wyatt caught a glimpse of a hand sinking beneath the waves or a shattered craft turning turtle. He hurried Josie into the deckhouse despite her pleas to be by him and returned to the deck. Already the *Pingree* was swamping. Searching over his shoulder Wyatt spotted the skipper, Captain Tomlinson, fighting the wheel to keep the ship headed into the wind. The only other crew member struggled to keep flotsam from the surrounding wrecks out of the paddle wheel.

"We're lost, Mr. Earp," a voice cried at his side. It was the governor's brother, pale and reduced to a violent trembling, his eyes wide like leather buttons set in a drained face.

"Not yet," Wyatt snapped. "Get the other men and everything that can hold water and start bailing." To help the paralyzed Pingree on his way, Wyatt seized him by his collar and the seat of his pants and launched him down the deck like he had done so many drunks as a peace officer.

Within minutes a string of frantic bailers handled their buckets, pots, and pans with the fervor that only possesses a sailor on a sinking ship. Even a bedpan was recruited as the men bailed for their lives. The passing wreckage of their unfortunate companion vessels and the drifting bodies of the drowned, staring glassy-eyed at them, only served to spur them to greater effort.

Shallow-drafted and flat-bottomed, riverboats were never meant to handle the swell and chop of a storm-tossed open bay. Besides, the *Pingree*, like the rest, was severely overloaded. Wyatt sensed the losing battle as the free board of the boat dropped closer and closer to the water. He worked his way along the sides of the paddle boat with an ax, cutting the lashings that held the extra weight that now threatened to drag them down like the other boats. As he grimly lightened the load, only a few protested until they saw his iron determination, then they quickly returned to bailing. Even in the face of death, Wyatt found amusement in what people had brought onboard. A porcelain bathtub, an iron-banded Wells Fargo combination safe, a player piano, and the complete works of Shakespeare— all splashed into the sea. Wyatt's last move was to roll Josie's steamer trunk overboard. With a twinge of remorse he remembered this chest held the baby clothes she still kept faithfully packed.

Abruptly, the *Pingree* burst out of the fog bank into the sunlight. The mouth of the Yukon was a hundred yards ahead. With one last grasp at its escaping prey, the gale lashed the boat, but its ensuing wave drove the sternwheeler forward. Surfing over the silted bar at the river's mouth, the *Governor Pingree* surged into the flat waters of the Yukon River, safe.

Wyatt turned and looked up at the boat's captain and received a salute from the seasoned sailor. Together, the two of them had saved the ship. Young Pingree capered back to where Wyatt stood looking back at the fog bank that hid the disaster in the bay.

"We did it! We did it, Mr. Earp," Pingree shouted. "We're

safe. It's all downhill from here. Klondike Gold Fields, here we come!"

Earp smiled thinly at the youth. "It's all *upriver*, Mr. Pingree," he corrected.

"Er, yes. Quite. I meant upriver." Pingree straightened his twisted collar. His hair was windblown and unkempt, his vest missing all but one button. "Say, did I see you throw my safe overboard, sir?"

"Was that yours?" Wyatt chuckled. "You are an optimistic sort, that's for sure. That safe could hold half the gold in San Francisco. It probably ought to have its own boat."

"To be sure, Mr. Earp." Pingree laughed. "But no matter. We're unharmed now, and I'll buy another one when I strike it rich. Maybe two or three. I'll even buy you one—in remembrance of this event." The man clapped his hands together in glee. "We're saved. Oh, I feel marvelous. I feel so alive. Does it feel like this after a gunfight, Mr. Earp? Surely, the worst is over, nothing ahead but a sore back from picking up gold nuggets."

Wyatt winced. Killing a man always left him feeling hollow, not happy. But he excused Pingree's boyish exuberance. "No, it doesn't feel like this after a gunfight, not in the least. And I think the worst is still ahead. . . . "

Wyatt's prediction held true. Steaming up the flat, milky waters of the Yukon, the paddle wheeler struggled against the rapid flow of main channels only to feel its way like a blind man among the braided streams where the river spread across open country. Precious hours fell by the wayside instead of miles as the *Pingree* ran aground on silt-hidden bars. The men would strip to the waist, swatting clouds of tiny black flies—wryly called no-see-ums—and mosquitoes and wade ashore in the icy water to man cables to winch the ship free.

More time was lost cutting cords of four-foot logs for the hungry boilers. Passage north between Holy Cross Mission and

Nulato found natives willing to cut wood for trade. Wyatt studied the change from the smiling round-faced Yupik Eskimos that peopled the lower reaches of the river to the dark, flat features of Athabascans as they progressed inland. They reminded him of the Apaches of Arizona, and he recognized some of their words as similar to those he's heard from the White Mountain and Chiracauah Apache. While these natives were friendly, their likeness to the warlike Apaches kept him on edge. Constantly he reminded himself that no recent uprisings had taken place, but he realized his old habits of survival died hard. Now he carried his pistol at all times.

As the natives turned more fearsome looking, so did the land. Where the river turned sharply east after Nulato, high cliffs and dense sloughs confused the landmarks. The vicious insects remained the same as did the limb-numbing water that sucked all feeling so that men slipped and stumbled through it on unfeeling feet. The banks grew more savage with deadly undercut shores and tangled sweepers of fallen spruce trunks that thrust up like pointed lances. More than one unwary boat died in these waters, impaled on shore sweepers or holed by those lurking beneath the turbid waters, and their keels and exposed ribs served as grim reminders to remain vigilant. Night travel became impossible, and the welcome sight of cut firewood along the banks grew uncommon.

But it was the vast emptiness that affected them most. Unlike in the West, the land lay quietly watching these interlopers like a lynx stalking a hare, watching and waiting for them to make a misstep. Miles upon miles of silent, shuttered forests surrounded the travelers, and that fact played heavily on each of the passengers' minds. Even the Michigan governor's brother grew more wild and unkempt to match the wilderness. His hair, before cropped close, now hung about his ears and touched his shoulders, while a sparse beard protected his face from stinging bugs, and he no longer brushed silt and mud from his torn suit. Only Wyatt remained outwardly unchanged, but even he was not immune to the spell of the Arctic. The cold nights stiffened his injured hip and played havoc with the old bullet wound in his shoulder, yet he kept his pain hidden. He found himself wondering at this madness that gripped them all. Driven by gold fever, Alaska Territory lured them ever onward into its dark heart while its grip relentlessly squeezed them to fit its mold. Wyatt realized the arctic's mold was immutable; one bent to fit it or one was broken.

Forcing them to race against the coming freeze, the land drove them to dangerous heights of frenzy. In his heart Wyatt knew the land would win another round. Time was running out. The bite of fall he had sensed at the mouth of the Yukon grew more obvious. A five-day delay to repair a leak, a wrong turn that led them three days into the Tanana River, and the daily chore of chopping firewood dragged on them like iron chains warped behind the boat while the days flew past. It was now September.

Returning to the *Pingree* one evening, Wyatt dropped his ax and paused to look at the trees on the far bank. The slanting rays of the sun fired the birch and aspen leaves into bold orange and yellow clouds as if they were glowing coals fanned by the sunlight from their setting in the deep shadows. The chill of evening settled over this backwater slough where the boat was moored, causing his breath to steam, the musty smell of high bush cranberries reaching his nose. He listened. Voices of the women fixing dinner carried across the clearing from the ship. But outside of them and the rustling of leaves in the wind, the enormous silence of the land persisted. Then he heard it, almost imperceptible at first, the sound grew steadily until there was no mistaking its origins. He jaw tightened and the hairs on the back of his neck prickled. He looked up and saw the source of the sound. Chevron after chevron of wild geese filled the darkening sky, piercing the silence with their strident calls as they fled south.

The morning dawned, cold and crisp, and brittle ice surrounded their boat. Their side slough also sported an icy rime extending from the shoreline and encasing stones and branches. Worse, chunks of slush drifted past in the mainstream of the Yukon itself.

The captain stepped up beside Wyatt and gestured at the river with his pipe. "I don't like the looks of that, Mr. Earp," he said. "Did you hear the geese last night? Those birds know when to clear out. They're damned smart that way. No dumb wild geese, and do you know why, Mr. Earp?"

"No."

"Because the dumb ones hang around too long and wake up one morning with their feet frozen in the ice and a hungry fox licking his chops beside them, that's why." The captain paused to light his pipe. He drew two mouthfuls of smoke while he frowned down at the waterline. "We ain't gonna make Dawson," he said flatly. "Not this fall."

Wyatt nodded. "I was afraid of that."

The captain gave Wyatt a hard look. "You? Afraid? I don't think you're afraid of much."

"Just a figure of speech, Captain." As usual, Wyatt parried the personal probe. Miles ahead men were staking claims and he was stuck here. The bitterness of coming so close yet falling short knifed into his stomach, but the captain would never know his frustration. Too many years of poker and upholding the law made masking his feelings second nature. "What do you suggest?"

"Well," and the captain's head disappeared in a cloud of pipe smoke but his headless voice continued. "If we try for Dawson, we're gonna get our butts frozen in the ice like some dumb goose. I say we try for Circle City. That's about three hundred miles from Dawson, and there should be plenty of empty houses there. Circle was a gold mining town before the big strike in the Klondike broke loose. Everybody left for Dawson when the news broke. Now the place is a ghost town."

"Sounds reasonable. If we freeze up on the river, we'll have to build shelters, and half the men here still don't know which end of an ax is for cutting," Wyatt said. "Let's try for Circle. Maybe Josie and I can travel overland the last three hundred miles."

They never made Circle City. The hard freeze hit four days later, just as they passed Rampart, still six hundred miles from their destination. With thick slabs of river ice battering the *Pingree*'s hull and threatening to pierce the green wooden planks, the captain reluctantly turned the boat around and retreated to a slough off the village of Rampart. Not as richly endowed with veins of gold as Dawson, Rampart still supported a handful of productive mining claims.

As Wyatt escorted Josie down the ramp he pointed out a tall man standing on the riverbank. "Look at that Stetson and the fringed buckskin jacket, Josie. See how his hat is uncreased. A Montana peak would be creased on all four sides, not rounded like his. That man has got to be a Texan."

"By God!" the man bellowed. "You must be Wyatt Earp!" He charged up the gangplank with his right hand extended. "I'm Tex Rickard."

Wyatt winked at Josie. "What'd I say?"

Rickard shook his hand warmly. "I saw you referee the Sharkey-Fitzsimmons fight. Your decision cost me five thousand dollars."

Wyatt arched his brow. Even in the remote corners of this world his past followed him. "No hard feelings?"

"Heck, no." Tex tipped his hat to Josie, mindful of his colorful language in the presence of a lady. "I always say if you can't afford to lose the money, you shouldn't be in the game. Besides,

I think you made the right call. It just didn't favor me, that's all."

"That's very gracious of you, Mr. Rickard." Josie flashed her most brilliant smile at the Texan.

"Hell—heck, ma'am. Call me Tex. Everyone else does. What good's a fortune for if you can't lose it at times. I've lost two in Dawson already, and I aim to lose a handful more." He swept the ice-lined banks of the Yukon with his fringed arm. "Looks like you'll be staying the winter in Rampart. The ice is in."

Wyatt nodded. "We thought about traveling overland to Dawson. What do you think about that, Tex?" Already he liked this boisterous, open-faced man, so opposite to himself.

Rickard pursed his lips like a judge passing a death sentence and shook his head vigorously. "Wouldn't waste my time there, Wyatt. Going overland now will be a bitch . . . er, real bad. And Dawson's staked tighter than a Scotsman's purse. Nothing left in Dawson unless you go into the commercial side, gambling, dry goods, whorehouses. . . . " Rickard stopped again. "My apologies, Mrs. Earp, for my blunt language. My mama would turn over in her grave, 'cause she raised me better than I turned out."

"You just go right ahead and speak freely, Tex," Josie smiled. "My ears can take it."

He beamed. "I knew you'd understand. As I was saying, Wyatt. Dawson won't pan out. There's plenty of creeks with color here in Rampart, besides it's part of the States. None of those red-coated Mounties traipsing around drinking their blasted tea and talking like they was first cousin to Queen Victoria herself."

"I guess it's decided then," Wyatt said.

"Great!" Rickard picked up one of their bags. "I've got just the cabin for you." Tex ambled down the ramp and climbed the low rise from the river.

The Winter Wolf

Wyatt followed with his wife. He stopped to look back at the *Pingree,* already encircled by slushy water. By morning it would be frozen in place. Rampart, he noted, sat on a pile of silt and river washed stones not more than forty feet above the river level; with the creeks feeding the Yukon rapidly freezing, the town appeared to be rising as the water fell. He imagined the reverse might well flood Rampart in the spring. Low hills populated with spindly spruce trees served as the village's backdrop while the Yukon formed the front yard. Small log cabins fanned out from a central two-story tin-roofed bulding flying the American flag from a peeled spruce pole. Just beneath Old Glory fluttered a white flag with the letters of the Alaska Commercial Company. A pole and plank boardwalk scarcely wide enough to roll a barrel down extended from the company building to what once was the Yukon's edge. But now it ended a good ten feet short of water.

Tex introduced them to Captain Al Mayo, who ran the company outpost, and his native wife Aggie. The squat Mayo, once a circus acrobat and one of the first white men in the region, welcomed the newcomers. Aggie, delighted at the arrival of another woman, pumped Josie over tea for the latest fashions from San Francisco. Soon the two women were chatting like long-lost cousins. The three men stepped outside to smoke cigars.

Mayo watched the wind snatch away a mouthful of smoke as he pointed to a small log cabin chinked with dried moss and sporting a sod roof. Scattered fireweed, dried to a deep purple and sowing its cottony seed, decorated the frozen grass. Wyatt felt the ground harden beneath his feet as they walked to the cabin and guessed the ground was freezing along with the river. A dusting of snow already powdered the rise.

"I can let you stay in that one," Mayo said. "It belongs to Rex Beach, but he's running mail."

Tex nodded. "It's a good, tight little hootch, Wyatt. Nothing fancy, but you'll be dry and warm."

"That's what counts," Wyatt added.

"Yup," Rickard agreed. "But Beach didn't build it. If he had, you'd probably freeze to death. He fancies himself a writer of sorts, not a carpenter. Always writing things down in his notebook. Says he's putting together a novel. Personally, I think he's collecting dirt on all of us to use for blackmail. That'll be his pay dirt, mark my word—our paying him off not to print our embarrassing asides when we're rich and famous. But I plan on shooting him and dumping him into the Yukon if he tries that on me." Tex exhaled and grinned at Wyatt. " 'Course you're already there, Wyatt. Wait until Rex meets you. He'll probably write a whole book about you."

Wyatt ground his cigar out on the polished gravel. "Infamous is more like it, I'm afraid," he said. "And I'm sure not rich."

Tex looked past Wyatt to the trail winding from the tree line behind the settlement. A solitary figure, rifle slung across his shoulder, trudged up the trail. "Well, here comes the builder, himself, Frank Canton. Do you know him, Wyatt? He built your cabin last winter on his way to Circle City. He's the deputy U.S. marshal for the Yukon district."

Judging from the man's stride and the way his eyes constantly searched in arcs about him, Wyatt already guessed the approaching man made his living with a gun, or at least had in the near past. Canton wore a fur trapper's cap with the ear flaps tied on top and a worn plaid coat that covered all but the tip of his holster, but his Marlin .45–.70 looked oiled and well cared for. Earp guessed he favored using his heavy rifle over his pistol, especially in the brushy Alaskan terrain. As the figure drew closer, his features, complete with dark handlebar mustache grew increasingly familiar to Wyatt.

Tex Rickard called out to Canton. "Frank, this here's Marshal Wyatt Earp of Dodge City and Tombstone fame. Come over here and meet him."

Wyatt winced at his introduction and noticed Canton stiffen. Instantly the two men sensed the other was on guard, but both hid it from Mayo and Rickard.

Canton stepped up to the three men. He grounded his rifle, the butt crunching into the gravel. His eyes masked his recognition of Wyatt. "Hello, Wyatt Earp," he said. "Are you marshalling here, too?"

Wyatt slowly extended his hand which Canton took just as slowly. "No, Marshal. Tex got that wrong. I'm just trying to get to Dawson, but it looks like my wife and I'll be spending the winter in your cabin."

Canton relaxed, noticeably. "Well, it's a good cabin. I'd still be in it now, except the government saw fit to make Circle the center of Yukon District, so I sold it to Beach."

"You two ever meet before?" Tex asked.

"No," both men answered.

"Thought you might have," Tex looked from one to the other, then shrugged. "Guess not. Hell, I was a town marshal once in Texas, and I never met either of you."

"The world ain't that small, Tex," Captain Mayo added. "What brings you back here, Frank?"

"I'm looking for Big Ed Burns. He's wanted for questioning back in Skagway. The Mounties sent word he passed through Dawson using the name of Ed Barnes. They said he was heading down river to Circle, but he's got past me. I figured he might be here. Also I was hoping the captain here might have my back pay from the last mail run. The government is seven months in arrears with my wages, and my credit in Circle is getting pretty thin."

"Well, you'll have to wait a bit longer, Frank," Mayo said.

"I got nothing for you except a wad of handbills for outlaws."

"Ed Barnes?" Wyatt questioned. "I knew him in Tombstone. He was a small-time crook. As I recall, he specialized in being a grip man."

"That's him. Knows all the secret grips and handshakes of the Masons and Odd Fellows and the like. Uses it to gain their confidence, then bilks them of their bank rolls. He worked with Soapy Smith and his telegraph service in Skagway."

"I heard about that." Tex chuckled. "Soapy would send telegraphs for five dollars and another five for the reply. Got a lot of confidential information that way and used it to fleece the unsuspecting stampeder. Trouble was, there weren't no telegraph from Skagway. He even made up the replies."

"Yeah," Frank Canton said, and picked up his rifle and wiped the butt plate clean of gravel. "Well, Soapy's dead. He and Frank Reid killed each other last July. Now his gang is busted up and running for cover, so I'm looking for Burns."

Wyatt's eyes narrowed. "Frank Reid was a good man, a good Indian fighter. I'm surprised Soapy stood up to him, let alone got a shot at him. He must have called Soapy's bluff."

"I heard Reid's gun misfired, so Soapy gutshot him before Reid drilled Smith through the heart with his second round." Canton looked away. "You seem to know a lot of people, don't you, Wyatt?" he commented.

Wyatt shrugged. "That comes with these gray hairs, I guess. I've met the good and the bad, but that doesn't mean much. I mainly try to mind my own business."

Canton seemed relieved. "That's good. Captain, I'm afraid I'll have to trouble you for a grubstake on my I.O.U. since the government seems to have forgotten about me. I promise to arrest myself if the note goes unpaid. But I need to keep heading downriver while the water's still flowing."

Mayo laughed. "I guess I can trust the U. S. Marshal. Come

on down to the store, and I'll outfit you, Frank." Mayo strolled off in the direction of his store.

Canton turned to Wyatt and smiled for the first time. "This job means a lot to me, Wyatt," he said simply. "I'm trying to make a good show of it. Here in Alaska a man can do almost anything he wants to, even make a fresh start. I appreciate your help."

Wyatt shook his hand again. "I'm just another stampeder, Frank. That's all."

Before another word passed, Canton shouldered his rifle and followed Mayo to the store. Wyatt walked along with him for a short ways while Tex relieved himself on a patch of blueberries. The Texan developed an aversion to the wild berries last year when he was forced to subsist on them for two weeks when he was snowed in a trapper's cabin stocked with nothing but dried blueberries. Now he urinated on them whenever the chance presented itself, taking a perverse satisfaction in doing so. As he buttoned his trousers, he watched Wyatt and Frank Canton talking in earnest. They shook hands again and Wyatt returned to Tex's side.

Wyatt looked down at the wet berries and their frost burnished leaves. "Remind me not to pick those," he said pointedly.

"Help?" Tex ignored Earp's aside, his curiosity aroused by the two men's conversation. "What did Frank mean by that, Wyatt? What help?"

"I don't know, Tex. Maybe he was trying to recruit me to work for him. But I'm not doing it. Now, I'd best collect Josie and move in before darkness sets in."

Later that evening Josie and Wyatt finished a meal of beans on the small cast-iron stove they had brought with them, rearranged the crates that served as furniture, and stepped outside their smoky cabin to look at the panoply of northern lights snaking across the satin black sky. Hissing in curving bands of green and purple with rose-tinged edges, the aurora danced for them alone as they watched in awe.

"How beautiful they are, Wyatt," Josie sighed, her head nestled against her husband's chest. "We could be the only two people on earth, and those lights would still perform for us with equal beauty. This land is fresh and wild, like the West used to be. We can make a clean start here, I just know it." When he didn't answer, she looked closely at him, studying his features in the flickering illumination.

"It seems that way, Sadie," he replied, his voice heavy and tired. "Just about anyone can start over. You know the deputy U. S. marshal that you met this afternoon?"

"That nice Frank Canton?"

"Yes. Only his name isn't really Frank Canton. It's Joe Horner. I recognized him from old handbills when I was in Tombstone. He's wanted for bank robbery in Texas. And here he's a deputy U.S. marshal for the entire Yukon district of Alaska, which has more gold that Fort Knox. Isn't that something?"

Josie continued to study his face. "Are you going to tell someone?"

"No, and neither are you. He and I had a long talk. He's dead serious about going straight, and he asked my help, so I'm going to give it to him. No one else knows about him, those handbills are over twenty years old and out of circulation, and I'm going to keep his secret. In this new country, a man ought to be able to start over."

"That's marvelous, sweetheart. But why are you so glum?" she asked.

"Because I don't believe that pardon extends to me. . . . "

"Why?" She struggled to keep all trace of alarm from her voice.

"Frank Canton told me something else when we talked

about Soapy Smith. That boy who leapt off the dock in San Francisco was there in Skagway. He survived, and his friends were with him, the one-armed one and the old gunman."

"Oh, my God, Wyatt! No! They're in Alaska?" Josie felt her fingers digging into his arm.

"Yes." Wyatt nodded. "And they were looking for me."

TWENTY-TWO

"Aha, at last a task fitting of my superior skills," Doc Hennison crowed as he laid his good shoulder against the tiller of their boat. He made a point of directing his comment especially at Jim Riley, who glared at him from the crate just forward of the helmsman's seat. Nathan and Wei-Li occupied the cramped space forward of the piles of crates and supplies lashed into their rough-sawn boat.

Riley turned in disgust and spit a long stream of tobacco juice over the gunnell a mere inch from Hennison's patched knee. He smirked inwardly when Hennison jerked his pant leg back in defense. He had nothing to say to Doc.

In fact, meaningful conversation between the two men had ceased three days before when they still had another two hard days of sawing remaining to finish the boat's planking. Whip-sawing the needed nine-inch planks out of green logs was said to test the will of two angels so that even they would be fighting in three days, and Riley and Hennison were never angelic. So the saw pit had its predicted effect.

Erecting the saw pit was easy, as was bribing the necessary person for the two logs needed to saw into planks, but after the three men had coaxed the log onto the raised frame and peeled it, the trouble began. The coarse-toothed whipsaw required one man to straddle the log while the other worked underneath. One pulled while the other pushed. It sounded simple enough, but the bottom man constantly ate a shower of sawdust, grating his nerves while compelling his aching arms to follow his partner's lead. While Nathan tried to work the bottom as much as possible, simple exhaustion still forced his two friends to whipsaw together.

Two to three times a day Nathan stopped his tasks to separate the men as they rolled in their pile of sawdust, fists and feet flailing. Then Hennison or Riley, whoever was on the bottom at the time the fight broke out, would complain that the other was deliberately not pulling his share and purposefully aiming the sawdust in their eyes and mouth and down their shirts. When Nathan suggested they strip to the waist while sawing, they then griped the shavings were being dropped down their pants.

Thankfully, the sawing was done. Two logs made the required number of nine-inch boards. The boat was pegged and nailed under the watchful eye of Superintendent Samuel Steele. Too many deaths that spring from claptrap boats prompted the man the stampeders called the Lion of the North to supervise all boats that now left for the trip down river to Dawson. That first breakup of the ice saw ten thousand boats head down the Yukon in a frantic dash for the gold fields. Some sailed in canoes, some built rafts, and some lashed barrels together with rotted rope. Many died. Miles Canyon and Whitehorse Rapids broke the flimsy boats and drowned their crew. The banks down river from those two deadly rapids were spotted with graves.

Build them long—eighteen to twenty-two feet was his standard—and build them strong, Steele commanded. Take your time building them, he said. The gold has no legs and will wait for you. A short boat would bob about out of control in the short, choppy standing waves at the narrows in Whitehorse Canyon while a longer craft had a chance.

Hennison shifted the tiller slightly to catch the breeze and watched their square canvas sail fill. For a fleeting moment memories of sailing during his youth crept over his defenses and flooded his mind with painful pictures of his past. First his heart warmed to the thoughts, but then the memories only served to magnify the enormity of his loss and how far he had fallen in his own eye. The spark of warmth in his chest turned to a penetrating ache, so he snuffed it out by biting on his lip until pain clouded all past memories.

Riley burrowed deeper into his cramped space and looked warily at the menacing fog bank that lay just off the shore of Lake Bennett. Ghostly apparitions emerged from the fog to follow them as a continuous line of fellow stampeders drifted after them. He sniffed the air for signs of rain, but his nose found nothing but the smell of fresh-cut cedar and aging summer grasses. Sudden squalls could turn Bennett into a nightmare of its own, but this time the weather preferred to wait and watch, perhaps to lull the unwary. Only the fog and the slightest breeze disturbed the mirrored finish of the lake's surface.

"Ain't natural, a man not having his feet on solid ground," Riley complained. "We'd have flippers instead of toes if that tweren't the case."

Doc, enjoying the gunman's discomfort off land, gave the boat a quick rock and watched Riley snatch the gunnell. "If you had your way, all men would have horses growing out of their asses so's they could constantly ride and not walk," he snorted.

Riley's free fingers cultivated his stubby beard as he studied the suggestion. "Why not? Four sure feet is a heap better than two pigeon-toed ones. A man on horseback is a winning proposition. You never heard of nobody drowning while his horse stood on dry land, did you?" He looked ruefully down at his cowboy boots and wondered who was wearing his spurs back in Skagway. This northern country had a way of separating a man from his best talents as well as wearing him down.

Horses and guns, Riley knew well, but the Arctic was no place for a horse. That left him only his weapons.

The wind died as the current swept them into the sluggish finger called Tagish Lake. The sail hung limply from its cross pole while the boat slewed along the shallows past wide swamps that lined both sides with irregular tussocks and clumps of blueberry, Labrador tea, and stunted alders. Even the air grew stale and rank with the stench of rotting grass and stagnant pools. Off to the left a marsh hawk hovered over the ground hunting field mice, causing Riley to feel like the harried rodent.

Around the bend the air shimmered and undulated as a cloud of living smoke hung before them. A distinct humming noise emanated from the mass. Nathan and Wei-Li watched the shadow draw closer, growing apprehensive but not yet able to identify what they saw. Then the reality struck home.

"Mosquitoes!" Nathan shouted back at his friends. "A whole fucking lot of them!" He swore uncharacteristically, but the cloud looked to contain thousands of the biting insects.

"Mind your language," Hennison chided him. "Riley and I still have hopes of making you into a gentleman. And—"

"Look for yourself," Nathan cut him short. His finger stabbed in the direction of the danger. That many mosquitoes could suck a man dry or drive him mad with their attacks.

Hennison rose from his padded crate and squinted ahead. His eyes widened in terror. "Jesus! You're right, boy! There's a hell of a whole fucking lot of them! What do we do?"

The mosquitoes waited, hovering directly over the river, waiting for the trapped voyagers to be dragged by the current into their wing-filled net. Inexorably the river carried them closer, working as the insect's ally. No shelter or escape existed on either side. Marshy swamp spread for a mile on both right and left, and the channel led straight through the expectant cloud. In a few moments their boat would enter the trap.

Frantically Nathan looked about. A scattered handful of rocks emerged from the river, boulders large enough to hole their craft or swamp it if hit broadside. The boat would require someone at the helm to avoid collision, but that helmsman would pay a terrible price. Instantly, the youth decided: It would be him.

"Everyone under cover, quickly!" he shouted as he scrambled aft. "Doc, up front with Wei-Li. Wrap yourselves in the blankets. You too, Jim. Keep down and seal any opening in the covers." He grabbed the tiller from the paralyzed physician.

"But, who'll steer?" Hennison protested. "Those rocks . . . "

"I will!" Nat yelled over the increasing hum of the hungry mosquitoes. "Now get forward. Hurry!"

Wei-Li screamed, rejecting his sacrifice, but one look from his grim face silenced her. Her heart sinking, she tore strips of silk from her undergarment which Nathan gratefully stuffed in his ears and nostrils. He turned up his collar, buttoned the jacket tightly about his neck, and turned to face his foe.

The cloud, wafting in the still air, so ethereal and gossamer, struck with the force of a hundred hammers. Thousands of hungry mosquitoes, driven by one desire only—blood to feed their eggs—attacked. Stinging, biting insects carpeted Nathan's face, clogging his mouth and blinding his eyes. Forcing himself to keep one hand on the rudder, Nat swatted and wiped at his tormentors until his face ran with his blood mixed with gouts of smashed bugs, and his eyelids grew heavy.

But the attack continued unabated. Each tiny aggressor held no thought for its own danger, only the need for blood. For every score Nathan killed, a hundred followed. As the boat drifted downstream, the cloud followed, mounting in ferocity.

Nathan's mind tottered on the edge of madness. Run, hide, jump ship, and roll in the weeds, it screamed. But the horrid drone masked those cries. Nathan found himself screaming without sound, choking as the creatures filled his mouth and bit his lips until the swollen tissue itself threatened to stopper his breath. But his eyes suffered most. His eyelids swelled until mere slits remained, and he battled near blindness to keep the boat in line. Ahead, the treacherous rocks dimmed to hazy patches, forcing him to guess his course.

Now, as if a part of the conspiracy, the channel narrowed and the current sped faster. The boat hit one rock as Nathan wiped his eyes, then it shuddered and careened downstream, wounded, with silty water seeping from a gash in its side. Unseeing now, Nathan kept his fingers locked on the tiller and prayed. He no longer felt the swarming attack on his swollen face, and he was beyond caring. Only the safety of the boat mattered.

An abrupt cloudburst spread a curtained veil across the curving water just ahead, but it was unseen by the youth. Unrelentingly the attack persisted until the boat hit the wall of rain, then the insects broke off their assault to retreat in the face of the rain. Past all caring Nathan dimly sensed the retreating hum as the cloud hung back, buzzing sullenly to await the next boat that the river would bring for it to feed upon.

The boat nudged ashore on the crowded silty bar just before the entrance to the deadly Miles Canyon. Most travelers stopped here to study and plan their next move in shooting the first deadly rapids. Boats, tents, and piles of cast-off goods littered the strip. Half swinging in the wash of the wider course, their craft grounded with a crunch and stopped.

"Hurrah! We're saved!" Hennison shouted as he popped from beneath his blanket. "We made it past those devils." But his words died in his throat as he saw Nathan fixed to the steering pole.

"Sweet Jesus," Jim Riley swore as he followed Hennison's gaping stare.

Locked to the tiller, white as death, sat an apparition dressed in Nathan Blaylock's clothing. Otherwise he was unrecognizable. Streaks and clumps of blood and black wads of crushed mosquitoes covered his face. Instead of the thin, boyish looks his appearance had changed to an eyeless, balloon-lipped grotesque with matted hair and swollen, doughy, lifeless flesh more akin to the belly of an overripe fish.

Hennison clambered over the supplies and placed his ear to the boy's chest. "He's barely breathing," Hennison gasped as he and Riley pried the boy's locked fingers from the tiller. "Help me get him ashore. He's going into shock. We need to keep him warm. I saw too many wounded men die this way from wounds that ought not be fatal. Somehow the humors congeal and impede the circulation."

A curious crowd of onlookers parted to let them pass. Riley begged the use of two stampeders' fire while they wrapped the shivering lad in blankets and forced warm tea between his swollen lips. Wei-Li held his head in her lap while Doc alternately elevated and massaged his limbs.

"I seen that before," a sleepy-eyed redhead grunted. "The boat behind us hit a nest of mosquitoes just like him. None of them survived. He ain't gonna make it, neither."

The man shut up when Riley's Colt tapped him between the eyes. He blanched and backed away into the protection of the crowd.

"Shut up, all of you," Riley hissed. *"He's gonna make it.* And the next fella I hear say otherwise, I'll kill."

The crowd faded away, returning to their plans for Miles Canyon, leaving the three to tend to the boy. The late summer alpen twilight settled over the group as they ministered to Nathan. Leaving Riley to force fluids, Wei-Li searched among the bushes outside the camp for herbs to reduce his swelling. She returned to layer his face with a poultice of rose hips and cranberry leaves.

For two days fevers and chills wracked Nathan at alternating intervals. Slowly the swelling subsided, and his eyes emerged unharmed from behind puffy lids. Another day and he was able to stand and walk several steps with Wei-Li's help. While Riley and Doc took turns nursing Nathan, the girl bore the brunt of his treatment, going without sleep for the first critical days.

Hennison bridled at the delays, but Riley used the time to best advantage by polling the Mounties and anyone knowledgeable about the dangers ahead. All voiced a fear of Miles Canyon, but Whitehorse Rapids below the canyon held the prize as the raft killer. No shortage of advice existed on these two places. Experienced river runners agreed on the best approach for both. Miles Canyon, with its hundred-foot-tall black basalt walls, seemed the most intimidating, especially the way the water boiled through the constricting gorge, piling up in midstream so the center of the river actually rode higher than the sides. Halfway through the gorge a monsterous whirlpool held the center. To survive one had to ride the wildly bucking hogback down the center then steer to the right to avoid the suck hole, and then shoot back to the left side to miss a rock in midstream waiting to spear the unwary.

Whitehorse Rapids was different. Roughly shaped like a dogleg, extending to the left, the rapids sprung suddenly beyond a white bluff that rose from the far right bank after traveling through an unremarkable stretch of lowland. The informed would note a danger post placed there by someone named Kelly. Suddenly the river swung to the left, exposing a shallow reef that caught the unsuspecting as the water accelerated through timbered shores to empty into a broad, placid basin marked with meadows on the right. But the basin acted like the sirens to lull the unprepared, for a reef stabbing from the left narrowed the course to less than sixty feet in width. Here the water tumbled over razor-sharp rocks in rooster tails, dragging the boats to their doom. Grave markers dotted the placid meadow beyond with those the rapids claimed, and shattered vessels and cargo littered the shoreline.

All these facts were well known, so carefully, almost painfully, the gunfighter used his nascent skills to copy maps and jot down notes. These he presented to Hennison, only to have them rebuffed.

By week's end Nathan's strength had returned enough to enable him to man an oar, so at first light the party shoved their boat into the main stream just as the patchy fog broke under the rays of the rising sun. The air was crisp and clear, portending the tail end of summer—a perfect day to spend on the river.

Silently they rowed into the current as Hennison, his hat cocked jauntily over one eye, handled the tiller with disdain. Winning big at poker last night did little to deflate his ego, so he discounted the tales he'd heard about what lay ahead. Besides, his head still spun from sampling the various stills at the post.

Riley noticed it first, a mounting roar better felt as a visceral sensation than heard as a noise. Then Nathan and Wei-Li, and finally Doc, marked the thunder growing ahead while the sky stayed clear and blue. The sound matched the increase in flow as the boat surged ahead of their paddles which now acted more like brakes. Hennison found it necessary to throw his body weight on the tiller to hold control. Doubt shadowed his thoughts as the craft slewed and yawed with the force of water. He opened his mouth to call for help, but the roar drowned his words.

A red flag, tattered by the wind, flapped its warning ahead, and a crudely painted sign on a weathered board proclaimed CANNON. The sheer, black walls of Miles Canyon shot into view and the little boat leapt into the chasm. Only luck kept them in the center, riding the ridge of water humped in the middle by the constricting walls. Nat watched the slick sides speed past. No place to catch hold if we go over, he thought. Luck again saved them from the midchannel rock, and Nat held his breath as the jagged spear lanced past just inches away.

Now they were past Miles Canyon, but the water continued its mad race toward Whitehorse Rapids. No one saw the warning post placed by the unknown Kelly to mark the start of Whitehorse Rapids.

The boat sped past the chalky bluffs and shot to the left. The waves ahead parted momentarily, and Nathan spied the telltale brown and gray smudges of rocks lurking beneath the milky waves.

"Doc!" he shouted. "Rocks ahead!"

His words came too late. The boat hit the submerged crags with a sickening crash and vaulted into the air like a hurdler tripped in midhurdle. The heavily laden craft flew for several agonizing seconds before its keel slapped back into the waves, then it raced on. Nathan and the girl were thrown half out of the boat but clawed back inboard. Waves poured over the thwarts and threatened to swamp the ship.

The boat broached and swung sideways as the current carried it through the right bend. Ahead, a second whirlpool, different from the one in Miles Canyon, appeared to drain the very center out of the wild river. Just behind boiled Whitehorse Rapid's notorious reef.

"Damn yer insolent hide." Riley swore at Hennison, leaning back so his curse stung Doc in spite of the noise. "I told you about this canyon and the rapids, and you didn't listen. So high and mighty with yer learning, but you ain't got the common sense God gave geese. We got to miss that damned suck hole and the reef beyond or we're goners."

Hennison's stark face bobbed in panicked agreement, but the water overwhelmed his efforts. "Help me, Riley," he pleaded. "I . . . I can't hold her." The knuckles on his hand shone white as his face while he watched the roaring whirlpool looming directly ahead.

Riley struggled toward the stern but the cargo lashed to the sides blocked his path. For a split second he weighed his chances of drowning now if he fell overboard versus in another minute when they hit the whirlpool. Then he rose to his feet and jumped for the stern. The rocking boat slipped away beneath his feet, leaving him clawing in midair. But the boat's movement carried it beneath him, and he dropped beside the panicked Hennison.

Together the two of them fought the tiller instead of each other, bending and bracing in tandem. Nature, in its perverse way, succeeded in yoking these two stubborn oxen to the same plow, something their own characters would never have allowed.

With both men's weight on the wooden handle, the boat edged away from the whirlpool to just skim its edge. But there was no time to celebrate. The more dangerous reef lurked ahead under a billowing rooster tail followed by two steep, standing waves. The boat needed to cross back to the right bank in the next few seconds or risk splintering on the rocks or nosediving into the standing waves. Again Hennison and Riley battled the river, but this time the river refused to give.

Their boat skimmed the reef only to dive nose first into the sharp wall of water standing behind the rooster tail. The overladen craft cleft the first wave, but its pull tipped the bow into a shallow dive. Water rushed over the sides, filling the craft and adding to its excessive weight. It hit the second wave nose pointing down. Here Superintendent Steele's wisdom of long boats proved correct. Their longer boat spanned the two wave crests and came to rest, one end jammed on a submerged rock while the other stood suspended in the midst of the second wall of water. There they hung suspended, thrashing and vibrating in the wild water, while the bow took on water. The lashings tore loose and their possessions broke away to race down the river. In its death throes, the boat had turned end for end, so Nathan and Wei-Li, once in the bow, now found themselves on the part grinding to bits over the buried stone ledge.

Pieces of the planking began to shatter under the terrible vibrations. The river shook the small boat like a grizzly with a hapless salmon. Another minute and the entire craft would shatter, spilling its occupants into the boiling waves to drown.

Nathan jumped from the boat onto the boulder. Scoured smooth by the water, the surface offered little foothold, yet the youth found one even with the water beating at the backs of his legs. Wei-Li watched, frozen in terror, her hand pressed to her mouth. Straining, he hefted the pinioned bow off the rock to set it free. The boat soared ahead. Nat made one desperate leap as the craft shot away. He landed half inside with his legs dragging underwater. Now the girl came alive; hauling with all her might she pulled Nathan to the safety of the vessel.

Draped over the shattered sides like dead men and drained of all energy, the four floated past the town of Whitehorse in pouring rain, oblivious to the steam vessels docked at its wharf, and on into Lake LeBarge. The half-swamped boat drifted in the current along the cliff-lined eastern shore, known for its lack of places to land and its murderous squalls that rose with sudden ferocity. But they were beyond caring, and so they drifted through another danger without knowing the risk. Fortunately, no storms struck as they passed, and by nightfall they nosed to a stop on a gravel bar at Hootalinqua where the Teslin river joined the Yukon and a telegraph wire ran from Dawson to Whitehorse. Exhausted, they limped ashore to fall asleep under sodden blankets behind the sod-roofed log cabins.

The next morning brought low scudding clouds and constant drizzle. After a hurried breakfast of rain-filled coffee cups and cold biscuits, the group reluctantly abandoned what little warmth they could coax from their smoldering fire of green spruce boughs and shoved off. Their patched boat rode higher with less than a fourth of their supplies recovered from the shore.

Onward they floated in silence, shivering in the constant rain while never knowing it was a mixed blessing. This stretch of the Yukon broke the back of many parties with numerous mosquito attacks, but the rain spared them that affront.

A chastened Hennison listened this time to Riley, and they floated past the Big and Little Salmon rivers and Five Finger Rapids with surprising ease. The protruding five fingers presented no problems. The next day they shot through Rink Rapids on the crest of rising water from the constant rain. Electing to pass Fort Selkirk they camped on the river bank outside Stewart City just eighty miles from Dawson City. Ahead, at the Junction of the Yukon with the Stewart, a Northwest Mounted Police post waited to check the stampeders before allowing them into the goldfields. With most of their required supplies lost in the river, they used the "midnight run" like so many others and slipped past under cover of darkness.

That evening, Wei-Li and Nathan sat on a spruce sweeper jutting into the river like some prehistoric reptile and watched the western sky awash in crimson and scarlet clouds. The sinking sun painted clouds' underbellies until it seemed they were afire, and their images danced atop the black mirror of the river. Nathan released Wei-Li's hand to point at the blaze.

He shrugged his shoulders in confusion. "This is a crazy place, Wei-Li. It keeps trying to kill us, but I . . . I like it. I never felt part of Arizona or Colorado, but I do here. I feel I could belong here. It's like each disaster is a test, and if you survive it makes you stronger, as if the land is challenging you. The table stakes are your life against part of the power of the land. If you succeed, you gain that power, that might. You keep on winning and growing until one day you lose. Then it's over, finished. You won't get a second chance. You die or leave broken, your power returning to the land. Does that make sense to you?"

Wei-Li knelt by a dark pool, careful to keep her back to him so the tears welling in her eyes would go unnoticed. "That is very Chinese, my love," she whispered. She dipped her hands into the icy water and withdrew them cupped together. Carefully she watched the water drain through her fingers and return to the river.

"You are like this restless river, my love. No matter how tightly I hold you, you will slip free and race away. Each trial only adds to your strength and makes it harder to hold you."

"Don't talk nonsense." He frowned. "I love you, Wei-Li. You know that. I want to marry you, and we will, in Dawson after . . . after . . . "

"After you kill this Wyatt Earp?"

"Yes, or after we strike it rich. But it has to be one or the other. I want us never to be poor again, never to be forced to do another's will because we need money." He held her tightly, the strength of his grip emphasizing his ardor.

She let herself mold to his muscular frame. "And I love you, Nathan. But the river cannot change to a rock no matter how much it desires to," she said sadly. "And it is your joss to be a river. To be restless."

"I don't believe in that joss stuff." He grew angry, fearful of her words. "And fate has nothing to do with it. A man makes his own destiny, not some tin god sitting on a mountain top. Believe me, I watched the sisters in the orphanage, and none of them could walk on water no matter how hard they prayed. And all their praying over Sister Bernadette didn't keep the whooping cough from killing her." He turned from her and fastened his hands on a splintered branch rising from the trunk, snapping it off at its base. Angrily he turned the severed limb over in his hand before flinging it into the dark waters.

Wei-Li stroked his arm gently and laid her head against his back. She watched the stick being carried into the darkness. "My joss may carry me away from you like that poor bough," she said softly. "But I would be happy if you never cast me aside."

"Never!"

The force of his response both frightened and reassured her. Silently she prayed to Quan Yin, the Goddess of Mercy, that the old sooth-sayer's vision was cloudy and that not all of it would take place, but so far it had been correct. . . .

She brushed back a strand of unsettled hair with her hand. This night she wanted to look her most beautiful. She planned this night, taking extra pains to appear desirable, using the tiny portion of French perfume she had hoarded since leaving Brackett's Store. With all but a few pieces of her makeup kit lost in the river, she had done wonders. Tonight she would be the most fertile, and she intended to make one part of the prophecy come true.

TWENTY-THREE

"So this is the fabulous Dawson City, the City of Gold. Looks like a dump to me," Jim Riley muttered as he looked about him. He stood on the seat of their battered boat and surveyed the town.

Three years ago the confluence of the Yukon and the Klondike rivers was swampy bog frequented only by moose. With the discovery of gold, a wily oldtimer named Joe Ladue staked a townsite claim and opened a sawmill. Now his "rectangle in a bog" of sawboards and slatted houses held thirty thousand people, slightly less than the population of Seattle. Surrounded by rolling hills striped in green, red, and yellow that proclaimed their rich mineral soil, and watched by the Dome, the tallest mount some twenty miles away, boxed-in Dawson sported three distinct faces: the waterfront, the main street, and the tent city.

Along the crowded waterfront majestic sternwheel riverboats rubbed shoulders with barges and the smaller stampeder's plank boats. Both had earned the right to be there. The sternwheelers had bucked the Yukon's currents and treacherous silt bars all the way from St. Michael at a cost of one hundred and fifty cords of firewood to stoke their boilers. Yet the tarred and planked boats belonged there, too. Veterans of the wild waters of Whitehorse rapids and Miles Canyon, they had suffered and succeeded and earned their place, many at great loss of life and property.

Set back from the bustling shore, clapboard saloons, stores, and restaurants lined the muddy length of the main street. Gaudy signs mingled with painted boards proclaiming services and wares of everything imaginable along the silt-churned street. Here one could buy almost anything, tailored suits from Boston, French champagne, and Cuban cigars. Prices were outrageous, but miners, denied of comforts, never complained. Nuggets and gold dust were the currency, and every store sported a scale.

Spreading out from the center of town, canvas tents and pole hovels sprinkled the rising hills like seeds scattered by the wind. These meager shelters followed the spiderweb of creeks that laced among the foothills to spread their white walls over the land like hoarfrost. More than a few shacks sat astride thousands of dollars of gold. From the distant Dome, Dawson looked like a dump strewn about by a marauding bear.

Riley stepped to the silty beach and puffed thoughtfully on a crumpled cigarette as he studied his neighbors. Home was their boat, moored along the stump-strewn bank with a hundred others. Canvas draped parts of the craft for shelter and four-inch stovepipes spilled smoke down river from the cast-iron Yukon stoves they carried to cook and keep warm. New arrivals lived on their boats for several days while they planned their next move. Some chose to work for others while the adventurous staked their own claims, and some simply hovered about their vessels in a state of shock.

Jim scanned the far bank of the Yukon. Shorn of all trees for lumber, yellow- and red-leaved willow and fireweed still colored the naked hills. He sniffed and his nose caught the pungent smell he had learned was high bush cranberry touched by a light freeze. That morning he awoke to find frost on their canvas cover, something he had been expecting for the last week.

Riley turned up his coat collar against the north wind. His mind told him what his senses already knew: Winter was coming.

His three fellow travelers slogged their way back to the boat while he watched them. Nathan and his girl looked tense while Hennison seemed ebullient from their scouting foray along the main street. Riley noted Nat was packing his pistol again. All three were splashed in mud up to their knees.

"What a place!" Doc crowed. "Thirty dollars for a gallon of milk, and six bits for a single egg. Would you believe that, and not even a fresh egg at that. I saw it outside Butler's Grocery. And forty dollars for a *pint* of watered champagne. Why, my elixir will fetch five dollars a pint for sure, maybe, ten dollars if I age it for a day and call it reserve stock." He fairly skipped over the pile of peeled spruce logs and the two layers of river boats between their boat in his excitement.

"Did you find out about Earp?" Riley asked, but the frown on the lad's face answered his question.

Nat shook his head. "No. But we know where to look. There's a place called the Grand Opera House that looks to be the biggest saloon in town."

Doc eyed the splintered remains of their riverboat, running his finger along the tar and pitch used to caulk the planks. "I can use this instead of creosote in my elixir," he said to himself. "And a touch of Labrador tea and spruce instead of juniper . . . "

"Doc!" Riley sputtered. "We ain't here for that! We're look-ing for Earp, remember?"

"Don't fuss. I know that. But I can whip up a batch of elixir while we're searching. The need is definitely here, and I can-not neglect my obligation to provide the populace with my cure-all."

Riley gave up. "At least I ain't seen no pigs here. Have some coffee while I finish my smoke," he suggested to Nathan. He handed the youth a steaming tin cup. "I ain't got but one more roll left, and I expect tobacco is too dear from the cost of things for me to waste it. Then I'll check out this Opry House with you. Doc can keep an eye on our goods with missy here, 'cause he ain't gonna be good for nothing 'til he gits his snake oil brewing."

Reluctantly, Nat gulped the hot java and waited for Riley to finish his cigarette. A growing uneasiness nagged at the back of his mind. Dawson was not what he expected. It was too big, too active, almost overwhelming in its feverish pitch. Gold was everything and the rest nothing. One could lose all focus here and easily join the rush for the yellow metal. That thought troubled him, and he forced himself to reread the now-tattered and ink-smeared letter from his long-dead mother, Mattie Blaylock. Smudged and faded in parts, her words rekindled his resolve. He studied the photograph as he had done a thousand times, then carefully refolded the scraps of paper and replaced them in his oilskin pouch. An observer might deduce he held a vast treasure rather than mere paper, but to Nathan, these torn links to his past were priceless; they held the key to his past and pointed the path to his future.

Trudging across the ankle-deep mud, the two arrived at an imposing frame structure complete with high, arched windows gracing its third story, and a central door opening to a rail-enclosed second story overlooking the entrance on the main floor. The entire facade sported a herringbone pattern of wood slats. Music and sounds of laughter spilled out the entrance to greet them.

"The Grand Opera House," Nathan said simply.

"It do look grand," Riley replied. He wiped his hand over his grizzled beard and tightened his gunbelt before they stepped inside.

Shouldering past a throng of muddied miners arguing in the foyer, they entered a packed room, filled with smoke, music, and human voices. At one end, five girls danced about a lighted stage to tunes from a five-piece band as bouncers sped about dragging drunken miners off the footlights. Opposite this stage ran a polished mahogany bar that stretched the entire length of the saloon. Heavy framed paintings covered the wall behind the bar, and red, white, and blue bunting—now browned by the constant smoke—decorated every corner. Poker tables and roulette wheels filled the space in between. For all its size, space to stand was at a premium.

Riley muscled his way to the bar and squeezed Nathan in beside him. "Two beers," he ordered.

The bartender slopped two overfilled mugs in front of them and waited patiently while Nathan dug two dollars out of his pocket. The man noted the coins, and said, "I take it you boys are new here."

"What makes you say that?" Riley asked after he wiped the foam from his beard. The beer was painfully green, but still tasted good.

"No offense, mister," the barman said as he wiped glasses with a stained rag while his eyes studied them, "but nobody pays in cash 'less they just got off their boats." He pointed to the scale to his right. "Dust or nuggets, that's the common currency."

Nathan followed the man's eyes and was startled to see gold dust littering the bar and pokes filled with nuggets on every poker table. Back at the stage, men were raining nuggets at the dancers, but the clatter was lost in the din.

"We're looking for someone." Nathan came straight to the point.

"Most everyone comes in here since our grand opening in July," the man grinned, revealing a shiny gold tooth. "Everyone 'cept the parsons and the women's temperance league. What's his name?"

"Wyatt Earp," Nathan replied.

The bartender stopped polishing. He glanced over the mahogany edge at the men's gunbelts. "I take it you men aren't miners," he said.

"Take whatever you like," Nathan snapped. "Do you know the whereabouts of Wyatt Earp, or don't you?"

The man stiffened. "Easy, mister. You need to talk to Charlie. He's the man to ask, not me." With that the man scurried away to the safety of the far end of the bar.

"Did I hear someone mention my name?" a voice boomed over the racket.

Nat spun around to face a giant dressed in fringed buckskin jacket and massive sombrero. A good four inches taller than Nathan, the man sported a thick handlebar mustache, and black hair fell in ringlets to his leather clad shoulders. Around his waist rode a brace of pearl-handled Colt .45s. He could have sprung straight from one of the dime novels Nathan had read at the orphanage. The giant grinned down at him and thrust his hand out.

"Charlie Meadows is my name, all six foot six of me," the giant thundered.

Jim Riley twisted around to see this wonder, his eyes widened, and he blurted out. " 'Arizona' Charlie Meadows!"

The giant peered closer at Riley, and his grin changed to a look of astonishment. "My God! 'Newton Station' Jim Riley, is that you? I thought you were dead!"

Riley jumped at the use of his name. His head swiveled from side to side, anxious that someone had overheard his name and knew the legend. But not a single head turned except to cast greeting smiles at Arizona Charlie.

"Hell, you can rest easy, Jim," Meadows rumbled. "This is Dawson. Gold is the only thing of interest here. That and maybe a trip upstairs with Squirrel Tooth Alice or that minx, Little Ruby, over at the Monte Carlo." Charlie eased up to the bar where the bartender already was pouring him a shot of his private reserve whiskey. At Meadow's prompting the waiter filled two more glasses. "You could be Jack the Ripper for all they care." Charlie chuckled. "Most all of the old crew from the runs in Arizona and the Black Hills are here. Why, look over there. That's Calamity Jane, the pride of Buffalo Bill's International Tour. She's a mite worn now." He pointed to a shabby woman nursing a drink at the end of the bar.

Riley shuddered at the remnant of the vibrant woman he'd met years ago. But he kept his poker face and sipped his drink while he looked up at Meadows. "Don't know no Ripper. Did he ride with the Hole in the Wall Gang or maybe with Bill Doolin in Oklahoma?"

"Nope, Jim. Not even close." Meadows wiped his mustache. "Where the hell have you been keeping yourself, Jim?" But his eyes studied Nathan intently. "And you might introduce your young friend."

"Nat, this is Arizona Charlie Meadows. Half the things he'll tell you are damned lies, and yer a fool to believe the other half."

Meadows doffed his sombrero and bowed low. "As eloquent an introduction as any I received in all my tours in Europe and Australia. But he left out I am a world-class cowboy, lassoist, trick shot, and showman."

"Do you know Buffalo Bill?" Nathan asked earnestly.

"Know him! Hell, son, I carried that thieving windbag out of more saloons than I care to recall. I toured England in his Wild West Show, worked with the Wirth Brothers' Show, and even performed in Australia before I started my own show." He downed another whiskey and sized up the raw-boned six-foot-two-inch youngster. "How old are you, son?"

"Sixteen. Going on seventeen."

"He's an orphan," Riley added.

Charlie's eyes took on a faraway look. "I was just sixteen myself when the Apaches killed my pa and my two brothers down in the Tonto Basin."

"I'm sorry about that, Mr. Meadows," Nat replied.

"Well, I killed a damned site more Apaches to even the

score. That's how I got the handle of Arizona Charlie, dedicating myself to rubbing out them savages in Arizona."

"How'd you git all the way up here?" Riley asked. The constant flow of whiskey was loosening his tongue.

"Crossed the Chilkoot Pass in '97 with a goddamned portable bar on my back, would you believe it?"

"I told you he lies like a fish," Riley warned Nat.

"It's the gospel. But I lost it when our boat swamped in the Horsetail. We had the godawful worst luck you ever saw. Lost the rest in a flood at Sheep Creek, horses ate poison grass and died, and we got wintered in on the Stewart River and missed the first rush. But I said to myself, Charlie Meadows, your bad luck is all used up now, so there's nothing but good luck ahead for you. And, damned if I wasn't right. Everything I touch in Dawson makes me money. It's embarrassing."

"How so, Charlie?" Riley asked as he held out his empty glass to the bartender for a refill.

"I bought up a few claims from miners, and they came in for me. Then I bought the *Klondike News* and sold that for a bundle. Now I just opened the finest saloon and theater in Dawson, this Grand Opera House, but I'm thinking of changing the name to the Palace Grand. It's sounds more classy to me."

"It do," Riley agreed.

Arizona Charlie gave Riley a hard stare, and his smile set hard at the corners. "But you didn't come to Dawson to muck for gold, Jim. Not the Newton Station Jim Riley I knew in Arizona. You couldn't stand to crawl in a badger hole for fear of being closed in. Remember when those White Mountain Apaches jumped us? All those rifle bullets kicking up dust around us? I packed into the nearest burrow I could find. But not you, Riley. You'd rather die than get shut in a hole. You stood out there in the open like a green Buffalo soldier and shot it out with those bucks. I never forgot that because I still think it was the dumbest thing I ever saw."

Riley stared at his glass and shivered involuntarily. "I hate being closed in, that's all."

"Right," Meadows pressed his advantage. "That's my point. It would take a steam engine to drive you into one of those mine shafts."

"We're looking for someone," Nathan interrupted. He'd never seen Riley like this before. It was worse than a fear of death. He knew death held no terror for the old man, but this was something different. Jim Riley was afraid of being trapped in a hole, and that fact made him seem more frail, more human than Nathan had thought possible. Instantly he moved to protect his friend.

A sly, knowing grin covered Charlie's face, and he nodded. "I thought as much. But, kid, you came to the right hombre. I know every living soul in Dawson."

"We're looking for . . . "

"Hold on, Nat," Riley interrupted. The ghastly pallor had faded from his face to be replaced by his usual ruddiness. The glowing potbellied stove and the whiskey had undoubtedly helped. "What's this information gonna cost us, Charlie? You always was known for yer hoss trading, and I figure this cold country ain't done much to soften yer heart."

A shrewd cast developed in Meadow's eye. "You two don't look to be rolling in gold dust, so I guess we're talking trade. What you got to trade, Jim?"

Riley shocked Nat by unbuckling his gunbelt. He held the polished revolvers up for inspection, twisting his wrist to let the lamp light caress them with its yellow glow. Arizona Charlie reached for the belt, but Riley jerked it out of his reach.

"Ah, not so fast, Mr. Meadows. These here irons are on the table as part of a wager. My guns if we lose, your information if we win."

Meadows clapped his hands together like a child with a newfound toy. "A wager! Damn you, Riley, you know me too well. Count me in. By the way, what are we wagering on?"

"That this boy can outdraw and outshoot you. . . . " Riley's voice was flat as a knife blade.

Nathan expected Meadows to erupt in laughter, instead he felt the man studying him with the cold, seasoned eye of a hangman. A circle of silence spread out from them like ripples in a pond as men watched them and whispered to each other.

"You're many things, Jim Riley, but you're no fool," Meadows said. "So this boy must be a hell of a good shot for you to risk your pistols." He walked slowly around Nathan, scrutinizing him, his hands, his gunbelt, and last of all, he marked the boy's cold gray eyes. Then he stepped back and folded his arms across his buckskin jacket. "Pick your target, son," he said.

A cheer filled the saloon, and men rushed to place bets on the contest. The crowd parted to reveal a straight path to the farthest wall of the opera stage, a good fifty paces distant.

Arizona Charlie motioned to the empty stage. "I ought to warn you, son, I used to shoot cigarettes out of my wife's mouth and glass balls out of her hands from that stage."

"He don't no more," someone shouted from the crowd. "Since he accidentally shot off part of her thumb last month."

"You're lucky she didn't shoot off *one of your balls,* Charlie!" another voice added, and the room dissolved in laughter.

"Mine aren't glass," Meadows retorted. "Anyway, I was drunk that night. I'm sober as a church mouse now."

He strode slowly to the platform, well aware he was in the spotlight he so dearly loved and relishing every minute of it. He flung his hat back over the bar and shook out his curls until they draped his shoulders. Carefully, Meadows selected two aces of spades from a nearby table and held them up for the crowd to appreciate. The group raised another appreciative roar as Charlie pinned them to the wall. He walked back to stand beside Nathan. While the showman removed his leather gauntlets with a practiced flourish, Nathan simply shucked his worn coat onto the sawdust covered floor and cinched his gunbelt tighter. His lack of concern brought mixed reviews from the spectators, and the betting renewed.

Meadows winked at Nathan. "Let's give them a show, son. It's good for business. Enoch, my bartender will count to three. We both draw on three and aim for the ace. Good luck." Then to the crowd he gave a true showman's wave and shouted. "Boys, I'm going to nail that set of guns over the bar after I win."

Nathan turned and faced the long corridor. Men jostled for a good view; out of the corner of his eye, he saw Riley betting his last twenty-dollar gold piece. Nathan wondered if Jim wasn't hedging his bets.

Both men stood shoulder to shoulder as the bartender raised his right hand with the towel, and the room fell silent. Enoch counted carefully to three and dropped his arm like a starting flag. Both Nat's and Arizona Charlie's pistols fired in a single report that shattered the silence and filled the room with smoke. A stunned silence followed while someone raced down to the cards and held them up.

Pandemonium erupted. Backlit from the stage's side lanterns, a single hole glowed in the printed black center of each card. The miners hooted and hollered, shot glasses crashed to the floor, and tables upended in the excitement.

"Why, the lad matched Arizona Charlie!" an astonished miner shouted. "It's a draw!"

Meadows studied the two cards that the man handed him. Laying one on top of the other, less than a hair's thickness kept the bullet holes from being identical. The giant showman raised his eyebrows. "Yup, I'd have to say it was a draw myself."

"Well, shoot again," someone shouted. "I got money riding on this, Charlie." A chorus of supporting voices echoed his sentiment.

Nathan took the cards from Meadow and held them up to the light. "No. My bullet is a hair off center," he said flatly. "Arizona Charlie won."

The losing bettors groaned and shouted in protest until Charlie held up his hands. "It's too close to call, boys," he shouted, his stentorian voice carrying over the protests. He waved his gloved hands over the crowd. "I'm not shooting any more holes in my brand new opera house, either. Not with what you thieving carpenters charge these days. It's a draw, and that's my final word. Those that don't like it can skedaddle. But they'll miss the round of free drinks I'm putting up to honor this fine, young sport. All you can swallow in the next two minutes is on me, boys. Go to it!"

That offer quelled all objection as the miners rushed for their free drinks. In ten minutes, the contest was history, relegated to memory while the men resumed their race to spend their hard-found wealth on cards and liquor. When evening arrived they would move on to spending it on women until the dawn broke. Then they would return to the harshness of their tunnels and mine shafts to muck out more gold.

Arizona Charlie led Nathan and Jim Riley to his private table at front row in the theater. As the cancan dancers were on break, the area was the quietest place in the building. Meadows poured three glasses of his private reserve and toasted his competitor.

"I like you, son," he said. One hand held his glass up in a salute while the other tapped his temple. "You're one of those rare breed, like myself. A man with talent *and brains.*"

Nathan grinned. "You know I beat you, don't you?"

Charlie faked an astonished look which he tried on Riley without success.

Riley bobbed his head while he clinked glasses with his old friend. "He did at that, Charlie. That was your card that was a smidgen off, not his. Nat switched 'em." The gunman leaned closer and sprouted a Cheshire cat grin. "And he beat you on the draw, too."

"No . . . ?" Meadow's denial lacked conviction.

"Yup," Riley insisted. "I was watching you two draw while these dirt diggers was ogling the cards, and Nat beat you plain as day."

Arizona Charlie tipped his chair back and braced an elaborate boot against the felt tabletop. He sipped his drink thoughtfully while his blue eyes studied Nathan. "That's what I said about brains. Nothing good would come of besting old Arizona Charlie in his own Grand Opera House." His eyes crinkled momentarily in all Nathan and Riley would ever receive of a begrudging grin. Then he turned all business. "You said you were looking for someone special. What's his name?"

"Wyatt Earp," Nathan said.

Charlie choked on his whiskey for a second, then recovered. "What business do you have with him?" Charlie asked.

Ignoring Riley's warning hiss, Nat answered directly. "I aim to kill him for abandoning my mother."

Meadow's eyes grew bright and hard as diamonds. His finger wavered in the air before coming to rest pointing at Nathan. "Blaylock? Blaylock! Mattie Blaylock. I should have guessed."

"You knew my ma?" Nathan asked. Deep inside him something cried out for some scrap, some fact to flesh out the photograph, even as another voice warned him not to press for painful news.

"Yeah, I met her once. In Globe, Arizona. An unhappy woman, no doubt about that. What happened to her?" he asked.

"She killed herself in eighty-eight."

Meadows regarded the young man like a wounded bear. "Sorry to hear that, son. When I passed through Globe she was hanging out with 'Big Nose' Kate Elder, drinking and . . . whoring."

"His leaving killed her, Mr. Meadows."

The showman squinted as he sorted his mind for buried facts while he held his hand up to cover Nat's upper lip. "Son of a bitch," he exclaimed. "I thought you looked familiar. With a mustache, you're the spitting image of Wyatt when he was younger. You must be his kid. I'd lay odds on it."

"You met him, too?"

Charlie shook his head. "No, just saw him a handful of times when he was working Dodge City with Ed and Bat Masterson. He was cold, but men said he was fair. I couldn't say for certain; never passed more than six words with him. But Bat sure put great stock in him."

Meadows switched his attention to Riley. "Jim, you never carried a grudge. Why are you in on this?"

"The reward," Riley answered, but he knew that wasn't the half of it. Nathan was like his own son now.

Arizona Charlie nodded sagely. "You'd do better to work for me, boys. The money's safer and you could call your own shots. I've got mining claims you could work, or do trick shooting on the stage with me, if you've a mind to. Believe me, you'll need something. Your grubstake won't hold out for long."

"Do you know where Earp is?" Nathan pressed.

"Yup. He's not here in Dawson, that's for certain. I heard he was wintering over in Rampart from some men who got frozen up on the Yukon river just north of here and packed in overland."

Nathan stood and extended his hand to Meadows. "I'm obliged to you, Mr. Meadows, for keeping your part of the bargain. Jim and I best be moving if we plan on getting to Rampart."

Meadows shook his hand warmly and sighed. "It'll be a fool's errand if you don't get there before the snow comes. The river's freezing up north of here, and once the snow falls, it stays for nine months. It's not like other places. Winter hunkers down and sits for a good while. The overland trail turns to pure hell with overflows and drifts deep enough to swallow a mule. Even the sourdoughs and the Indians won't try it, except for this crazy Swede who ice-skates here with the mail once in a blue moon."

Nathan nodded. "Well, then we'd better get moving. Thanks, again."

He turned and walked back into the saloon and along the polished bar with Riley at his side. This time the miners stepped respectfully aside or tipped their hats, clearing his path to the door. Nathan buttoned his coat against the chill in the foyer. He frowned down at melting pools of dirty slush tracking in from the closed entrance. Opening the etched glass door, he stepped onto the boardwalk. He stopped so suddenly that Riley bumped into his left shoulder.

A heavy blanket of snow was already falling.

TWENTY-FOUR

RAMPART, ALASKA.

Josephine Marcus Earp hummed a nameless tune only half remembered from her show days. Always restless, she had complemented the life her husband led, following the gaming tables from one mining camp to the next, blowing like a tumbleweed in the wind to the latest gold or silver strike. She had seemed to thrive on living in tents and out of packing crates. But these last eight months with Wyatt in Rampart came closest to her having a real home, and she found it to her liking.

Outside their tiny cabin she gave the moose-hide blanket an energetic snap and watched the wood chips and dust sail into the warm spring wind. The sun felt good on her face, and its steady persistence already was remaking the land, exposing patches of frozen ground and flattened grass. Melting ice steadily dripped from the cabin's eaves and the hoarfrosted glass and through the sod roof as well.

Josie squinted into the sun's glare and smelled the air. It was sweet and fresh and whispered of spring, not fouled with the stench of creosote and tar, or the biting tang of mercury vapors found in the mining camps. She sighed as she looked back through the open door at their bed of birch and willow poles and the packing crates that served as table and chairs. Aggie Mayo had helped her sew calico curtains for the windows and donated a crock washbasin when theirs was broken. Aggie and Captain Mayo, as everyone called him, were great friends, helping warm the long winter nights with their Thanksgiving and Christmas parties. Seeing the glowing woodstove reminded her of Wyatt sniffing about her first pot of moose stew with his mustache frozen stiff as a board. With his lynx fur trapper's hat, wolverine trimmed parka, and mukluks, he seemed to belong to this land, and she was hard pressed to remember him sitting astride old Dick Nailer and sweating under the Arizona sun with his straight brimmed hat and leather chaps.

Snuggling beneath the moose and caribou robes while watching the northern lights, life had seemed simple and straightforward without gunfights and intrigue. But she knew they would be moving soon like the spring water.

A clod of dirt dropped onto the top of her head.

"Hello down there, Sadie girl." Wyatt waved at her from the sod roof. A mischievous grin covered his face, and he watched her with his shirtsleeves rolled up as he leaned on a hoe.

"Wyatt!" She shook the dirt from her hair and pretended to be angry. "That's not amusing. What are you doing up there, prancing around like a schoolboy? You'll fall off and break your fool neck."

His smile broadened, and he crouched down, bracing his hands on his knees to be closer to her. "I've got a surprise for you, my dear, but you've got to be sweet or I won't show it to you," he said.

"What is it?"

"These!" He proudly displayed a fistful of radishes and stringy onions, the largest no bigger than her little finger. "Fresh from our garden."

Josie placed her hands on her hip and regarded him like a prankish child. "Where on earth did you find those?"

"Why, I've been growing them, sweetheart. The snow's melted off the sod up here and the sun heats it up like a regular hothouse while the ground down there is still frozen solid. I planted these beauties less than a week ago, and here they are.

With all this sunlight they just shot up. I swear they even grow in the moonlight. So tonight we dine on fresh vegetables." He waved the produce like it was a royal flush.

"Who would believe it." She laughed at her husband, stripped to shirtsleeves with hoe in hand. "Wyatt Earp, famous lawman and gunfighter, growing a garden on the sod roof of his log cabin. I certainly wouldn't, and I know Allie and Virgil won't either, when I write to them."

All at once an ear-shattering crack filled the air and rolled across the surrounding foothills. Echos returned the sound in lessening degrees. Josie spun in the direction of the sound as Wyatt leapt from the roof to land by her side. Instinctively, she fled into the safety of his arms.

Another report, equally loud, followed and the ground quivered beneath their feet. A series of low rumblings and cumbrous grinding shook the river bank, extending to their wobbling cabin.

"Earthquake!" Josie screamed.

"No, look!" Wyatt pointed to a massive slab of ice that now rose from the previously flat frozen surface of the Yukon River. As they watched in awe, the block climbed ponderously onto the back of the intact portions of ice then stopped. As it did so, its tons of weight sent wide cracks radiating across the ice in all directions. More rumblings occurred, and another slab crawled upward to jut from the river like a massive knife blade. Medium and lesser groans and squeals joined until the chorus of noises drowned all other sounds.

"The river's breaking up, Josie," Wyatt shouted over the din. "Let's watch it from the roof." He pushed her up the crude ladder until the two of them looked down on the awakening Yukon.

A third island sprung free of the river's frozen grip to edge upward at an acute angle before slipping back into the water with screeches of protest. Now the spiderweb of cracks widened, and dark, silty water boiled through the fissures and ran across the icy surface. With a last, enormous protest, like some monstrous birth, the Yukon broke free, sending slabs and chunks the size of small islands spinning and colliding as the entire frozen surface of the river lurched downstream.

Wyatt and Josie watched dumbstruck at the power and force of the frozen surface staggering ponderously on its way to the Arctic Ocean. Imprisoned for eight months, the Yukon was again free to execute its will. For over an hour the two stood and watched the endless parade of broken ice moving down stream. Sometimes the blocks would slam, protesting, into each other to form an ice dam. Then the river would overflow its banks and escape around the blockade, but eventually the dam would yield to the constant attack of more ice, and the whole thing would collapse with thunderous noises and tumble away.

Ambling along this frightening display a small figure approached their cabin, sidestepping the fresh pools of overflow and blocks of ice as if they were mere rain puddles. It was Captain Al Mayo. For all his casual demeanor, he could have been out for a Sunday stroll. He stopped and looked up at Wyatt and Josie.

"Morning, Wyatt," he said. He tipped his hat to Josie. "And to you too, Mrs. Earp. It's a fine spring day, isn't it?"

Josie looked down quizzically at him. "More than that, Captain Mayo, or didn't you notice all the commotion in the river?"

Mayo glanced over his shoulder. "Oh? The breakup? It's something for sure, but I've seen more than a few, Mrs. Earp."

"Well, it's certainly breathtaking to me," she continued. "And it's one of the strangest things I've ever seen."

Mayo looked at Wyatt. "It's not so strange as what I just saw back down the trail about half a mile. A man's out there talking to a bunch of ptarmigan." He shook his head at the sight of this person on his knees, pleading and coaxing a cluster of the Arctic's version of the sage hen. "Damnedest fool thing I ever saw. He's telling them to stay put!"

Wyatt burst into peels of laughter, dropping his hoe in the process. When he regained his breath, he explained. "That must be Wilson Mizner. He's staying with us for a few days. He's new to Alaska, but a game fellow. He offered to hunt for supper."

"So?" Mayo looked puzzled.

"Well, I told him the way we hunt ptarmigan is we herd them into groups of a half dozen at a time, back off so the shotgun pattern spreads out, and get them all with one shot. He's pledged to bring home a dozen with only two cartridges."

"Good thing you didn't tell him to cross the river. The damned fool might have tried it as well," Mayo snorted as he turned to study a block of ice twice the size of his trading post grinding over the shoreline. He recalled the two cabins swept away in last year's breakup. "Well, I didn't come here to talk about that nut." He paused to hold up a crumpled envelope. "Charlie Hoxie, the customs man, brought two letters for you from St. Michael."

Wyatt followed Josie down and read the letters while Mayo hung around. Any news in Rampart was a delicacy to be shared with the rest if possible. So Wyatt read their contents, then reread them out loud.

"One's from Mr. Ling, and the other from Tex Rickard." He paused to let his words sink in. Rickard, always restless, had rushed down the frozen river with all its perils when news broke of a new gold strike at Anvil Creek north of St. Michael on Norton Sound. "You remember Ling, Josie, he runs the Alaska Commercial Company store in St. Michael. He wants me to open a canteen there. I can sell cigars and beer for ten percent of the take."

Mayo whistled. "That's a good deal, Wyatt. I'd take him up

on it." He dug the toe of his boot into the frozen ground, toying with the thawing surface. His network of information cast a wide web, and news reached him from natives, trappers, and freighters traveling in all directions. "Dawson and the Klondike are all panned out, I hear. All the rich claims are staked, and the big commercial companies are moving in, buying up the smaller claims and setting up to do large scale placer mining. One man told me they're bringing in a gold dredge, actually freighting its parts in by dogsled."

"I suspect all the commerce is tied up, too." Wyatt smiled wistfully. "I guess we missed that stampede, Josie. In spite of ourselves."

She took his arm. "They'll be others, don't worry about it, dear."

"That's what Ted Rickard writes. He got to Anvil Creek. They're calling it Nome now after another stream, Nome Creek. He says even the sands on the beach are full of gold. People are panning right on the beach, and others are working the creeks back from the beach and finding more gold."

Mayo scratched his head. "Tough decision to make."

Wyatt stared at Josie. "Well, we could head back down river to St. Michael, and if we don't like it, we can go to this Nome. What do you think, Josie?" He waited for her answer.

She smiled, loving him all the more for honoring her with the decision in front of Captain Mayo. "I think we should go. Your garden won't furnish enough food for more than one meal, so we'd starve to death if we stayed here. And I've seen enough of the Yukon river to last me a lifetime."

The breakup seemed endless, grinding on her nerves like fingernails raked over glass and sapping her resolve. Josie wondered if the frightening sounds that shook their little cabin might not portend the coming of cataclysmic events in their lives.

"I'm going to miss you two," Mayo said. Inwardly he was

glad. He planned to hurry them along. With the river breaking up, a flood of miners and stampeders fleeing their failures at Dawson would be clogging the river. Mayo's keen mind had pieced together other disturbing rumors coming from Dawson as well. Gunmen, held fast there by the winter, planned to assassinate his friend Wyatt. Now the river's opening meant Wyatt was free to travel—but so were his stalkers.

✶ ✶ TWENTY-FIVE ✶ ✶

Jim Riley fanned the air with his Stetson to clear the smoke and peered anxiously into the dark hole. More smoke roiled upward from the pit, escaping into the cold spring air and wafting away to mingle with a hundred similar plumes of smoke emitting from drift mines pockmarking the side of French Hill.

High above Eldorado Creek, site of one of the fabulous gold strikes, miners toiled on French Hill, mucking through the white gravel laid bare by spring rains and uprooted trees used for shoring up the mines below. French Hill held gold, but it kept it close to its vest, and success or failure followed only upon the hill's whimsy. Millionaires sprinkled French Hill, working their claims within spitting distance of paupers. Nothing separated rich from poor but the glint of gold dust in their pans; both lived in filth and poverty, fighting scurvy, hunger, darkness, and the ever-present cold. Both lived in drafty stick shacks, and chopped slabs of frozen bread with axes while they burned what precious wood they had to thaw the frozen ground they worked rather than waste it to keep warm.

Riley backed away from the smoke pouring from their mine and wondered how Nathan and Doc Hennison could stand it down there. Try as he might, the gunman could not force himself to climb down the rickety ladder into that pit, even for an instant.

Mortified by his weakness, Riley had confessed to his friends of the time near Bisbee when a cutbank, weakened by the rains, had collapsed on him. He was chasing a stray calf down a gulch one minute only to be buried up to his neck the next. Unable to move, the young Riley felt his horse quivering beneath him while it suffocated. For two days he sat astride his dead mount, encased in mud as hard as concrete with only his nose and eyes exposed. When the other hands found him and dug him out, he was babbling like a madman and half blind from the sun. That was over thirty years ago, but the fear of being trapped like that never left him.

So Riley toiled above ground, doing the work of two men to compensate for letting his friends down. There was plenty to do. Stoking the tiny steam boiler they used along with the underground fires to thaw the muck, foraging farther and farther afield for firewood, and cranking up the windlass that brought buckets of thawed pay streak to the surface. In the winter that dirt quickly froze, but Riley worked long hours into the night, panning for gold inside their pole shack.

Riley scrambled about the rim of the shaft, taking care not to kick any loose rock down the hole. Forty feet below his two friends were inching along a side drift no more than three feet wide in search of the elusive yellow metal. With candles tied to tin cups for headlamps, they were burning some of their valuable firewood to thaw the frozen shale. Then they would chisel the bedrock with a pick, back out along the drift to send it up in a basket for Jim to pan.

Riley pondered the dangers drift mining carried. Shafts collapsed or flooded from underground springs. And thawing the muck with fires poisoned the air. All three had helped pull miners from their mines, limp and cold with their dead faces always a ghastly blue. Bad air almost got Nathan on one occasion, but for his candle sputtering and going out from lack of fresh air. Seeing that, the lad dragged Hennison to the shaft, and Riley had winched them gasping and choking to the surface.

All winter long they had grubbed their claim with little to show for their labors. The gunman sighed. It looked like their luck this spring would be no better. He checked the hole again. No dirt had come up in the last twenty minutes. Riley was worried.

An unnerving scream echoed up the shaft walls, and the windlass rope jerked frantically. Instantly, Riley was cranking the handle, spinning it as fast as he could. Had the drift collapsed? Had a tongue of trapped swamp gas licked out and turned his friends into flaming torches in that frozen hellhole. The screams continued, and Riley redoubled his efforts.

The black-smudged face of Doc Hennison shot to the surface on the gunfighter's frantic efforts. Doc's wild white eyes and his opened mouth contrasted vividly with his blackened skin.

"We're rich!" the physician squealed. "Rich!" He scrambled out of the basket and flopped onto the muddy ground, his legs kicking in the air.

"Damn!" Riley released the handle and dropped backward onto his haunches, gasping for his breath. The freewheeling windlass spun like a propeller, and the bucket dropped back into the hole. "I thought you was dying from those screams."

"Look! Look! Look!" Hennison's chant accompanied the wild kicking of his legs. "Gold!" Waving in the air in time to his feet, a gold nugget glinted from his fist. "We got this bugger, and he's got brothers down there!"

"Lemme see that." Riley slid on his seat over to the gyrating Hennison. He pried the nugget from Doc's fingers and bit into it. "Gold, all right," he said in amazed tones. "I can't believe it."

The bucket rope jerked unnoticed as Riley gave a snort and

dove on top of the laughing snake oil salesman. The two rolled in the mud like children, laughing and punching each other. Nathan's head appeared above ground to view this scene. With no one to haul him up, he was forced to pull himself up the line hand-over-hand. He swung one leg onto solid ground and walked over to the celebration. More nuggets filled his pockets.

"Looks like we're rich, boys!" Hennison laughed up at Nathan as he wiped mud from his eyes and spit out a glob of dirt. "All our damned work finally paid off."

Nathan's smile glowed like a beacon from his sooty face. "You found it, Doc, you surely did. I can't wait to tell Wei-Li." Nathan's throat constricted as he thought of his love bravely enduring the hardships of this last winter. Refusing all offers to work in the White Chapel District as a whore, she had suffered most (from the darkness and isolation while the men worked together at the mine). But she never complained. Nathan smiled to himself. And soon the baby was due. Now they would have whatever they needed, whatever they wanted.

"Yes, I did, didn't I!" Hennison crowed. "I sluiced it out of that drift wall with my private hydraulic system." Both he and Nathan dissolved in laughter.

"What's that?" the puzzled Riley asked.

Nathan bit his tongue to stop laughing. "Doc peed on the side of the tunnel, and lo and behold, that nugget cometh forth in all its glory."

Hennison managed to puff his chest out while lying flat on his back. "Only the superior force of my stream of urine got the job done. Not bad for an old man, eh? Hell, I've half a mind to go into town, drink a gallon of beer, and come back here to piss the whole side of French Hill away. Who needs hydraulic giants anyway, when you've got me? I'm a walking wonder, that's what I am." He sat bolt upright as an idea crossed his mind. "Hey, do you suppose my privates are some sort of gold locating device? I mean, I could have watered down any place in that tunnel, but I chose that specific spot. What do you think?"

Riley combed his fingers through his mud-coated hair as he gave Doc a reproachful look. "God sakes, you call yourself a doctor. You done pickled what sense you ever had with yer snake oil to be thinking like that. Who ever heard of a man's short arm pointing to gold? If anything, it looks for women!" Before Hennison could protest, Riley nailed him with a handful of muck, and the two resumed wrestling in the thawing mud heaped around their mine.

When the two men paused to catch their breath, they saw Nathan staring down into the valley. A frown spread across his face as he watched a column of black smoke rising from a cluster of shacks. Unlike the smoke issuing from the drift mines, this smoke mixed yellow and gray as well as black, indicating more than wood was burning. Besides, it came from an area without mines. The distant clang of Dawson's handdrawn fire wagon reached their ears.

Hennison struggled to his feet and followed Nathan's gaze. He shrugged. "Just another fire, Nat."

Slapped together at random, Dawson was no stranger to fires. Packed canvas tents, board houses, and slum sheds made good tinder for tipped kerosene lamps and woodstoves driven to their maximum against the arctic cold. Scarcely a week passed without hearing the clang of the volunteer fireman's bell. Even "Arizona" Charlie Meadows's Grand Opera House burnt down only to reemerge from its ashes as the Palace Grand Theater.

The smoke spread and tiny bursts of flames presented as yellow flickers against the drab gray landscape. Now Riley was on his feet, and his heart sank.

"It's coming from my house!" Nathan cried. He started to run.

When Doc and Riley reached the edge of town, the flames were almost out. The wind and a sudden rain did more to stop the fire than the efforts of the handpumping hose of the volunteers, but two entire blocks of hovels were gone. Riley searched with difficulty for Nat's shack amid the smoldering and charred ruins, for all familiar landmarks were gone. People wandered around the remnants of their dwellings, poking the smoking ash for anything to salvage and breathing a thankful prayer it was Spring and not forty below zero.

They found Nat kneeling beside Wei-Li. He had rigged a crude shelter to keep the rain off her and placed her on a charred door covered with a blanket. Riley choked when Doc stooped to raise the blanket to examine her burns, and even the war-hardened Doc winced at what he saw.

The black hair, glossy as a raven's wing, was burnt until only a dirty stubble remained. Hennison stared at the swollen lids and lips as he searched for some landmark of her former beauty. Dark, leathery patches of deeper burn covered her face and body to mix with angry red blisters swelling even as they watched.

Nat looked up imploringly at his friend even as he fondled her charred hand. "Help her, Doc," he begged. "Please, help her." His voice trailed off like a little boy's.

"I . . . I'm not, not, a doctor anymore, Nat," Hennison pleaded. "Please don't ask me to . . . " But the look from his young friend's eyes stopped him.

He felt Riley's hand on his shoulder. "Go on, Doc," he said, "do the best you can."

Hennison kneaded his forehead with his dirty hand. "I . . . I saw burns like this during the war. We've got to get her to the hospital."

336

Ever so gingerly, Nat lifted Wei-Li and carried her to a makeshift litter. Then he and Riley carried her the length of Dawson's lone street, ignoring the curious stares, until they arrived at St. Mary's Hospital and Catholic Church at the foot of the Dome. Nat looked up at the cross jutting from the peaked entrance of the long two story building. Feelings of foreboding flooded his mind, and the images of hell and damnation drummed into him at the orphanage filled his thoughts. Doc led the way, kicking open the door.

A weary-looking nun in equally worn habit hurried to intercept them. "Please," she whispered. "This is a hospital, for heaven's sake. We have sick people here."

"What the hell do you think *we have here*, sister?" Doc roared. "Where's Father Judge? Tell him his old friend, the blasphemer Hennison, is here. We need his help."

Shock registered momentarily on the sister's face to be chased away by a look of sadness before she composed herself. She dropped her head as she answered. "Where have you been? Father Judge is no longer with us."

"The hell you say!" Doc swore at her. He waved a nugget in her face. "Don't worry about getting paid. We've got money." Wei-Li's obvious suffering was causing him great anxiety, something he thought had been scorched from his very being by that terrible war. The fact that he felt it now was all the more disturbing. "Gone?" he pressed the distressed nun. "Gone where? Get him back, now! We have a seriously ill patient for him."

The sister seemed unable to answer. Instead she removed her wire framed glasses and wiped them on her robe. Only the thin clack of the rosary beads at her waist broke the silence.

Nat looked up imploringly at her. "Please, sister, we . . . we don't come here often. Most all our time is spent in the mine. We've been working it all winter."

The nun replaced her glasses and composed herself.

"Father William Judge is dead." She sighed. "He died this last January."

"Died?" Hennison thought of the care-worn Jesuit priest who always had a kind word for him, calling him his blaspheming friend. Father Judge had come to Dawson from Fortymile in the winter of 1897, one of the first to respond to the gold rush. Single-handed he caused St. Mary's Hospital to be built where he worked day and night caring for the sick. During the awful winter of '98 when typhoid, influenza, and starvation struck, he earned the name of "Saint of the Klondike." When Doc last saw him in November, Judge looked years older than forty-five, worn out by his ministrations.

"How about someone else?" Riley asked.

The sister shook her head. "There's no one. Sister Agnes and the others . . . we're doing the best we can for the time being."

Nat looked at Doc. "You've got to do it, Doc," he pleaded.

Riley stepped up behind Hennison as if he expected the man to bolt for the door. "You can do this, Doc," he said. "You don't need no two arms to treat Wei-Li."

"You're a doctor?" the sister asked.

The color drained from Hennison's face as he slowly nodded his head. "It's been a while," he said slowly. "But, at least, I'm more sober than I've been in thirty years. So let's get started before I lose my nerve."

With infinite care, they carried Wei-Li to a small room separate from the crowded ward. There Doc and the sister bathed her burns, peeling away the broken blisters, then covered them with cloths soaked in boric acid. Thankfully, laudanum was administered, and the girl, temporarily released from her torment, fell asleep.

Hennison spent the night hovering at Wei-Li's bedside while Nathan sat in the only chair and held her hand. Jim Riley watched, propped against the door. At every possible opportunity Doc ladled tea and soup between her swollen lips. When dawn cast its sallow illumination through the room's window, the doctor was still at work, but his past experience weighed heavily on his heart. Still, for his friend Nathan's sake, he struggled on.

Sometime after even in the morning, Hennison awoke to the light touch of Sister Agnes, the other nun with medical training. Quietly, he followed her out of the room into the open ward.

"Doctor," Sister Agnes said. "How is your patient?"

Hennison stared bleakly at the nun. Except for her sable habit her round face and short stature belonged to any of a thousand Austrian hausfraus, save for the chronic fatigue that marked her face. Her accent confirmed his guess.

"No one has called me doctor in a very long time," he said. "More often they call me a quack."

She smiled gently. "A quack doesn't stay awake all night fighting to save someone's life."

He hung his head, stung unexpectedly by the compliment. Years of scorn and self-derision had prepared him for all manner of attack except a friendly one. "A fool might," he said.

Again, the sister smiled. "I leave that judgment to Our Lord. May I ask a favor?"

"What?"

"A Han Indian was brought in early this morning from his village of Moosehide. He's quite ill, and I'm not sure of his diagnosis. Could you possibly look at him?"

Too tired to argue, Hennison followed the sister down the long ward, his eyes drifting from left to right over the rows of beds. Automatically, a part of his brain, locked away for years, opened and he began to tick off the diagnoses of those he passed. The ward was sparse but notably clean with white-sheeted cots carefully arranged. The smell of camphor and wood alcohol added to the aura of cleanliness. At the fourth to the last bed on the right, the sister stopped and drew back the covers of a quivering native, doubled into a ball while he coughed blood-tinged sputum. His eyes burned red in his bronze face, and his lips appeared a dark purple.

Hennison examined the man, lifting his shirt to inspect his back, and tapping out the area of dullness at the base of both lungs. He called for a light and used the oil lamp to scrutinize the man's skin. A scattered rash covered the man's face and back, almost lost against the background of his burnished skin.

Stepping back he washed his hands and dried them on a towel the sister provided. "Measles," he said flatly.

"Dear God." Sister Agnes sighed. "There will be more, then. Many more. Few Indians have ever been exposed to measles, I'm afraid."

"He has pneumonia as well, both lower lungs. I suggest you burn some more camphor and try to get some boiled milk into him. Willow bark extract might help to break his fever."

Sister Agnes nodded. "Yes, doctor. Would you like to see the other patients—that is, if you're not too tired."

"Why not?"

For the good part of the morning, Hennison and Sister Agnes walked the wards, sharing their experience and tapping the buried knowledge in his head. Doc found her strong and sturdy, having been raised on a farm in the Tyrol. Together they made a whole physician, her two hands expertly following his advice, setting a broken limb, lancing a boil, and cutting away frostbitten toes.

But always he returned to the room that held Wei-Li and his friends to feed her soup and water mixed with salt to battle the loss of fluids from her burns.

Four days passed at an agonizingly slow pace, matched only by the constant suffering of the girl, yet her inner steel shone through as she never cried out once under the torture of being bathed and having her dressings changed. Whenever Nathan held her hand, which was almost constantly, she managed a smile for him. That was about the only part of her he recognized, her even white teeth and her coal black eyes. But now they were surrounded by painful and swollen tissue. Still, Nathan sat by her side, dreaming of her lost beauty and hoping for a miracle. And all the while, Wei-Li refused more laudanum to protect her unborn baby and to keep her thoughts crystal clear while she planned.

On the fifth day she sent Nathan away to find some spring flowers, asking especially for a handful of the tiny purple vetch that grew near their mine on French Hill. Reluctantly, he released her hand and stumbled away. Before he left she gazed into his eyes and pressed her swollen fingers gently against his lips.

"You are my river," she whispered. "And you own my heart, forever. Be always strong."

After he left with Riley on his heels, she called Doc to her bedside. "Take the baby," she rasped. "Every day my weakness robs him of strength and a chance for life. I feel him growing weaker. He kicks less."

Hennison blanched. "Wei-Li, I can't! *You'd never survive the operation.*"

"You must!" She held onto his coat desperately, her fingers like claws. "I am finished. You know that!"

He hung his head, unable to face her and the terrible truth of her words. "I can't," he said. "I won't do it." He hurried out of the room as she spat invectives at his fleeing back.

Wei-Li looked at the painted ceiling and prepared herself. The bitter Hennison had acted just as she had expected. He would be of no help unless she bent him to her will, and she was prepared to do that. She studied the peeling paint on the cedar boards and wondered at the winds of fate that had blown her so far from her home in China to this frozen land. A fleeting moment of regret crossed her mind as she recalled her favorite jasmine that she would never see. The old lady who read my fortune told the truth, she thought. She just did not tell me all of it. Now I must make the rest of it come true. Now I must protect my son.

Wei-Li turned her head to look out the window. The drab hillside with its smoking plumes from drift mines greeted her. She turned back to look at the ceiling. This land held no warmth for her. Instead, she focused on her last image of Nathan, care and concern covering his handsome face. She smiled. "Be strong, my love," she whispered.

Then she reached beneath her pillow for the razor sharp knife.

"God in Heaven! Doctor! Come quickly!" Sister Agnes screamed. Her eyes started out of her head at the sight in front of her.

Wei-Li lay dying on the bed, surrounded by a pool of clotted blood. The crimson stains contrasted starkly with the pale tone of her burned skin. The room reeked with the sickly sweet smell of fresh blood. In one hand she still held the bloody knife with which she had opened her womb while her other arm protectively cradled a kicking infant boy, coated in his mother's blood.

Hennison flew into the room and stared in horror. "Jesus Christ Almighty," he sobbed, bitter tears blurring his vision. "What did you do, Wei-Li?"

She smiled defiantly, her voice barely a whisper. "You were too weak," she said. Then her head rolled to one side as she died.

Sister Agnes crossed herself and fumbled with her rosary, unable to comprehend this dreadful reality. Only the infant's cry mobilized Hennison. He wiped his tears clear and gently lifted the baby from Wei-Li's still arms. He tied off the umbilical cord and used Wei-Li's knife to cut the cord. Turning the instrument over in his hand like a poison snake, Doc turned to face Sister Agnes with the struggling baby.

Nathan and Jim Riley stood in the doorway staring at him.

The fresh-picked purple vetch dropped from Nathan's hand as he viewed the sight of his love enveloped in blood-soaked sheets with her belly cruelly opened and her unseeing eyes staring at the ceiling. His gaze fixed on Hennison with the congealed knife in one hand and bloody baby in the other.

"Doc!" he gasped. "You killed Wei-Li! You butchered her!"

"Nat, I . . . I didn't . . . "

"You killed her." The tone was not the poisonous one Hennison expected, not full of hate and fury, but one filled with abject misery. It was what one would expect of a child robbed of all dreams, all hopes, and all attachments with friends and loved ones.

"No, no, Nat. She . . . she," Hennison fumbled for words. He stepped toward his friend still holding the damning evidence.

Nathan recoiled in horror. "Get away from me, you butcher!" He backed out the doorway, knocking aside a tray of instruments, and fled out the entrance into the cold.

Doc looked imploringly at the ashen Riley. "I didn't do it, Riley. Honest. She . . . she did it herself . . . to save the baby." His voice came in short, sobbing pants.

Riley squeezed his eyes as if to shut out what had befallen his friends; but he knew when he opened them, the tragedy would remain. "I gotta go after him, Doc," he said. "You understand. He's my pardner."

"What about me. Aren't I your friend, too?" Doc asked.

Riley grinned ruefully at the irony. For most of his life he'd been without a single friend, and now the fates were forcing him to choose between the only two friends he might ever have. "Yes, you are," he said. "But Nat needs me more right now, I think. I'll try to talk to him, but I don't think he'll listen. Not just yet."

"What about the gold mine?" Hennison pleaded after the departing back of Riley. "What about our gold?"

"You take care of it," Riley replied. "And see to the baby."

In the morning, no signs of Nathan Blaylock or his friend, Newton Jim Riley, were found in all of Dawson or its surrounding hills.

TWENTY-SIX

NOME, ALASKA TERRITORY, 1900

Wyatt trudged along the beach and stopped to light his cigar. He exhaled thoughtfully and watched his smoke float away from the black sands and in the direction of the low hills behind the town. Like Dawson, the newly renamed Anvil City had sprung up overnight. Gold dust found on the sandy beach and in its draining creeks lured those unlucky miners from Dawson, and they arrived in the thousands just as hungry for fortune. A once vacant beach now held strings of wall tents and board shacks while people jostled shoulder to shoulder with gold pans sifting the sand. Without a way to stake a claim in the sand, the miners worked the soil upon which they stood and anything in reach of their shovels. Most of the men on the beach knew him, but they were too busy these days to greet their own mother.

Wyatt smiled as he recalled their arrival. It was almost as if Norton Sound had welcomed them, for the ship voyage from St. Michael was undisturbed and took less than two days. Without a pier or dock, the ship anchored offshore, and small boats and lighters carried them into the shallows. Then a giant stevedore clad in rubber hip boots carried his startled wife ashore.

What they found surprised them. Nome was a hell on wheels, wilder than Tombstone in its own frozen way. This place was as different from Rampart or Dawson as the moon. A churlish river looping to the sea outlined Nome's beach and

Richard Parry

little else. No trees, no mountains, no waterfalls marked Nome, only rolling hills of tundra and salt marshes of knee-high sea grass. *Flat* best described Nome. Since it was without trees, the whine of sawmills, so common in Dawson, was never heard. Instead, the sounds of Nome were hammering, night and day, of boards brought from far away, and the incessant clack of rocker boxes sifting the gold-bearing sands.

He turned away from the beach and ground his way to the main street running parallel to the beach. Crossing a plank bridge, he watched the water running from the creek into the sound. A lot of water had flown under those boards since they had arrived over a year ago. Charlie Hoxie and he had built the Dexter Saloon together, Nome's first two-story structure in the middle of town. They wryly called it the "Only Second-Class Saloon in Nome," but it was by far the best, surpassing the bars owned by his friends Tex Rickard and Lucky Baldwin. Furnishing the Dexter had led Wyatt back to San Francisco and more encounters with fleas and storms at sea. But now the Dexter sported the finest polished bar and posh gaming rooms upstairs.

Not everything this year was good. His brother, Warren, was dead, shot to death in Arizona. The cigar snapped in Wyatt's fingers as he remembered the bitter news. Self-defense the jury said, but those twelve men were paid off just as was Warren's killer, Johnny Boyett. Self-defense! Wyatt snorted and tossed the tobacco fragments angrily into the swirling water. All Warren had on him was a small pocketknife when Boyett fired two shots at him in that saloon in Wilcox. When Warren asked Johnny for his gun, Boyett drilled him through the heart at point-blank range.

Wearing a badge cost them all too much, Wyatt thought. First Morgan and then Virg with his crippled arm, and now Warren. The retribution went on forever, it seemed. Tombstone and the Clanton feud still hung like a shadow wherever he

346

went. Never again, he vowed, would he put on a badge. The price was too steep. When push came to shove most honest citizens would shut their doors in your face, and justice was a joke. Town officials went with the money, and that meant turning their backs on their lawmen if need be. And that just left men like Morgan and Warren dead.

But he was learning to play their game. You could still have your justice, or was it revenge? The secret was to keep it secret. No more shoot-outs in the middle of town like the O.K. Corral. No more witnesses. That only made trouble for you afterward.

Wyatt smiled grimly. He and Virgil had buried Warren in public, and then they buried Boyett in private. That rat wasn't so brave drawing against a man with a pistol of his own. No one would ever find his unmarked grave. It was fitting justice that they planted him on the road between Globe and Wilcox that Warren drove for the stage.

He sighed. All he wanted was to be left alone. Handling the Dexter and his interests in a handful of mining claims was enough. But it was starting all over again. Gold brought out the worst in men. Trouble was coming.

Wyatt threaded his way up the packed street and stepped into his saloon. Built with lumber from Canada and filled with mirrors and draperies from San Francisco, the Dexter was a thing of pride for Wyatt. Upstairs had thick carpets and coal-fired stoves, but sawdust still buffered the saloon's first floor from the invasive sand and mud. Behind the polished wood panels and wallpaper, more sawdust served as insulation. The smell of beer, oak, and cigar smoke greeted him as he stepped up to the long bar.

"Someone to see you, Wyatt," his bartender said after he placed Wyatt's customary cup of coffee and a fresh cigar at his elbow. The man rolled his eyes to the potbellied stove and the knot of men standing around its cheery warmth.

Wyatt removed his hat and ran his hand over his iron gray hair. Matched with his gray eyes, his salted hair imparted the look of a lone wolf to him more now than ever. He'd been expecting this visit, but not looking forward to it.

"Looks more like a damned committee to me, Ike," he mused. "You don't see a rope with them, do you? Or maybe a bucket of tar or feathers?"

Ike snickered and moved away as one man approached. He wore his bowler on the back of his head like a dandy, and Wyatt noticed all his clothes were brand new. Puffed up with self-importance, the man swaggered over to Wyatt with a drink in one hand. He switched his drink and extended his right hand for a handshake. Wyatt guessed the show was more for the four other men than to impress him.

"Wyatt," the man almost was shouting over the general hum of the saloon. "How are you today?" Obviously, he wanted the others to hear him.

"Fine, Charlie. Just fine," he shook the hand of Marshal C. L. Vawter while he studied the man. Vawter and his wife were friends from St. Michael, especially his wife and Josie. But he'd changed since transferring to Nome, and his new duds cost more than an honest marshal could afford.

"Glad to hear it, Wyatt. I want you to meet my new friends." Vawter's tone left little doubt what kind of friends they were—influential friends. The marshal beckoned to the others.

Wyatt suppressed his fleeting disgust. He wasn't lily white himself in most people's eyes, and this was Alaska. Bending the law or looking the other way happened, but not without some reward.

The introductions began. "Wyatt, you know Mr. Hume and Mr. Beeman."

Wyatt nodded to the two lawyers whose office was down the street.

"And this is Alexander McKenzie and his associate, Mr.

Hubbard. Mr. McKenzie has just arrived in Nome and is certain to play an important role in settling these mining claim problems, Wyatt. A very important part, I might emphasize. He's president of the Alaska Gold Mining Company."

Wyatt watched Vawter bowing and scraping to McKenzie. Well, at least I know who's holding the top cards, he thought. I don't even have to guess what happens next. I'll bet this McKenzie comes at me like a sidewinder.

But the stocky McKenzie surprised him. His attack was direct and blunt as a splitting maul. He didn't even offer his hand.

"Earp, I'll come directly to the point. Washington is disturbed—greatly disturbed—about the foreign threat to American wealth here in Nome, and I'm here to correct the problem. With your help I can make you extremely wealthy."

"Foreign threat, Mr. McKenzie? What would that be?" The remark would have been amusing, but Wyatt judged this man to be dangerous. Certainly Canada was undaunted by the foreign threat, since ninety percent of Dawson and the Klondike were Americans.

"Why, the half-civilized Laplanders robbing the gold that rightfully belongs to American citizens."

"I believe you are referring to the three lucky Swedes, Mr. McKenzie. United States mining laws allow anyone to file a mining claim."

McKenzie tapped a sheaf of papers in his pocket. "President McKinley signed a new civil code in June to correct that problem, and I'm here, *directly at his wish,* to do just that. Vagaries in the mining law can be remedied by administrative action."

Aha, thought Wyatt, they couldn't get Congress to change the law, so they mean to steal the claims by rigging the court. That's the card up their sleeves. He remembered Johnny Behan and the ranchers in Tombstone trying the same thing. So Vawter was going to be the Behan of Nome. Times change and places change, he noted, but the game is still the same.

Vawter added, confirming Wyatt's assessment of him. "You'd be wise to play along, Wyatt. This is a sure thing."

McKenzie leaned closer. His cologne failed to mask the whiskey on his breath. "Judge Noyes, the new federal judge, and Joe Wood, the district attorney, are my men. I control this town now. I can be a powerful friend, or just as powerful an enemy."

Wyatt puffed thoughtfully on his cigar. He blew a protective cloud to counter McKenzie's perfume. "Well, Mr. McKenzie, I'm just a saloon keeper, and that's all I plan to be."

McKenzie glowered. "Not what I would have expected from a famous gunfighter, but a wise second choice." He stomped out with his followers scurrying behind. Vawter raced ahead to open the door, and he left it open.

Ike swore to himself, stopped polishing his glasses, and ambled in the direction of the chilling draft.

"Leave it open for a minute, Ike," Wyatt ordered. "This place has a bad odor. We ought to air it out."

Young Mr. Pingree, the governor's brother, raced through the door, his face glowing with excitement. He dropped a worn canvas cloth tied with string on the bar beside Wyatt then slapped both hands onto the shiny wood.

"Did you bump into my recent visitors?" Wyatt asked. Pingree was a frequent customer, known to be working hard on a placer claim on Anvil Creek.

"Yes, who are they? Marshal Vawter nearly pushed me off the walk to make room for the others."

"Trouble," Wyatt answered. "Best keep clear of that lot, Pingree."

The young man looked puzzled until his gaze fell on his parcel. "Wyatt! I did it! I finally struck it rich. Look at this!" He loosed the string and spilled the contents across the bar. A handful of gold nuggets clattered over the wood. "And there's more. You never should have thrown my safe overboard, Wyatt. Now, I'm going to need it."

Wyatt watched the man fingering the yellow metal with loving care. He smiled. He liked Pingree for his excitability, something Wyatt knew he lacked. Wyatt recalled that Josie often called him a stick-in-the-mud with a poker face. "Congratulations, Pingree. Have a drink on the house to celebrate."

The man wiped his face with both hands as if assuring this was no dream. "No, Wyatt. I'm buying for the house. And now I can pay back the money I borrowed from you."

"First I'd put those nuggets in the bank and double-check that your claim papers are all in order."

Pingree frowned while his fingers chased the golden lumps back into the worn bag. "I don't trust the banks, Wyatt. Your safe is as big as theirs. Can I stash my find with you?"

"Sure. Ike will make out a receipt for you. But check on your papers. I've seem more than one fortune lost by shoddy paper handling. And you know people are jumping claims faster than frogs catch flies."

Pingree nodded hurriedly and raced back out the open door. "Good idea," he called over his shoulder. "I filed with Hume and Beeman."

Wyatt narrowed his eyes. Hume and Beeman were with McKenzie.

Ten minutes later Pingree returned mystified. "I went to their office, Wyatt, but it was locked. And its only two in the afternoon. So I walked around the side. I saw Hume and Beeman through the window working like madmen over a pile of papers that looked like mining claims. That McKenzie and Marshal Vawter were with them. I tapped on the window, but Vawter told me to go away, that they were closed. He said something about official business. What does it mean, Wyatt? What's happening?"

Wyatt poured Pingree the drink he'd promised and watched the man gulp it down. "I'm not sure what it means," he said. "We'll just have to wait and see what they're up to."

But inside, he knew. The trouble was here.

⋆ ⋆ TWENTY-SEVEN ⋆ ⋆

YUKON RIVER BELOW NULATO,
ALASKA TERRITORY, 1900.

Jim Riley awakened with a start. His limbs twitched and his eyelids fluttered for an instant before he was fully alert. Blinking the snowflakes off his lids, he looked about and his heart sank. He had emerged from one nightmare directly into another. In his sleep, those he'd shot stalked him seeking revenge; in reality, the country was doing the same.

The freak summer snowstorm continued. While the Yukon River still flowed—a ribbon of silvery silt-laden water—gouts of snow rafted down stream and the green landscape now was white. Willows and birch trees bent in graceful loops almost to the ground under the weight of the wet snow. Three feet of snow flattened the grass.

A cow moose with her spring calf emerged from the tree line across the river like a shadowy wraith, and Riley's stomach called out in hunger. But they were too far for a shot, and he had no way of crossing the swollen river. Besides, he was too weak.

The sudden storm had struck without warning, almost like a final blow. It was as if the land, having noticed their plight, determined to finish them off. It wouldn't take much more, Riley admitted.

Most of a year had passed while he and the heartbroken Nathan wandered the wilds of Alaska, skirting the sparse towns and living off the land like wild animals. Without will or direction Nathan followed the rivers and the changing winds while the wounds to his heart healed. And Riley had remained by his side. During that time the boy had grown into a man of eighteen years. His eyes still carried a glint of the pain he felt whenever he saw a spray of purple vetch, but he bore his grief in silence on his sinewy frame. He spoke less and watched more now, Riley noted. The gunman knew the signs well. Nathan's boyhood was ended, just as painfully as Riley's had in spite of everything the gunman had done to protect it. Now, just when they were heading back to civilization, disaster struck.

A silent sweeper, hiding round the riverbend and half submerged, had swamped their canoe, leaving them stranded with few supplies and only their handguns and a precious slab of smoked bacon. For two weeks they had battled the brush and cutbanks as they struggled down river. Carving tiny slices from the bacon and eating grass and leaves, their strength lessened each day. Four days past, a marauding grizzly bear drove them from their camp and ate the last of the smoked meat. Then the snowstorm hit. More frozen than not and starving, Riley figured they were finished.

Nathan shifted beneath his blanket of leaves and spruce boughs. He looked briefly at the moose fading into the curtain of snow.

"You couldn't hit her from here if you tried," Riley whispered. His voice sounded foreign in its softness.

Nathan laid his head back on a branch. "I wasn't thinking of that. Seeing her with her calf got me thinking about Wei-Li and our baby."

"I didn't get much time to look, but he was packing a short arm, so he's a boy for sure," Riley replied. Just this talk left him shaky, but it was the first time Nathan had mentioned them since that terrible day in Dawson.

"It would have been nice to see him," Nathan said. "But I

guess I won't ever. Do you have any regrets, Jim? I mean about anything you really would do different."

Riley forced his wandering mind to focus on the issue. "Hard to say, son. Seems to me, I never had much choice in the matter. But sometimes I regret killing all those men. I suspect they'll be gunning for me when I gits to hell." He dropped back and stared at the snow filling his vision overhead. His eyes were playing tricks on him. The shadows moved and he started. His nightmare was coming to life. The gaunt specters of those he'd slain were shuffling in on him.

Nathan closed his eyes. He recognized the warm glow spreading throughout his body that came when one froze to death. It didn't matter now. "I know Doc didn't do that to Wei-Li. She was hinting about something like that to save the baby, I could tell. I just couldn't bring myself to believe it. I'm sorry about that misunderstanding, too. . . . " Nathan knew his words were slurring together, so he stopped and let the warmth continue.

"Do you suppose this thing with Wyatt Earp is all another misunderstanding, Nat?" Riley asked dreamily. He felt the warmth as well. Freezing ain't so bad, he decided, not like being gutshot or broken up inside by a horse fall.

But Nat never answered, slipping down the last of his thoughts into a cozy darkness.

Riley raised his head for a last look. The shadowy apparitions stood just inside the line of trees, wavering with the curtain of snow. Jim waved feebly at them. "Sorry I kilt you-all, boys," he stuttered. "You got a perfect right to haunt me, but you better hurry 'cause I'm dying too."

The shadows stirred.

Riley chuckled. "Come on in, boys. Don't be shy." Then he sank back and joined Nathan in chasing that black river.

The figures moved cautiously around the bodies. The largest threw back his caribou hood, revealing straight black

hair brushed back from ears dangling dentalium shell orna-
ments, and knelt over the bodies. He handed his bone-tipped
spear to another brave as he ran his fingers over Nat's dark
beard and pulled open Nat's shirt. His dark eyes widened in surprise at the pale white skin, and his nose wrinkled as he sniffed
its foreign smell. Carefully, he placed his ear to the lad's chest.
He nodded up to the others, then examined Riley similarly. He
sniffed the smoky bacon smell where Riley had wiped his hands
on the front of his tattered shirt before comparing it to the
smell of the slab of bacon they had taken from the stomach of
the bear they had killed.

A smile spread across the face of Chief Sesui of the Telida
tribe as he straightened up with the men's gunbelts. He motioned his warriors to lift the two, and then the group moved
off along the riverbank. Stopping just twice to feed the white
men with ground moose meat mixed with berries, the party
reached their village well into the long arctic twilight.

Intrigued by these pale-skinned men whose salty meat was
stolen by the grizzly, the Telida nursed them back to health,
learning much in the process about the strange race that sailed
up and down the Yukon in great canoes that belched fire and
smoke. In three weeks Riley and Nathan regained their strength
and said their good-byes to the natives who saved their lives.
Riley parted with his buffalo skinning knife as a gift to Chief
Sesui, and fended off offers to marry one of the leader's daugh-
ters. Under the expert guidance of the Telida, the men were
led across country and handed over to the Koyukon Eskimos
who brought them to Holy Cross, the combined mission and
trading post dating back to the Russian Fur Company. Riley
needed no further help to locate the saloon.

"I still think you should have taken old Chief Sesui up on
his proposal," Nathan chided his friend while they leaned on
the makeshift bar in the town's tavern. "You and that daughter
made one handsome pair."

"I ain't no squaw man, let alone the marrying kind," Riley protested through a foamy beard. He wiped the beer from his face and licked his fingers. "When I gits the itch for female companionship. I prefers to rent."

Nathan sipped his beer thoughtfully. The fingers of his left hand toyed with the jade dragon hanging from his neck while his thoughts drifted. But four men at a table were studying them intently. Nathan continued to sip his drink while he tightened his gunbelt. Riley caught the movement and did the same. Slowly, almost imperceptibly, the two edged apart to separate themselves and make them less easy a target.

"Do we got a problem, Nat?" Riley spoke through the side of his mouth while fixing a silly grin on his face.

"I don't know, but those men over there are watching us, and I don't think it's because we remind them of their mothers. I recognize one from Dawson. He was in Soapy Smith's gang, I think."

The largest of the four rose and swaggered over to the bar. Nathan noticed he wore his pistol on the left in a butt-forward cross-draw. A glass of beer occupied his gloved right hand. But his left hand was without a glove. He turned to face Nathan.

"Don't I know you, mister?" the man growled. "You look familiar to me. Ever been in Dawson?"

Nathan beat him to the punch, shifting to one side to block the man's left hand. "We've been lots of places, friend. But I'd remember you if we'd met. I don't know many men who use a left-handed back-draw like Bill Hickok."

The man's face dropped in amazement, then he broke into a broad grin, exposing buck teeth with a wide cleft in the center. "I'll be damned. You know your stuff. But you're too young to know Hickock."

"I ain't," Riley retorted. "And I taught Nat half of what he knows. The other half is pure meanness."

"You two look like you can handle yourselves." The man

pointed to their exposed holsters. "Most of the cheechakos here don't know a Mexican loop rig from moose shit. It'd take them a week of Sundays to clear their pistols. You boys ever do any regulating?"

Riley nodded. "Pleasant Valley and a few other places."

"I thought so. You got that look for sure. My name is Big Fred Walsh, and these others are my associates, Bastow Page, Tom Fisk, and Paul Stackhouse. We used to work with Soapy Smith in Skagway, except Stackhouse was in the O'Leary gang." Walsh studied their shabby dress. "You boys looking for work?" he asked. "You look like your grubstake didn't pan out, if you don't mind my saying so. Let me buy you some steak and eggs, and lets talk."

The steaming food vanished down Riley's mouth, and he helped Nat clean his plate with a chunk of bread before he released a satisfied burp and leaned back. All the while Big Fred had talked. "Nome, you say?" Riley hiccuped.

"Yup, that's the deal. These crazy Laplanders are stealing gold that rightfully belongs to the U. S., and Mr. McKenzie of the Alaska Gold Mining Company is following court orders to stop them. Our job is to help enforce those orders. I'm on the way there now."

"What about the law?" Nathan asked.

"The U. S. marshal is with us, can you believe that? But the problem is too big for him, and the army's strapped as well. They can't enforce the law. So we're on the side of the law for once as Special Regulators. Old Soapy'd roll over in his grave for this deal. The pay is two hundred dollars a week and a bonus for each claim we clear for the receivers. What do you say? Are you in?"

Nathan looked past Big Fred while he pondered the empty feeling he still felt where his heart belonged. Riley waited for him to speak.

"Oh, I forgot to mention the other things," Fred interrupted his thoughts. "The judge is cleaning up all the other loose ends in Nome, too. We get paid to help on that. Another five-hundred-dollar bonus for each saloon we . . . we transfer to the company."

"Transferring saloons to the gold company?" Nat asked. "What kind of deal is that?"

"Well," Walsh explained. "Not the Alaska Gold Company, but it's another holding and investment company owned by Mr. McKenzie. Actually, it kills two birds with one stone, and we get paid for both. These saloons are behind on their taxes, so we encourage the owners to hand them over. Besides, one of the saloons belongs to a troublemaker that the miners look up to. With him out of the way, things will be a hell of a lot easier."

"What's his name?" Nathan asked.

"That old gunfighter, Wyatt Earp."

"Earp?" Riley watched that dangerous look flicker in Nathan's eyes. In some way the lad blamed Wyatt for Wei-Li's death, along with himself.

"You know him?" Fred asked.

"Yeah, we know him," Nathan replied. His voice was hard and even like a knife edge. Here was the opportunity to make something right, to close a chapter of his life. "Count us in."

Two hours later Riley tightened the cinches on their borrowed horses and entered the tavern to get Nathan. The young man was finishing a letter which he handed to the bartender.

"Time to scoot, Nat. We're going overland to Nome. I'll be damned glad to part with this Yukon River. It's been nothing but bad luck for us. What ya got there?"

"A letter. The next riverboat will take it down river. It should get to Nome before us."

Riley squinted at the address. "To Wyatt Earp, eh? I take it ain't no birthday card."

"No," Nathan said. "I'm telling him I'm coming for him."

359

Wyatt cradled his cup of coffee as he pondered the turn of events. The warmth it imparted to his hands did little to help the chill he felt. Trouble was an understatement for what was taking place. If Mr. Pingree had any doubts what the piles of papers in the law office were, he had none now.

Within hours of arriving McKenzie and the new Judge Noyes turned the town on its ears. McKenzie's secretary in his gold company instantly rose to senior partner in the former law firm of Hume and Beeman. All those papers were court orders placing the richest mines on Anvil Creek into receivership for their "protection" while the judge studied them. Protection turned out to be McKenzie's Alaska Gold Mining Company working the claims round the clock, robbing them of all they were worth while Noyes stalled.

The theft expanded blatantly, even those uncontested operations. McKenzie strutted around town declaring himself above the law while Marshal Vawter and his regulators cracked heads and drove miners off their land. Now he was after the other source of gold in Nome, the saloons.

Wyatt looked up at his friends, John Clum and Dave Unrah. Clum, once owner of the *Tombstone Epitaph,* was now the postmaster of Nome, and Unrah was the manager of Lucky Baldwin's saloon. Clum and Wyatt went back a long ways to the

Clanton troubles and the scourge of Tombstone's "Cowboys," and both were no stranger to what was happening here.

"Do you mean to tell me, Vawter and his Spoilers just raised the bond to *twenty thousand dollars in gold?*" Clum sputtered. "The ten thousand wasn't good enough? Why, it's out-and-out robbery!"

"Yes," Unrah said. Perspiration dripped from his forehead although the air was damp and chilly, and his veins stood out above his collar like ropes. "Vawter said Judge Noyes approved it. Wyatt, what are we going to do? They're deliberately blocking the sale of Lucky's saloon with all these shenanigans. First it was that ridiculous, trumped up lien of twenty-five hundred dollars for taxes, then the ten-thousand-dollar bond *in gold,* now this. They know Lucky's facing a foreclosure notice. He'll lose the entire property!"

"And Judge Noyes is in with the lot," Clum snarled. "It's just like the old days in Tombstone. All the crooked politicos. Wyatt, we ought to get a party up and lynch the lot of these sons of a bitches."

Wyatt suppressed his amusement at that. Nineteen years ago they rode a trail of vengeance, and the stigma of that still haunted him. Yet, here Clum was ready to do it again, dapper fedora, potbelly, and all. "Have you taken a good look at yourself in the mirror lately, John? We're not the spring chickens we once were."

Clum smoothed his ruffled silver mustache and snorted. "The hell you say, Wyatt. We can still lick the bunch of them. They're just bullies and thugs, scared to face a real man. It's easy pushing miners and storekeepers around." He shook his fist. "Why, we may be gray and a bit long in the tooth, but we've got experience and we're not afraid. The toughest animal I ever hunted back in Arizona was this old, grizzled wolf. A winter wolf, that's what he was. A wolf in the winter of his life, not spring or summer, but tough and smart as an owl. And that's what you are, Wyatt, a winter wolf."

"You keep flattering me like that, John, and I'll be forced to give you another free drink," Wyatt replied.

"Damnit, Wyatt!" Dave Unrah swore. "These bastards are running roughshod over everything. Even committing murder. Those last three suicides sure as hell were nothing of the kind. You knew Sven Lundstrom. He loved working his mine, and he was planning on sending to Seattle for his wife next month. He'd never hang himself. Not in a million years. And all those sudden drownings? I don't believe it."

Wyatt sipped his coffee. It had grown cold. "All right, Dave. Give me a couple hours to raise the twenty thousand in gold. I won't let Lucky lose his Baldwin, not on my account."

"But what's to keep those skunks from just raising the bond again?" Clum asked.

Wyatt reached behind his bar and withdrew a length of Manila hemp used to secure the beer barrels. He handed the rope to Unrah. "You tell that son of a bitch, Vawter, I raised the gold with my friends, and if we have to raise anything else, it will be him—on the end of this hemp!"

That evening Wyatt stepped outside the Dexter and breathed the salty air. He thrust his hands into his pockets, and his hand touched the letter the right one held. He withdrew it and opened it. Tilting it to take advantage of the low slung sun, he reread the writing.

"I'm coming to get you, you son of a bitch, for deserting my mother," he read out loud. The letter puzzled him. If it was meant to frighten him, it wasn't working. Dying never did. Perhaps that was why he could squeeze his trigger so coolly, taking his time in a gunfight to aim, when all others were carelessly throwing lead with their frightened jerks. Was this part of McKenzie's tricks to drive him off, to seize the Dexter? The miners begged him to lead them, to stand up to McKenzie and Noyes, but Wyatt had vowed not to follow that route.

No, he decided, this letter was something different. His mind drifted back to the dock at San Francisco, then to the warnings Tex Richard let slip about the boy in Dawson. Maybe that was it. He'd keep his eye open. The town was filling up with toughs brought in by McKenzie. Perhaps this letter writer would be one of them. In any case, he could do nothing now. He'd have to wait and see.

Wyatt stepped wide of the corner as he headed in the direction of the tent city where he and Josie lived. In spite of the grandiose Dexter, they still lived in a wall tent, something that irked Josie constantly. He'd promised her a house, but lumber and carpenters were hard to find now with the building boom. Soon the Dexter would be surrounded by similar buildings.

"Wyatt! Help me!" a voice cried out from the side alley.

Wyatt saw Pingree struggling with four toughs. Two held him while the other landed body blows to the frail youth. Marshal Vawter stood to one side.

"What's going on here?" Wyatt demanded. "Let Pingree loose."

"He's drunk and disorderly and resisting arrest. So mind your own business, Earp," Vawter retorted.

"I am not!" Pingree protested. "I'm planning to take a petition to San Francisco to remove Judge Noyes and the Spoilers, and they're trying to stop me, Wyatt! Help me!"

"Let him go, Vawter," Wyatt ordered. "He doesn't sound drunk to me. I'll be responsible for him. You have my word on it."

Wyatt barely saw the blur that struck him from the darkened alley. He ducked but not fast enough. The next thing he knew he was being hauled to his feet with his arms pinioned behind his back.

"So, aiding and abetting this criminal, are you, Earp?" Vawter snarled into his face. "Maybe you need a lesson, old man."

"So this is the famous Wyatt Earp," a harsh voice snapped. Wyatt turned his head to recognize Fred Walsh and Ed Burns, two new members of McKenzie's regulators. "He don't look so tough now," Big Fred sneered.

Vawter's face poked into view and Wyatt focused on the bright marshal's badge pinned to his chest. A wave of bitterness engulfed him as he noted the irony. Morgan, Virgil, and Warren had worn badges, but they had done so with honor.

"I don't like your threats, Earp," Vawter said. "You'll see that we know what to do with a piece of rope as well as you do. Take Pingree to the jail, and teach Mr. Earp to keep his nose out of things that don't involve him."

Burns swung the sandbag with all his might. The sack, used to hold gold dust, crashed into the side of Wyatt's head, stunning him. Then the beating began in earnest. Always using the weighted sandbags, Burns and Stackhouse flailed away at Wyatt's head, chest, and stomach while Walsh held his arms. Vawter watched with his arms crossed.

"That's enough," the marshal ordered after Wyatt slipped into unconsciousness. "He won't be able to sign over the Dexter if he's dead. Lock him up, too: interfering with an officer in the discharge of his duty." He laughed. "I don't want him killed just yet."

Wyatt's swollen eye opened a crack. *You just made a big mistake not killing me while you had the chance.*

Josie's eyes widened in horror and her hand leapt to her mouth to stifle a scream. The bruised, disheveled man coughing blood and swaying before her scarcely resembled her husband.

"Well, are you going to invite me in?" he rasped hoarsely.

His wry smile looked all the more terrible against his battered face.

"Wyatt! My God! What happened?" she gasped after she recovered her wits.

"I fell."

"You fell? You fell off of what? Good God, Wyatt, there isn't a mountain tall enough around here for you to fall off and look like this!"

"You'd be surprised, Josie."

She guided him in out of the night and laid him on the cot. With trembling hands she washed his cuts and bruises and helped him out of his coat. He winced as she removed his shirt, and tears filled her eyes as she touched the cruel bruises covering his back and ribs. Then her fear turned to anger.

"What kind of animal would do this to you, Wyatt?" she sobbed. "What kind of man? Tell me his name, and I'll kill him, I swear to God!"

"Now, now, Josie." He patted her hair. "Don't you be swearing. It doesn't become a lady like you."

"But . . . "

"No buts. A little licking now and again is good for me. It keeps me from thinking too highly of myself, and it keeps me tender for sure."

She dabbed at her eyes. "I was so worried about you. When they brought the terrible news about poor Mr. Pingree . . . "

"What about Pingree? He's still in jail. They let me out on bail before him."

"No, Wyatt. He's dead. They say he hanged himself in his cell. Didn't they tell you?"

Wyatt squeezed his eyes tightly shut, but that couldn't keep out his thoughts. That was what Vawter meant about the rope. Pingree had paid the price for Wyatt's remark.

Wyatt moved off his back, testing the injuries. No bones broken. But his coughing still brought up streaks of blood. Still his ribs felt intact. He reached under the cot for the pistol he kept there and placed it by his side. First, he'd sleep, then in the morning he would decide his moves. What he needed now was rest.

But his sleep was fitful. Morgan and Warren haunted his dreams, and Doc Holliday appeared to sit on the foot of his bed and smile at him. Wyatt jerked awake. The predawn glow was just painting the side of their tent with its creamy pink tones. Josie lay asleep in a chair by the bed. His twelve-gauge shotgun lay across her lap. He smiled when he saw it. She'd been guarding him.

Wyatt checked to make sure Doc Holliday wasn't actually sitting there, the dream had been so real. Damn, Doc, he thought. You looked real good. Still young, still strong, like the old days. Not like me, gray and stiff. He remembered their last visit together in Glenwood Springs. Both knew it was their last visit, and Doc was dying. They'd talked of many things, but never of growing old.

TWENTY-NINE

Nathan held his finger to his lips and drew Jim Riley aside as they strode down the darkened alley. The gunman slowed his pace until the other three regulators drew ahead. Glancing around, Nathan started to speak, but a warning glance from Riley silenced him. Big Fred Burns, the unofficial leader, appeared suddenly from the darkness.

"What you boys waiting for? The rest are up ahead." He jerked his head at the backs of the four men turning the corner.

Riley fumbled with his pants. "Gotta take a leak, Fred. We'll catch up in a minute."

"You need the boy to take a leak?"

"We stick together," Nathan replied, trying hard to hide his growing dislike for Walsh. The man was an obvious bully.

"And a man my age could use all the help he can git." Riley smiled lamely.

Walsh grunted a dozen noises that passed for laughter. "Well, I don't care if he holds it for you, old man, but make it quick. We got work to do." He hurried off.

Riley watched his receding back as he rebuttoned his fly. He spit onto the darkened ground. "I'm developing a powerful dislike for that hombre. What'd you want, Nat?"

Nathan spoke rapidly in short whispers while his eyes darted about for the others. "Something real bad is going on here,

Riley. Yesterday, after we split up, I went with Bastow, Fisk, and Stackhouse to evict this so-called dangerous foreign alien from his claim out on Discovery Number 10."

"Yeah?"

"Well, they didn't just kick him off. They beat him near to death with an ax handle. Broke his arm and all the fingers on his right hand. And they enjoyed it, Riley. It was like the Horner Brothers all over again!"

Riley scratched his beard. "Yeah, same with the group I joined. These boys have a mean streak, that's for sure."

"That's not all, Jim. The alien they were beating was scream-ing all the while *in English!*"

"Yeah? I guess foreigners can learn English. I know a little Spanish, but that don't make me one."

Nathan gripped the front of Riley's coat. "He was yelling and cursing with a southern accent! He was as American as you and me."

Before Riley could reply, Bastow Page returned for them. "Come on! Big Fred wants you to see this."

They trotted after him, turning the corner to stop in the shadows of a frame hardware store. Beyond, lines of wall tents glowed in the cloudless sky. The moon was not yet up, but its glow lightened the hilly backdrop, casting long dark tongues of shadow over the unlit camp. Far to the west an ink black cloud, drawn across the sky like a straight line, smothered stars as it ominously rolled toward land. A storm was coming.

Walsh waited until they joined the group. He squinted at his pocket watch but looked up as Tom Fisk arrived, sweating and out of breath. "Well?" Big Fred asked. "Is he still there?"

Fisk nodded while he caught his breath. "Yeah, he's there. They're having some kind of a meeting."

"Good. Let's do it then," Walsh said. "That's his tent over there." He pointed to one glowing from a coal oil lamp within.

Nathan shot Jim a warning look, and the two hung back

while the others surrounded the tent. Swiftly, they cut open the canvas side and the five others rushed inside. There was the sound of things breaking. Then a woman screamed. That unexpected sound galvanized Riley and Nathan into action. Drawing their pistols they rushed through the slit.

Inside, Stackhouse and Bastow Page struggled with a half-naked woman as she kicked and punched at them. Part of a blanket covered her head, but her nightgown was torn, exposing her legs. Tom Fisk rambled about the tent, breaking things at random, while Ed Burns knelt on the floor examining a handful of papers. A strong clinical smell wafted from a broken bottle near the opening in the side. Walsh stood with his hands on his hips, overseeing the operation.

"Damn. The bitch broke our bottle of chloroform. Try to keep her quiet," Big Fred ordered.

"It ain't easy," Page protested. "She's fighting like a wildcat." He clamped his hand over the cover where he guessed her mouth was only to be rewarded by her teeth snapping down on his fingers. He cried out in pain and slammed his fist into the side of the woman's head. Her body went limp, slumping back into Stackhouse's arms.

Burns looked up at the exposed flesh and licked his lips. "My, she's a pretty one, ain't she?" he said as he rose. "Be a shame to pass her up now she's cooperative." His hand shot out and groped her breast as he pressed against her hips. "Bet she'd want it, too. It's been a week since we beat up her husband, but the licking we gave him ought to put him out of the mood for a month." He unbuttoned his pants.

Stackhouse licked his lips and loosened his grip. "I'm next, Ed."

"Leave her be." Nathan's voice shattered the night.

Heads turned to stare at the dark tunnel of Nathan's .45. Beside him, Jim Riley added the muzzles of his two pistols to the ante.

369

"Are you crazy?" Walsh sputtered.

"He wants her for himself," Burns protested.

"Leave her alone, Ed," Nathan repeated, "or I'll kill you on the spot."

"You can't take us all," Walsh warned.

"You ain't oughta be too sure of that, Big Fred." Riley grinned. He spit a stream of tobacco onto Walsh's boot. "Cause you're the biggest target. Now do as Nat says for I gits to skinning my irons. I ain't known for my patience."

Suddenly, the woman's knee shot up, driving hard into Ed's groin. He crumpled with a strangled groan, and she broke free of Stackhouse to slide to the floor. The covers slid off her head.

Josephine Earp glared up at them like a trapped panther. Her chestnut curls covered half her face, and an ugly bruise covered one cheek. Still, her head jerked from side to side ready to launch her attack. Her molesters backed away from her and the pistol barrels, turned, and then fled into the night.

Nathan holstered his pistol and handed Josie the blanket to cover her nakedness. "I'm sorry about all this," he said. "We never knew what they planned."

Her breathing slowed and her vision cleared. A light of recognition shone in her eyes as she identified his face.

"You! You're the one!" she said.

"Yes," he said slowly. "I'm his son."

Then he and Riley vanished into the darkness.

★ ★ THIRTY ★ ★

"I'll kill every goddamned one of them!" Wyatt spoke with deadly coldness as he buckled on his gunbelt and checked the loads in his shotgun. He kicked an upturned stool aside and retrieved a box of shells. Purposefully, he crammed his pockets full of cartridges. The long-barreled revolver hung from his hip, waiting.

Josie reached up to touch his hand, causing him to stop and kneel by her side. Ever so gently he touched the bruise on her face. In that instant he turned from killer to concerned husband.

"It's not worth risking your life for, Wyatt," she pleaded. But she knew her words fell on deaf ears.

He gave her a piercing look. The killing fever had resurfaced in him. "Are you saying it's all right to beat up my wife?"

"I just don't want you to get hurt. You're all I have, Wyatt, and I couldn't live without you. Nothing is as important as that."

He kissed the top of her head before getting to his feet. "Don't worry, Josie. I know how to handle mad dogs. I won't let them bite me."

"McKenzie and Noyes are too powerful, Wyatt. You can't kill them. The army will hang you if you do."

Wyatt tucked the blanket around her shoulders. "Those two are like an evil octopus with arms reaching into everything.

The way to handle them is to cut off their arms. One at a time. Quietly. With no fuss."

He turned and strode outside. It was morning, but black storm clouds blanketed the sky, casting the landscape into an eerie gloom without sun and without separation of a molten lead sky from the pewter sea. Only the spindrift and white horses prancing on the wind-whipped water distinguished the two. Storm waves already attacked the low-lying beach, driving even the most fanatic prospectors away as the water rolled into the town. A barge, torn free from its moorings, heaved from side to side as the sea leisurely battered it to pieces on the shoals. Nome hunkered down to ride out the storm.

Wyatt studied the scene. Soon the rain would arrive hard on the heels of the wind to lash the land with icy sheets. No one would venture into that maelstrom, no one in their right minds. He smiled grimly. Conditions were perfect for retribution.

Bastow Page drove his boot into Nathan's ribs, but the young man simply grinned back fiercely and tensed his muscles against the ropes that bound him. "And you thought you could hide from us," he guffawed. "I thought you was smart." He leaned back against a rotting windlass and a pile of moss covered boards.

"I never expected you'd find us in the Chinaman's laundry," Nathan admitted. The longer he kept Page talking the more time he had to plan his escape.

"Hell, we didn't find you. The Chinaman sent his daughter to tell us. They're all afraid of us. You ought to know that."

Riley groaned beside Nathan as he regained consciousness. Trussed like Nat, the gunfighter flopped onto his side and spit out a clot of blood from his split lips.

"Sorry I got you into this, Jim," Nathan apologized.

"We're pards, ain't we? And partners stick together, thick or thin."

Page looked up as Tom Fisk climbed over the rim of the cliff and walked along the bluff to them. "What's the plan, Tom?" he asked.

Fisk produced a bottle of rye, took a lengthy pull before handing it to Page. "Well, Bas, Fred wants us to keep it nice and quiet. These boys have just got to disappear."

"Why can't I just shoot them?" Page complained.

"Fred don't want that. He don't want no word to get out about our own boys stepping out of line. He says that'd be bad for business." He jammed his hat down over his ears and turned his coat collar up as the rain began to pelt them. "Shit, here comes the damned rain."

Bastow Page shivered. "How we gonna do that?"

Fish walked over to the abandoned mine shaft and dropped a rock into the black hole. A remote splash greeted his ear. While he peered down the flooded shaft, the rotted timber he held onto gave way and a slide of dirt cascaded into the murky water. Dug in search of the mother lode, the shaft was abandoned the previous year when sea water flooded the drifts. Now it stood abandoned, its water level rising and falling with the changing tide. "We drop them down this hole. No shots, no nothing."

Jim Riley closed his eyes, his worst fears now realized. Since that landslide in Arizona, he had carried the fear of being buried alive again, and now it seemed certain.

"Wait!" was all Nathan had time to say before Bastow rolled him into the hole. He tumbled headfirst down the shaft into the oily water. Another splash announced the arrival of Riley. With arms and legs tied, Nat struggled against drowning. Disoriented in the dark water, he kicked out, but only succeeded in driving his head into the slimy side of the mine shaft. His lungs screamed for air and threatened to burst while he thrashed around for the surface.

His head surfaced just when he thought he could hold his

breath no longer. Beside him, a wild-eyed Riley was slipping under the water. Nat caught Riley's shirt with his teeth while he treaded water. Struggling as best he could, he kept both their heads above the brackish muck.

"Let me loose, damnit!" Riley protested between gulps of air. "I'm dragging you down, Nat! Save yerself."

"Partners!" Nat growled between his clenched teeth. But despair filled his heart. He couldn't tread water much longer. Already his legs were growing numb in the icy water.

Two shots exploded above his head. The sound, amplified in the mine, reverberated against the walls. They're shooting at us, Nathan thought. Better a bullet in the head than choking in this slop.

But a geyser of water rose beside them as another body hit the water. Nat turned to look directly into the astonished eyes of a dead Tom Fisk. A bullet hole burnt the skin in the center of his forehead. Then, a lariat loop dropped over his shoulders and cinched tight.

"Hold on!" a voice commanded. "I'm pulling you up."

"I can't let go of my friend," Nat croaked back. "He'll drown if I do."

"Well, I can't pull you both up," the voice replied with a slight edge of exasperation.

"I'm not letting go!" Nathan responded.

"Damnit, let go of him."

"No!"

"I ought to let you two sink. I can't pull the two of you up."

"I'm not letting go!"

There was a silence that seemed to Nathan to stretch for a lifetime.

"Oh, hell. Okay, hold on while I think of something," came the answer.

Nat heard the creak of wood, and he remembered the half-rotted windlass discarded by the miners. Abruptly, the rope jerked tight, cutting into his chest as they began to ascend. He wrapped his legs about Riley while they rose, twisting, toward the surface.

As his head leveled with the ground, he saw Bastow Page lying face down in a spreading pool of blood. He also saw that the storm had broken in all its fury. Sheets of rain marched across the landscape like a hail of bullets, and bolts of lightning illuminated the watery curtains. The loud crack of thunder sundered the constant roar of the wind and the nearby waves. Nat and Riley kicked themselves over the slippery rim and rolled, panting, onto their backs. The rain hosed the muck from their faces.

Another bolt of lightning lit up the sky and Nat found himself staring into the face of Wyatt Earp.

"I got your letter, son," Wyatt said as he stepped forward and removed a Bowie knife from his boot. He cut their bonds and stepped back while the two men sat up.

Nat wiped the rain from his eyes and squinted at his father. Wyatt was studying him just as closely. Earp kicked Nathan's gunbelt over to the lad, and Nathan reached for it.

Jim Riley snatched his wrist. "Hold on, here! Ain't you two got somethin' more to say to each other afore you gits to shooting. This don't make no sense. Here you save the boy's life just so you can shoot it out!"

"It's a matter of honor, Jim," Nathan replied. "Stay out of it."

"Honor!" Riley sputtered. "That don't amount to a sack of pig shit if you does the wrong thing! He jus' saved our lives, boy! That gotta count for somethin', or I ain't taught you a damned thing! I swear, you two must be kin. I ain't never seen a pair of stiffer necks in all my born days!"

Nathan eyed the tall man facing him, studying the raw-boned features, the straight brown hair, the quarter moon mustache laced with silver, and the pale gray eyes like his own.

They truly looked alike. "Why did you leave my mother?" he asked.

"Mattie?" Wyatt sighed. "More like she left me—for whiskey and laudanum. She was drifting out of life long before I ever met Josie or left Tombstone. There just wasn't much left of her except an empty shell by that time."

"What about me?" Nat pressed.

"I never knew you existed. Never laid eyes on you until that time in San Francisco. I reckon that was Mattie's revenge. She knew how much I wanted a son." His voice lowered. "I still do."

"Are you saying my mother put me in an orphanage all that while and never told you about me?"

"It's the truth, whether you believe it or not. She never visited you once, did she? If I'd known about you, I'd have walked barefoot over the Rockies to see you."

Nathan's head spun as he sorted his facts and jumbled emotions. His father was nothing like he expected. Wyatt had saved his life without placing a single condition on that act. Here he stood ready to fight him if necessary. And Wyatt left the choice up to him. It didn't fit with the evil picture painted in Mattie's letter. This man more resembled the hero Nathan remembered from his dime novels. What he'd heard in his short time in Nome matched that impression well.

"I don't know what to think anymore," Nat admitted.

"Well," Wyatt relaxed. "No hurry on that. We're twenty years late as it is. A few more days won't matter." He turned his back on them and walked over to the body of Bastow Page which he rolled into the mine.

"Eighteen," Nathan corrected.

Wyatt squatted on his heels and looked into the shaft. "Eighteen? You're big for your age. Got a full beard, too," he said. He studied Riley for the first time. "This man been looking after you?"

"Been a few years," Riley admitted proudly. "More like he's nursing me, now."

Wyatt smiled for the first time. He pointed his finger at Riley. " 'Newton Station' Jim Riley," he said. "I thought I knew your face from the old handbills."

"Jesus," Riley swore. "How come every Jack in Alaska knows about me? Don't nobody know I'm in disguise except me!"

"I wouldn't worry about that if I were you, Riley. Those were very old posters," Wyatt said. He straightened and flicked his slicker, but the rain doused it in seconds. "I'm rooting out rats today, and I've got three to go before the rain ends. So I'd best commence where I left off."

Nathan buckled on his revolver. "Mind if we come along?"

Big Fred Walsh wiped his hand across his greasy beard and shielded his eyes from the torrent. Page and Burns should have been back by now. He paced around the shack his regulators used for headquarters. It was set along the dunes south of the beach. The location was perfect, remote enough for their work, yet convenient enough for communicating with McKenzie and the judge. He blinked the rain from his eyes and tried to concentrate on business. But the long legs of Josie Earp kept interrupting his thoughts. After they finished with Wyatt, maybe she'd be worth a visit, he thought.

He spotted two figures approaching down the beach. Their dark shapes stood out against the pounding surf, but the lashing sheets of rain obscured more detail. He stepped out onto the beach.

"Fisk! Page! Is that you?" he shouted over the storm. One of the men waved his right hand over his head while they kept walking.

Ed Burns stepped outside at the sound. He walked over to stand beside Walsh. "Looks like the boys finished their assignment, boss."

The rain intensified, blurring everything in sight, until the two groups were a few feet from each other.

"Did those two beg for mercy when you stuffed them in that shaft?" Big Fred asked.

"Not quite," came the reply. A flash of lightning bared the faces of Wyatt and Nathan Earp and their pistols leveled at Walsh and Burns.

"Don't go for your guns," Wyatt ordered. "I wouldn't want to kill you two without a fair fight. Now back out onto the beach, both of you."

"I ain't going, Wyatt! You can't shoot me. What I'm doing is all legal!" Walsh hoped he protested loud enough for Paul Stackhouse to hear him from the shack. He slowly raised his hands as he looked past Nathan to see Stackhouse poke his head out the door, then disappear.

"The hell you say. You put your filthy hands on my wife," Wyatt snarled. "And you tried to kill my son."

"Your son?" Walsh started, but he continued to stall as he watched Stackhouse emerge from the side door and slink along the side with a Winchester held to his shoulder. Another two feet and Stackhouse would have a clear shot.

Jim Riley stepped around the corner of the shack and emptied both barrels of Wyatt's ten-gauge into Stackhouse. The double charges nearly cut the man in half. He flew backward into the grass where the blast threw him, dead. Riley looked down at the body. "It ain't no fun for a bushwhacker if they's the one gits whacked, is it?" he said to the corpse. Then he waved to Wyatt. "All clear here," he said.

Wyatt kept his eye on Walsh the whole time, watching him blanch at the sight of his man going down. "Start walking backward," he commanded.

Like some sort of deadly minuet the four men backed slowly onto the beach and into the raging surf. The lightning intensified and the wind rose to a fevered pitch in anticipation of the

378

impending fight. When they were above their knees, Wyatt stopped and holstered his Colt. Nathan followed suit.

"Now's your chance, Fred," Wyatt snapped. "But you won't find me as easy as beating defenseless women."

Walsh swallowed hard and glanced sideways at Ed Burns. Burns was licking his lips while his fingers inched for his revolver.

A colossal bolt of lightning froze the four men as they drew. Two shots split the howling wind, so close that they sounded like one, followed instantly by the deafening crack of thunder. Wyatt and Nathan stood together with their pistols smoking and watched Big Fred Walsh and his lieutenant, Ed Burns, pitch forward into the waves. Their bodies bobbed about with arms outstretched until the outgoing tide caught them and they began to float out to sea.

"No evidence," Wyatt said flatly. "And no publicity."

Jim Riley waded out to them and watched the losers floating away. He looked at Wyatt and Nathan and grinned. "I ain't gonna say who was the fastest, 'cause I don't want to start no family arguments, but I'd hate to live on the difference."

As if on signal, the storm broke and the rain ceased. The clouds parted and a ray of sunlight leapt from the low horizon to bathe the beach and the dunes obliquely in golden light. Even the wind lessened. Only the pounding surf continued to mark the storm that had passed.

Wyatt waded ashore. He turned his pistol over in his hand, then holding the long barrel, he handed it to Nathan.

"Some things can never be set straight, and it's no use trying," he said. "You grew up without me to guide you as I would have liked. And I will never know the pleasure of raising a boy. But you've grown into as good a man as I ever could have hoped for. I have nothing of value to offer you but my love and this pistol. You'll always have my love and my respect, something not every man can give his son. Use the gun to protect yourself and only draw it for a just cause, and it will never let you down. *But you must never carry the family name.* Doing that would curse you with my sins and make you a marked and hunted man. The greatest legacy I can give you is the freedom to follow your own destiny."

On that windswept Alaskan beach, Wyatt hugged his son for the first time, fighting back his tears. But these tears were different from those he had shed upon the premature death of his other son. These were tears of pride and happiness for a part of him that would live forever.

★ ★ EPILOGUE ★ ★

Without tentacles, Alexander McKenzie and Judge Arthur Noyes were powerless to stop a delegation of miners traveling to the Ninth Circuit Court of Appeals in San Francisco. On October 15, 1900, two deputy United States marshals arrived by steamship to arrest McKenzie and Noyes to stand trial in San Francisco. The power of the Spoilers was broken.

Wyatt and Josie Earp sold the Dexter Saloon a year later for a profit of over $80,000 and left Alaska, never to return. Thinking about his experience in Alaska, Wyatt remarked while on the departing steamship, "She's been mighty good to us."

Wyatt Earp never admitted to anyone that he might have a living son.

For Nathan Blaylock and Jim Riley, the adventure was just beginning. . . .